D1765926

Gift Aid Fiction
£

0 029310 066520

CREATURES OF SPIRIT

BLOOD AFTER DEATH

A. K. AKAR

A Fortis Vult Publishing Book

All Rights Reserved
Copyright © 2024 D. Anderson

Editing by Jessie Anderson
Formatting by Damian Jackson
Cover and Illustrations by A. K. Akar

Hardcover Book ISBN: 978-1-7780408-9-4
Paperback Book ISBN: 978-1-7383431-1-9
Electronic Book ISBN: 978-1-7780408-8-7

BELIKE

This is a work of fiction that bumps into history. If there are any similarities between real people and events and the characters and events in this story, then they are artifacts of the aforementioned collision and are coincidental.

BEWARE

"History is a nightmare from which I am trying to awake."

— JAMES JOYCE

Bewritten

Viking tradition speaks of a world where slain warriors fight and feast forever. They call it Valhalla. Vampire tradition speaks of a similar world. We call it Earth. The witch-born one, she who befouls our kind and our way, must be cast off its face, in ashes, from the fires of the white oak.

— Blood Sea Scrolls, 1358 CE

Part 1

PROLOGUE

JANUARY 13TH, 1758

The Palace of Versailles shone as Louis XIV, the Sun King, decreed it would. Bright moonlight reflected off its facade into the night sky and lit the sculpted gardens that stretched to the west from its north and south wings. The glow poured life into the eyes of the statues that watched over the gardens but blinded them to the battle being fought in the *Orangerie*.

In the shadows of the fruit trees a hulking man and a lithe woman grappled, fighting for the dagger that was clenched in the man's fist. Unable to break his grip on the knife the woman grabbed his wrist and hauled on it, hammering her back into a tree trunk and driving the blade deep into the flesh between her ribs. Nose-to-nose with the man, as her blood oozed over his hand, she watched him sneer in her face and then nod over his shoulder to the graybeard he was protecting.

The old man grinned and stepped forward to thank his bodyguard but froze when a loud crunch shook the big man to his core. His smirk drooping, he whispered the guard's name then cried out as his limp body flew at him through a web of low hanging branches. Eyes

3

bulging, he threw up his hands to fend it off but was slammed down under its dead weight onto a flagstone path.

Groaning, the patrón heaved the corpse off his chest. Its head rolled loosely and, retching, its former master kicked it away. Then, spitting and cursing, the old man struggled to stand up as the steady beat of boots on stone grew louder in his ears. Gaining his feet at last, he swayed and squinted at the pale, black-haired woman who stopped an arm's length away, pulled his guard's dagger from between her ribs, and dropped it on the frozen ground.

"So, the tales are true," he wheezed. "Well, know this *witch*. I am Don Micael Bartolome. By appointment, Royal Emissary of King Ferdinand VI of Spain. You will not have his gold. It is mine!"

Bartolome lunged at the woman, but she slapped aside his clawing fingers, grabbed a fistful of his hair, wrenched his head back, and plunged her fangs into his throat. Her crimson irises flared as she drank in his lifeblood, his hatred, his greed, and his treachery. When he ran dry she plucked a scroll from inside his cloak and tossed him on top of his guard. After a quick inspection of the scroll's wax seal, she turned her back on the dead men, marched out of the *Orangerie,* and mounted the Hundred Steps staircase.

As she jogged up the steps toward the palace she glanced down at the don and hissed, "I am no witch."

LONDON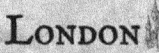

CoS 1758

LE HAVRE

LOUISBOURG

PARIS

VERSAILLES

HALIFAX

LA ROCHELLE

ASTURES

North Atlantic Ocean

Nassau

ELIMINA

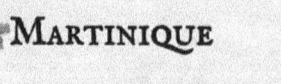
MARTINIQUE

CHAPTER 1

QUADRILLE

JANUARY 13TH, 1758

The view of the western horizon from the south wing of the Palace of Versailles was spellbinding. Captivated, Léonarre Poisson, Regent to King Louis XV of France, drank it in through his office window. When a door closed quietly behind him, Poisson spoke to his visitor but kept his eyes fixed on the horizon.

"Our beloved Louis is of a mind, given the fortune he has sunk into it, that the fortress at Louisbourg ought to throw a shadow from its perch on the edge of New France, across the Atlantic and onto the walls of his palace here at Versailles," he sniffed in contempt.

Pulling his gaze off the skyline, Poisson let it linger over the contours of the silhouette he cast on the windowpanes. Tut-tutting, he patted his coiffure, plumped the ruffles at his cuffs, and tugged on his fitted jacket as his guest approached. Their footfalls echoed throughout his rococo-infused office, but he ignored the racket.

"It may be true that the grandeur and strategic import of the fortress are unmatched in the New World," he continued, striking a pose for himself. "However, the expense of maintaining it is draining France's treasury."

Poisson leaned in close to the glass, smoothed an eyebrow and then straightened his back.

"Needless to say, his royal highness will not be amused if its upkeep reduces his allowance to the point where he must curb his spending on his household and appearance," he resumed, his voice snapping like a whip. "*That* would spell trouble for everyone. The dungeons would overflow. People would be stretched on racks and, worse yet, we all might be force-fed English cuisine. All of which brings us to our little get together this evening, the outcome of which, hopefully, will help us avoid such unpleasant eventualities."

Preened to perfection, Poisson smiled brightly at his thirtysomething reflection, loving the look of his fair skin, almond eyes, angular cheekbones, and slender physique. His grin faded, however, when crackling talons of light crept out of the window lattices and clawed at his mirror image. Scrabbling across his ornate jacket, they tore into the gaping maws of the three-headed dog on the coat of arms resting over his heart.

Poisson scratched at the embroidered crest but stopped when he began to fray its threads. Narrowing his eyes, he pressed his hand against the windowpane and rubbed tight circles over the vision in the glass, jerking it back when frost bit his skin. When he turned his hand over to inspect his palm he shivered as icicles melted on its surface and icy water trickled down his wrist.

With a shudder, he shook off his jitters and swung around to welcome his caller. Coming out of his turn he was stunned to find a woman, rustically attired but clearly of noble rank, standing on the opposite side of his gilded desk, rather than grizzled old Don Micael Bartolome. Loose tresses of lustrous black hair shaded her eyes and clung to the corner of her jaw and the fine line of her pale neck. The rest of her thick mane washed over wide shoulders and fell to her waist.

The curves of her honed physique were wrapped in the furs and leathers of a cloak. Cinched around her waist was a sword belt, slung so that her scabbard rested low against her right hip. Poisson's jaw slackened in astonishment at the sight of the woman but, seeing her gaze fixed on the door barring entry to the antechamber to his left, he clapped it shut.

"You are startled," she said. Her manner bore the lessons of the Spanish court. Hints of amusement studded her observation.

"Yes . . . no. Not at all, *Doña Señorita?*" Poisson fumbled his greeting.

"Marquaisa. You were expecting me," she replied, her eyes aimed at the anteroom door, her hand playing with the jeweled hilt of her rapier.

"No . . . yes. I mean, where is Don Bartolome?" Poisson asked, squaring his chest and fighting to regain his composure.

"Don Bartolome is gone," Marquaisa answered, looking Poisson up and down.

"Gone?" Poisson repeated, his rosy cheeks going pale.

"He was consumed," she explained. Her eyes glistened and her voice took on a husky undertone.

"Oh, I see, the consumption," Poisson's knitted brow unwound in comprehension. "How awful. You have my deepest condolences."

Don Bartolome's stand-in stared through the French regent.

Taking his queue, Poisson pressed on delicately, "Don Bartolome and I were about to conclude, on behalf of our divine monarchs, a most sensitive agreement in which—"

Poisson cut off his narrative and tensed as Marquaisa reached into the folds of her cloak. When, with a flourish, she extracted a scroll he relaxed and watched it uncoil smoothly under the weight of the seal of Ferdinand VI, King of Spain. His eyes sparkled with delight as the contract poured out of her hand and she pointed at the signature below its bottom line.

"The terms are accepted," she stated.

Barely breathing, Poisson stretched his arms across his lavish desk and allowed Marquaisa to place the linen into his open hands. Cradling the sheet, he paused to admire the exquisite calligraphy with which it was inscribed. He then combed through the pact it articulated, from its somber introduction to the blessing at its conclusion and exhaled slowly as he scrutinized Ferdinand's signature.

Only then did he offer Marquaisa a scroll sealed with Louis XV's signet.

"What do you think the Marquis of Ensenada, your former prime minister and champion of détente, would think of this arrangement?" Poisson sneered. "Ferdinand exiled him for suggesting an alliance with France, did he not?"

Marquaisa accepted Poisson's scroll and secured it within her cloak, ignoring his dig.

"*Caballero,*" she nodded curtly and took her leave without waiting for a reply.

Grinding his molars at her abruptness, Poisson watched the tight-lipped Spaniard stride out of his bureau. When the double doors latched behind her, he cleansed his lungs of sour air and his spleen of a string of slurs against her, Spain, and Ferdinand. Only then, after he had expelled his vitriol, did he look down at the open scroll on his desk and smile.

"D'Acier, join me, if you please," he called to his left.

Trémont D'Acier stepped from behind the hand-carved door of the antechamber as if it were his partner in the dance the fashionable crowd were calling the *quadrille*. A decade younger than Poisson, like the regent he had weaponized his emotional illiteracy; both men were remorseless, but where Poisson was calculatingly manipulative, D'Acier was dangerously sadistic. As was his habit D'Acier's wardrobe was black on black, leather over silk. His streaked, ruddy hair was held up in a top knot from which a flowing tail fell over his right shoulder and down his chest. Scars acquired in duels were etched into the corners of his azure eyes and scored his brown cheeks. Tall, strong, and effortlessly graceful, he drifted to his post behind Poisson and listened.

"Ferdinand believes he has acquired New France, *half of the New World*, for a mere ten tons of Spanish gold," Poisson chuckled as he summarized the terms written on the scroll.

"Then he is, in fact, the fool you believe him to be. Well done, my lord," D'Acier congratulated Poisson, his deep voice rumbling like boulders grinding in a ships' ballast tank.

"Indeed, he is. I would dearly love to be present when he makes his announcements to our darling Louis and that hypocrite Pitt, who persists in selling himself as England's *savior* while denying he is its prime minister, regarding his intentions to exercise Spain's sovereignty over its newly acquired territory," Poisson giggled, nasally. "It should give the three of them sufficient cause to prolong their ridiculous war. When they do, Trémont, you and I will be provided ever more opportunities for profit."

D'Acier cleared his throat and eyed the crevices, known to conceal eavesdroppers, in the walls of the expansive office. Poisson grinned at his aide's caution and waved his hand over the document laying on the polished surface of his desk.

"Kindly alert our friend, Commandant de Chaffant, as to when and where he will receive the treasure he is to deliver to Louisbourg," he tasked D'Acier. "You will find the details in the contract."

D'Acier stole a look at the scroll, then went back to scanning the surrounding nooks and crannies.

"See to it, also, that a message makes its way to Pitt informing him that Louisbourg will not be reinforced. Our Mediterranean fleet is bottled-up at Cartagena."

"What an incredible coincidence," D'Acier observed, slily.

"To be sure," Poisson agreed, smoothly. "Do make a point of connecting the dots for that dolt. Tell him in very plain terms that it was I who helped his Commander Osborn trap the imbecile de La Clue and our fleet. Now, despite their wretched incompetence, the British will easily be able to make Louisbourg their gateway into *Nova Francia*."

"I will explain it as if to a child, my lord," D'Acier assured the regent, with a smirk.

"Splendid, but do leave out the bit about British ineptitude," Poisson edited himself, casting a sideways glance at D'Acier. "Last of all, instruct Pitt as to when and where his invading army is to make its landing and remind him that it will be at Louisbourg where he will find the gold he will accept in exchange for our freedom."

"The British," D'Acier curled his lip in loathing, "They will betray you, my lord."

"They will think the better of it," Poisson countered, tapping his desktop, lightly, with his knuckles. "Pitt knows me. So, he knows that at the first whiff of treachery I will see to it that his booty is cast into the wind or into the drink. If that happens, then all he will have to show for his folly of an expedition will be a ruin of a fortress stacked upon a rock in the middle of nowhere."

"That is well," D'Acier conceded then, his tone turning acidic, demanded of his master, "But what of the king's watchdog, Aubergine? Let me kill him before he informs Louis of his suspicions concerning you and I."

"You will do no such thing!" Poisson scolded his aide, rapping his desktop sharply. Then, feeling rather than seeing the young man bridle, he softened his tone and reassured D'Acier, "Neither, I might add, will the 'king's watchdog,' as you have so eloquently named him, be acting on his intentions, as you have so astutely articulated them. I had a special friend of mine visit Aubergine to convince him to do otherwise. Rest assured, he will no longer be sticking his snout where it does not belong."

Pleased with his cleverness, Poisson stepped around D'Acier and returned to his window and the view it provided of the distant horizon.

"Who knows? In time his highness may forgive us for excluding him from our enterprise," he hazarded, nonchalantly. "After all we will have rid him of a bottomless spending pit that returns nothing to France other than stinking rodent hides and toothless refugees."

D'Acier bit his tongue rather than contradict Poisson's delusions.

"All that aside," Poisson returned, abruptly, to matters at hand. "We have a more pressing concern. Namely, Lady Marquaisa. What thought you of our new friend?"

"She is free of fear, my lord," D'Acier opined, peering at the double doors through which the Spaniard had departed. "But she sought to burden you with it. Did she succeed?"

Poisson turned his shoulders, slightly, toward D'Acier and without looking at his aide warned him, "You know better than to ask that of me. You know, also, that in a blink I could snip out your insolent tongue and dump your mongrel hide back into that rat-infested hole off whose floor I scraped you."

"You asked. I answered," D'Acier shot back, shrugging his shoulders. "Pity you didn't like what you heard."

"Well met, my good young man," Poisson complimented his protégé, then shifted his attention to his manicure. "I'll admit, she *medusified* my brain for an instant. Her news of Don Bartolome's demise and her utter disregard of *our king's* contract—it took me days to duplicate Louis's signature, by the way—had a certain shock value. However, I do believe my dig at Ensenada made for a stylish recovery. But, enough about me. What else did you think of her?"

"She will do her duty as she sees fit"

"Meaning?"

"She will do as she pleases."

"That is a woman's prerogative. Your point is?"

"She intends to make the gold her own."

"That is as true for her ladyship as it would have been for the dearly departed Don Bartolome. Anticipating as much you've taken precautions, yes?"

"Yes, our pet cutthroat, the one at whose back I've had a crop since he was a weanling, has been instructed to slaughter the bearer of your scroll, whoever they may be. Once that is done, he is to ride to Paris to deliver the scroll by his own hand to the Spanish," D'Acier explained, his voice keen with bloodlust.

Poisson nodded in appreciation at the reflection of D'Acier's tapered back, then drew a sharp breath. Feigning innocence, he inquired of his retainer, "Perchance, Trémont, does this cutthroat of ours ride a dapple-gray stallion?"

"He does, my lord," D'Acier's reply was piqued with curiosity but he kept his eyes on the doorway at the far end of the office.

"Then he has completed his mission posthaste!" Poisson's report dripped with sarcasm. "As we speak he is on parade in the avenue below. Well, most of him is."

D'Acier turned his head towards the window.

"The torchlight is weak. But, from this distance it looks as if he has lost his sword arm, *and* the back of his head, *and* suffered a multitude of other wounds, any one of which would have been fatal," Poisson itemized the assassin's injuries. "Thankfully, he appears to have bled out elsewhere other than on the stallion."

"Squids!" D'Acier cursed as if his croquette ball had jumped a wicket.

Bested by curiosity he slipped to his post behind Poisson and stared into the street.

"I appear to have underestimated the Spaniards," he admitted through grinding teeth.

"Agreed," Poisson concurred, crossing his arms over his chest. "I'll wager it won't happen again."

The regent watched the corpse topple from the saddle.

"Well, there you have it my young apprentice. The witch has flung the gauntlet at our feet," he announced, then spun around and smiled at D'Acier. "Being the gentlemen that we are we have no choice other than to pick it up and accept her challenge. This we shall do by outrunning her to Louisbourg, snatching the treasure from under her nose, and lifting the yoke of life from around her neck!"

"Indeed, we shall, my lord," D'Acier vowed and bowed his head to Poisson.

"Indeed, we shall!" Poisson declared rubbing his hands together. "Meanwhile, D'Acier, let us revisit the topic of *refugees*. I trust you have prepared this evening's sample with your usual flare and in the style that most appeals to my peculiar tastes?"

"I have, my lord," the retainer confirmed, his lips stretching into a feral snarl, a lupine glow filling his eyes as he stood aside and let the regent pass, "They await your pleasure in the antechamber."

CHAPTER 2

PAWN

JANUARY 13TH

PARIS, FRANCE

A chain of dead highwaymen lying in their wake, a horse and rider bound for Paris stepped onto a straight stretch in a winding backroad. Trees fell back from its shoulders and the dusting of snow on its dirt surface turned it into a smooth white line that pointed east to the city's lights, which flickered under a broad wave of cottony clouds that were drifting westward. Enticed by the open road the horse lengthened her stride, happy to stretch her legs after negotiating countless twists and turns.

An Asturcón from the mountains of northern Spain, the mare was tall for her breed. Sorrel with four white stockings, a star, and a streaked mane and tail, Elazuna was correct in her confirmation, muscular, and tireless. On a loose rein, she loped along in the soft footing and the light snowfall, careless of the threats that surrounded her and her rider.

Sitting tall in her saddle, the reins in her right hand, her rapier in her left in a long low tail guard, Marquaisa kept her eyes moving. She scanned the road and the forest for anyone or anything that might try to stop her from reaching the capital. Her body quiet, her long black hair free, she gave not a moment's thought to the men she had slain, including the three at Versailles whom she left as a message for Poisson.

A heartbeat, tapping around the barren branches, reminded her the message had yet to be passed forward. A flaming arrow, shot high over her head, introduced her to the person within whom the heart raced. From its highest point the shaft plummeted to the road and buried its tip in the ground a few strides in front of Elazuna. Horse and rider slowed to a halt and watched the ball of fire fizzle in the snow. Elazuna snorted at the wisp of steam that drifted into her muzzle, then turned on her haunches to size up their attacker.

"Be still, or I'll put the next one in your eye!" a boy squawked from his hiding spot.

Elazuna sighed and shook a cloud of snowflakes out of her mane, showering Marquaisa, who brushed them off the fur trim of her cloak. As the flakes fell to the ground, a second arrow zipped past her shoulder.

"I told you to be still!" a foot stamping on the ground punctuated the reminder.

As ordered, Marquaisa froze, but pinched the reins between her fingers to stop Elazuna from charging.

"Good!" the boy yelped, his voice cracking. "Now, drop your sword."

Marquaisa held her left arm out to her side and loosened her grip on her jewel encrusted rapier. She let its hilt slide slowly down her palm but caught the pommel between her thumb and forefinger. After raising her arm slightly, she opened her hand and let the sword plunge point-first into the snow.

As she lowered her arm a lanky teenager wrapped in rags sidled into view, one hesitating step at a time. Freezing temperatures had leeched the warmth from his dark brown skin, leaving it the color of day-old dishwater. Tangled ringlets of black hair, the bronze high-lights in which had paled, fell past his shoulders. His nose was long and wide and dripped steadily. His lips were cracked and peeling. His eyes were round, brown, and red-rimmed and he kept them locked on Marquaisa as he tipped the point of his last arrow at the snow.

"Get off. Slowly, mind you," he said, blinking sweat and tears from his eyes. "Then walk from the horse to me."

Marquaisa eased her right leg over the pommel of her saddle and dismounted. Showing him that her gloved hands were empty, she squared her chest and started walking at the boy, nodding to Elazuna in passing. As she approached him the boy took a sharp breath and drew his bow to its fullest, making the staves creak. Disregarding his threat, Marquaisa advanced on him until his arrow nicked her cloak, at which point she raised her hands to shoulder height.

"Okay. Okay, good," the teen stammered. "Now, I really don't want to hurt you. But I also don't want you chasing me. So, turn around and put your hands behind your back."

Marquaisa did as she was told. When her hands touched together at the small of her back the youth dropped his bow and fumbled with a length of rope that was looped around his waist. Choosing to not make a move, Marquaisa waited patiently while he bound her wrists.

"My sister taught me how to do this. Then she would . . ." he said wistfully, a singsong accent adding a lilt to his reminiscences.

Rather than ask him to finish his tale, Marquaisa stood silently while he robbed her coin purse and unbuckled her scabbard. She then allowed him to help her kneel in the snow.

"There, that's done," he puffed, wiping sweat off his brow with the sleeve of his torn coat. "Strange how I am dripping wet, yet the snow does not melt in your hair."

Declining the opportunity to engage in small talk, Marquaisa stared up at the boy.

"Anyway," he checked himself, catching her hint. "I'm going to take your sword and your horse and ride away now. Please don't cry out for help. Someone truly nasty might hear you and, like I said, I wouldn't want you to be hurt. Just try not to freeze to death."

Satisfied his plans, his advice, and his concerns were properly regis-tered with his victim, the thief scuttled away from her toward her horse. On his way he pocketed her money, strapped on her scabbard and sheathed her sword. He then hopped on her horse, dug his heels into its flanks, and stole her away at the gallop. Elazuna opened up under his balanced seat and quiet hands and fixed her sights on the lights of Paris. Glad to be given her head she ran hard until she reached the outskirts of the city where she slowed to a trot, then to a walk to let the boy catch his breath.

When he relaxed, fully, she bolted. Shocked and nearly unseated the youth clung to her mane as she sped up deserted lanes and down narrow alleys. Unable either to slow or steer her and unwilling to bail out and splatter his brains on cobblestone pavers the boy bent at his waist and wrapped his arms around her neck. When she braked hard at an inn that backed onto the Seine River he held on tighter to avoid cart-wheeling over her head.

Leaning against a hitching post outside the inn, her arms crossed over her chest, the woman he left alone on the road in the snow and the cold waited for her horse to stop skidding. The sparks and grit that kicked up from the toes of Elazuna's shoes bounced off Marquaisa's boots and she arched an eyebrow at the mare. Then, scowling at the juvenile, she leapt on behind him, took up the reins, and peeled away from the inn at the gallop.

"Oh, no, no, no! I robbed a witch!" the teenager wailed. "I'm sorry Your Majesty! I'm so, so, so sorry. I'll give back what I took. Just, please don't kill me or turn me into something awful like a pig, or a turnip, or—"

Marquaisa clapped her hand over his mouth to silence his blather. With her other hand she helped Elazuna find her way to Notre-Dame cathedral. Were the night clear, the cathedral's rose window would have twinkled in the moonlight. Under the cloudy sky, however, it was as dull as the stone that held its glasswork together. Equally empty of life, the streets that surrounded the gothic colossus were cast in shadow.

Near the square that fronted the cathedral Marquaisa guided Elazuna into an alley that offered an angular view of its grand entrance. Careful to stay hidden in the dark, she nudged the boy's feet out of the stirrups and, holding him firmly, dismounted. The instant their feet hit the ground she jammed him against a wall, her chest pressing into his back, his nose rubbing the bricks.

His body pinned by hers, his mouth clamped shut by her right hand, with her left hand Marquaisa drew the rapier he stole from her and pressed its point under the corner of his jaw. At its touch he squirmed, but he cut short his struggles when she dug the tip of the blade into his skin and cut loose a trickle of blood. Its ruby sheen and sweet scent made her twitch, but she clenched her teeth and bit back her cravings while the boy quieted down.

When his heart stopped pounding Marquaisa turned his back to the wall, reset her hand gag and her blade, and squeezed him into the masonry with her body. Taller than her captive, she forced him to look up at her. Frightened, he shut his eyes, but with a twist of her sword she popped them open again.

Marquaisa read his naivety in their roundness, his energy in their gold flecks, and his humor in the fine crow's feet at their corners, and grinned. Her smile widened, slightly, when a hard nub pushed up her thigh into her pelvis. It pulsed in time with the teenager's heart, and he blushed as he fought to curb its growth. Showing an ounce of mercy where normally she would grant none, she dropped her hand from his face and shifted her body weight off him. But her sword point stayed where it was and to make her meaning plain she raised a finger to her lips and shushed at him for quiet.

"Sorry, Your Highness," he squeaked. "I didn't mean for that to happen. It's just, well, I've been like that for as long as I can remember. Will you be killing me for it and, well, everything else?"

"Not yet," she replied. "What is your name?"

"Thierry Dubusset," he whimpered, spilling his name over his lips. "Wait, why not?"

"You remind me of someone," Marquaisa grumbled, lowering her sword.

"Really, what is his name?"

"Ryhu. Like you, he is a fool. He thinks the world is magical no matter how bad things get for him."

"Let me guess," Thierry ventured. "Things are about to get very bad for me."

"No," Marquaisa snapped, and punched Thierry in the chest. "But you will be made to earn the gold you stole from me."

"You're giving me a job?" Thierry, asked through a cough, puzzled by his good fortune. Then, thinking it too good to be true, he added, "Wait, what do you want me to do?"

"Piss someone off."

"I can do that."

"I know," Thierry's new employer quipped and held out her hand. "Give me back my scabbard, then go and stand at the entrance to the cathedral, under the rose window. When two men, Spanish men, approach the church make them chase you into this alley. Run by me and do not look back. When you are far away use my gold to start a new life. Do you understand?"

"Yes, I'll go find my sister. She's in the New World. But wait, what will happen to you?" Thierry's voice broke over the last word.

"Only that which I choose," Marquaisa replied, taking back her sword belt and scabbard and sheathing her blade. "This you should understand, by now."

"You mean, you let me—"

"Go," she interrupted and pointed him at the church square.

Thierry looked both ways before ambling out of the alley, whilst scratching his throbbing dong and rearranging the tattered pants that barely kept his ebony buttocks a secret. Marquaisa watched him blunder across the square as she backed deeper into the alley and bumped up against Elazuna. The mare's expression was colored with doubt.

"He'll be fine," Marquaisa assured the horse, gripping and re-gripping the hilt of her sword.

Below the stained-glass window Thierry shuffled his feet and played with himself. Occasionally, he flung a thumbs-up sign at the alley, the meaning of which was clouded by his preoccupation with his genitalia. Whatever the intended message the signal was entirely lacking in discretion, given a key element of the boy's assignment entailed not divulging the presence of his handler.

"Shush!" Marquaisa hushed Elazuna for blowing her nose at the boy.

At that moment Thierry stopped fidgeting and focused on a street to his right, which branched off the square. Stock still, he stayed at his post until two men marched into view. One of the men was middle-aged, swarthy, and dressed in the style of the Spanish court. The other was younger, taller, brawnier, and clad in the armor of a conquistador.

Certain they were the men for whom he was waiting, Thierry hurried into the middle of the square and thumbed his nose at them. The men stopped in their tracks and reached for their swords, trying to decide what he was up to. Deciding he was harmless they laughed at him and resumed their conversation only to be interrupted, yet again, when the boy spat a stream of slurs at them.

Roaring their offense, the Spaniards drew their swords and stormed the square in pursuit of Thierry's scrawny butt. Slippery as a rabbit, he scampered out of their reach and disappeared down the alley in which Marquaisa was concealed. His eyes wide with excitement, he waved and smiled brightly when she flashed him a thumbs-up as he sprinted past her.

"Adiós," she bid the lad goodbye, quietly, knowing he would not hear her farewell.

Thierry's footfalls fading, Marquaisa stepped into the center of the alley. Making a fist of her left hand, she planted it on her hip and propped her right hand on the handle of her scabbarded sword. Elazuna looked over her shoulder and blocked the alley with her body. Cloaked in shadow, they awaited the arrival of the Spanish delegation.

Yelling dire threats and tripping over one another the two men scrambled into the alley. Gaining traction, they ran a few steps at full stride before stumbling to a halt a sword's-length from the woman who loomed up before them. In an attempt to regain a measure dignity, the courtier doffed his plumed hat and bowed, while the conquistador stood at attention and clicked his heels. Marquaisa yawned at their salutations.

"*Señora,*" the nobleman greeted her, swallowing his affront at her ill manners. "Please allow us to pass. We have business with the street rat who just ran by you."

"Your business is with me, not with the boy," Marquaisa countered.

"Stand aside, whore," the warrior growled at her, sticking out his chest.

"You mistake me for your mother, *General*," she mocked the soldier and stood her ground. "Kindly shut your trap while the grown-ups are speaking."

"Hold, Hernandez!" the noble barked to stop his guard from taking a cut with his sword at the sharp-tongued woman. "I wish to hear what the *señora* has to say."

"You are Quintano, Ferdinand's errand boy," she obliged, aiming a finger at the courtier. Then, while extracting a scroll from her cloak added, "Everything I would tell you is written on this. As you can see, it bears the seal of the King of France."

"Where is Don—"

Elazuna, her voice deep, throaty, and grating cut off Quintano's question.

"Silence that stupid beast, or I will put her to the sword," Hernandez threatened, drawing his Toledo steel blade.

Marquaisa started into a retort but stopped when a sweet aroma filled the ally and Thierry's shaggy, severed head soared over her shoulder and slapped on the pavers at Quintano's feet. Speechless, she and the two men stared into the boy's vacant eyes. Rage flooding her every fiber, she stuffed the scroll back into her cloak and tore out her rapier.

"Rodriguez, you idiot!" Quintano shouted at the conquistador strutting down the path up which Thierry had disappeared. "You were to wait until I had the pact in my hands!"

"You mean you don't have it yet?" Rodriguez carped, testily. "Hernandez, didn't I tell you he is as useless as a—"

Elazuna spared everyone the aggravation of listening to Rodriguez's insults by kicking him in the throat and breaking his neck.

As he slumped, Hernandez raised his sword high over his head to deliver a death blow to the wench who had slighted his mother.

Marquaisa waited for him to reach the top of his windup. Stretched to his limit, Hernandez revealed the chink in his armor; between his cuirass and his shoulder plate his unprotected armpit was exposed. Spotting the opening Marquaisa struck, driving her blade into the gap, across his chest cavity, and out his left shoulder.

Stunned, Hernandez dropped his sword. As it clattered on the cobbles behind him Marquaisa yanked her sword free and let him fall to his knees. The edge of a wave of thick blood dribbled over his lower lip and, choking on it, his eyes bulged as her blade sliced through the air at the lump in his neck.

Encased as it was in its helmet, the soldier's head landed with a *clang* on the stone floor of the alley. Blood from his slashed throat and his punctured chest poured down his kneeling frame into a pool that flowed towards the toes of Quintano's boots. Marquaisa splashed through the gore and slapped the nobleman with the back of her right hand, gashing his cheek and sending him piling into a brick wall. On top of him before he could recover, she hauled him to his feet and licked a ribbon of blood off his face.

"Stop, hag!" Quintano shouted at her, anger and desperation coursing through in his plea. "We fight for the same cause!"

"What cause?!" Marquaisa screamed in his face.

"The glory of Spain and her Empire!" he yelled back at her, hiding his fear.

"There is your Empire in all its glory," she grabbed his chin and jerked his head around to look at Thierry. "So full of promise and so dead before knowing it."

"You set your trap," Quintano grit his teeth and shoved her away, covering over his shame with a show of false bravado. "I set mine."

"You knew of Bartolome's treachery," Marquaisa snarled, punctuating her deduction with a low growl.

"Ferdinand is no fool," the courtier snapped at her, a defensive quiver breaking down his posturing, "Judging by your presence here, neither are you."

"You thought Thierry was Bartolome's," Marquaisa hissed at him, in a rage. "So, you butchered him. I should kill you, just like I killed—"

"Bartolome?" Quintano guessed at the finish of her sentence, squirming under her rapier. Then, thinking he saw a hint of memory flicker in her eyes, he dared to change his tack, "Thank you for your service, *señora*. You have made a success of my mission. Or, should I say, you will once you hand me that scroll."

Marquaisa replied by jamming the point of her sword into Quintano's coat over his heart, ready to run him through. The Spaniard gasped as she channeled her weight and strength down the blade. Razor sharp it cut through the cloth and was about to lance his skin when she stopped.

"You shall have it on two conditions," she told him, grabbing a fistful of his garish topcoat and pulling him tight to the tip of her rapier. "First, you will deliver it to the king like the pawn that you are. Second, you will tell no one, not even Ferdinand, of my part in this affair. If you do, then know this: I have your scent and I will find you. When I do you will watch me eat everyone you hold dear. Then I will feed you your entrails, until you shit them out your ears, and leave you to drown in your own excrement."

"I will abide by your first condition not to appease you, but because it is my duty," the nobleman replied, grasping for his dignity. "As for the second, what would I tell Ferdinand? A woman whose name I do not know killed the traitor, Bartolome, to obtain the writ that contains France's pledge. Then, she and her horse slaughtered my guardsmen to protect it. And to top it off, for services rendered, she asked for nothing in return!"

Quintano laughed, spitefully, and looked up at the night sky.

"First, Ferdinand would relieve me of the scroll," he predicted, turning his glare on Marquaisa. "Second, he would shut me away, forever, thinking I've taken leave of my senses. So, no, you need not fear *señora*. Where your role in this enterprise is concerned my lips are forever sealed."

"For your sake, they had better be," Marquaisa warned him crowding into his personal space.

Using his pant legs as rags she cleaned her rapier, then retreated a step and sheathed it with a flourish. After it clicked home she reached into her cloak, pulled out the sealed paper cylinder and held it up to his eyes for inspection. Then, rather than hand it to him, she made him take it from her.

"Go, now, Quintano," she ordered him, pointing at the cathedral. "Before I have my mare make a meal of you."

Removing his hat and pressing it to his chest, the Spanish emissary bowed and scraped. He then did a brisk about-face and with Marquaisa's mocking laughter ringing in his ears strode out of the alley.

"Too bad about the boy. I thought he might make good his escape," Marquaisa told Elazuna as she knelt and shut Thierry's eyes. She dipped a fingertip in his blood and studied the bead before tasting it. It was cold, but sweet. "Otherwise, that went well. Xi would agree. She also will be glad to have new gold to count, courtesy of Ferdinand."

Elazuna stamped a front foot, eager to quit the cramped alley.

"Demon horse," Marquaisa teased the mare and swung into her saddle.

Blood clinging to the hem of her cloak painted the horse's hind quarters. Feeling its clammy touch Elazuna got herself going at a canter and looked for the shortest route to the Seine. When she reached it she headed west, putting at their backs the false dawn that was creeping into the sky ahead of the rising sun.

CHAPTER 3

POMPADOUR

JANUARY 27TH

DUCLAIR, FRANCE

A pencil-thin sunbeam shot through the knothole in the wooden door and smacked into the sleeping guardsman's brow. The heat it carried seared the soldier's skin. But, stuck in his nightmare-plagued slumber, he could only paw at the prickling.

Blind groping brought him no relief, so he curled into a ball and wedged himself deeper into the corner of the roadside tavern in which he had taken refuge during the night. Drained by days and nights of riding and, after his horse died under saddle, running, he was too spent to switch spots. Nor would he open his eyes for fear of what he might see when he woke.

Shut so tight as to squeeze out trickles of oily tears, the soldier's eyelids shielded his vision from the glaring wave of sunlight that washed into his hideout when its front door boomed open. Two men, wraith-like in silhouette, stood in the portal. One leading, one following, they waded through the rays of light that broke past their slim frames. High and tight to his ears, the collar of the guardsman's coat muffled the sounds of their approach.

"Give him a kick, D'Acier, if you please," Léonarre Poisson, stylishly sleek in a buttery soft, knee-length, tan leather coat, matching pants, tall black riding boots, and beaver plush, ostrich feather trimmed tricorn hat, requested of the man on his left.

"With pleasure," Trémont D'Acier replied, sportively, flicking the long tail of his top knot over his shoulder and straightening the lapels of his deep, matte black leather overcoat as he took a stride past Poisson.

Dignity a distant afterthought, D'Acier located the sleeping man's posterior and slammed the pointed toe of his jodhpur-booted foot into it with the same force he used to break down the tavern door. His torpor caved in, his fists crashing into the wall, his feet thumping the floor, the guardsman roared out of his doss and lunged at his attacker. Expecting as much, D'Acier caught the soldier by the collar of his crumpled white great coat, drove him back into the wall, and slapped him hard across the face.

"Mind your manners, Rousellot," D'Acier growled and gave the soldier a shake. "Or it will be my sword up your arse instead of the toe of my boot."

"Forgive me, my lord," Rousellot blubbered in reply, his lips flapping sloppily like fish spilled on a wooden deck, "I did not know it was you. I thought it was her, come to claim me at last."

"To whom, exactly, are you referring," Poisson asked, smoothly, sliding into the wide-eyed man's field of vision.

"Oh, Your Grace, thank goodness you're here," Rousellot whined and wrang his hands together. "It was horrible!"

"D'Acier, please sit the captain down," the Regent directed his retainer, then waited for Rousellot to pull himself together. "Now, Lucien, tell me what happened."

"It was terrifying, my lord!"

"So you've said," Poisson replied quietly and squatted down to look Rousellot in the eye. "Bring us wine, D'Acier."

"She's terrible. Absolutely horrifying," the guard whimpered.

"There now, you've exhausted the combinations of *terr,' horr,'* *'ible, and 'ifying,*" Poisson teased Rousellot and patted him on the shoulder. "So, take a breath and think back to the start of your mission, right after I sent you after that wicked woman."

"The woman," Rousellot repeated, his eyes rolling. "Yes . . . yes . . . Paris. Notre-Dame. Bodies, headless bodies. Blood everywhere."

"Are you saying you killed her?" Poisson, eager for clarity and, if possible, closure, tightened his grip on the captain's shoulder.

"Non, non, mon seigneur," the soldier moaned, shaking his head. *"She* killed *them.* I think. Then she left. But I followed her. She was headed this way."

"Merde," Poisson cussed. *Shit.*

"Shit, shit, shit!" Rousellot shrieked, tugging on his hair. "Still, it gets worse!"

Bottle of wine in hand D'Acier walked into the thick of the exchange. Head cocked a few degrees to the side, he shifted his eyes left and right, from Rousellot to Poisson, while breaking the bottle's grip on its cork. When the stopper came free he smelled it out of habit, then handed the bottle to Poisson who sniffed its contents and nodded his approval.

"Well done, D'Acier," the regent complimented his man on his selection then offered the wine to Rousellot. "Drink, Lucien."

The captain licked his lips and snatched the bottle. No sooner was it in the soldier's hand than it was plugged into his mouth and he was sucking it dry. After it yielded its last drop he pulled it from between his lips and hugged it tight.

"Impressive," Poisson declared, his distaste for Rousellot's guzzling transparent. "Now, you were saying you followed the woman."

"Woman?" Rousellot slurred, then clamped his eyes shut and buried his chin in his chest, his lips near the mouth of his bottle. "I saw her feed. She took down a wolf by herself! I watched while she ate it. That is when she saw me. I've never seen eyes like hers; solid black, shot through with blood red veins. When I looked into them I saw myself as she saw me. *As prey!* So, I ran. I've been running ever since. For hours, no, days at a time."

Poisson stood up and looked down on the broken man. Disgust on his face he ordered D'Acier, "Kill him. He is of no use to me."

"Wait! I am not useless!" Rousellot pleaded, his eyes shifting in D'Acier's direction.

"Really?" Poisson countered, challenging the soldier. "Then tell me plainly. Did the woman follow you here?"

"Woman?"

"Have I said otherwise?" Poisson asked, his tone grating. "Yes, the woman you followed into and out of Paris. The one you say ate a wolf."

Rousellot took a sharp breath and, cackling, he matched Poisson's tone, "You idiot. I was talking about her horse. Not the woman, you imbecile. Her horse!"

"Kill him, D'Acier. Now!"

Hungrier to save his own life than D'Acier was to end it, Rousellot clubbed the retainer with the wine bottle before he could make a move. Thick and blunt, the base of the bottle bounced off D'Acier's brow, leaving a deep imprint on his dark skin. Bent on splitting D'Acier open the soldier then aimed a backhand swipe at D'Acier's face, meaning to rake the bottle from the corner of his jaw to the bridge of his nose. D'Acier swayed out of its path. But his limbs leaden, he evaded neither Rousellot's pumping knees, nor his pounding feet and was knocked down and trampled upon by the bottle-wielding brawler.

Compensating for his retainer's burst of ineptitude, Poisson lopped-off Rousellot's head. The force of the chopping blow dropped the soldier's body on the spot, while his head spiraled into the air. It sprayed loops of blood as it tumbled through a steep arc, until it plopped down on the floor. When it landed it rolled into a tread-worn pocket in the stones and stopped, upside down, its wide eyes gaping through the inn's open door.

"I do so *hate* verbal abuse," Poisson told the back of Rousellot's topsy-turvy head, stretching out his last word in his credo as if he were snuffing out a candle between his fingers.

With no apology forthcoming from the disembodied skull, Poison shifted his focus to the body that once carried it. Its movement staunched in mid stride by its beheading one of its knees had ended up tucked under its belly, the result being its derriere was pushed upwards at a rude angle. Poisson ambled around the protruding posterior and wiped his blade on its round cheeks.

"Must I do everything, D'Acier?" Poisson asked his aide, while inspecting the finish on his sword. Dissatisfied, he went back to polishing it on the dead man's buttocks.

"I was merely confirming you still have your touch, my lord," D'Acier explained, still flat on his back on the floor, his coat bunched up under his back.

"You will be glad to know that I do," his governor reported, checking his blade once more. Pleased with its polish, he planted its point in the floor and posed heroically, "Not that you would have witnessed as much. You being in your repose."

"Yes, it's a pity I was too busy being concussed to catch your act. I'm sure you were stellar," D'Acier grunted and sat up in time to see Poisson slap Rousellot's backside with the flat of his blade, then sheath it. "I'm certain, also, you'll be repeating the tale, *ad nauseam*, for the entirety of the crossing to Louisbourg."

"Of that you can be assured," Poisson promised.

Willing to wait not a second longer for his retainer to peel himself off the floor, Poisson offered him a helping hand. D'Acier inspected the appendage before accepting it and allowing himself to be hauled to his feet. Once he was standing, his master locked arms with him to keep him upright and steered him towards the door.

"Oh, look, there's Rousellot," Poisson feigned surprise, then hoofed the guardsman's head out of their way and into a darkened corner of the inn.

"What thought you of his tale of the woman and her horse?" D'Acier asked, gripping the doorframe with his free hand as he and Poisson walked into the sunlight.

"Lunatic ravings for the most part," the regent snorted, while helping his apprentice up the steps of their carriage. "The one exception being the fact that Lady Marquaisa is alive and at large."

"You think her a threat," D'Acier said what Poisson left unspoken.

"You need not. She is nothing. You have the blessings of a king, which I know not how you obtained."

"She is a nuisance," Poisson corrected his aide as they sat, facing one another in the carriage's passenger compartment. "As for securing his majesty's backing, that was a trifle. The challenge lay in convincing my cousin that our expedition had merit, without disclosing its true purpose."

He rapped the outside of the carriage door with his knuckles to tell their driver to roll on and remembered knocking, with equal alacrity, on the door of one of the king's reception halls at Versailles two weeks earlier.

"Jeanne Antoinette Poisson, Madame de Pompadour, *cousin* to you," King Louis XV had drawled, sounding vaguely apathetic but undeniably authoritative, from deep in his lounge chair. Leaning on his elbow, he eyed Poisson as he strutted into the great room, hat stuck in the crook of his arm and weaving his way through a wonderland of partially clad women, discarded clothing, powdered wigs, silver platers covered in half-eaten food, and wine bottles, some full, some empty, some cracked and leaking their contents onto Persian rugs, "Chief Mistress to *us*, she was."

"Yes, thank you, Your Majesty," Poisson acknowledged the unnecessary reminder and stepped over a slick of red wine that was smeared across the marble floor in front of the pedestal upon which king's chaise lounges resided, "She was worthy?"

"She was the world to us, as we were to her for a time," Louis recollected, wistfully. Naked under an open, pink, ankle-length silk robe, he twirled the end of one wave of his long mousy brown hair around one of his fingers. His skin fair, his muscles smooth, his oval face cleanshaven, were he younger than his forty-eight years he might have been considered more pretty than manly, were it not also for the extraordinary length and girth of the body of his penis. "Now she belongs to the queen. A lady-in-waiting is she."

"Yes, Your Majesty," Poisson acknowledged that of which he was already aware and kept his eyes averted from Louis's king-sized, horizontal erection, of which the regent was painfully aware, "She is serviceable?"

"She runs France," the king admitted without a hint of a qualm, while scratching the underside of his hard-on. "Neither the queen, nor I have interests in the affairs of state. Marie prefers music and the company of her courtiers. I like it here, in my stag room, with my play-mates. You may borrow one or two of them if you wish."

"By Your Majesty's leave, I shall," Poisson accepted, bowed in gratitude, and choked down a gag, "When the timing is more opportune."

"Oh, bother," Louis moaned and flopped onto his back, his stiff penis waving at the orgies of fornicators painted on the ceiling of his bower. "Very well, to business. Jeanne tells us you wish to go on an excursion to New France to inspect, on our behalf, the fortress that bears our name."

"I requested that honor, yes, Your Highness."

"You are aware of the risks, yes?" Louis cautioned his regent while tracing in the air the curves a dark-skinned female reveler who was captured in the picture of the sex party. "Not just in the crossing, but also in that you will be putting yourself at the front line of a war?"

"The risk to France will be greater if the fortress is unfit to defend her honor, Your Majesty," Poisson sermonized, carefully concealing his contempt for what he considered was the folly known as honor.

"The connection between the health of that backwater and the wellbeing of our crown eludes us," the king countered. As he wres-tled with Poisson's dogma, the tip of his finger came to an abrupt halt at a compilation that featured a woman entertaining two men simultaneously, one anally and one orally. "But Jeanne thinks the initiative is well advised and has warranted that we should grant it our approval."

"I will make it a point to thank my cousin," Poisson assured the king. Then, holding his breath, asked Louis, "What say *you*, Highness?"

"You must promise us that you will neither be lost at sea, nor killed by either a savage or an Englishman. Though the difference between the latter two *also* escapes us," Louis stated his conditions, grappling with his beliefs, as well as his pulsating shaft.

"I promise, my lord," Poisson swore, and bowed to his king, happier to look at the veins in the marble floor then the ridges of the king's rod.

"So be it. You have our blessing, young Poisson," Louis sighed, then sat up straight in his chair and covered himself with his robe. The touch of silk exciting, he continued to toy with his manhood as he heaped more blessings on Poisson, "You shall also have the use of the royal carriage of your choosing for transport to Le Havre. It will be stuffed with coin enough to ensure comfortable passage for you and your man and also to pay for any repairs to our fortress you deem are essential."

"You are too kind Your Majesty," Poisson bowed, again.

"Yes, we are," Louis agreed, petulance poisoning his largesse. Then, waxing melancholy, he added, "Now, go. We will embrace you only upon your safe return, for we deplore farewells."

Glad to have been released from his audience, Poisson made an about face and started for the exit, but came to an abrupt halt when the king called out his name.

"Léonarre Yvain Poisson," Louis pronounced all three names as if he was scolding a child. "What are you not telling us?"

Poisson spun into a second about face, squared his shoulders to the king, and put his neck on the line, "Just this, Your Highness. I have masterminded a plan to sell New France to Spain. However, rather than return the proceeds to you, I will keep most of it for myself. The balance will be given to the British, whose invasion of New France I have enabled by trapping our fleet at Cartagena, to help fund their conquest of the New World."

As his mouth fell open the king stood up and, the head of his engorged penis nodding at Poisson from between the folds in his robe, stared at his regent. Poisson nodded back, looked Louis in the eye, and smiled. Louis watched his regent's grin widen and, slowly, matched it with one of his own.

"You dear, brave, impetuous young rascal," the king laughed and stamped his foot, making his rigid royal scepter waggle. "You jest to spare us from worrying for your safety."

"Indeed, Your Highness," Poisson forced himself to share in the laughter.

"Now, no more games, *monsieur*," Louis demanded, stifling his chuckles and sitting down on the edge of his seat. His manhood returned to its silk wrappings, he pet it, absently, and asked, "What surprises will you be bringing back for us?"

"Would that I could tell you, Highness," Poisson apologized, feeling a sudden pang of desire to aid the king in his quest for sexual gratification. "However, my cousin has sworn me to secrecy. If I were to break my pledge, she would be most displeased."

"Oh, yes, there is that," Louis concurred, drumming his lips with the fingertips of his unoccupied hand. "Things would get very ugly. Though not so much for us as for you."

"Too true, my lord," Poisson conceded, then took a deep breath to temper his cravings.

"Very well," the king relented and started stroking himself hand-over-hand, "A surprise it shall be. Oh my, but we shall be all of a dither until you return. Go. Go, go, go. Now, you young pup!"

Poisson bowed and pivoted sharply, then marched out of the king's flesh house, hastily, before yielding to his baser appetites. As its doors closed, Louis cut loose a belly laugh.

"Mastermind, indeed!" he guffawed and banged on the arms of his chair with his hands. "Nadège, you saucy little vixen, my dam ready to burst. Bring your nubile body to me, this instant, and open my flood gates with your candied lips!"

Startled by the banging of his carriage as it rattled over ruts in the road, Poisson grabbed the cushioned arm rest of his bench. His posture warped by the jostling of the coach, he shifted his bones back into alignment and cast his eyes through the window next to his seat. Warmed by the sun, which was following his trek west to the coast, the land was shedding the film of frost that had taken hold of it overnight. The thaw reminded him of the trickle of ice water that rolled down his wrist and chilled his bones when he first met Lady Marquaisa, which meeting was followed by his tête-à-tête with his cousin and, subsequently, his audience with the king.

"And that, D'Acier, is how we came to be riding in his majesty's carriage, endowed with his coin, and protected by his seal," he wrapped up the tale of their path to good fortune.

In appreciation, D'Acier hacked out a honking snore and snapped off a full body twitch as his demons shredded his dreams. Poisson snorted quietly at his retainer, then nudged the sole of his booted foot to calm him. He then recited to himself the mantra of torments to which he would subject the Spanish witch when he caught her, until he fell asleep, a razor-sharp smile on his face.

CHAPTER 4

CHANCERY

JANUARY 31ST

LA ROCHELLE, FRANCE

Hours had passed since the sun had set. What little heat it provided during the day followed it when it tumbled over the edge the earth. Abandoned to the cold and the dark, the port town of La Rochelle fired lamps to light its winding lanes, and hearths to warm its worldly-wise citizens.

Untouched by the warmth, chill air wafting over the harbor coaxed icy mists from its tepid water. Knifing through the vapors, a longboat skimmed across its still surface. Powered by the strong backs and sinewy arms of the two seamen at its oars, the rowboat rushed towards a sandy beach that was bracketed by a pair of stone piers.

Wedged into the prow of the boat and looking like its figurehead, a lanky cabin boy in a short, blue, woolen fearnaught jacket, baggy trousers that reached down to just below his kneecaps, and bare feet watched for hazards above and below the waterline which might pierce the small craft's hull. Strands of his straight blond hair strayed across the soft ridges and shallow planes of his face, but did not stop his eyes from tearing up in the cold. Blinking hard, the teenager cleared his eyes and then wiped the watery tracks off his face with his sleeve as he called out the countdown on the approach to shore. His voice, light and crisp, was octaves above those of the sailors milling about in the streets beyond the beach.

Sitting on the bench at the stern of the longboat, Captain Aleron Duvauchelle leaned back and stretched his bowed legs. A tall tricorn hat added back the inches in height that were subtracted by his warped pins and his bulky greatcoat added width to a chest and a pair of shoulders hollowed and stooped after long years as a seafaring merchant. He chose not to disguise the gray in his shoulder length hair and grizzled beard. Nor did he hide the hardened intellect that laughed at the world through his blue eyes.

When his longboat struck bottom sooner than expected and his young lookout was thrown over the rail, he belched out a laugh. He added a round of applause when the lad somersaulted and, catlike, landed on his feet in the surf. Then, seeing both of his men-at-oars dumped on the deck, their booted feet kicking in the air, their canvas long coats flapping, their wool caps skewed on their heads, he slapped his knees.

"Well done, Mister Beaufort!" Captain Duvauchelle guffawed. "Now, see if you can get her beached without capsizing her!"

While Beaufort tugged their little boat to shore, Duvauchelle helped his sailors get up off the deck and straighten their gear.

"Weapons check, gentlemen," he ordered them. "We wouldn't want anything going off unexpectedly or jamming when we need it most."

"All clear," the men reported after inspecting the pistols tucked in their belts, the swords belted to their hips, and the daggers hidden in their boots.

"Clear," the captain replied after examining his own weapons cache. "Permission to come ashore, Mister Beaufort!"

"Granted, sir!" the boy chimed.

"Thank you!" Duvauchelle bellowed over his men's heads, then pointed at the water. "Shall we, gentlemen?"

The three men vaulted over the sides of the boat into water that rose above their ankles and drenched the tails of their coats. Spray and foam hit the captain's trousers and the stains spread as he dragged himself onto dry land. The oarsmen bumped Beaufort playfully in passing, then took up their positions at the edge of the beach, keeping their eyes on the town to their front, and the piers by which they were flanked.

"Good man, Saro," Duvauchelle praised Beaufort, rubbing the crown of his head with his thick knuckles. "Now, take this pistol and guard the boat. The boys and I have a bit of business to take care of in town. But we'll be back within the hour."

"Aye, sir!" Saro said, seriously, and stuffed the gun into his pants.

"Remember," the captain placed his hand on the youth's shoulder. "Warn the blackguards before you shoot. If you have to shoot, aim to kill. After you shoot, draw that sword of yours. Cuz, whether you hit'em, or miss'em, they'll come runnin' and you'll have to hold'em 'til we gets back'ere. You good with that, lad?"

"Aye, Cap'n!".

"Very well, Mister Beaufort, you now are in command," Duvauchelle deputized the boy, then shouted at the other members of his team. "Right, you two! Let's turn over the rock under which that swindler Fauchelevant keeps himself hidden and see what he wants us to take off his greasy hands."

His gait rolling, Duvauchelle churned through the sand to the street that fronted the harbor and was joined by his two men. The trio stamped sand off their boots, then swaggered up the lane, heading north for Fauchelevant's shop. Leading the way, the captain stuck his head into the doorways of the inns he frequented, greeting their owners. Declining, politely, their invitations to stop-in he stayed his course, eager to conclude his meeting with his supplier without delay.

Near the mid-point of their trek, the lane curved up and away from the seafront. Shops, warehouses, and homes closed in on the three men, from both sides, and lamplights became fewer and farther between. A few steps into their climb up the shallow incline they heard a door creak open and saw the lamp above it flicker to life and splash a puddle of light on the empty street.

Warily, the captain and his men angled for the opposite side of the narrow road. As they came alongside the open doorway, a craggy-faced man wrapped in a heavy blanket and sitting in a rocker struck a match and sucked its flame into his pipe until the tobacco crammed in its bowl began to glow. Cross-eyed from the effort and the first hit from his leaf, he coughed out a cloud of smoke, then smiled and waved at the passersby.

Calmed by his harmlessness the sailors returned his greeting, but kept walking, the crunch of their boots on the cobbles echoing off the tightly packed buildings. Slackening their pace as the road steepened, they looked back over their shoulders as a stream of pebbles pinged down the hill behind them. The instant they turned their heads, a door on their left swung inward and Duvauchelle was hauled through the opening into a blacked-out shop.

From the street, his men heard display cases toppling over, boot heels scuffling, and their captain spewing profanities. Focusing on his cussing, they charged into the shop to rescue him. In their hurry, they slipped on broken glass and crashed into collapsed shelving but made it to the storeroom at the back of the shop, through whose unhinged door Duvauchelle's voice was blasting.

Shouting his name the duo ran into the unlit room, swords drawn, and pistols cocked, and were blinded by two torches that burst into flame before their eyes. When they threw their hands in front of their faces to shield their eyes they were disarmed, kicked in their groins, rammed into a wall, driven to the floor, and forced to sit next to the man they'd come to save. Their unseen attacker held the torches close enough to their faces that their skin blistered, and long enough that they understood it was in their best interests to silence themselves.

"Those two over there were your executioners," the bushwhacker told Duvauchelle, while waving a torch at a pair of dead men propped against the wall opposite the one against which he was propped. Then, flashing the flame over two more corpses, continued, "These two were to supposed to murder your escort. You've made some very bad people very angry, Captain."

"Occupational hazard," Duvauchelle shrugged, unfazed by the threat and how she dealt with it. "Who are *you* here for?"

"Myself," Marquaisa replied, letting the glow from one of her torches light up her smiling face, her tone telling Duvauchelle the answer to his question was patently obvious.

"And what do you wish for yourself?" the merchant asked, eyeing her disturbing dental arsenal.

"Valhalla, with a twist," Marquaisa quipped and arched an eyebrow when Duvauchelle's face went blank. "You know, a world where the virtuous are rewarded with endless rounds of feasting, fighting, and fucking. The twist is, I'm going to be the richest, most powerful fucker of them all. So, I'll decide who gets to stay, versus who gets condemned to an eternity of torment; cast away to a world where damned souls plague each other with endless cycles of lying, cheating, and corruption. You know, the world of politics."

Duvauchelle gawped at her.

"But, that wish is not yours to grant," she stated the obvious for the captain, taking her two torches in one hand and dismissing her rant with a snap of her fingers. "So, instead, you will provide me and my horse passage to the New World. You're headed that way, are you not?"

"Yes, but . . ." Duvauchelle vacillated, reflexively rubbing his thumbs and forefingers together.

"But?" Marquaisa scooched in close to Duvauchelle and, the flames of her torches flaring, rested her elbows on her knees, crossed her arms, and rested her chin on top of them.

"What's in it for me?" Duvauchelle went straight to the point.

"There is the merchant about whom I have received such sparkling reviews! Excepting, of course, what these cretins had to say about you," Marquaisa grinned at Duvauchelle and turned away from him to she set fire to the four dead men. She then answered the captain's question, "You will walk out of here with your skin intact and you will have my protection for the duration of my stay on your ship. It is an offer that you will not regret accepting."

"I am already regretting it," Duvauchelle griped, his mind having been made up for him.

"Nonsense, it is far too soon for that," Marquaisa teased the captain and tossed her torches into the crowded recesses of the storeroom, "Save it for tomorrow, when I evict you from your cabin."

"What?" Duvauchelle spluttered.

"Now, it's time for you to attend to your business with that wicked man, Fauchelevant," Marquaisa reminded him and helped him off the floor. "He has some excellent cinnamon in stock and I persuaded him to sell it to you at a deeply discounted rate that will set you up for a handsome profit. You can imagine how *those* negotiations went, I'm sure."

She placed his tricorn hat on his head and popped it firmly in place.

"And do be choosey in his cellar," she advised him while guiding him, arm-in-arm, through the wreckage of the shop and out its shattered doorway. "He claims the vintages of the '40's are the finest to be had. However, his palate is as misguided as his estimations of his manly endowments are exaggerated. Go for the stuff bottled in the 30's."

She steered the captain and his men up the hill, towards Fauchelevant's.

"I will return your prize cabin boy to you tomorrow morning. Saro is so young and innocent. I know that you could not live with yourselves if you fled like cowards, leaving him behind to die horribly. Or worse, to be corrupted. Or, even worse, both," Marquaisa smiled, fiercely, at the captain and his men. "Meet us at the beach, just before dawn. I expect, at that time, you will be pleased to welcome my horse and I aboard the good ship *Camille*."

She spun on her heel, ignoring their objections, and started down the hill for the seafront. The lamp still was lit above the old man's doorway, so she slowed down to thank him for helping her ambush Duvauchelle and his men. When she reached his doorway, however, she was struck not by the rich smell of his tobacco blend, but by the coppery scent of his blood.

Still in his rocker, cozy under his blanket, the old man sat dead. Four puncture wounds scarred his neck. The gold coin she'd given him to light his match to signal her was hammered into the middle of his forehead and a horse's bit cleaved his mouth.

"Elazuna," Marquisa hissed and bolted down the hill.

When she reached the seafront road, without breaking stride, she turned right and sprinted north. In moments, she reached the edge of town and the stables where she was boarding her mare. At full speed, she smashed through the barn doors and found her horse standing in its stall looking back at her, bleary-eyed.

Without hesitating, Marquaisa pushed up the sleeve of her coat and raised her arm to bite her wrist and extract the cure for her horse, but froze when she heard an object whirling at her from the opening that, until she demolished them, was filled by barn doors. A blink of an eye before it slammed into her temple, she pivoted and let a six-pointed silver star whiz past her ear and between Elazuna's, and burry itself in a wooden beam at the back of the mare's stall.

Without waiting for another one to come flying her way, she charged the thing with no heartbeat standing between the shattered doors.

She hit it at full speed, lifted it off the ground, and pounded it into the dirt, yards from the barn. A massive blow from one if its fists rocked her head sideways, but she shook it off and punched back harder, driving her fist into the middle of its masked face. The impact produced a loud crunch and her attacker, whoever, or whatever they were, went still.

"Who are you?!" she snarled, sat on its chest, and tore off its mask. "Vlad! What are you doing? And why are you wearing that ridiculous outfit?"

"Owwww!" Vlad yowled, touching his flattened nose, then wiping a tangle of his frizzy long black hair off his face. "Damn, girl, you really *do* pack a punch. Enough to break my mask and wreck my whole samurai vibe; that's what the rad armor's all about, by the way."

"Sorry," Marquaisa didn't apologize and punched him a bit lower, breaking his front teeth and loosening his fangs, top and bottom. "It's just like the Chancery to send a half-wit they want rid of after me."

"Now, that's just hurtful," Vlad whined and wiggled one of his fangs with the tip of a finger, then smoothed his Fu Manchu moustache down both its sides to their ends, which fell past his chin. "Why so *aggro (aggressive),* babe?"

"Let's see. You murdered an old man in my employ, poisoned my horse, and tried to kill me," she counted his wrongdoings from the past quarter-hour on her fingers, then grabbed him by the throat. "Your head stuffed in your bladder should convince the lord chancellor to leave me alone for at least another hundred years, *babe.*"

"Wasn't him!" Vlad choked, grabbing her wrist. "Freelance!"

"Great, I'll put that in a note and nail it to your forehead," she squeezed Vlad's neck harder. "He'll be happy to know he has one less rogue in his camp."

"Ruggg?" Vlad gurgled and frowned.

"Yes, *rogue.* Freelance work is forbidden," Marquaisa growled while bouncing the back of Vlad's head off the hard ground. "It's written in the charter your sire read to you and which you signed on your first night. Who is your sire?"

"Don't know," Vlad rasped when she let go of his windpipe. "I was in this dive getting wasted—I was still pretty messed up from that whole *'Impaler'* phase I went through—and the hottest chick ever, present company excluded, walked in. Next thing I knew it was tomorrow, she was in bed beside me, and I had the *all-time* hickey on my neck. I opened the curtains to catch a few rays, she burned to a crisp, and I've been on my own ever since."

"I had to ask," Marquaisa grumbled and bopped him in the shoulders with her open hands. Then, shifting her weight and sitting back on his stomach, she stamped one bootheel one of his gauntleted hands and jammed the other under his chin and pushed. "Okay, we'll deal with your sire issues later. Who hired you to kill me?"

Vlad squirmed and worked his jaw in and out, and side to side against the sole of Marquaisa's boot. She watched him closely, savoring his struggles, and after a time allowed him to lever his mouth open wide enough that he could answer her question. But, as he was about to spill, he was interrupted by Elazuna's groaning. A moment later, the mare crashed to the floor of her stall.

"Oops," Vlad giggled when Marquaisa jerked her foot out from under his jawbone. "Looks like all the tobacco juice in the old man's blood is as bad for her as it was for him."

"Mierda! (Shit!)," Marquaisa cursed and ran into the barn. When she reached her mare's stall, she stopped and bit her wrist. She then waded into the straw bedding.

Laying on her side, Elazuna surged, trying to stand up. Quickly, but quietly, Marquaisa calmed the mare and knelt in the straw. When the horse settled, her mistress showed her the open wound in her wrist and she licked the healing ichor until her eyes cleared.

"Dude!" Vlad hooted from his backside, propping himself up, stiffly, on his elbows. "You totally care about that stupid animal!"

Marquaisa did not reply to his taunt.

"Wait!" Vlad gasped and rolled onto his feet, the plates of his armor creaking. "That means the witch left a sliver of soul somewhere in that oh-so-tight bod' of yours. *Mmmm,* what I wouldn't give to taste a bit of the sugar locked in all that steel."

Marquaisa reached, slowly, for her rapier.

"Oh, wow," Vlad snickered, banging dust out of the joints in his leather, wood, and metal suit. "No wonder they're so hot-to-trot to drop the true death on your butt. Having a soul, even *uno pequeñito (a tiny one),* is the ultimate *faux pas (no-no). Mucho, mucho* worse than being a vampire for hire. Even someone as uneducated on the Charter as me knows that."

Marquaisa inched her sword from its scabbard.

"I can see what you're doing down there, all stealthy-like," Vlad called out. "Sheath that blade. Or, while you're nursing that brute, I'll go up to the loft and finish off the kid you left sleeping in the hay."

Marquaisa stilled her hand.

"He told me he's going to the New World," Vlad badgered her. "Wild guess. You're going there too."

Marquaisa did not move.

"Got it," Vlad said, scratching his head and gazing up into the night sky. "Okay, here's the deal. You go off to the New World and do . . . whatever. I'll say I closed the contract on you, get paid, and disappear.

All I need is some proof I did the job. That sword of yours will do the trick."

From within the barn, Marquaisa's rapier spun through the air between the splintered doors. Flying faster than Vlad could react, it caught him square in the chest and broke through his breastplate. Stingingly sharp, it pierced the flat bone in the middle of his chest, severed his spine, and staked him to the ground.

"So that's what it feels like," he wheezed and squinted at the sword sticking out of his body.

With both hands he grabbed the blade and tried to free it from the soil and his body. Farting with the effort it cost him, the palms his gloves were quickly shredded, his hands went slick with blood, and he lost his grip on the sword. Pinned, he turned his head, frantically, from side-to-side, searching for an escape. Finding none, he could only listen as Marquaisa walked out of the barn, then watch as she stood over him, her legs straddling his waist.

"Gas bag," she scoffed.

"Okay, new deal."

"Silence," she shut him up and planted her butt on his hips.

Without saying another word, she grabbed a handful of his hair and jerked his head out of the dirt. Her eyes locked with his, she crammed her slit wrist between his teeth and made him drink. He bucked, then took what she gave him until she pulled herself free and dropped his head.

"*This* is the deal," Marquaisa said, yanking her rapier free from the ground and scraping its edge against his bones and his armor. She then leaned over and went nose-to-nose with Vlad. "By the witchborn blood that now clings to your every miserable fiber, you are mine to do with as I please, until I see fit to release you."

"Shit!" Vlad swore.

"If I say so, yes, and in the color of my choosing. *Capiche?*" Marquaisa grabbed his chin and nodded his head for him. *Do you understand?*

"Totally," Vlad squished his bloody hands into fists and popped a double thumbs-up.

"Good. Tell me who hired you," Marquaisa picked up her interrogation where she had left it off.

"No clue, man," Vlad blurted, puzzled as to why he answered her question so readily. He confused himself further by adding, "It was a friend-of-a-friend thing."

"Very well," Marquaisa accepted his explanation, knowing he now could do nothing other than tell her the absolute truth. With a shove against his chest, she pushed herself off Vlad and onto her feet. She then began to pace, up one side of him then down the other, thinking out loud as she walked, "First, you will choose your friends more wisely. Second, in my absence, you will nurse Elazuna back to health. Third, while you tend to my mare, you will spread the word that *Camille* is bound for Saint Pierre, on Martinique, weighed down with rich cargo. Fourth, when Elazuna is fully healed the two of you will find the one who contracted your services. Fifth, when you find them, you will keep your distance from them, while keeping your eye on them. Like you, they too are mine. Clear?"

"You bet, Boss. Anything else?" still flat on his back Vlad welcomed her direction, nodding eagerly while, at the same time, wincing at his enthusiasm.

Without hesitating, using her rapier, Marquaisa cut off the ring finger of her right hand.

"Nasty," Vlad cringed, and without thinking covered his crotch with his bloody hands, "And not exactly what I had in mind."

She then trimmed out a lock of her hair and wound it around the severed finger. Using the blood that was dripping from the stub on her hand, she saturated the hair. Working quickly, she rolled the gory sausage between her palms until the hair and blood mixture hardened into a crust.

"The crust will preserve the finger. The marquis cut carbonado ring it bears will be recognized as my own and will be the proof you need to get paid. But *do not* give it to those thieves at the Chancery. Keep it safe and on your person at all times" she commanded Vlad. "Use your prize money to pay for your travels and to buy some decent clothes. If you run out, Elazuna will know how to get more."

"Far out," Vlad replied, shuddering at the site of Marquaisa's muti-lated hand. "Hope that thing grows back the way you want it to."

"Me too," she muttered to herself, narrowing her eyes at the nub as she waited for it to scab over. When the black shell sealed itself shut, she snapped out more commands for Vlad, "Now, on your feet. Take the boy, Saro, back to the beach and stay with him while I fix my horse and convince her to work with you, rather than eat you."

"Sure thing, Chief," Vlad sprang out of the dirt and accepted his orders, wondering why he was feeling so good about doing so. As she walked away he called after her, "Best boss ever!"

"A warning," Marquaisa called back to him as she disappeared into the barn. "Do not linger over long with other vampires. If you do, they will catch my scent upon you and kill you instantly."

"Yeah, great," Vlad mumbled and bunted some pebbles with the toes his leather boots. Then, knowing she was not listening, he added, "Hey, thanks for the job, man. Sure, keep the shuriken. It's from Nihon, by the way. What's that? Yeah, absolutely, when you get back we'll hang out. Have a few laughs. It'll be awesome."

CHAPTER 5

BULLDOG

FEBRUARY 3RD

LONDON, ENGLAND

Orbs of lamplight hid the stars that winked at the frosted streets of the West End of London. Home to the Thorney Island Retreat, known otherwise as the Palace of Westminster, the West End also gave up a patch of ground in St. James's Square to the unofficial residence of Britain's unofficial leader, William Pitt, the Elder. Pitt refused to be formally invested as the nation's prime minister, preferring instead to call himself its savior.

His residence, to which the number ten was affixed, was stacked five stories high, was dead center on the northern edge of the square and commanded a view of the park located in front of it and Pall Mall beyond. Its centerpiece was an octagonal great room that rose three floors through the heart of the flat and which was capped by a doomed ceiling that arced up into a hexagonal skylight. The glass canopy allowed sunshine and moonbeams alike to rain down upon the residence's principal occupant while he charted the course of the British Empire.

Less concerned with the fate of the realm than he was with navigating the traffic on Pall Mall, Colonel James Wolfe hurried toward St.

James's Square, where he was to make his way to house number ten and present himself to Pitt. Taller than many men, he also was slimmer than most, qualities that were exaggerated by the long grey overcoat he was wearing over the red jacket, white trousers, and black knee-high riding boots of his dress uniform. Head up, chest out, and shoulders back he made a crisp right turn into the square and politely tapped the brim of his black tricorn hat with his cane, excusing himself to the man and woman walking arm-in-arm whom he narrowly avoided knocking down.

Their and his honor preserved he picked up his pace until, near the top of the square, his path crossed with that of a fellow officer who could easily have been his twin.

"Evening, Barnes," Wolfe greeted his peer with a polite, but perfunctory nod of his head.

"Bugger off, Wolfe," Barnes scowled and marched past Wolfe, clipping the colonel's shoulder as he went by.

"What's the matter, Barnacle?" Wolfe asked, letting the force of their collision turn him around just enough that he could see his assailant hurrying on his way. "Daddy's bankroll not big enough to buy you *this* promotion?"

Barnes pivoted and while backing down the street spat at Wolfe, "Gutter snipe. You're neither officer material, nor a gentleman and you know it. Stop wasting your breath and everyone else's time. Go back to Kent and your barrow."

"You would miss me, I think," Wolfe bantered and took a few casual steps toward Barnes. "So, for your sake I'll stay. Look me up in the Daily Post while you're at tea with your mumsy and I'm off campaigning in New France."

"Braggart," Barnes threw a parting jab at Wolfe, then resumed his march out of the square.

"Poltroon," Wolf shot back. *Coward.*

"Conquering," a woman whispered in his ear, her voice like a soft breeze sifting through green spring leaves.

Wolfe, leaning on his cane and savoring the sight of Barnes scurrying away with his tail between his legs, arched an eyebrow and,

without looking her way, set aside the Kentish provincialisms that sometimes slipped out during heated exchanges and replied to the woman in as refined a manner as he could muster, "That is my intention, my lady."

"Then, why did you not say so?" she inquired, speaking into his other ear.

"Did I not?"

"You did not."

"What did I say?" Wolfe asked, knowing full well what he had said, while peeking back over his right shoulder.

"You said you would be 'campaigning' in the New World" she reminded him, knowing he needed no reminding, while circling around him, to his left. "What you really meant was conquering it."

"Am I that obvious?" Wolfe asked, turning his eyes her way as she rubbed shoulders with him.

"Transparent," she answered. Tall, straight, and strong, she walked by him without looking at him. "In fact, right now you are wondering, 'Have we met?' In short, we have not and, given you are about to embark upon a crusade that is hazardous in the extreme, I expect we never will."

"Then, my lady has me at a loss," Wolfe called to her as she feet touched the edge of a patch of the square that was untouched by lamplight.

"I doubt there ever will be a day when that can be said truthfully about anyone, where you are concerned," she ventured. "Good night, General James Peter Wolfe. Racine and duty are calling you."

"Colonel," Wolfe admitted, chewing on the title.

"Hmmm, I think not," she mused as she disappeared. "Barnes, pig though he may be, was correct. You are no officer. What he and his ilk fail to see, however, is that you are so much more. You know it in your heart. Show Pitt."

"Pitt is a horse's—"

"Get your arse in here, Wolfe!" a voice born of the parade ground thundered from the top of the square. "We haven't got all night!"

"By the three-eyed toad of Twickendon!" Wolfe swore. He whirled around in time to see a man in a bright red jacket dive into number ten. "Is that you, Amherst? Answer me! Craven! Stand, I say!"

Wolfe mounted his charge on Pitt's household and 'Rule Britannia!' pierced the air. Racine, the home's fossilized guardian, whistled the tune through his parched lips while standing his ground at the gateway to the estate. Bent and stiff, his white hair flowing over the collar of his black tailcoat, he was armed with a bottle of port and a silver dinner bell.

"Young man," he croaked, stopping Wolfe in his tracks the instant he waded into the light cast from the front porch. "Must I give you a lesson in decorum?"

"Am I to be judged on my knowledge of it?" Wolfe challenged the majordomo.

"Only if you persist in behaving as if you have none," Racine barked, forcing Wolfe to bite his tongue. "You and the Lords Amherst and Pitt may cast ceremony to the wind whilst you confer with one another, if you wish. However, while you are in my charge you will conduct yourself in a manner befitting that of an officer in the British army."

"My standing in that regard is the subject of much debate," Wolfe informed Racine, bitterly. He knew that when his candidacy for the promotions that would add up to the realization of his carefully cultivated ambitions was considered, his eighteen years in military service typically were cancelled out by his well-earned reputation for not tolerating stupidity in anyone and for bludgeoning it and them, bluntly and mercilessly, if and when he ran into them.

"Get used to it," Racine advised him. "When you are a leader everyone will doubt everything about you. You must, however, never doubt yourself."

"Were you under my command you would know that I never do," Wolfe assured the old sage. "Speaking of which, Pitt and Amherst have kept the real savior of Britain from doing his duty for long enough. Wouldn't you agree?"

"That's more like it," Racine registered his approval of Wolfe's attitude with click of his heels. "Follow me, my lord."

The craggy butler shuffled through a one hundred- and eighty-degree turn, then pottered up the short walkway and onto the narrow porch of Pitt's residence. After a brief wrestling match with the handle of its black-lacquered front door he cracked it open. When its glossy face formed a right angle with its frame he stood aside and made way for Wolfe, who strode into the foyer and removed his hat and overcoat. Expecting his outerwear would be taken off his hands he held it out for Racine, who let it fall into a heap on the stone floor as he wobbled toward the staircase that wound from the ground floor up to the first floor. Leaving his gear where it lay, Wolfe hoofed-it up the stairs behind the ancient footman.

"I met a woman in the street," he said, peeking over Racine's shoulder.

"Pursue her no further," the warden commanded as he made the right turn from the first landing onto the second flight of stairs. "What she has is catching."

"What? No! Not *that* type of woman," the colonel blustered. "She was a lady. She spoke knowingly of Pitt."

"So, she acts as if she reads The Post," Racine huffed. "Scene one in a pantomime, I'm afraid. Scene two will find you waking up in an alley in your skivvies, robbed of your purse and beaten to within an inch of your life by her cronies. I repeat, stay away."

"Speaking from experience are you?" Wolfe needled the old man. "Never mind. That was indelicate of me. Anyway, I'm more interested in the lady."

"*Casanova,*" Racine poked back. "Think you're the world's greatest lover?"

"Hardly," Wolfe declined the comparison, angling to the right and onto the third flight in the staircase. "I am merely curious. She gave me the impression that she was here, tonight, in the company of Barnes and Pitt."

"Barnes the jackal, you mean," the provost snorted. "Indeed, he was here earlier and, yes, there was a lady on his arm. A woman of grace, refinement, and beauty. Far too good for the likes of him."

"Her name?"

"What would you do with it if I gave it to you?"

"Most likely nothing," Wolfe grumbled. "She made it clear she expects never to see me again."

"Then be unexpected," Racine chided him as their stair-climb ended and he trundled off toward the open door of Pitt's study. "Lady Katherine Lowther would expect nothing less."

"Really? Well, I can do unexpected. I am nothing if not unconventional."

"Really? I've heard you're quite mad."

"Slanders spread by nameless, monied, pretenders who call themselves officers, but who lack the mettle it takes to be one and the honor to stand by their words."

"Oh, yes, *honor,*" Racine sighed. "Word has it you're fanatical about it."

"Without it life and victory—words that are interchangeable, as far as I'm concerned—are as worthless and as vile as rodent turd."

"Bullshit," William Pitt, the Elder, leader of Britain and arbiter of hogwash, stood in the doorway of his den, resplendent in his bulky red robe and fuzzy slippers. In between sips from his brandy snifter and sounding like Antony asking his friends and countrymen for a loan of their ears, he pooh-poohed the words by which Wolfe professed to live his life, "I don't give a fig about honor. Nor should you, Wolfe. Take the win any way you can get it. That's what I say. What about you, Amherst?"

"Cheers! Couldn't have said it better myself. Now, be a good sort and pass the brandy, if you please, Pitt," seated with his back to the wall and a clear view of the doorway and still wearing the red coat he flashed on Pitt's doorstep, his white waistcoat and breeches and black splatterdashes now plainly visible, General Jeffery Amherst puffed on a cheroot. His voice sounding like corked iron horseshoes clattering on frozen cobblestones, he shouted at Wolfe, "Dash it all, what are you waiting for, Wolfe? Get in here!"

"There you have it, Colonel. Straight from the man who will be your commanding officer during the invasion of New France," Pitt waved his decanter at Amherst before filling the general's glass. His eyes sparkling next to the bridge of his aquiline nose, he winked at Amherst, "Give no quarter, eh Jeff?"

Biting like a lumberjack's axe into tree bark, Wolfe objected, "I will conduct myself—"

"As you did at Culloden?" sitting forward in his chair, his drink and his cigar forgotten, Amherst jumped down Wolfe's throat. "Where you disobeyed a direct order?"

"From a coward to butcher—"

"Or, as you acted at Rochefort?" planting his snifter on a side table and wedging his stogie into an ash tray, Amherst interrupted Wolfe again. "Where you took the lead when your commander did not?"

"The general was—"

"Incompetent. Derelict. A hazard to his men and the mission," Amherst listed his former colleague's failings in rapid-fire succession, his voice rising as he rhymed off the flaws.

"Your words, sir," Wolfe deferred.

"Aye, and I stand by them," Amherst grated, rising from his chair and stalking over to Wolfe until they were toe-to-toe. "Just as I stand by this. You will be Brigadier to me in America, but not here at home. My peers would mutiny if I made you one of them. In return, you will give to me the Rochefort version of Wolfe. If Culloden Wolfe rears his head I will cut it off."

"You can't cut a proper fart, let alone a man's head off his shoulders," Wolfe dismissed Amherst's threat out of hand. "So, stick your Sevenoaks hogwash up your flat, forty-year-old arse. If you want me you'll take all of me. Otherwise, you and your expedition can be damned."

"Ha!" his cheeks glowing, Pitt laughed at the two fighting men. "You were right after all, Jeff. He *is* the man for the job."

"We shall see," Amherst promised. Still glaring at Wolfe, he tested the colonel, "At the very least, he can't be any worse than the other louts on our short list."

"Is that so?" Wolfe weighed Amherst's opinion of him against his own and, bent on not sell himself short, drove the first stake into the ground, "Well, you can count on me being, *at the very least*, dearer than the others."

"This is not a negotiation," Amherst made a play at correcting Wolfe.

"It certainly is," Wolfe persisted. "You two tossers know I'm your man. You just said as much. So, my promotion will apply equally at home as abroad. I will be kitted out in style, at your expense. I also will be assigned an aide, who you also will pay for, who will look after said kit whilst keeping the two of you out of my hair."

"You will walk out of here with your kit and your man guaranteed," Amherst allowed then, after glancing at Pitt, put his foot down. "You will assume your rank when you board *HMS Princess Amelia*. You will wear it in the colonies, then you will vacate it the instant you set foot back on these isles. Take it or leave it."

Wolfe narrowed his eyes and measured Amherst's resolve, for a moment, before offering him his hand, "Taken."

"Splendid!" Pitt crowed and threw back a shot of brandy. "Now that's settled, if you would Jeff, please take your seat. Wolfe, stay where you are."

Amherst reclined in his chair and, smelling his brandy, asked Pitt, "What of the French fleet?"

"Bottled up by Osborn at Cartagena. Louisbourg will not be reinforced," the leader of the nation reported, rubbing his hands together. "What news of our asset in the fortress?"

"Installed and reporting as planned," the general replied. With a slight shake of his head, he elaborated, "The French suspect nothing."

"Incredible," Pitt wondered at the news. He then turned his eye on Amherst's brigadier and issued his orders, "Wolfe, get your affairs together and report to *Amelia* in forty-eight hours. She'll be sailing for Halifax before month-end."

"I'll report when it damned well pleases me," Wolfe countered, the hairs on the back of his neck bristling. "I'll not be spending one second longer than is absolutely necessary on that scow."

"Oh, yes, the sea disagrees with you. Shameful of me to forget," Pitt chortled along with Amherst. "Very well, but report in good time.

If you do not, then your next promotion will be to a dungeon in the Tower of London. Have I made myself clear?"

"Crystal," Wolfe replied, crisply.

"Good. Begone," Pitt dismissed Wolfe then rounded on Amherst and, his voice going quieter with each word he spoke, continued scheming with the general. "Now Jeff, about the invasion, I have in my hand a letter from our friend in which are specified . . ."

Wolfe bowed to his hosts, who ignored him, then turned and marched out of the octagon, followed by Racine, the old man's cracking, popping, and wheezing drowning out the voices of the two grandees. The sound of Pitt's office door shutting brought Wolfe to a halt at the top of the winding staircase. Tracking their numbers with his fingers, he counted the steps in each of the three flights as he waited for Racine. When the old man finally caught him up, they locked arms and picked their way slowly down the stairs. Upon reaching the foyer, Wolfe fetched his hat and shook out his coat before shrugging into it.

"That went well, I thought," Racine rasped.

"I suppose so," Wolfe muttered. "That is, if you think the move from expendable, thirty-one-year-old colonel to sham, thirty-one-year-old general is an upward one."

"It will be if that is what you make of it," Racine snapped. "On the other hand, you could shirk your duty and mope about and in so doing prove to Amherst that your doubters are correct. That you're nothing but a lowborn grunt."

"Ha!" Wolfe guffawed as Racine hauled the front door open. "Very well, you old bulldog. When the place and time are right, I shall be Brigadier General James 'Puppet' Wolfe."

"Pirate," Lady Katherine Lowther, standing alone in the porch light, the hood of her green velvet overcoat pulled up and casting her eyes and cheeks into shadow, edited Wolfe again.

Wolfe caught his breath and lowered his voice, "Was that not the very word I used, my lady?"

"In fact, you said 'puppet,'" she jogged his memory. "No doubt out of bitterness from coming away from your audience with less than you desired. But, like all pirates, you will recover your losses and then some."

"Your appearance here has started me down that path already," Wolfe assured Lady Katherine, bowing and ignoring Racine's choking cough. "How can I be of service?"

"The cad Barnes, in something of a snit, has deserted me," Katherine recounted, laughing quietly. "In consequence, his life is in jeopardy. My steward will surely murder him for allowing me to walk the streets alone. However, his life might be spared if I am escorted home by a suitable stand-in. Do you know if there is any such person about?"

"Indeed, I do," Wolfe replied and wrapped his arm around Racine. "No man is finer than Racine. He would be honored to do your bidding. Unfortunately, he must attend to the two bumpkins upstairs, neither of whom would be considered suitable by anyone's standard. So, it appears as though I am your and Barnes's last hope. I am no Racine, mind you, and I am not ashamed to admit it. No one man can match him. But I will do my best to make you safe in his stead, if my lady will have me."

"You are too kind," Lady Katherine dropped a curtsy. "I am honored."

"The honor is mine, entirely, my lady," Wolfe returned the compliment, donned his hat, and offered his arm to Katherine.

Racine watched the couple stroll into the square and mumbled to himself, "Well, that was unexpected."

CHAPTER 6

CHARRED

FEBRUARY 21ST

ATLANTIC OCEAN, TRADE ROUTE SOUTHWEST TO THE
FRENCH CARIBBEAN

Matte gray clouds soaked up the watery dawn light and cast shadows on the ocean surface, lending it a greasy black sheen that hid the prowlers in its depths. Sandwiched between the rolling waves and the dome of clouds, winds swirled and spanked the backsides of *Camille's* sails. Her riggings straining, the sleek merchant ship snared the airy currents in her canvases and used them to surge ever farther southward in her sprint for the French Caribbean.

Standing by herself at *Camille's* stern rail, her black cloak wrapped tightly around her naked body, Marquaisa sipped from the bottle of wine that dangled between the forefinger and middle finger of her right hand. The vintage, which she'd plucked from a case Captain Duvauchelle selected from Fauchelevant's cellar at La Rochelle, took the edge off her cravings but contributed nothing to her recovery. Still sapped of strength from recruiting Vlad, propping up Elazuna, and regrowing her ring finger, her conviction to protect rather than eat

Duvauchelle and his crew was waning. With each passing night the swabbies were looking warmer and tastier.

To help quell her bloodlust she shifted her focus to the northern horizon. The bump on its curve, which she spotted just before nightfall, had turned into a blob that was rising and falling with the waves. It was tracking to *Camille's* course, it was gaining on her, and it was without doubt unfriendly.

"She will have you by tomorrow morning," Marquaisa reported to Duvauchelle when he reached the top of the stairs that lead to the poop deck.

"Hard for her to have anything if she's on the ocean floor," the captain replied, tipping back his tricorn hat and squinting at the blob. "We'll sink her the instant she comes into range."

"Not if she can outgun you, which is more likely than not," Marquaisa countered. "Save your shot, your crew, and your cargo. Stay out of her reach for the day. Let her catch you later tonight. I will do the rest."

"Those your orders?" Duvauchelle asked, defiantly, straightening his hat and hooking his thumbs in the wide leather belt that reached around his ample waist and held his overcoat shut.

"My promise," Marquaisa reminded the captain and took a sip of wine.

"Right," Duvauchelle snorted and gripped *Camille's* stern rail with both of his hands, "Your vow of protection. Tell me, in what world does surrendering without firing a shot equate to protection?"

"My *orders* did not include surrender," she corrected the merchant, and frowned at an imperfection in her pedicure, "They never do."

"Well, bully for you," the captain scoffed, then gave her a hard look. "If we're to neither sink her, nor surrender to her, then our plan must be to ambush her. Do tell, from where exactly do you suggest we pounce upon her to her utter surprise?"

"I will pounce," Marquaisa informed Duvauchelle, cryptically, without making eye contact with him, "You will take possession of her, on my command."

Duvauchelle turned his whole body to face Marquaisa, and leaning on the elbow he had rested on the rail asked her, "Alone? You think you can take that ship all by yourself?"

Marquaisa gave the captain a sideways glance and confirmed his understanding of her intentions, "If you do your part, yes,"

"And my part is?" Duvauchelle pressed, leaning her way, his eyebrows raised.

Marquaisa executed the quarter-turn required to face Duvauchelle, tilted slightly toward the captain and told him what to do, "Stay out of my way,"

Duvauchelle's face fell in disbelief and his shoulders slumped. Then, sneering at the absurdity of her plan, he looked up into her eyes and asked her to repeat what he thought he heard her say, "Stay out of your way? That's it?"

"Yes," Marquaisa replied, curtly, then doubled down on her proposal, "You *and* your crew."

Duvauchelle turned his back to the rail, shoved his butt against it and laughed, "This I have *got* to see!"

"No, you do not," Marquaisa countered, swinging around to locate the pursuing ship. "Stay below, listen, and imagine. What you envision you can forget. What you would witness would stain your every waking moment and wring the sweetness from your dreams."

The memory of his introduction to Marquaisa, in the back of the shop at La Rochelle, still fresh in his mind, Duvauchelle stopped chuckling and went along with her, "As you wish, then. We'll stay below, out of your way. Anything else?"

"Smoke. Plenty of it. From the galley. Starting now. At midnight strike the sails and wake me," she instructed Duvauchelle as she strode away from him toward the staircase that dropped down to the main deck. "You know where I will be."

"Yes, you'll be in my cabin," he groused at her turned back. "I hope you're comfortable."

"I am," she said, padding down the stairs without a backwards glance.

"You're also mad," he snapped at her as he hustled across the poop deck. "Wait. No. I'm the one who's crazy! I must be, for agreeing to this scheme of yours! It's lunacy! Do you hear me, witch? Sheer lunacy!"

"I am no witch," she replied, her tone matter of fact. "Fortunate are you."

"Is that a question?" Duvauchelle shouted from the top of the stairs as the door to his cabin closed.

Using her heel, Marquaisa pushed the hatch fully shut. Silent and still, she took in the smells of the blacked-out room. It stunk no more than usual. She was on her own.

"Shit," she cursed, spun around, and slammed home the deadbolt that locked the entrance.

Clenching her teeth, she pressed her forehead against the door panels and squeezed its handle until the iron began to creak. Hearing its objections she released it, but the moaning persisted. Her eyes shut tight she listened to the keening and, recognizing her own voice, silenced herself.

Though she knew she was by herself, she glanced sheepishly over her shoulder. Certain, once and for all, no one was watching she bumped her head against the wooden door. Her hunger relentless, her pain unforgiving, she promised herself if her plan of attack went sideways, then everyone, including Duvauchelle, his crew, and the ne'er-do-wells who were chasing them, would die horribly.

Her mind quieted by the prospect of a killing spree, she stood on her toes and dug her nails into the lip of the shelf above the door. With a tug of her arms and a kick of her leg she swung up and onto to the ledge as if she was mounting Elazuna. From its edge, she rolled onto a canvas laying between two of the joists that were holding up the deck on which, moments earlier, she'd been standing watch.

Before she curled into a tight ball she unbuckled her sword belt and hugged the scabbarded blade to her chest. Calmed by its familiar feel she let *Camille* rock her until she fell deep into the sleep of the dead. As she drifted into darkness, dreaming of blood and fire, she giggled at images of sticky red fluid being licked up by searing orange flames and reduced to crackling black ashes.

Orange under black, blazing arrows poured from the night sky into the walled-in town nestled in a valley in northwestern Hispania. Kayza of the Lugones, General in Gausón's revolutionary army, watched the pinpoints of fire blossom into flames that scorched everything in the hamlet. Old friends and neighbors whom she had known for most of her twenty-five years, including those who had chosen to be Romanized, perished in the blaze, or were cut down by the legionaries who charged into the town on the heels of the barrage. The villagers who listened to her warnings on what it meant to be pacified by Rome, and who now were scattered up the slopes behind her, gripped their makeshift weapons tighter and lurched toward the inferno that was swallowing their homes.

Kayza turned Elazuna, her tall Asturcón mare, sharply on her haunches to face her followers and roared, "Stay where you are! I will bring the Romans to you. When I do, kill them all!"

Their angry howls filling the air, she pointed her mare at the burning town and kicked her into a gallop. As they neared the village terrified shrieks and feral baying surged over the ring wall that encircled it, drowning out the pounding of the Asturcón's hooves. When they reached the collapsed gates of the settlement Kayza pulled up. In a bank of firelight, her blond ringlets glowing, her bronze cuirass shining, her chestnut mare steaming, she waited for the Romans who were hunting her to pause long enough in their bloodletting to see she was within easy reach.

A double take by a soot-smeared centurion, followed by the chain of expletives he barked at her, at once told her she'd been spotted and triggered her attack. Ripping twin blades from scabbards strapped to her back she pushed Elazuna into a headlong charge at the Roman who recognized her and the troops who were rushing to reinforce him. Surprised she blitzed them, rather than run away, the soldiers wavered. Sensing their confusion, she crashed into their ragged line and slashed them with her swords while her mare trampled them with her hooves.

Bruised and bleeding the Romans retreated, clearing the way for her to strike deeper into the town in search of more targets. She found them in the legionaries who were laughing at the charred remains of buildings and bodies lining both sides of a narrow lane. Weaving up the smoke-filled corridor at top speed Kayza worked her blades like scythes, cleaving limbs and severing heads from men too slow to dive out of her reach.

Their fun spoiled, the soldiers who survived her assault screamed at Kayza and, leaving behind their mutilated brothers, chased after her. As they entered the village square, which was serving as an impromptu field headquarters, the centurion leading the pursuit saw her sheath her swords and draw from her boot a dagger, which she flung at his commander. The knife clanged off the officer's helmeted head, the force of the blow nearly unseating him from his gray stallion.

To save himself from being dumped in the dirt the officer tightened his grip on his reins, sat deep in his saddle, and pushed his heels down in his stirrups to balance himself and his fretting mount. As he wrestled with the stud, he shot looks up and down the narrow arteries that branched off the square, searching for signs of his attacker, and was rewarded with a glimpse of an apple-bummed chestnut horse galloping for the hills that backed the burning town. Raging at the fleeing horse's buttocks, he dug his heels into his colt's flanks, and stoked by the whooping and hollering of a phalanx of his men, raced ahead of them after the beast.

Kayza heard the yelling and hooting reaching out to her from deep in her wake and brought Elazuna from a gallop down to a canter. As the mare eased her pace and caught her breath the destruction that surrounded them took shape. Tasting bile in her mouth, Kayza shouted a torrent of curses that deafened her to the bawling of the legionaries nipping at her and her mare's heels.

Her resolve to bait them into her trap hardened, Kayza kept Elazuna at a lope until she saw a child, further up the street, running toward one of the village's toppled gates. Lithe, with long flaxen ringlets not unlike her own, the little girl was no more than seven years old. She also was very fast. But, fleet as she was, the legionary who was chasing her with his sword drawn was gaining on her.

"No!" Kayza yelled and launched her horse onto a collision course with the bloody-minded soldier.

A stride short of being run down, the trooper heard the mare's hoofbeats and cut to his left. In the corner of his eye, he saw the horse's head, neck, and shoulder flash into the space he vacated. He neither saw, nor felt the blade that cut through his spine at the base of his skull. Rent from his lifeless body, his head hurtled into the grit and ash in the road and spun to a stop with its face planted against a smoldering timber.

Elazuna galloped past the disembodied head and skidded to a stop in front of the child, where Kayza dismounted her quickly. The tiny girl, unable to evade horse and rider, balled her fists and attacked them. Dropping her swords, Kayza knelt down on one knee and caught the child in her arms, squeezing her tight while she kicked and punched with all of her might. She let the girl fight for a moment longer, then took her shoulders n her hands, held her at her arm's length and, smiling, looked her in her tear-filled, blue eyes.

"It's all right, little one," Kayza whispered to her, gently kneading her shoulders and arms. "He is gone. Soon, you will be safe."

Her tears streaming over the grime on her cheeks the child glanced back, fearfully, over her shoulder, then up at Kayza's grin, before quickly looking down at the dirt that was caked on her bare feet.

Dipping her head and searching for the child's eyes, Kayza asked her quietly, "What is your name?"

"Xhaka," the little girl squeaked and reached out to touch Kayza's cuirass with the tip of her finger.

Kayza folded her bent leg under her buttocks and pushed her knee into the dirt. On both knees she shuffled in closer to Xhaka and with one hand lifted her chin, "Hello Xhaka. Where are your mother and father?"

"No father. Mother left me. She went with the soldiers," Xhaka sobbed and wrapped her arms around Kayza, hiding her tears by pushing her face tight to Kayza's bronze breastplate.

"Then you must be brave," Kayza told the little girl, easing out of her embrace, "As brave as when you fought me, just now. For I need a warrior." Then, wiping teardrops from Xhaka's face and brushing stray ringlets out of her eyes, she asked Xhaka, "Are you ready?"

"Yes," the child answered, her voice shaking, her hands clutching Kayza's arms.

"I knew it," Kayza told her, then kissed her forehead, picked her up, and carried her to Elazuna.

"I'm a good rider," Xhaka piped-up, taking the reins in one hand and, with the other, patting the mare on the neck after Kayza sat her in the saddle.

"Of course you are," Kayza replied, crossing the stirrups in front of the pommel of the saddle. "This is Elazuna. She will take care of you. Run with her into the hills. Find the people from the village. Tell them my orders are they must follow you to Lancia, where they will find General Gausón. Elazuna knows the way."

"What about you?" Xhaka asked, anxiously.

"I will catch up with you after I teach those bad Romans some manners," Kayza assured the girl, tossing her head at the oncoming horde. "Off you go now. I will see you soon."

True to her word, Xhaka pivoted Elazuna on her haunches, expertly, and in a few strides had her sprinting to the gate and out of the guttering town. Kayza picked up her swords and watched them run until her view of their flight was blocked by a cordon of legionaries. Waiting for one of them to make the first move, she was surprised when it came not by way of a sword, or a spear. Rather, she was struck from behind by a piercing voice.

"Kayza of the Lugones. General in the army of the rebel Gausón. Pain in my ass. You are surrounded. Lay down your swords," the Roman officer demanded. His use of her language was strained, but the edge in his voice left no room for negotiation.

"If I refuse?" Kayza negotiated, keeping her back turned to him.

"I will send my men into the hills to exterminate the vermin from this rat trap who are cowering among them, including the runt for whom you just gave yourself up. Her suffering, and eventually her death, will be your final visual experiences on this earthly plane. You then will die in abject failure and unimaginable pain," the Roman recited his list of threats, then sighed. "Why must it always come down to intimidation and violence with you people?"

Kayza whirled her blades in her hands, and ignoring his question badgered him, "The real question is why *you Romans* resort so swiftly to such tactics and their bedfellows, brutality and murder. I would say it's because *you Romans* are nothing more than greedy swine. But, that would be an insult to pigs everywhere."

"Thank you for that meaningless digression, General," the Roman said abruptly. "Now, give me your answer. Will you lay down your swords, or will you condemn your people to needless suffering?"

"If I do as you demand?" Kayza continued negotiating.

"Your people will be spared. Rome will rebuild this town, along with all of the others we have razed in our quest to ferret you out, yet again," the man droned on. "Do I really need to repeat myself? I mean, this is what, our third, no our fourth time at this is it not? At this point you know the conditions of your surrender better than I. You also know, very well, that speaking in your tongue gives me a sick headache."

"Is it the language or is it from me beaning you with my knife?" Kayza needled the soldier.

"Yes, that was nasty *and* unnecessary," the Roman decided as he dismounted and took a step into the shrinking circle that surrounded Kayza. "Give me your answer, now. I cannot forever keep these savages from cutting you to bits and eating you for their bedtime snack."

Kayza took another moment's pause, then wheeled about to face the Roman. Looking him in the eye, she stated her terms before dropping her swords, "This is *not* a surrender. It is an infiltration."

"Call it what you like. I call it, *victory Roma!*" the officer declared, jabbing the sky with his fist and drawing raucous cheers from his men. "I am Augustus Caesar, Emperor of Rome, and I claim you and these lands in its name and for its glory!"

"You are an asshole," Kayza opined, her declaration lost on everyone but Caesar.

"So say you, for the time being," Augustus rejoined. "However, very soon your feelings will change. To me, Char!"

Legionaries standing behind Caesar allowed a tall pale woman with braided red hair to walk into the ring. Her nose was straight, her lips were full, and her naked body was as white and as hard as polished ivory. Her green eyes fixed on Kayza, she bypassed Caesar and circled his prisoner, eventually coming to a standstill in front of her. Then, stepping in close to Kayza, she kissed her, sparking excitement and jealousy among the soldiers who were crowding in on them. When she sensed the men were about to riot, she pulled herself away from Kayza and licked her lips.

"Pretty thing. I do like a challenge," she said in a voice loud enough for all to hear.

"Fine. Great," Caesar said, tapping his leg with the flat of his sword. "Can you do it?"

"Yes, my lord," Char replied.

"Roman whore," Kayza snarled at Char.

"I am neither Roman, nor a whore," Char shot back, wagging a finger at Kayza. "I am of your tribe. In fact, I am the mother of the filthy brat whose worthless life you just saved. I am also a witch."

Kayza's teeth clashed together and she narrowly missed biting off Char's finger. The witch did not flinch, but her eyes rolled up in their sockets, showing off their whites. When they came back into focus, she shivered and smirked at Kayza.

"That was interesting," she snickered, steadying herself. "I do believe you've just given me a peak into what the future holds in store for you, my dear."

"Tell me," Caesar order the witch.

"Yes, my lord," Char obeyed. "The precise details elude me, but I can tell you this much. You will point her down the path that leads to the fulfillment of her destiny."

"Just as I prophesied," Caesar crowed and stared through the smoke at the stars. "After you make her love me I will take her as my queen. I then will rule the world, with her and the heirs she produces for me at my side."

"That is, indeed, what you told me, my lord," Char agreed with the emperor, bowing her head to conceal her contempt for his blind arrogance.

"Well," Caesar blurted, looking down his long nose at the witch, "What are you waiting for? Get on with it!"

Without uttering another word, Char clasped her hands together and knit her fingers, clenching them tighter and tighter until they glowed. A spectrum of colors flowed over their ridges and traversed their lengths, jumping and darting wildly. When they turned radiant blue she unlocked her fingers and grabbed Kayza by the shoulders. At her touch the battle-hardened warrior's knees buckled and she flopped on the ground at Char's feet. As her eyes shut, she caught a whiff of smoke drifting from the ruins of the village and thought it strange it reeked of burned potato peelings.

Foul and cloying, the smell of smoke coming from *Camille's* galley jolted Marquaisa out of her reverie. "Romans," she grumbled, scratching her nose, "What a bunch of barbarians."

Taking care to not thump her head on the surrounding woodwork, she uncoiled and let her shins dangle over the edge of her shelf. Still hugging her rapier, she listened for the sounds of Duvauchelle and his crew going about their business. Hearing none, she paid silent homage to the captain for playing his part in her plan. The clatter and scrape of grappling hooks clawing at *Camille's* decks, overhead, told her it was time to play hers.

A Visit[1]

'Twas a night of pitch darkness, and on Camille's deck
A lone creature stirred, no pulse in her neck;
Her long hair was black, by a cloak it was hid,
In her hand sharpened steel, of her foes it would rid;

The crew lay in wait below in the hold,
Their heads full of visions of diamonds and gold;
And Captain in his armor, his men at his back,
All armed to the teeth for a surprise attack,

Camille was the bait, a prize for the taking,
Her treasures westbound, good time she was making.
But slower she was than the shark in pursuit,
By dawn it would have her, and the loot in her boot.

Her crew showing panic, she took lame at the gallop;
Her sails all entwisted, by fire she'd burn up.
So chase became capture, before she was lost;
"O're take'er," cried Sharkey. "No matter the cost!"

By hook and by crook, they caught her right quick;
And grappled on fast, a dirty old trick.
More vulture than magpie, they crowded their rail,
And whistled and catcalled, convinced they'd not fail.

"Now Dimwit! Now Damfool! Now Prongtoe, and
    Varlet!
On Cobweb! On Clinker! On Dogmeat and Braindead!
To the lines! Use your backs and haul her in tight!"
Old Sharkey then called out, "Get ready to fight!"

No warning the beast on Camille did require.

She ran cross the ropes like a bird on a wire,
To Sharkey, the Captain, and chopped off his head;
Then drank of his lifeblood, she the undead.

Her body grown stronger with one bloody sip,
She turned her attention to taking the ship.
Her blade weaving death strokes, she broke the
    first wave
Of pirates attacking but sent to their grave.

Stone cold, wicked fast, her eyes hard and flinty,
She killed all on deck, her heart void of pity.
Then racing below to press forth the slaughter,
She mowed down the gunners, their blood ran like
    water.

But four did she spare, on later to dine,
All well fed and healthful, she'd age them like wine;
With a spank on their buttocks she ran them up top,
Where she chained them and gagged them, their
    bleating to stop.

In the quiet that followed, she heard a soft bump,
From inside Sharkey's cabin to whose door she did
    jump;
Off the hinges she tore it, and cowering there,
Was Hobnob, the slave girl with curly brown hair;

She spoke not a word, but ran straight to the raider,
To bind her arms 'round her, the monster, her savior.
The last thing expected on buccaneer boat,
The blood fiend enwrapped her in old Sharkey's coat.

With the girl in her coils, cross the lines Kayza skipped,

To Camille *and her crew, whose bloodlust she'd pipped;*
"Battle's won. She Wolf's *yours, save the four at her*
   mast.
Good night to all. It's been a blast!"

---

1. Not to be confused with Clement Clarke Moore's *A visit from Saint Nicholas.*

CHAPTER 7

BOUNDING

MARCH 10TH

ATLANTIC OCEAN, TRADE ROUTE WEST TO HALIFAX

Wolfe had known a few good nights, but they were distant memories that were becoming more like dreams than happenings in which he had been an a participant. His head heavy, greyed-out images of a meeting with Amherst and Pitt, spent hammering out the terms of his ascension to the rank of brigadier general, drifted past his mind's eye. Faded and frayed, the harder he fought to bring them back into focus, the more rapidly they wrinkled and aged.

Though they too were paling, Wolfe's recollections of Lady Katherine Lowther were not as washed out as those involving his commanding officer and the self-styled savior of England. Shivering, he remembered, after escorting her ladyship to her flat on Mortloch Road and delivering her into the hands of her guardian, the redoubtable Malvor Galbrith, being able to think of little else other than seeing her again. This he conveyed in a letter he hand delivered to Galbrith and, to his surprise, not only could the man-bear read, but he also graciously consented to the request for an audience with his ward. High tea was arranged and Wolfe presented himself at the lady's door, at the appointed hour, for the first of a series of fixtures that grew more intimate as the date of his departure for the New World drew nearer.

Wolfe was enchanted by Lady Katherine's warmth, wit, and worldliness, as well as her countenance. Nine years his junior, she was tall and graceful, her elegance offset by her unruly dark brown hair, which bounced over her shoulders and down her back and accentuated her lively brown eyes and playful smile. Wolfe also cherished her touch, which he came to know by monopolizing her dance card at high society mixers, and strolling with her, arm-in-arm, along London's lamplit lanes. On one such occasion when they reached her flat, Kate, as she preferred he call her, surprised him first with a kiss and then by steering him, gently, through her front door.

Once inside Kate took him by the hand and led him up a winding staircase and down a dimly lit hallway whose walls were hung with souvenirs from the time she spent on Barbados with her father, Britain's governor on the island. Ornate masks, leering, laughing, and fierce were paired with heraldic shields and fearsome spears, bows, and blades that were, to Wolfe's trained eye, less ornamental than they were battle-ready. The exotic armory gave way, at the end of the corridor, to her spacious personal chambers. Overlooking the road, they featured a cluttered, book-lined studio, a sweet-smelling lavatory, a colorful dressing room, and a sumptuous four-poster bed piled with an assortment of soft blankets and pillows.

His heart thudding, Wolfe followed Kate as she made a beeline for the bed, littering the route with the clothing she shed as she went. Taking her example and matching her pace, he kicked off his boots and shrugged out of layers of outerwear until he rendezvoused with her at the footboard. For a moment they regarded one another, she curvy and glowing in her lingerie, he lean and angular in his undershirt and clam diggers. Liking what they saw, they freed each other from what remained of their modesty and, kissing lustily, tumbled into the bedding in breathtaking pursuit of the pleasures that are found only in shared visceral desires.

Waves of heat rushed through their hips as they joined in a cascading climax that at once sated and whet their appetites. On board for a second course, as they rolled and clutched each other, the surge of warmth Wolfe felt became a gurgle of nausea. Then a swell of bile hit his palette in acrid reminder of his current reality. He no longer shared a bed with Lady Katherine, in her flat on Mortloch Road. Rather, he was bedfellows with a debilitating case of seasickness, on the *Good Ship Amelia*.

Bone-chilling and waterlogged, the so-called 'direct route to the New World' felt more like a roundabout drag. A voyage of the damned, it was an unrelenting, rising, falling, windy ordeal plagued by long stretches of mind-numbing boredom that were interrupted by agonizing cycles of stormy misery. Wracked by queasiness, his gut spasming from rounds of gagging and vomiting, Wolfe yearned for respite from constantly feeling deathly ill. His brain caught in a vice whose clamps were engraved with the names *Anguish* and *Torment* he eased himself out of his cot, clinging to the hope that he might, for a time, simply feel rotten.

Shaking from the effort it took to stand upright, Wolfe's face locked itself in a nausea-induced look of distaste that was rendered demonic by the greenish hue of his skin. As off color as it was, however, his hide was as thick as shield armor and he made a point of ignoring the concerns for his health expressed by Major Isaiah Brock, the *aide-de-camp* assigned to him by Amherst. He preferred, instead, the merciless ribbing of Amelia's crew and the soldiers with whom he was sailing, to which he was about to subject himself yet again.

"Sailing, sailing, over the bobbing main," Agsun Swift sang from his post at *Amelia's* wheel, the instant Wolfe appeared on deck. "Afternoon Guv'na! What do you think of my song, so far?"

"Afternoon, Aggie," Wolfe burped and peered up at the helmsman. "It's genius. Sheer genius."

"Here's thankin' you, Guv! You're a fine gentleman, to be sure," Swift gushed, the whole of his thick body rocking in time with the ship. "Me, I'm thinkin' it's a bit off. I mean, to me, *bobbing* just don't sound right."

"Let me guess. You would like me to suggest some synonyms," Wolfe hiccupped and braced himself against the ship's rail.

"Oh, no, sir. Nothin' dirty. It's a song for the kiddies, after all," Swift objected, his full red beard shedding salt spray as he tussled with the wheel. "See, I've some words in mind that's different from bobbing. But they means pretty much the same thing. I'd like you to tell me which one of 'em's best."

"That's what I just . . ." Wolfe bit his defensive tongue, tightened his grip on the sip's rail, and invited Swift to proceed. "Please, do go on."

"Say no more!" Swift exulted, sucked in a chestful of sea air and launched into his solo. *"Sailing, sailing, over the heavin', droppin', pitchin', churnin'—"*

"Thank you! Thank you, Aggie! That will be quite enough," Wolfe gagged, raising his hand to the helmsman in surrender. "I need hear no more, for I have a suggestion for you. Actually, I have two."

"That's amazin'!" Swift exclaimed, leaning over the spokes of the wheel and ogling Wolfe. "Let's 'ear 'em."

"Right, then," Wolfe agreed and fought down a dry heave before granting Swift's wish, "When you return to England do one of the following: either go to the Tower of London and enlist in the Torturer's Guild, or gather together a troop of wayward minstrels and wander far and wide sharing your musical talents with the world."

Swift laughed out loud and slapped his thigh and sent *Amelia*, momentarily, off course. After a quick correction he congratulated Wolfe, "Good on you, my old son. But you forgot about my song."

"I've done nothing of the kind," Wolfe disagreed. "The word you are looking for is—" Wolfe choked as his mouth filled with brine from a wave that broke against *Amelia's* hull. Coughing out salt water, he bellowed, "Buggerations!"

"Nope. That word won't work, sir," Swift deadpanned. "Too many parts to it. Breaks up the beat. Nice try though, Guv."

"Thank you, Aggie. Carry on," Wolfe ground out his appreciation through his clenched teeth.

Cold, wet, and queasy, he pivoted stiffly, clung to the ship's rail, and started unsteadily for the bow. Brock, dry and clear-eyed, met him at the halfway point of his trudge. Wolfe was a hand's span taller than

Brock. Though shorter and lighter than his commanding officer, Brock's shoulders were wider, his arms were thicker, and his legs were sturdier. Where Wolfe was jocular and spirited, Brock, in his early twenties, was as stoic and reserved as someone possessed of twice his years and experience. His speech was refined, his manners were impeccable, and his kit was unfailingly immaculate. His nose was straight, his jaw was square, his smile inspired confidence, and in sum total Wolfe saw in Brock the nearest thing to soldierly perfection as could be found in either branch of the service, army or navy, in any country in the world. What he lacked was experience in leading troops in the field, and Wolfe had made it his mission to school the young man in that aspect of his profession. Side-by-side they walked what remained of the length of the main deck and mounted the companionway that rose to the forecastle.

"How fare the rank and file?" Wolfe asked his aide when their feet were firmly planted on the planks of the raised foredeck.

"Bored, sir," Brock reported, sidestepping in front of Wolfe and turning his back to the wind by which his senior officer was being buffeted. "But they've yet to use it as an excuse to kill one another."

"No doubt that idea of yours to draft them into the service of the ship's crew is helping us to avoid that eventuality," Wolfe complimented the young officer. "That was good thinking on your part, Brock"

"Thank you, sir," Brock bowed, slightly, at the waist and grabbed his hat to stop it from blowing overboard.

"It is I who should be thanking you," Wolfe replied, his body swaying. After a moment's pause, he moved on to the true purpose of their meeting. "Now, to the matter of furthering your education in the arcana of military strategy. Let us once more consider the puzzle that is the fortress at Louisbourg. Piece together for me, in as few words as possible, its posture and defenses."

"Yes, sir," Brock obeyed, his expression hardening as he concentrated. "The fortress stands roughly three hundred miles east of Halifax. It sits above the western rim of a bay that is ice free year-round. Its cannon cover all of the points of the compass and its walls are built so as to enable their defenders to pepper attackers with small arms cross-fire. Small islands at the mouth of the bay host artillery outposts, as does Lighthouse Point, which is directly opposite the fortress."

"So, it's a bit of a prickly pear," Wolfe understated the obvious, staring down at the deck. He then looked Brock in the eye and challenged him, "How do you plan to defeat it?"

"The French will block the entrance to the bay by scuttling what ships they can. So, the navy will be hard pressed to sail into the bay and batter the fortress at close quarters," Brock theorized, without hesitation.

"Not that they'd hit anything, even at close range," Wolfe interjected. He then apologized, "Do pardon my editorializing, Brock. Please, go on."

"By your leave, my lord," Brock accepted Wolfe's prompt. "First, I'd have the navy take out the gun posts on the islands and the point. Then, I'd have them hit the fortress proper. While they're at it, I'd land the army a bit to the east of Lighthouse Point, then march it around the bay, blow up the main gate of the fortress, and take it by storm."

"Alright, if I'm hearing you correctly you are proposing surgical artillery strikes on the batteries, a diversionary bombardment of the fortress, and a surprise attack at its front door," Wolfe summarized Brock's recipe for success in the coming campaign.

"Yes, sir," Brock confirmed, his voice tight with nervous excitement.

"Interesting," Wolfe commented. "You combine muscle with deception and daring. Remind me to not trifle with you when we are playing at cards."

"Yes, my lord," Brock laughed quietly and breathed easier.

"You show promise, my young stalwart, and this first version of your plan is a good beginning," Wolfe commended his aide. "Still, there remain items within it that will benefit from some additional thought. For instance, exactly when would you bring the army ashore and how would you get it to Louisbourg's front door without its being seen."

"Yes, sir. Thank you, sir. I'll run through it again," Brock enthused.

"I know you will," Wolfe reassured his aide, bopping him on the arm with his open hand. "We'll catch up on it tomorrow. Meanwhile . . . lookout!"

Amelia's prow split an oncoming breaker, shattering the wave into arrays of sodden projectiles that washed over the forecastle and soaked Wolfe and Brock. As the deck planks shed the flood that followed the watery explosion, the two soldiers gasped and scrubbed the spray off their overcoats. Having rid themselves of layers of loose water, they shook off the drops that clung to their hands, and at last heard the heckling of the ship's crew.

"Swift!" Wolfe yelled at the helmsman, who was leading the barracking. "Demon spawn that you are! Thank you for *not* warning Brock and I of the oncoming deluge!"

"Nothin' to it, Guv," Swift called out to Wolfe, between guffaws.

"Quite the opposite, I'm sure!" Wolfe yelled back at the sailor, quelling a laugh of his own. "But let's never mind that. Your little prank has inspired me. I now have the word you need for your song!"

"Here's hopin' its better than the last one!" Swift joked.

"Indeed, it is," Wolfe assured him. "The word you are looking for is *bounding*. You know, 'Sailing, sailing, over the *bounding* mane!"

"Umm, well, okay," Swift hemmed and hawed. "It keeps up the rhythm and it sounds about right. But, what does it mean?"

CHAPTER 8

TRADE

MARCH 12TH

ATLANTIC OCEAN, TRADE ROUTE SOUTH TO THE GOLD
COAST OF AFRICA

"What it means is the high seas are a rolling, breaking, foaming frontier that liberates us from our petty lives and gives us leave to be weightless and wild," Léonarre Poisson, dandified in his fitted, gold silk, embroidered coat, matching waistcoat, knee-length breeches, linen stockings, black shoes, and favorite beaver plush, ostrich feather trimmed tricorn hat, waxed poetic, as he breathed in salt air and scanned the watery horizon, beyond which lay the southern hemisphere.

Standing beside him, his black silk shirt clinging where he had sweat through, the tail of his top knot bound in a low fade, Trémont D'Acier heaved a sigh and leaned against the rail of *Maëlle's* upper deck with his back turned to the ocean.

"Yes, Trémont, *I know,*" Poisson conceded, drawing out the last two words of his confession, "Since we cast off from Le Havre you've made it abundantly clear. To you, riding the waves is dreary monotony. So, I am left to wonder, whatever shall we do to relieve your boredom?"

He pivoted slowly, giving up his view of the ocean in favor of the scene unfolding next to *Maëlle* in the sun-drenched port town of Elimina, on Africa's Gold Coast.

"I've got it!" his almond eyes shining above his angular cheekbones, Poisson clapped his hands and answered his own question, "We'll go to the market and buy you a couple of toys! In fact, I might even treat myself to one or two, since I've been such a good boy lately."

"Fine," D'Acier sulked, sticking out his lower lip and playing the spoiled child. "But I'll not be sharing mine with you or anyone else."

"Brat. I expected as much," Poisson poked his protégé in the ribs. "I am expecting, also, that you will be the embodiment of tact and diplomacy during our walkabout among the unwashed."

"Screw diplomacy," D'Acier snapped and leaned back on the ship's rail, crossing his strong arms over his sinewy chest.

"You will do no such thing," Poisson insisted. He wiggled his arm under and around one of D'Acier's and proceeded to escort him through the men and matériel on the crowded deck. "Rather, you will listen whilst I bestow upon you all of the knowledge you will ever need on the topic of diplomacy. Which knowledge you will immediately translate into observable behavior."

"If you say so, my lord," D'Acier muttered, dragging the heels of his black leather shoes across the deck.

"I most certainly do," Poisson insisted while navigating toward the gangway that angled down from the ship to the wharf. "Now, be a good little savage and listen to what I am about to tell you. It will serve you well today and in the days, weeks, and months to come."

"Fine, fine, do your worst," D'Acier relented and tilted his ear closer to Poisson.

"You know I will," Poisson replied, a sly grin stretching his lips thin. "You also will find, D'Acier, that the rules of diplomacy are deceptively simple. They are as follows. First, you must have my back, just as I will have yours. Second, you must *watch* my back, just as I will keep watch over yours."

D'Acier nodded slowly, concentrating fully, and waited for more bombshells of wisdom to drop. When it was apparent no more were falling his way his shoulders slumped. Underwhelmed by the lesson, he smoothed a few stray hairs off his forehead and tweaked the bindings of his manbun.

"Forgive me for reminding you, my lord," he rumbled, straightening up his body and bringing their stroll across the ship's main deck to a halt, "But we already do those things."

"True," Poisson agreed, patting D'Acier's forearm, while making a show of watching what was going on around him, "But we do them within the confines of the king's court, where we know all the players and everyone knows the rules. Out here in the wild we are out of our element, and while the rules of the game may be the same the stakes are much higher. At home you might lose face if you commit a *faux pas (social impropriety)*. Out here, if you offend, then you will lose your face in the most literal way you can imagine."

"Then, let us simply stay on the ship," D'Acier attempted to reason with the regent.

"We represent the king of France, dear boy," Poisson took his turn handing out a reminder. "If we fail to show our faces among the locals, then they will be grievously insulted, and as I've just explained take it out of our hides."

"That would make for some much-needed excitement," D'Acier perked up and did a cursory visual inspection of the people on the wharf, checking for worthy opponents.

"Perhaps," Poisson hedged, restarting their walk to the plank. "But in the aftermath you would find yourself either skinned alive or facing the prospect of a long voyage without toys with which to play."

"Alright," D'Acier sighed, again. "If you would please be so kind as to explain to me the nuances of the diplomacy game as it is played hereabouts, then I would greatly appreciate it."

"It will be my pleasure," Poisson announced as he mounted the gangplank.

Poised at the top of the narrow bridge, the king's regent waited for all eyes on the wharf to turn his way. When they did he smiled brightly and waved happily. In return he was showered with roars of approval and rounds of applause. He bowed in gratitude and as the clamor faded helped D'Acier onto the wooden ramp. Poisson then led the way down its length toward the people who were jostling with one another to be first to greet them.

Scanning the mob from left to right, then back to front, D'Acier spoke into Poisson's ear, "The nuances, my lord?"

"Oh, yes," Poisson chirped. "They are thusly. First, you must agree with all that I say, visibly, but not too enthusiastically. For you can count on the fact that whatever I say, I mean the exact opposite. Second, if some misguided soul sees fit to attack us, then by all means disarm and subdue him. But do not kill him. To do so would deny the local authorities the opportunity to exercise their self-appointed rights to torture, maim, and slaughter one of their own."

The rules laid bare, Poisson plunged into the throng that was crammed onto the wharf. D'Acier, cheeks spasming from his efforts to remember how to smile, dove in after his benefactor and kept his eyes peeled for faces as grim as his own. Grins were the order of the day, however, coaxed out by Poisson, who told everyone he met how thrilled he was to see them and complimented them on the quality of their merchandise.

"What a delightful reception. Thank you! Thank you, all!" Poisson, hand over his heart, trumpeted his appreciation across the wharf. He then turned his attention to a nearby knot of traders and prevailed upon them, "My good men. Might one of you be so kind as to direct my friend and I to the market?"

Eager to help, the merchants pointed their fingers at the far end of the wide boulevard that rose through the heart of Elimina. Wedged into the armpit of West Africa, the port town was ripe with riches from every corner of the known world; guns and armor from France, sugar and rum from the Antilles, spices and silks from the Far East, and flesh from the African Interior. The weapons and the luxuries were abundant on Elimina's docks. The slaves could be had only from its market.

Stacked on top of the plateau that capped the boulevard, a tall stone wall crested with thorny battlements and spikey lookout towers defended Elimina's market. Built of rock hauled off mounds churned up when the landscape was being shaped, its face was roughhewn and gritty. In the middle of the craggy façade, under an arch of soot-blackened stone, the grill of an iron portcullis scowled at everyone either unwise enough, or unlucky enough to look through the gaps in its bars.

Perspiration dotting his forehead after his hike to the market, Poisson squinted past the rusty lattice and focused on its open square. Wanting to be sure of what he was seeing, he leaned closer to the grate, taking care to avoid touching it. His eyes fixed on the market square he raised his hand and flicked a finger, signaling to D'Acier to join him. When his aide reached his side, Poisson greeted him, "Here you are at last. I thought I'd lost you to the scantily clad mavens peddling their fleshly wares in the street."

"I was tempted, my lord," D'Acier admitted. "But I chose our mission over a fleeting moment of self-gratification."

"Shame on you, silly boy," Poisson teased then, pointing into the square, changed the subject. "Look in there and tell me what you see."

D'Acier glanced through the bars of the gate and reported his observations, "I see a cannon aimed directly at us. I estimate its fuse will burn down and the gun will fire in three seconds."

"I thought as much," Poisson replied and stiffened his back. "Very well, brace yourself."

The warning was lost on D'Acier, blown away as it was in the blast wave that roared out of the square and over the harbor. In its wake shreds of singed wadding swirled in the smoke that spewed from the mouth of the heavy gun. Rocking in its blockish mount, its barrel hummed in counterpoint to the laughter that chased the explosion through the gate.

"What and infernal racket," Poisson complained as he patted down his hair. "Still, it was somewhat subdued compared to the salutations So-and-So normally bestows upon his guests. I wonder what is ailing him?"

"I'll tell you what will be ailing—what did you call him?" D'Acier fumed.

"So-and-So. It's his name," Poisson replied. "Now, do tell, what afflictions will beset him?"

"Knocked out toothitis, blackened eyetropy, and kicked-in nutsemia, to name a few!"

"An impressive collection. However will he contract them?"

"I shall hammer them into him."

"Good old blunt force. Trémont, you really are too predictable," Poisson said, shaking his head. "But that is my fault. For too long you have been my battering ram. It is high time I taught you to be less transparent and more invisible. I shall begin immediately. Laugh with me."

"I find nothing amusing in what just happened." D'Acier protested hotly.

"Perhaps. From your perspective," Poisson noted, shifting his eyes in the direction of heavy footsteps approaching from the square, "But it is So-and-So's oldest and best joke and he *never* tires of it. So, laugh. Laugh. Laugh!"

"Léonarre Poisson!" So-and-So boomed in coarse, Dutch-accented French. "Stop hiding in the smoke and come into my arms!"

"So-and-So, you old scoundrel!" Poisson returned the greeting. "Open this wretched gate and I'll do just that!"

"Ghajdoo, you Ashanti dog, raise the curtain for our guests!" So-and-So yelled through the smoke at his gatekeeper. As he emerged from the haze, his white caftan billowing around his ample frame, his sandals slapping the soles of his puffy feet, the Dutchman drew a bead on Poisson, "So, Léonarre, you still find my little prank amusing. I was hoping you'd forgotten it and would soil yourself as you did when I first played it on you."

"I might have, were I not expected to set a good example for my associate," Poisson confessed and directed So-and-So's attention to D'Acier. "Allow me to present monsieur Trémont D'Acier, Adjunct to His Majesty, King Louis XV of France. You will find that his mind and mine are as one. Monsieur D'Acier, I give you So-and-So, Lord of the Elimina Market and Impresario Extraordinaire."

"An honor, sir," So-and-So and D'Acier greeted one another as the market's gate locked in place over their heads.

"Now," the slave lord commanded. "Get in here and let me hold the two of you. I wish to smell the glory of France!"

Poisson and D'Acier did as they were told and were rewarded with a massive, handsy bearhug by the massive, handsy Dutchman.

"You carry with you the scent of the court," So-and-So said, dreamily. "Power mixed with intrigue and a healthy dose of debauchery. I love it! And your attire, Léonarre! Spectacular! The cut and the colors are so modern and so marvelous. Tell me, did I feel the touch of French silk?"

"None other," Poisson confirmed, striking a regal pose for his host.

"I knew it!" So-and-So exclaimed, rubbing between his fingers a fold in the skirt of Poisson's jacket. "Tell me you brought some for me."

"Enough for you and all your playthings," Poisson did as he was told, again.

"You always spoil me you naughty man," So-and-So chastised Poisson, while smiling broadly at him. He then squeezed himself between his two visitors, and with an arm wrapped around each of them swaggered into the market square. "Come and we'll see if I can do the same to you."

Smoke from So-and-So's cannon hung about the gateway and drifted lazily into the open-aired square. The clouds obscured the cages that were built on top of one another, against the inside of the bastion's chunky wall. Its acrid odor deepened the palpable despair that permeated the market's every inch.

Warmed by the ambiance, Poisson rubbed his shoulder against So-and-So's and asked, "Why do you insist on calling this a square when, in fact, it is an oval completely bereft of corners?"

"For how long have you wanted to ask me that question?" So-and-So wondered out loud before offering an answer. "Well, my friend, the reason I call it 'the market square' is to avoid confusion. Chaos would rein and my business would collapse if it started calling my square 'the market *oval.*' In your academies, did they not teach you how to manipulate society for the purpose of turning a profit?"

"Strangely, no," Poisson drawled, matching his host's sarcasm.

"They did, however, teach us how to count and, by mine, your pens are holding exactly zero occupants. Save the one whose tenant looks and smells more like a cow patty than a human being."

"Fortunately, for me, the market for flesh is insatiable. Always has been. Always will be," the slave trader forecast. "No sooner do Ghaj-doo's Ashanti brethren bring me a fresh supply of newly defeated rivals, than my countrymen, as well as representatives of enterprises based in Britain, Spain, and a dozen other countries are at my door demanding I sell them my entire inventory."

"Good for you, indeed," Poisson congratulated the agent of cruelty. "But bad for me. I promised D'Acier a toy or two."

"Now, now, don't be blue, Léonarre," So-and-So consoled Poisson. "I always keep the best and most pleasingly twitchy under the lash for myself. It is from this stock that you and Trémont, my newfound friend, shall have your pick."

"You are too kind," Poisson flattered his host. "However, I must decline your most generous offer. I came here not to take advantage of you, but to engage in fair trade."

"And you shall," So-and-So assured Poisson. "The items you extract from my collection will be taken as payment for the services you are about to render to me."

"That sounds like a proposition at which we would be foolhardy to turn up our noses," Poisson inferred.

"You might call it foolhardy. I'd call it suicidal. For you know I will not accept 'no' for an answer," an evil undertone cut through So-and-So's voice and the sunburned skin on his cheeks turned a darker red.

"Now, don't get grumpy you great bear. You know very well I am incapable of refusing you," Poisson chided So-and-So and patted the big man's flushed cheek. "Just tell me what you have in mind."

"Grumpy, you say? Well, I suppose I am a bit cranky. For days I've been wracking my brain trying to determine a way out of a most sour pickle. Then, out of the blue, you show up at my door and the light of inspiration bathed me in its splendor. The thought that there was even the slightest possibility it might be snuffed out made me cross. Do forgive me," So-and-So apologized and opened his arms to Poisson.

"There is nothing to forgive, old friend," Poisson consoled the Dutchman and accepted his embrace. After giving So-and-So a squeeze, the regent took a step back and, feigning concern, asked the slave master, "Do tell. What has you so vexed?"

"Not what, but who." So-and-So corrected the Poisson and steered he and D'Acier toward the sentient dung pile the regent spotted earlier.

"That is Irian Fortess. Formerly, a captain in Louis's royal infantry,", So-and-So pointed at the long, gaunt, grime-encrusted man chained to the back wall of a cage. "Of late, he is a soldier of fortune. He came into my possession a fortnight ago when he broke into my kennels. His plan was to steal and pimp-out some of my bitches and use the cash to purchase passage to the New World. Can you imagine? Him, steal from me?"

"What's that? Who's there?" Fortess asked, dragging himself to his feet, his chains clinking. "In the name of His Majesty, King Louis XV of France, I demand you release me!"

"You know damned well who it is, you swine," So-and-So snapped at Fortess and banged the bars of his cage with his pudgy fist. "You also know that it is by my say-so you continue to draw breath. So, keep your mouth shut or I will have the girls remind you, yet again, what *their* lives would have been like if *you'd* had your way with them."

On reflex, Fortess clamped one hand over his crotch, the other over his butt hole and squeaked, "I would rather die."

"There you have it," D'Acier chimed in, "Kill the wretch. Better still, if you will allow me, I will happily do it for you."

"What? No! Who said that?" Fortess squawked.

"We, as in you or I, cannot," So-and-So declined D'Acier's offer. "He is the subject of an arrest warrant issued by a certain monsieur Aubergine, a man with whom the two of you are no doubt familiar. According to the warrant, he is to be returned to France where he will be tried as a deserter and then hung."

"Poor Fortess," Poisson affected pity, then shared with So-and-So a deduction he had made. "You wish me to return him to France."

"As we discussed," So-and-So reminded Poisson, "You will be rewarded."

"Indeed, I shall be" Poisson agreed. "So shall you, I presume. There is a bounty on Fortess's head, yes?"

"A handsome one," So-and-So confirmed, then deflected. "But do not trouble yourself with trifles. It will be reward enough for me to be rid of him."

"On the contrary, it will trouble me not one bit to sling you a sackful of Louis's money," Poisson smiled generously and shook So-and-So's hand, sealing their agreement. "Bundle him up and cart him off to *Maëlle* with instructions from me to stow him in the brig."

"I shall summon the girls!" So-and-So announced, cheerfully.

"Splendid!" Poisson voiced his approval. "Now that's been taken care of, let us cast our eyes upon the specimens you have so kindly set aside for Trémont and I."

'I can think of nothing I would rather do," So-and-So bowed and made way for his guests, opening a path that led them away from Fortess. *"Après vous, messieurs." After you gentlemen.*

Indulged by So-and-So in his private showroom for the remainder of the day and into the evening, Poisson and D'Acier departed from the market near midnight, passing by Fortess's empty cage as they made their way back to *Maëlle* with a quartet of tall, dark, chained women in tow. The ship, having been unburdened of the freight destined for Elimina and having taken on fresh provisions, departed the port the following morning bound for the French island of Martinique, in the Caribbean. When they reached open waters Poisson tasked his two newly acquired chattels with retrieving for him the newest male addition to *Maëlle's* retinue. In their absence he had his table set for lunch, placed two chairs such that they faced one another from opposite sides of the table, and sat himself in the one whose back faced the door. When his girls returned he gestured to them to seat Fortess in the chair facing him and to chain themselves to his bed.

Fortess sat still and held his breath for a long moment, then opened his eyes and immediately wished he had not. What he saw was too good to be true, which meant he was either dead or mad and he couldn't decide which was worse because neither one was the state in which he wished to live out the rest of his life. No, he was going to be filthy stinking rich with a huge house and stables full of fine horses and a big green yard crammed with gilded carriages looked after by an army of servants who also cleaned his huge house and fixed luscious meals for him whenever he wanted and served them with chocolate that he didn't have to share with anyone ever. Chocolate. And tarts. Lots of tarts. The pastry kind and the female kind.

"Pardon?"

"Pardon what? What pardon? Am I pardoned?" Fortess heard himself say.

"Pardoned of what?"

"I beg your pardon. I am Irian Fortess, captain in the army of His Majesty, King Louis XV of France," Fortess recited his mantra. "That savage, So-and-So, said my behavior was unpardonable. But he was wrong and so are you. You're wrong. Wrong I say."

"Pardon me."

"I'll do nothing of the kind," the captain pouted and curled himself into a ball, sticking his hawkish nose between his tucked-up knees. "But I will kill you when I get out of this cage."

"Excuse me?"

"Excuse is just another word for pardon. You can't fool me," Fortess declared. "Just like I know the smells of food, and wine, and fresh salt air are pretend. Just like you. You're not real. It's just So-and-So playing another one of his awful tricks to make me go mad. Well, I'm not mad. Not mad."

"Of course you're not mad. But you have had a bit of a nasty time. That's all behind you though. So, open your eyes again and join me for lunch, Captain Fortess."

Fortess was confused and more than a little sad because he wanted the whole thing to be real and at the same time he wanted it all to go away because if it was pretend he would cry and . . . he opened his eyes and peeked over his knees.

"There you are."

"*Where* am I?" Fortess asked.

"Here, where you belong, in my quarters on His Majesty, King Louis XV's ship, *Maëlle*, bound for Louisbourg, in the New World. I am Léonarre Poisson, Regent to His Majesty, your host, and I am pleased to inform you that you will be serving his majesty in the battle to keep New France out of the hands of his enemies."

"Which of his enemies?"

"Any who express enmity toward him."

"That is a long list."

"Which is precisely why I need a man of your quality," Poisson flattered the madman. "You will, naturally, be rewarded handsomely for your service. But never mind that. We will have plenty of time to discuss the details of your duties during our voyage. For now, let us partake of the fine fare chef has laid on for us."

"Ummm, okay, sure," Fortess stammered. When his knotted limbs untangled he remembered his manners, "I mean, thank you, sir."

"Think nothing of it," Poisson replied. "Now, I could not help but notice how tall and strapping you are for someone who is at most, what, twenty-five years of age? And, you must be oh so brave, given your perseverance in the face of So-and-So's cruelty. The ladies' hearts must go all atwitter at the sight of you."

"Ladies?" Fortess said with a start. "So-and-So's ladies attacked me in my cell. I think one of them hit me on my head. Next thing I know, I'm here. How did I get here?"

"I'm afraid So-and-So's plan, since he could not break you, was to end you," Poisson lied. "It was the ladies' task to carry out the deed. Fortunately, my man, D'Acier—you will make his acquaintance later —caught up with them before they chucked you off Elimina's peer and brought you to me. You cannot imagine how glad I was to find you were, for the most part, unharmed."

"For the most part," Fortess mumbled, distantly, as in his mind he tried but failed to take an inventory of all his damaged parts.

Poisson kept his eyes trained on the former captain, alert to the possibility he might lash out violently in his confusion. He also kept his finger on the trigger of the flintlock pistol resting in his lap, under the table, ready to send a lead ball into Fortess's brain pan if he showed a speck of malice. But instead, in place of anger, a spark of reason flickered in the lunatic's eyes.

"I am in your debt. Yours and monsieur D'Acier's," he noted, solemnly. "How shall I repay you?"

"My dear Captain Fortess, the only debt you owe is to yourself to fulfill your promise to serve His Majesty," Poisson replied, his voice thick with false sympathy and phantom patriotism. "As a friend to you and as a loyal subject to His Majesty I will support you by placing you in position to make the best use of your considerable abilities during our mission in the New World."

"And monsieur D'Acier?" Fortess asked, a hint of mistrust in his voice.

"What of him?" Poisson replied, irked at being put on the spot by a crazy person.

"Does he too speak for the king?" Fortess's tone shifted, abruptly, to one of longing for reassurance.

"He does, but only after I tell him what to say," Poisson guaranteed him and eased his finger off the trigger of his pistol.

"Bien!" (Good!) Fortess exulted and stood to attention. "What would the king have me do?"

"Two things," Poisson replied, amiably but sternly, 'First, you must eat and you must exercise as you will need your strength. Second, outfit yourself in proper attire. Flouncing around in a state of nakedness lends itself neither to sailing on a ship, nor to waging war. You may do these things in the order and at the times that suit you best, but see they get done."

CHAPTER 9

SPAWNLING

MARCH 14TH

ATLANTIC OCEAN, TRADE ROUTE SOUTHWEST TO FRENCH CARIBBEAN

Saro could think of nothing he would rather do than carry messages from Captain Duvauchelle to Lady Marquaisa. Thing of nightmares though she was, since she took him hostage at La Rochelle she sweetened his dreams whenever he slept. Always, they were the same . . .

Her sudden silent attack. Her strong arms holding him tight to her body. Her hair flowing over his face as she raced into the darkness beyond the edge of the town. When they reached the farm, her pushing him into a haystack, his shirt front bunched in her fist and her warning him against wandering off or calling for help. His eyes wide he searched not for an escape, but for a way to etch her every feature into his memory. Her eyes blood-red, her face oval, her skin clear and smooth, he touched it with trembling fingers . . .

He stilled his shaking hand by balling it up, then used it to tap on the door of the cabin the lady had usurped from the captain. The instant he stopped knocking, *Camille* pitched her bow upwards, toppling him into the door, his forehead, elbows, and knees drum rolling down its length. Digging his fingernails into the wooden doorframe, he stopped the downward slide that would have seen him sandpapering the door with his face.

With a sharp shove he separated himself from the door, straightened his blue fearnaught, and smoothed his blond hair. Steadying his legs, he stood at attention and awaited a reply to his knock. As he waited he looked to his left and found *She Wolf*, formerly the property of Old Sharkey, some fifty yards away tacking easily alongside *Camille*.

A corsair, she was sleek and deadly, with a dozen gun ports each on her port and starboard. Gifted to Captain Duvauchelle by Lady Marquaisa, the captain had plundered her and enslaved the surviving members of her crew, making them dispose of their dead mates, cleanse the decks of their gory residues, and pilot the ship under the watchful eyes of his most hateful men. Loath to scuttle her for fear of missing out on the price she and her crew would fetch, but concerned the reek of piracy might stick to him, Duvauchelle kept her at arm's length and made it no secret he looked forward to being rid of her.

Saro watched her cut through the surf and wished he could make her his own. With her, he would see the world on his own terms and underscore his name with a reputation for being a man with whom one did not trifle. Caught up in his imaginings he jumped at the sound of a wave slapping *Camille's* hull and turned his attention back to the door, expecting to find it shut.

Instead, it stood wide open. Standing in shadow inside the captain's quarters Lady Marquaisa studied him. At the door's threshold, bathed in the light of day, her curly brown hair and tanned skin glowing, a woolen blanket layered over a full-length coat, Hobnob dragged her sea green eyes off *She Wolf* and locked them with Saro's.

"No more *drrreaming Sarrro,*" she burred, then grabbed his belt and hauled him through the doorway and into the cabin, "It is time for us to *rrremove* your *rrrandy* eighteen-year-old head from the clouds."

"You are here to convey the captain's warning regarding the galleon that is tracking us and which he hopes I will deal with in the same way as I did *She Wolf*," Marquaisa informed Saro, backing him into the door as it clicked shut. "I am here to tell you that you will serve me, or you will die, here and now. Make your choice."

His hand steady, Saro touched her cheek with his fingertips and brushed the end of his thumb over the tip of one of her fangs. Closing his eyes, he exhaled slowly as fantasy and reality melted together into a softly shimmering pool. It rose and fell with *Camille* and Saro swayed in time with it until he peeled open his eyes, his mind made up.

"I shall serve myself, my lady," he said, his voice quiet and steady.

He felt her take his hand in hers and slide it down the length of her neck to press it against her frozen heart.

"That was not one of your choices," she said, squeezing his hand. "But for you it is the correct one. Always remember that you are the fool who made it."

"*Rrremarkable,*" Hobnob remarked, stepping in close to Saro and Marquaisa and looking from one of them two the other, while nodding her head enthusiastically. "Let us celebrate *Sarrro's* liberation by *burrrning* Duvauchelle's ship to the waterline!"

"Protect this ship I did pledge to do, not make a pyre of it," Marquaisa reminded Hobnob, keeping her eyes locked with Saro's.

"*Rrregrettable,*" Hobnob grumbled, her eyes shifting from side to side in their sockets as she rifled through her repertoire of mayhem-causing strategies for an acceptably violent alternative, "Then I shall slit the captain's *thrrroat* to mark the occasion."

"He and his crew are included in my pact," Marquaisa informed the pirate spawnling, ruefully.

"*Rrrats!*" Hobnob *errrupted.*

"They were consumed," Marquaisa told the fiend, sharply, then gave Saro his hand back along with a suggestion. "Tell Duvauchelle you now are in command of *She Wolf.*"

"He will call me a mutineer and hang me from the yardarm," Saro predicted, resignedly.

"On the contrary, he will wonder what took you so long,"

Marquaisa corrected the boy and began circling him. Her Spanish accented French rolling, she built Saro's pitch for him, "He also will welcome the news that Hobnob and I will accompany you, that you will return to him the crewmen he posted to *She Wolf*, and that you will use her to get the Spaniard who is pursuing him off his tail."

"A fine way to begin building your reputation," Hobnob said in Saro's ear, following Marquaisa and orbiting around behind him.

"Only if the two of you have read him correctly," Saro hesitated, doing his best to keep his eyes on the two shark ladies.

"Stand here one second longer and it is your eulogy I will be reading," Marquaisa assured him as she came to a halt behind Saro and slapped him on the buttocks.

Saro yelped, spun on his heel, dodged around Marquaisa and, forgetting the door was closed, stubbed his toe and thumped his nose on the solid oak. Blinking away the pain, he yanked it open and fled from the cabin. His ears ringing with the aftershocks of bashing his bean on the door, he could barely hear himself think. Still, as he clambered up the gangway to the poop deck, he overheard Hobnob ask Marquaisa a question that made his bowels churn.

"Are you *sure* we *rrread* the captain correctly?"

"Soon we will know," Marquaisa replied, walking around behind Hobnob, wrapping her fingers lightly around the girl's throat, and whispering in her ear, "Now, let us begin."

Desperate to know what Hobnob was up to, Saro slowed his ascent of the stairway and peeked over its railing. But as Hobnob emerged from the cabin with her blanket wrapped cowl-like, over her head, Duvauchelle's voice filled his ears.

"Come to me, Saro!" Duvauchelle beckoned his attendant. "Tell me of the plans the witch has concocted for the Spaniards!"

Eyes wide, words sticking in his throat, Saro rushed to obey and lost his footing on the slippery steps. His misstep broke the logjam of words piled-up below his Adam's apple and they burst out of his mouth in a yodeling howl. Airborne and in rapid descent, his warbling was accentuated by the windmilling of his arms. By chance, one of his flailing hands struck a post in the railing and he grabbed it. Anchored, suddenly and securely, his flight jolted to a halt and he slammed down on his back on the stairs, winded, his eyes glazed over and straining to focus on the main deck.

"What in the name of the sea serpent's shithole are you playing at?" Duvauchelle yelled from his station on the aft deck. "Stop carrying-on and get up here and tell me the news!"

His shoulder blades aching, Saro rolled onto his stomach and crawled to the base of the stairway. Pawing at the railing, he lurched to his feet as clouds of pain billowed behind his eyes. Then, slowly, his head throbbing, he made his way up the stairs and onto the deck.

"Well, what did she say?" Duvauchelle snapped at the cabin boy.

"What she said does not matter," Saro replied, deciding to throw caution to the wind, "I am now in command of *She Wolf*."

"Say again," Duvauchelle growled, bunching his fists and butting them against his hips.

"I will use her to lure away the Spanish," the boy ignored the captain's demand.

"Saro," Duvauchelle's voice took on a warning tone.

"I will send back the men you posted to *She Wolf*," Saro hurried on.

"Good of you," Duvauchelle rumbled, and started swaggering across the deck toward the boy.

"I also will take Lady Marquaisa and Hobnob with me. So, they will be out of your cabin and out of your life," Saro said, the words coming faster and his voice rising higher with each step Duvauchelle took toward him.

"It keeps getting better," the old salt barked and grabbed a fistful of the hair on the top of Saro's head.

"She said you would *like* that last bit," Saro squawked and stood on his toes to ease the tension in the roots of his hair.

"I think I'll hear it from her with my own ears," Duvauchelle growled into Saro's face.

He then cranked Saro's head around until the teenager was looking back down the stairs he had mounted moments earlier, and gave him a kick in the arse to get him moving toward the main deck. Saro wobbled down the gangway, then shuffled across the deck to the captain's cabin.

Its door was shut tight, so Duvauchelle shoved Saro into it, face-first, and pinned him to it while he pounded on it.

"Show yourself, witch!" Duvauchelle bellowed. "Or I'll stake this mutinous little bastard through his traitorous heart to this bloody door!"

Saro grimaced when the point of the captain's sword pierced his back. But as it ground into his skin Saro uttered not a peep. Instead, he balled his hands into fists as solid as the ballast rocks in *Camille's* bilge. His dreams about to be cut from his soul, he pivoted to face the man he used to call 'Captain,' the end of whose blade scored a line around his jacket until it rested over his heart. When their eyes met, something heavy crashed on the floor in the captain's quarters and the old man blinked.

"Fuego!" someone shouted.

The order to fire rang out loud and clear from the gun deck and a split-second later a blast from a single cannon shook the main deck. The shot blew a hole through the hull, above the water line and below the forecastle. A hail of wooden shrapnel ripped into the surface of the ocean.

"No!" Duvauchelle howled and spun away from Saro.

As he turned Duvauchelle lost his traction and started to fall, but before he hit the deck Saro caught him by his jacket collar. The veins in his forehead and neck bulging, the captain turned on the boy and batted away the boy's hand. Then his lips peeled back to reveal his decaying teeth and he raised his sword high to deal the lad a killing blow.

"Yes," Saro disagreed with the captain and punched him squarely between the eyes.

The old man's head snapped back and his arms went limp. His knees buckled and he collapsed, twitching, at Saro's feet. The waves of tiny spasms loosened his grip on his sword until it popped out of his hand and clattered on the deck.

"Well, *shiverrr* me *timberrrs,*" Hobnob purred in Saro's ear while looking over his shoulder at the cold-cocked captain.

"That would be Lady Marquaisa below deck then," Saro ventured, watching Duvauchelle convulse.

"None other," Hobnob replied, chuckling at the captain's spasms.

"Why?" Saro asked, confused.

"Ask her yourself," Hobnob answered and lifted his hand to wave it at the blanketed wraith striding toward him, down the length of the main deck, with four healthy looking human specimens in tow.

"My lady is well?" Saro asked Marquaisa, while reclaiming control of his hand from Hobnob.

Marquaisa nodded and replied, *"Gracias."*

"I am glad," Saro said, sounding more anxious than relieved. "You went below."

"I collected my things," Marquaisa countered, tilting her head, minutely, at the humans standing behind her. "Their names are *Uno, Dos, Tres y Cuatro.* They will serve you."

"Thank you," Saro accepted, knowing not what else to do. Trying to sort things out, he then asked Marquaisa, "And the cannon was?"

"Amusing," she informed him, one corner of her mouth crimping into a tiny grin.

"Duvauchelle would disagree. But I am grateful," Saro said, seriously, and added, *"Gracias, mi señora."* Thank you, my lady.

Marquaisa stepped past Saro, rubbing shoulders with him on her way to Duvauchelle's quarters and, her smirk widening, paid the new captain her respects, *"De nada, Capitán."* You are welcome, Captain.

Puzzled by to look on Marquaisa's face, he understood one of the causes of her grin only after she was in the cabin. Preoccupied with their conversation as he was, Saro had not felt Hobnob sliding her hand down the front of his pantaloons. Knowingly, carefully, she vetted his swelling package fully.

Her examination complete, she withdrew her hand and as she followed Marquaisa stated her findings and made a prediction, "By the *rrrod* of *Rrrasmus,* he *rrreally* likes you, my lady! But he will love me!"

CHAPTER 10

TRRROUBLE

MARCH 19TH

ATLANTIC OCEAN, TRADE ROUTE SOUTHWEST TO FRENCH
CARIBBEAN

I n summer the North Atlantic is frigid. In winter it is a viscous
glacier. Bitter and murderous, surviving its crossing requires that
one skim nimbly over its surface and hope it does not take notice.

Her eyes colder than the icy death the ocean promised, Marquaisa
stared over *She Wolf's* stern rail into its depths, searching for the ones
who ruled their darkest, most dangerous recesses. More lethal than the
waters that were their domain, they stalked its currents primed to seize
their prey or pick a fight. To them, she knew, she and her type were a
prized catch. Not only tasty, but also promising immortality.

For ages she had wanted to bend one of them to her will. She knew
the odds were in favor of her perishing in the attempt. But the risk was
trivial when weighed against the possibility she might be able to move
about the Seven Seas without having to hitch or hijack rides.

"Solve how to drink salt water I must do first," Marquaisa said to
herself as, at the limit of her vision, a sinewy tail shimmering in a spectrum of colors and crested with thorny spikes snapped a greeting and a
challenge at her. Promising herself she would take up the gauntlet, she

pulled back the hood of her black cloak and received the person who was silently ascending the gangway to her rear, "Answers you are seeking, Captain Saro Beaufort of the *She Wolf*."

"How did you know I was—"

"That is not the question you wish to ask."

"Actually, its questions," Saro confessed.

"Choose the one the answer to which you do not already know," Marquaisa recommended.

"Okay," Saro agreed, his voice cracking. "What . . . what are you, exactly?

"Death."

"No," Saro protested. "You are not evil, you—"

Saro grunted as Marquaisa pounced on him and clamped shut his windpipe in her fist before he could move. Faster still, she encircled him, wrapped her arm around his chest, and squeezed his ribs. He writhed, but she held him fast, and in a low voice, before he blacked out, spoke into his ear.

"Life and everything else I want I do take from the living. Good and evil be damned. Must needs be this the reputation that also precedes you."

Feeling him go limp, Marquaisa loosened her grip and let him collapse. The sound of his head thudding on the ship's aft deck punctuated his swoon and he lay still. Offering him no aid she waited and after a long moment he sucked in air and coughed.

Satisfied he would live, she unbuckled the sword belt that held her cloak shut. Unfettered, it billowed and slipped off her naked body. As it piled up around her ankles, she slung the belt over her shoulder and around her chest, and strapped her rapier across her back, its pommel next to the pointed tip of her left ear. Then, catlike, she leapt onto the ship's rail, ready to dive, but paused when she felt a familiar set of eyes burning into her back.

"Verrry instrrructive," Hobnob thanked her tutor.

"The Spanish are mine," Marquaisa replied, eyeing the galleon's lights flickering against the blackened horizon. "Saro did well taking *She Wolf* and ridding himself of Duvauchelle and his crew. But he is not yet ready for things bigger than beating up the ones who put him down. Change that and I might make use of him *and* you, Hobnob with the curly brown hair. Twenty years you have seen, but wiser than that are you. Fare thee well, Sea Witch."

"*Whateverrr* you are, *trrrouble* are you," Hobnob returned the compliment, drawing a smile from Marquaisa, who then sprang from the rail into an arcing dive that ended with her knifing into the surf with hardly a ripple. Hobnob shook her head and grinned at the performance, "Show off. My eye is upon you."

When on dry land Marquaisa used her lungs not to breath, but to make herself heard when a fist, a blade, or a bite were out of the question. Those occasions were rare and as a result her lung capacity had shrunk to the point where it lacked the volume to help her float. So, buoyant as a clay brick, to stop herself from sinking she swam hard. When she swam on the surface she kicked up a bright rooster tail. While underwater she spun out a bubbling, long-tailed cone that streamed off the tips of her fingers and toes.

A body length deep in the black brine, she drove herself toward the sounds of waves slapping against the galleon's hull. Far behind her and well below her a torrent of water churned, and a low rumbling growl reached out to her. Her challenge accepted, the race she wanted to run was joined.

Stepping up her pace, Marquaisa shot forward tearing chunks out of the distance that separated her from the Spanish ship. Closing yet quicker was the gap between the soles of her bare feet and the double rows of teeth that lined the jaws of the harr dragon chasing her. Whipping is spiked tail, it surged nearer the surface, the water rushing over its scales making them ring and warning Marquaisa she needed to swim faster still.

Dead ahead of her, under full sail, the warship rode the surf in pursuit of *She Wolf* and her crew, determined to avenge the losses the pirates had inflicted on Spanish treasure ships. Minutes earlier, the galleon's crew laughed when it looked like Old Sharkey finally came to his senses and turned and ran, rather than challenge them. Now they jeered as he sparked up his tail gun and popped off a shot that sizzled through the air, then fizzled when it plopped into the ocean nowhere near their bow.

Marquaisa heard the hot cannonball *ping* when it hit the water and cracked to its core in the intense cold. A moment later, the crackling was drowned out by the clanging of the galleon's bell and its crew's cries of alarm. The uproar on the ship sliced into the waves and infuriated the sea serpent, the sound of whose charge was the cause of the panic that gripped the mighty vessel. When it breached and drew a breath before burrowing back under the surface the sailors howled in anguish at its knurled skull and singing scales.

Marquaisa paused to savor the wailing of the seamen and to tease the beast bearing down on her. "Hello, Nesbit," she greeted the creature. Then, after reading the unrelenting craving in its eyes, spun away, drawing it deeper into its collision course with the galleon.

Baited, Nesbit swept after Marquaisa and thrust himself out of the water into a tall rainbow arc, the treasure at the end of which was her well-aged physique. Cold winds scraped water down his back and off his tail and froze the stream in a glittering parabola that rose from and fell into the waves. Near the midpoint of his flight, Nesbit rolled and turned his pale belly skyward and, his large eyes fixed on the trail his quarry was cutting through the undercurrents, took aim at his target. Accompanied by the screams of every living soul aboard the galleon, onto whose main deck it appeared he would crash, Nesbit dove, straining his every inch in his effort to snap up his prey.

A hair late, his teeth clashed together a whisker behind her kicking feet. But, as he plummeted he clipped one of them with a fin and knocked Marquaisa into a twisting head-over-heels spin. He then swatted her with the flat of his tail and sent her hurtling into a face-plant against the galleon's keel.

"Mierda!" Marquaisa cursed. *Shit!*

Rocking and rolling, the massive ship plowed forward through the rush of waves raised by the sea monster's dive. Walls of water buffeted Marquaisa, and she bounced along the ship's hull until she shot off its tail end. Floating freely, with Nesbit's chittering laughter filling her ears, she lunged and dug her fingernails into the ship's rudder before it skated out of reach.

"Find you in your loch, I will, Nesbit," she promised as the ship towed her away from the sniggering sea serpent. "Ride you I shall."

Preoccupied as she was with sassing Nesbit, a sharp course correcting swing of the ship's rudder gave her a jolt and nearly broke her grip on it. But she hung on and started clawing her way up its length. When she reached the water line a blast of salt spray blurred her vision and she fanned on her attempt to latch onto the ship's hull. Off balance, she clung to the rudder with one hand, and as her body snaked through the surf fought against the water that bubbled off the ship's stern and kept her submerged.

When, at last, she got her head above water she heard men shouting from high up on the aft deck. She was sorting through what they were saying when a heavy net spread out beneath her and was cinched up around her, tangling her in its webs. A series of quick, hard tugs by the crew shut tight the mouth of the net and pulled her out of the water and onto the deck, dripping and snarling.

"What is it?" a seaman asked as he backpedaled away from the tangled mass.

"It's a mermaid," another seaman declared, pointing at Marquaisa in wonder.

"How would you know, Balasco? You can't tell a fish from a fig tree," yet another seaman chided his mate. "Anyways, whatever it is, that monster out there wanted to kill it. So, we need to do what it did not."

"Look, its tearing apart the net!" the backpedaler shrieked. "Kill it! Kill it now!"

"Stand aside!" a commanding voice snapped, growing louder at it neared the seamen.

"But Capitán Roxas, it's—"

"Get out of my way, or I'll flog the lot of you!" Roxas barked harshly at his men.

The sounds of bare feet retreating across the deck filled the silence that followed the captain's orders. As his men withdrew, Roxas marched up to the net and studied the creature hacking its way loose from its entanglements. Patiently, he waited until its head and shoulders broke free before pounding the butt of his musket into the gap between its eyes. Prudently, he kicked it to make certain it was unconscious. Then, keeping his eyes on it, he issued his next set of orders.

"Balasco, bring me the weapon strapped to its back. The rest of you, lock it in our deepest, darkest, coldest hold. If it survives our voyage, then we will leave it to the inquisitors at Ferrol to decide its fate."

CHAPTER 11

PLAYTHING

MARCH 21ST

ATLANTIC OCEAN, TRADE ROUTE TO FRENCH CARIBBEAN

Warm and light, a gentle breeze flitted across Kayza's cheek. As it slipped by her ear, it left behind a quiet lilting beat. As soft as the gown that hugged her and the generous fur throw that covered her, it lifted her spirit. Smiling, sleepily, she realized she was hearing herself giggle and, thinking it odd that she thought it odd, she felt happy.

Dismissing as drowsiness her muddled thinking she sighed contentedly and rolled over, and as a gossamer blue film dissolved in the watery layer of her eyes she found she had company under her blanket. Her shoulder brushed against her bedmate's back and she held her breath, expecting they might flinch in startled reaction. When none occurred, she discarded the apology she was cobbling together in favor of a closer examination of the woman lying next to her.

Lean, but with generous curves, the roundness of her thighs and buttocks spoke of time spent in the saddle, while the tone in her arms and shoulders said she was well-known to labor or combat, or both. Her skin was clear and the light tan that gave it luster was unbroken by pale swatches left behind by clothing. Evidently, whether working or fighting, she preferred to do it in the nude, her only concession to modesty being long, wavy, auburn hair that might, on a calm day, conceal a few of her body parts.

"You are wicked," the nudist said, her voice heavy with sleep.

"How are we here, like this?" Kayza asked in reply.

"At Your Majesty's bidding, of course," the sun devil whispered, turning over to face Kayza. "I am here to please."

"Very well . . ."

"Char."

"Very well, Char. Please me."

Char pecked Kayza lightly on the cheek, then the lips, then pulled her into a deep kiss. Keeping her lip-locked, she feathered her fingers down Kayza's spine and traced the crevice between her cheeks. Then, moving smoothly, she slid under Kayza and eased her thighs over her hips. Their pelvises joined, she held Kayza by the waist and pulled their sweet spots together.

Kayza arched her back when Char started pushing, rhythmically, and held each successive beat a little bit longer. No longer needing Char's help to move in time with her, Kayza grabbed her wrists and pinned them to the bed, over her head. Char took a sharp breath and struggled against Kayza's grip but could not free herself. Then, closing her eyes in surrender, she thrust herself into Kayza with mounting urgency. Thrilled, Kayza held her down and pushed herself into Char, while Char squeezed her tight with her thighs until their shared heat was too much to bear and, together, they convulsed in a grinding climax that left their chests heaving and their bodies quivering.

Her hands still clutching Char's wrists, her breathing settling, Kayza smooched her on the lips and nibbled on her neck, making her laugh. Then, after a last, shuddering flex of the muscles of her back and hips, she wriggled off Char and collapsed on their throw. Beside her, Char hummed in satisfaction.

"Is Your Majesty pleased?" she asked Kayza.

"For the moment, yes," Kayza replied.

"Then, if it pleases Your Highness, I will take my leave," Char begged pardon.

"I said, *for the moment*," Kayza reminded her attendant. "Stay where you are."

"But, Your Majesty," Char objected. "I am required elsewhere."

"Don't, *Your Majesty* me," Kayza cautioned the fretting woman. "I am . . . I am . . ."

"Augustina."

"Yes, thank you. I am Augustina," Kayza accepted the reminder. "Gods, that's an awful name. How typically Roman of Augustus to choose something so derivative. You must call me Tina. In addition, I will decide where you are required, and for the foreseeable future that will be with me. If anyone, Augustus included, thinks otherwise then I will make it my business to convince them of their wrong-headedness."

"Yes, Your . . . Tina."

"Good!" Kayza burst out, clapping her hands. "Now, I know you like your birthday suit, but let's find you some clothes—risqué but tasteful—then go out in the sun and have fun getting ourselves into trouble!"

Fun in the sun was opposite to the way in which Marquaisa was spending her time in a hold onboard a Spanish galleon. She was, however, in deep trouble, a fact of which she was reminded when Capitán Roxas rousted her out of her sweet dreams.

"Not that I care, but was that laughter I just heard?" Roxas asked her, his voice coarse, his tall frame in silhouette against the weak light outside the hold. Without waiting for a reply, he swished the sword he was pointing at his prisoner. "My compliments, your rapier is remark-able. Light but not weak, hard but not brittle, and *sooo* sharp. I wager I'll retire on the fortune I get from selling the gems in its handle."

"Serve me," Marquaisa replied, sifting her fingers through the remains of the net that once ensnared her. "Take me to Louisbourg, or you and your crew will die. Make your choice."

"I serve the Spanish monarchy—"

"That was not one of your choices."

"—and I certainly do not operate a ferrying service for monsters."

"Then you and your crew are dead," Marquaisa informed the captain, matter-of-factly.

"As are you," Roxas rejoined, chopping crosses in the air with Marquaisa's rapier.

"You have no idea," she growled and threw at the captain the stale bread his crewmen had thrown at her.

Roxas swatted at the half-loaf with the rapier, but missed and took the mouldy bun on the chin. Dry and brittle the bread landed with a *crack* when it hit the deck, spreading crumbs in every direction. No rats hurried to claim the bounty.

"As are we all," Roxas concluded and tipped the rapier's blade back, casually, onto his shoulder.

"Fool," Marquaisa snorted. "If you are so easy with death, then give me my sword and I will show you to its door."

"When I die it will not be by your hand," Roxas chuckled and leaned against the doorframe.

"Yes, it will," she assured him, totally confident in her prediction. "Now, get out of my hold and do not come back. Go and live what little life you have left."

"Heed your own words, foul hag," Roxas shot back, pushing himself off the doorframe and taking a step toward the object of his scorn. "For when I deliver you to the inquisitors at Ferrol they will waste no time deciding your fate and how you will meet it."

The captain paused, anticipating a retort. When none came his way he stepped back and, sniggering, continued, "If it's any comfort, you won't be alone. Before we return to Ferrol I will have captured *She Wolf*, claimed her booty, and consigned her to the depths. Those of her crew who survive will share your fate which, as I intimated, will most assuredly be an excruciating death."

"You are stupid," Marquaisa ignored Roxas's prognostications. "Worse, you waste your time. If you had any wits, then you would have known the instant I washed up on your deck *She Wolf* does not warrant your attention. She is pathetic. She picks at scraps left behind by the real wolves of the sea. So, there will be no glory and even less of a prize for taking her. Believe me when I say, I would not be here if I thought she was endowed with any prospects."

"Believe this," Roxas riposted, flicking the point of Marquaisa's rapier at her heart. "Your presence here defiles this ship. Furthermore, the *prospects* available to you here are limited to starvation, torture, and death. Just deserts for a greedy, disloyal harpy"

"Thank goodness I have good teeth, hair, and fingernails," Marquaisa dismissed the captain's insults. Adding emphasis to the last virtue she listed, she tapped the tips of her nails on the hardwood floor of her hold, their rapping akin to the sound of a blacksmith's maul hammer striking red hot steel on being forged on an anvil. "The fact is, the monarchy to which you pledge loyalty has, fittingly, sent you on a fool's errand. *She Wolf* is nothing compared to the one on whom you really ought to have your sights trained."

"Do tell," Roxas sarcastically requested enlightenment.

"The one who has her sights set on you," Marquaisa hinted, untangling her feet from the net and crossing her legs. "The one your men whisper about."

"Rajani?!" Roxas exclaimed, not quite believing what he was hearing.

"The very same," Marquaisa placed a tick next to Roxas's answer, clapping slowly to congratulate the captain on the wiliness of his deduction.

"Ha! That scow?" Roxas guffawed and tilted his tricorn hat up off his forehead. "With *Savannah* and her sixty-four guns I outclass *Rajani and* her captain. If I am *lucky* he will challenge me. For if he does, then he will discover he has again bitten off more than he can chew. Just as he did when he botched his raid on Saint-Pierre, the so-called 'Paris of the Caribbean.' Yes, if fortune smiles upon me, I will happily add *Rajani's* name to my list of conquests, right below *She Wolf's*. Doing so will fill me with almost as much joy as will watching what is left of you, after the inquisitors have finished with you, burn at the stake. Sleep well witch."

"A witch would make of you a plaything," Marquaisa informed Roxas as he slammed home the bolts of the door and her hold went black, "I am no witch."

CHAPTER 12

CRAFT

MARCH 31ST

ATLANTIC OCEAN, TRADE ROUTE SOUTHWEST TO FRENCH CARIBBEAN

Fraught with nothing remotely resembling peril, all of the pieces were in place for *Maëlle's* voyage from Africa's Gold Coast to Martinique, one of the sugar islands in the French Antilles on the eastern edge of the Caribbean Sea, to be the epitome of idyllic boredom. By no means overpowering, the southeasterly trade winds mustered enough energy to keep *Maëlle's* tall, sleek frame gliding over the ocean, full speed ahead, while spinning barely a ripple off her prow. Vast, featureless, and capable at a moment's notice of rising up and swatting down any who tested themselves against it, instead the Atlantic rolled and swayed, gently helping *Maëlle* on her way. So, on a steady west-northwest bearing, she happily stretched her legs, her timbers warmed by the tropical sun.

While *Maëlle* soaked up the sun, its heat, combined with the mounting number days on board, gradually eroded the thin layer of civility that enabled her passengers and crew to coexist peacefully. Fortess's physical fitness regimen, which involved his climbing and swinging, ape-like, among the riggings became less a harmless amusement and more an irritating distraction. D'Acier, piqued at having worn out the toys gifted to him by So-and-So, tossed them overboard, moved on to Poisson's and quickly turned their alternating cries of agony and extasy into grating annoyances. Poisson, his nerves jangling over the antics of his two mentees, converted his angst into anger, which he vented through increasingly aggressive swordplay with crewmen who initially were complimented by his challenges, but who eventually had to be coerced into accepting them as they typically ended with their visiting the ship's surgeon.

Together, the extreme animalistic, sadistic, and antagonistic behaviors formed a witches' brew that, if it was allowed to boil over, would have reduced *Maëlle* to a saline mass of dissolving flesh, bone, weapons, canvas, and wood. Fortunately for all aboard her, the pervasive sense of endlessness that fueled the fire beneath the brew was stoppered by the sighting of the island of Martinique. With the next port of call on the voyage within view, the edginess that was rife on *Maëlle* receded and the thin fabric that concealed the baser instincts of her riders repaired itself.

Martinique was governed, on behalf of King Louis XV of France, from Fort-Royal. But Saint Pierre, a few miles to its north, was bigger, richer, and more glamorous. Neither *Maëlle's* captain, nor Léonarre Poisson, the king's regent, was the least bit interested in becoming entangled in political wranglings. So, the capital was bypassed and *Maëlle* continued up the west coast of the island until, graceful as ever, she glided into the bay that fronted Saint Pierre.

Expert seamen, captain and crew navigated their ship through the many tall-masted merchants at anchor in the bustling port and eased her up to the dock where, assisted by sure-handed wharfies, they brought her in for a well-deserved rest. As her lines were made fast a team of deckhands cast out her gangplank to their onshore compatriots, who secured her to the wharf. Then, when they were certain the ramp was steady, the swabbies scattered to secluded spots on the main deck to make way for the captain and his three guests.

Turned out in their finery, D'Acier in red, Poisson in white, and Fortess in blue, the three men graciously accepted the captain's invitation to be the first to take leave of the ship. Their many thanks ringing in his ears, from the ship's rail the captain watched over their descent of the footbridge and then their first few steps on dry land. Safely on their way, he eyed the lines that linked his ship to the quay and weighed, in his mind, the consequences that went with waiting for them to return against those that might accompany cutting the lines, casting off, and leaving them to their fates. As if his mind was being read he saw Poisson, his white hat, coat, and trousers shining in the bright sunlight, test the heavy ropes as he walked the length of the ship, giving the last one in the set a hard tug before leaving *Maëlle* behind.

"Gentlemen," Poisson addressed D'Acier and Fortess airily, "Methinks, in light of our recent bouts of savage behavior, that if the captain had his druthers he would leave us stranded on this isle."

"Screw him," D'Acier submitted, waving his hand, dismissively, at nothing.

"Seconded," Fortess agreed, bowing to D'Acier.

"Motion carried," Poisson closed the item for discussion and changed topics. "Fortess, your exertions have put you in fine fettle. You are to be commended."

"Thank you, my lord," Fortess replied and returned the honor. "My compliments on your growing prowess with the blade. You are becoming quite formidable."

"You are too kind," Poisson feigned humility. "Though D'Acier might disagree with you if, that is, he left my dollies alone long enough to evaluate my form."

"The procession of your sparing partners passing by my quarters on their way to the surgeon tells me all I need to know," D'Acier countered. "You are almost ready to challenge me."

"And that, Fortess, is as near as D'Acier will venture to paying someone a compliment," Poisson declared, patting the fencing virtuoso on the back. "Come, let us locate the nearest drinking establishment so we can toast my ascension to the ranks of 'those who are nearly good enough,' before our friend Mount Pélée, in whose forbidding shadow we crawl like ants, erupts and wipes Saint Pierre off the face of the earth."

With Poisson leading the way, they strutted up the wharf toward the town, remarking as they went on the repair work recently completed on a number of its sections. They attributed the work to regular maintenance, but their assumptions were challenged when they reached the harbor front. From one end to the other, the sun-bleached facades of its warehouses were riddled with pockmarks and the mouth blown glass panes of their windows were punctured with round holes. Then, as they strolled up the main street in the town's shopping district, they witnessed stores operating at full capacity despite their frontages being boarded over, their awnings smashed, and their doorways damaged by fire. Even the shingle hanging above the entrance to the largest tavern on the street was worse for ware, holes having been shot through the name it bore, changing it from *The Bilge* to *T Pilg*.

When the three of them stepped into the saloon and stood side-by-side their vivid attire stood out in stark contrast to its muted décor and the soiled clothes sported by its regular patrons. For the most part, they were dockworkers or sailors, all hard-bodied and flinty-eyed, with thick, calloused hands, and grim, scarred faces. For a moment they suspended their drinking and hushed conversations to take the measure of the three newcomers then, visibly unimpressed, went back to swilling their booze and mumbling incoherently.

D'Acier bridled at the chilly reception and, after scanning the bar's patrons, said to Poisson, "My lord, we should leave this place. Rabble as low as this are not fit company for one such as yourself."

"While a quick exit might be prudent," Poisson reasoned, "It most certainly would be boring, and we have had our fill of boredom on *Maëlle*. So, I think we will stay. Besides, there is a matter of import I need to discuss with Captain Fortess, and this is the perfect venue for confidential discourse."

"As you wish," D'Acier gave in, not at all pleased. "To the bar it is. Follow me."

Zigzagging his way through the tables, while taking care to not allow his suit to be soiled by any of *The Bilge's habitués (regulars)*,

D'Acier found a path to the bar. Constructed of hardwood and polished to a high gloss, it was close to three feet deep and stretched across the width of the room, giving customers ample space to imbibe without having to rub elbows with one another. The barkeep, who was big, broad, round, bald, and of Euro-Carib descent was ready to take their order when they bellied up.

"I am Brice," the bartender introduced himself to his newest customers, dropping the *I am not nice* qualifier from his *nom de guerre (pseudonym),* "What can I get for you gentlemen?"

"Hello Brice, I am Poisson. This is Fortess and this is D'Acier," Poisson returned the greeting and nodded first to the man on his left, then the man on his right. "What drink is most popular with your regulars?"

"Grog, sir," Brice informed Poisson, to the regent's bewilderment.

"Rum diluted with water," Fortess translated for Poisson.

"I see. Do you serve anything else?" Poisson followed up.

"Indeed, sir," Brice replied and produced three identical bottles from under the bar, itemizing his selections as he placed one in front of each man. "Grog, grog, and grog."

Poisson arched an eyebrow at Brice's furrowed brow then smiled and placed his order, "Well then, grog it shall be my good man! These three bottles will do splendidly!"

"Excellent choice, sir," Brice complemented Poisson, then completed their transaction. "That will be three francs, please."

"There's twice that amount in it for you if you care to answer a question," Poisson bargained with the barkeep, while digging around the loose change in his pants pocket.

Brice's furrow deepened and he placed his clenched fists on the bar, "That *sounds* generous, sir. Whether or not it *is* generous will depend on the question. But, fair warning, if I don't like what your askin' about I'll take my six francs, and more, and bounce your candy asses out into the street. *Comprenez vous?" Do you understand?*

"Of course," Poisson asserted and placed on the bar, between Brice's fists, the six francs he fished from his pocket. "Now, I've heard it said Saint Pierre is the 'Paris of the Caribbean.' But instead of a city of light, I have found a town in disarray. Who or what caused the damages?"

The furrow in Brice's brow stayed fixed in place and his eyes flashed with anger. To Poisson, it looked like he and his entourage were about to be ushered, unceremoniously, out of *The Bilge*. However, rather than being given the boot, he got an answer to his question.

"Pirates," Brice growled. "Brutal, bloodthirsty pirates. Like I've never seen 'afore. Bare-chested, barefoot, baggy pantaloons, heads wrapped in dyed bandages, chitterin' in some strange language. And *tough*. Mean as alley cats. Snuck into the bay after dark. Lit up the town with their cannon. Came ashore and raided our shops and storehouses. Killed, no, *butchered* our folk. Soldiers cornered one of 'em. A woman, they said. Had her dead-to-rights, they said. But she went through 'em like they was butter. Shot two of 'em dead. Cut three more to within an inch of their lives. Took all their muskets and ran off, angrier'n black thunder, screamin' a name over'n over. *'Heriki,'* or some such. One of their Gods, maybe. Then they all just disappeared. Poof! Like they wasn't ever 'ere. 'Cept for all the damage they left behind. Like I said, never seen the like of it."

"Terrifying. So sorry for making you relive your nightmare," Poisson responded to Brice's story, his compassion for the man contrived. "Here, take what I have and treat yourself and the rest of your guests to a comforting splash of grog."

Poisson proceeded to pour the contents of both his pants pockets into the palm of Brice's hand. As the stream of coins flowed onto the bar the big man's furrows unfolded and a gap-toothed grin spread across his moon-shaped face. When the shower of silver and gold stopped it was his turn to arch an eyebrow and, as he did, he reached across the bar and shook Poisson's hand. Then, without a word, he retrieved four more bottles of grog and, with three of them dangling between the fingers of one hand, set about visiting all of his customers, refreshing their glasses or giving them swigs from the bottles.

Turning his back on the festivities, Poisson snickered then huddled with D'Acier and Fortess, "We must acquire *Heriki's* proper name and find out if his services are for hire. A man such as he could come in handy in the months to come. Speaking of which, Captain, as I mentioned earlier there is a matter, most secret, we must discuss."

Fortess was all ears, "I am the soul of discretion."

"I know you are and forgive me for waiting so long, but I had to be sure you were recovered from your ordeal with So-and-So before burdening you with this information. You are, so here it is," Poisson lowered his voice. "The British are planning to storm our fortress at Louisbourg. But we will push them back and drive them to the west, away from the fortress gates to a place known to us as *Anse de la Cormorandière*. The British, stupidly, call it Freshwater Cove. How can a cove fed by the ocean be freshwater? But I digress. You will play your part at the cove."

Fortess leaned closer to Poisson, "What do you require of me?"

"You will command the detachment of infantry guarding the cove," Poisson informed the captain. "You will resist the British landing until it is clear you will be overrun. You will then lead your troops in a strategic retreat back to the fortress, drawing the British after you."

Fortess looked puzzled, "How will this help us defeat the British?"

"An excellent question," Poisson complimented the soldier. "This part of the plan you must take to your grave. As we speak our Mediter-ranean fleet, formerly based at Cartagena, is sailing for Louisbourg. Its arrival will be timed to coincide with the British build-up to the siege of the fortress. They will see neither our ships, nor the reinforcements they are carrying until it is too late. They will be trapped between the fortress's guns and the men and arms of our fleet. The British expedi-tion will be crushed, and France will emerge victorious."

Fortess's jaw dropped, "Brilliant! Let us raise a toast to certain victory!"

With their teeth, Fortess, D'Acier, and Poisson pulled the corks from their bottles of grog and took long pulls of the light brown spirit. Then, buoyed by liquor and the prospect of playing a hero's role in the defeat of the British invasion of New France, Fortess went on a tour of the saloon, glad-handing the clientele, toasting Louis and all things French, and drinking his way into a stupor.

Watching the mood in the bar elevate from somber to celebratory,

D'Acier shook his head and said to Poisson, "That was easier than I anticipated it would be. He accepted your story verbatim."

"What can I say," Poisson shrugged. "He trusts me. Yet more proof that despite his physical recovery, Fortess is and always will be a madman."

CHAPTER 13

CARDS

APRIL 1ST

ATLANTIC OCEAN, TRADE ROUTE WEST TO HALIFAX

Another night. Another storm. Another block of time in Wolfe's life spent clinging to the sweaty sheets of a too small bunk in a pocket-sized cabin, seesawing between exhaustion-induced nightmares and seasickness-spawned hallucinations.

In his dreams, Wolfe was with Kate. They were dancing at a society social, keeping time with a Viennese waltz. Together they turned, effortlessly staying in step with one another and the couples with whom they shared the floor. Then, as the song neared is crescendo and they began turning faster, the floor started rotating, and a breeze tugged at their hair and clothes. Soon the room was spinning like a top, sometimes level, but mostly tilting every which way. Kate was thrilled, but he was frightened it would turn over completely, fill with freezing cold salty water and sink, and he and Kate would never see or hear from one another again. His fear of losing her always woke him, thrashing, from his dream.

Then his hallucinations would begin. The most terrifying took hold when he saw his reflection on a piece of silverware, or a pewter mug, or the water in his wash basin, or any number of shiny objects. No

118

longer someone he recognized, the face baying, snapping, and glowering back at him was that of the madman his detractors said he was, vainglorious, covetous, wrathful. In a word, loathsome. That he was able to shake off the vision, understanding what it was, he hoped meant he still clung to a shred of his sanity. He wished he could shake off his seasickness as just readily and get some real rest.

"Halifax," Wolfe said to himself as *HMS Princess Amelia* rose, then fell yet again. "Halifax is where I am going and Halifax is where I will be in a few short days."

"The dream, again, sir?" Isaiah Brock, Wolfe's *aide-de-camp,* asked sleepily. His voice, drifting down from the top bunk, was barely audible above the sounds of the west wind battering *Amelia* and her efforts to keep it from breaking her apart.

"Aye, lad," Wolfe replied, talking through the strain that went with keeping nausea at bay. "Apologies for waking you, again. At least it's too dark for anything to trigger the hallucinations."

"If my lord wishes, I can shine a matchlight on my silver pocket watch so he can see his reflection," Brock offered, innocently, unable to stifle a giggle.

"Very funny, whelp," Wolfe grumbled and scrubbed his face with his dry hands to help rid himself the aftereffects of insomnia. "Clearly, you've been spending too much time in Aggie's company. So, would you like to continue to torment me? Or, will you have a sudden lapse into decency and play at cards with me, and so assist me in my efforts to free myself from the bonds of my wretchedness?"

"A difficult choice, my lord," Brock continued tormenting his commanding officer and sat up in his berth, his naked shins dangling over its edge.

"Making hard decisions is the lot of an officer in the British army," Wolfe repeated learnings Brock had already assimilated. "Allow me to make this one for you. Get your arse down here and bring your playing cards with you. I will supply the candle and the match, seeing as the last time you attempted to light a candle our cabin nearly went up in flames."

"Yes, my lord," Brock obeyed, fighting a losing battle to control his laughter.

"What the blazes!" Wolfe blustered at Brock, while taking a swat at his bare feet. "Have your laugh and be done with it, man! And stow the *my lord* business. Coming from you it sounds more like *you imbecile.*"

"Yes, my lord," Brock blurted then, realizing what he'd said, fell back in his bed laughing and swinging his feet.

"Are you quite finished?" Wolfe asked after a moment and sat up in his bed, folding his white nightshirt over his knobby knees, which he had tucked into his chest.

Brock burst into another fit of laughter.

"Fine, I'll just wait," Wolfe sulked, speaking to the underside of Brock's mattress.

Brock tried to suppress his hilarity, but the effort made things worse.

"I'm glad my suffering is the source of such profound amusement for you, Brock. You will make a fine officer," Wolfe pouted and bumped the back of his head against the wall of his and Brock's cabin.

"Thank you, sir," Brock squeezed out his appreciation while catching his breath.

"You're welcome," Wolfe replied. He then backtracked on one of his cracks, to avoid offending his aide. "Don't be put off by my sarcasm, Brock. I meant what I said about you being officer material. Now, kindly climb down from your perch so we can get on with our game of *Vingt-et-Un.*" *Twenty-one.*

Wolfe lit a candle to help his aide find a landing spot in what little space the cabin offered. Brock took advantage and hit his mark on the cabin floor, then straightened his nightshirt and sat down on the sea chest in which he kept stored his and Wolfe's kit. When Brock was settled, Wolfe placed the candle in a holder fastened to the wall and then watched his aide shuffle and deal the cards. The effort it took to focus his eyesight on the card faces gave him a headache, but as he concentrated on the game he gradually forgot the pain.

"What is the first thing you will do when you are on leave at Halifax?" Brock asked Wolfe as they went through the motions of playing their game.

"I will walk about the town, out of uniform, and attempt to be a civilian," Wolfe stated his intentions as if he was planning an assault on an enemy stronghold. "I am curious to know what it will feel like to be accepted as an ordinary man, rather than feared because I am a soldier."

"An interesting choice of pastime," Brock commented after a reflecting on Wolfe's reply, as well as the hand he had dealt himself. "For my part, I have never felt feared when I am in uniform, in public. I have seen contempt, envy, and grudging admiration on the faces of people I've passed in the streets at home, but never fear. It's likely that's because I'm not considered a threat, as I might be if I was part of an invading or occupying army."

"Astute of you to make the distinction," Wolfe commended his aide. "That having been said, as you and I very soon will be part of an invading force you must prepare yourself for the inevitability the subjects of our conquest will fear you. That being the case, you must make a promise to yourself to not use their fear to your advantage when you make contact with them. You also must accept the fact that no matter how respectful you think you are being, you will be subject to their deep and abiding hatred."

"If that is so, then how do I stop from hating myself?" Brock asked as he lowered his hand and watched Wolfe think through his answer to the question.

"I can speak only for myself when responding that query," Wolfe prefaced his reply, his voice softening as he showed his cards. "My answer is I cannot. I have been in the trade long enough that I can hide my self-loathing behind bravado, or officiousness, or humor, or any number of other devices including, yes, overt brutality. But when I lack the energy to sustain them, they collapse like a house of cards under the weight of the contempt I have for things I have done or been part of, and what I have made of myself as a result."

"I am sorry, sir," Brock said the only thing that came to mind.

"Officers never say, *sorry,* young Brock," Wolfe wagged a finger in the air and pretended to lecture his aide, their game forgotten. "They might say, *my apologies,* occasionally. But they never say they are sorry. You must explain to me the difference between the two, after you have figured it out," he challenged his ward, then continued. "In sum, use what I can share with you from my time as an officer to make the time you will have as one better. Speaking of which, how goes your work on our plan for the invasion of New France. Wait! Before you answer, know this; the fate of England's burgeoning empire, and as a result that of the world, rests upon your shoulders."

"My plan is complete," Brock reported, full of confidence.

"Splendid! Let's hear it!" Wolfe exclaimed, leaning in toward Brock.

"Yes, sir," Brock obeyed, tilting forward slightly and speaking just above a whisper. "It begins with the demolition, by the navy, of the batteries on the islands at the entrance to the harbor and on Lighthouse Point. After those tasks are completed, the army will make landfall east of Louisbourg. East, even, of Lighthouse Point. We shall shelter behind the North Cape . . ."

Brock presented the details of his plan over the next fifteen minutes. When he concluded, his commander was laying on his back with his eyes closed.

"Your plan is excellent, Brock," Wolfe said dreamily. "I shall present it to Amherst and the Council, at Halifax. I expect they will tweak it, if for no other reason than to make themselves feel important and useful. It will remain, however, essentially yours. Well done."

"Thank you, sir."

"One more thing," Wolfe drawled through a yawn. "All plans fall apart the moment the first shot is fired. So, your next task is to think through the answers to the *what if* questions. You know, 'What if this, that, or the third happens?'"

"Yes, sir. I'll begin straight away," Brock promised. "Can you suggest where I should begin."

Wolfe whooped out a chest-rattling snore.

"Good night, General Wolfe," Brock said quietly, then licked the tips of his thumb and forefinger and extinguished the candle on the wall.

In the darkness, he climbed up into his bunk not realizing, in his fatigued state, he did so without having to balance himself against the motion of the ship. That the west wind had abated, the rain had ceased, and the ocean had calmed also escaped his notice. *HMS Princess Amelia* had smooth sailing ahead, all the way to Halifax.

CHAPTER 14

SIREN

APRIL 2ND

ATLANTIC OCEAN, SOUTHWEST TRADE ROUTE TO FRENCH CARIBBEAN

A haunting siren song floated above the slumbering ocean. Soft cords coaxed from a sarod's strings and soothing melodies sung in a young woman's voice swayed with the starlight that reflected off the still water's surface. Comforting and enticing, the music drew a silent Spanish galleon slowly into its embrace.

Behind the warship, blacked-out and reeking of bad intent, a tall three-masted predator crept into her wake. Crowded at the stalker's rail and poised to strike, her crew made not a sound as she glided up the port side of the galleon. When the great ship of the line came within range, on silent command they loosed their grappling lines and snagged their quarry. Heaving on the ropes, they pulled the two ships into close quarters and made ready to drop their boarding ramps to bridge the final few feet of the gap between the vessels.

Crouched low behind their starboard rail, the raiders braced themselves for the Spanish counterattack. A few of them, itching for a fight, glanced over the rail but saw no signs one was imminent. Rather, the galleon appeared to be empty and the siren song drifted, unbroken, over her decks and across her square sails. Eager to not lose their advantage they turned to the man who had signaled them to cast their hooks, keen to know what they were to do next.

"Hold," Captain Mario Ortona Enriquez, dressed in all black, his top, breeches, and boots skintight, his wavy back hair tied back in a ponytail, whispered to the man on his right, who passed it on, sending the order sizzling through the ranks. "Vishnu, Ganesh, Yuval, with me. Let's go have a look."

In unison, three short, sharp, stabbing swords hissed out of their scabbards. Enriquez checked his pistol for what, to him, seemed like the hundredth time since they got within striking distance of the galleon. Satisfied it was ready, he winked at his three lieutenants. Maratha from the Indian subcontinent, they wore their turbans wound tight above the vermillion-colored, smiling crescent moon tattoos inked on their foreheads, their printed calico tops and slops loose, and their feet bare. Sheens of sweat, drawn out by the promise of a close quarters fight to the finish, shone on the dark brown skin of their necks, their thirst for blood borne out in the wicked smiles that gleamed from underneath their bushy black moustaches. Cracking a smile of his own, Enriquez led the three warriors through his horde of cutthroats to the nearest one holding a boarding ramp and gave her the nod to lower the plank.

No sooner had the ramp clapped down on the galleon's rail than, with practiced ease, the four pirates sprinted across its length. When they reached its end they hopped off, touched down lightly on the main deck, and fanned out smoothly, searching for clues they'd been lured into a trap. None were revealed, but the ship's torches showed the deck was awash with evidence of a more sinister kind of mischief. Splashes and streaks of blood coated the deck boards and were crisscrossed with parallel tracks that led to the ship's rail. What appeared to be the door of a cargo hold, it hinges torn out, lay on top of a flattened body.

That there were no survivors and the ship was adrift told Enriquez the members of her crew had gone mad and slaughtered one another. His voice hushed he summoned his lieutenants and reversed with them, slowly, in the direction of their ramp while stating his verdict on the galleon, "Gentlemen, I fear our hunt has been for naught. *Savannah* is cursed. Let us leave her for the crows."

When they reached the bridge to their ship they formed a tight knot around it, at the rail. Enriquez nudged Vishnu with his elbow, telling him to make good his retreat. After a quick nod to his captain, the pirate pivoted to mount the plank and froze. At the same instant, Enriquez, Ganesh, and Yuval sucked in their breath as the remains of an iron deadbolt, presumably the one that at one time held shut the door that presently was squashing a swabbie, clattered down upon and rattled around the main deck.

"Ahem," a lady-like voice drifted down from the aft quarter deck.

Enriquez cursed under his breath then, with a few swift hand gestures, sent Ganesh and Yuval to the galleon's starboard stairs. When they reached them, pistol in hand and Vishnu at his heels, he started creeping up the portside steps, his movements mirrored by the two men on the opposite side of the ship. Near the top of the stairway, he crouched and snuck a peek between a pair of the posts supporting the banister. He squinted at the dark, smokey deck, trying to catch a glimpse of the woman who was seeking his and his men's attention, but had to shield his eyes when the huge stern lantern suddenly blazed to life. When his eyes finally adjusted to the light he saw a man turned out in the uniform of a Spanish naval officer, its cut and braid indicating he was the ship's captain, standing in front of the mizzen mast. As befit his rank, the captain stood proudly at attention, his gaze aimed beyond the forecastle and far out over the ocean. The woman was nowhere to be seen.

Enriquez stood up straight and raised his gun, aiming it at the captain, and stomped up the remaining steps to the quarter deck. Vishnu, Ganesh, and Yuval, their blades ready, stormed the deck equally noisily.

"What happened here?" Enriquez demanded of the captain.

The Spaniard shifted his eyes in Enriquez's direction and was about to answer, but was cut short by the sounds of steel slicing through flesh and grating against bone. Caught between two scything blades scissoring his neck from behind, the captain's head popped off his shoulders and spun through the air until it thudded on the deck and rolled to a stop at Enriquez's feet. Helped on its way by a kick from behind, the captain's body then crashed down, spewing a stream of blood that lapped against his head. Standing in the space vacated by the captain, head bowed, hands by her side, each gripping a bloody sword, a black-haired, broad-shouldered woman stood stock still, her naked body splattered with blood.

"Suchika sings and plays sweetly," she said, her voice husky, her critique erudite.

Enriquez cleared his throat and began, "My lady . . . ?"

"Marquaisa," the killer gave Enriquez the name he did not ask for, then told him what he did not know he was thinking, "You were expecting me."

Certain the woman was the last person he expected to meet on a Spanish warship, Enriquez returned to the topic of the music that accompanied his and his lieutenants' foray onto *Savannah*, "My lady Marquaisa is too kind."

"I assure you, I am not," Marquaisa imparted unwanted information on Enriquez and rested her foot on her victim's back.

Enriquez changed course, "I am—"

"Mario Ortona Enriquez," Marquaisa did the honors for the captain, "Capitán of *Rajani*, grandson of Don Miguel Enriquez, the Grand Archvillain. You are accompanied by your lieutenants, Vishnu, Ganesh, and Yuval, late of the Indian subcontinent. Tell me, how does a Spanish pirate claiming notorious Puerto Rican descent end up in command of a Mughal warship?"

"My lady is well informed," Enriquez, masking his unease over the accuracy of her intelligence, avoided her question, "She also, clearly, does not require whatever assistance I might provide. I believe, therefore, I am here by her design."

"You are," Marquaisa confirmed the captain's belief.

"The question, 'Why?,' springs to mind," Enriquez followed up, eyeing the severed head that was resting at his feet.

"To serve me by taking me to Louisbourg," Marquaisa replied and pointed one of her swords at the head that was occupying Enriquez's attention. "Roxas would not. I know you will not make the same mistake."

Enriquez dragged his eyes off Roxas's hemorrhaging brain bucket, cleared his throat, and ventured, "Then you also know my next question."

"Yes, the matter of your compensation," Marquiasa deduced, the pirate's motivation patent.

"Indeed. I am, after all, a businessman," Enriquez submitted while attempting a humble smile.

"You are a scallywag," Marquaisa reminded the rogue. "Your payment will be this ship and its contents and, if our mission to Louisbourg is a success, a five percent share of the gold we liberate from the French."

"My lady is generous and I would love to grant her wishes," Enriquez dissembled. "However, given the risks, I must insist on a fifty percent share."

"The *risks* are irrelevant. Your life and the lives of your crew were forfeit the instant you set foot on this ship," Marquaisa countered, stalking toward the pirate. "You will take a ten percent share and not a speck of gold dust more."

"Thirty percent, or I will be unable to live with myself and, thus, I will have no choice but to sink this ship, scuttle *Rajani*, and accept a watery grave."

"Fifteen percent," Marquaisa relented and before Enriquez attempted further parley grabbed him by the throat and smiled at him, showing off her array of pearly white weaponry. "Take it or it will be *me* who relieves you of the burden of living, and it will be *me* who enjoys the spoils of capturing this tub, and it will be *me* who captains *Rajani* to the fortress at Louisbourg. Deal?"

In reply, Enriquez, who was certain he could see his reflection on her tooth enamel, croaked, "Deal!"

"Shrewd of you," Marquaisa congratulated her new partner and let go of his throat but kept her eye on his throbbing carotid. "Although I might have gone as high as eighteen percent, given the risks."

"I knew it!" Enriquez lied while massaging his Adam's Apple.

"Nevertheless, I thought it best to have mercy on you and end our negotiations."

"Mercy," Marquaisa made the word sound like the punch line of a bad joke. "Count on it you will be shown none, especially if you leave Suchika behind as you did when you abandoned her to the French on Martinique. She sings of your betrayal in her song, as well as what will happen to you if you do it again. Her catalogue of tortures is impressive. I look forward to sharing notes with her."

Relishing the rapid exodus of color from Enriquez's face, she stripped Roxas of his great coat and, before wrapping herself in it, smelled the blood that clung to it. Heady with the coppery scent, she looked at Enriquez and his men hungrily. Their bodies tensing under her stare, the four men squared their shoulders and gripped their weapons tightly.

"Well met," she complimented the foursome, then invited them to follow her. "Shall we?"

Without waiting for a reply, she leapt over the portside rail and landed, without a wobble, on a grappling line. She then tiptoed across the swinging rope without putting a foot wrong. Aboard *Rajani*, the crew greeted her arrival with showers of applause and an uproar of cheering.

Still standing on the castle deck of the galleon, a pool of blood coagulating around his boots, Enriquez boasted, "I could do that with my eyes closed, if it wasn't so dark."

CHAPTER 15

BOONDOGGLES

APRIL 10TH

NASSAU, THE BAHAMAS

An offshore breeze carried Nassau's stench across the harbor to *Rajani*, where it added body to the smoke that seeped from the lamps that lit her decks. Its odor and texture robust, the mixture took some of the edge off the sharp notes in the song that wove its way from below deck up to Enriquez, who was leaning on his ship's stern rail.

"Which of my virtues are you singing about tonight, Suchika?" the captain wondered out loud. His weight on his elbows, he gazed at the surface of the harbor's still black waters and admired his reflection. Having swapped his form fitting, jet black, night raiding gear for his long, scarlet, high-collared, wide-cuffed, button-festooned coat, wide silk sash, wool knee-length breeches, tall boots, and lace-trimmed tricorn hat, he was the image of piratical swagger. The black goatee, now neatly trimmed, added an edgy, rakishness to his appearance that carried over into his attitude and bearing.

"She sings of Martinique," Marquaisa answered the pirate's question, extracting from him a squawk of surprise and a scrambling about face. "She still has not forgiven you."

"Forgive me, my lady. I did not mean to ignore you. I did not see you in the shadows," Enriquez's voice cracked, and his cheeks reddened.

"Suchika is the one from whom you must beg forgiveness," the lady replied, still shrouded in darkness. "Otherwise, it could go as badly for you as it did for the soldiers in Saint Pierre, if not worse."

"She knew what to expect," Enriquez mounted his defense. "To the soldiers her actions were unexpected, as I expected."

"She killed two of them and maimed several more as you may have expected. However, she then had to chase down your forsaking hide to avoid being captured, unexpectedly," Marquaisa reminded him. "By failing to apologize to her you risk sharing a fate similar to that met by the unsuspecting soldiers."

"I am forewarned," Enriquez thanked her with a bow. "I am also forgetting my manners. I am going ashore this evening. Nassau is a cesspit of crime, despite what its current governors would have you believe. So, it is an excellent place to sell a used galleon, one of which recently came into my possession. It also has a fine pastry shop, and I find myself craving the taste of a sweet fruit *Mag-Pie*. Would you care to join me for a bite?"

"Choose your words wisely," Marquaisa suggested, grimly. "You may crave sweets. My palate is more sophisticated."

"Can I take that to mean you are confirming the gossip the crew share when they whisper about you?" Enriquez probed, cautiously.

Stepping from the shadows, Marquaisa corrected him, "I mean *vamanos*." Let's go.

Darkness parted before her, sticky black tendrils clinging to her and losing their grip on her only when she moved into the lamplight. Slithering off her cloak they left behind oily trains that streaked her hooded black cloak and the ridges and planes of the carved blood red demon mask that hid her face.

"I was wondering what happened to my cherrywood cutting board," Enriquez said, trying to sound offhand.

"You are startled," Marquaisa concluded, watching him recoil from her.

"*Sí.* I mean, *no,*" Enriquez babbled. To stop himself he ushered Marquaisa to the stairs that led down to the main deck, stepped aside, bowed, and slipped on his invitation, "Demons first."

Marquaisa stopped and stood beside him, studying him from behind her mask. "Very well," she said. "After you."

"What?" Enriquez squeaked.

"You said, 'demons first.' So, lead on."

"What?" Enriquez repeated. Then, summoning his nerve and recovering his manners he accepted her deferral, "Oh, yes, please follow me, my lady. Your landing craft awaits."

When they reached the dinghy they were greeted by Enriquez's three Maratha lieutenants, all wearing fresh pheta turbans, and wrapped in their brightly colored cotton kurta pajamas, loose-fitting pants, and sandals. Ganesh and Yuval were manning its oars, while Vishnu was standing in the pinched nose of its prow, a spyglass jammed in his right eye socket, scanning the town's seafront. He quit his surveillance neither when they boarded, Marquaisa to stand at the stern and Enriquez to sit in front of her on the aft bench, nor when the rowboat was winched down the port side of the ship, nor when it splashed into the water. However, when it rocked left and right in response to Ganesh using his oar to energetically cast off, Vishnu was joggled out of his fixation on the shoreline and into an arm-waving, feet-dancing, torso-contorting balancing act that barely kept him and his spyglass from plopping into harbor.

The scalding exchange of blistering curses between the two Maratha warriors, into which Yuval unhesitatingly inserted himself, ricocheted off *Rajani*, as well as the hulls of all the ships in the immediate vicinity. Loud though it was, their yelling was lost in the riot of noises that was spilling out of Nassau into its harbor. Raucous laughter, shouted oaths, screams of pain, drunken singing, crackling gunfire, and the clanging of swords took turns coming to the fore of a chaotic symphony whose movements were punctuated by the splashing of bodies as they hit the water after being thrown off any one of a number of jetties. Stretching away from the piers and into the town, at odd angles, its maze-like streets were crammed with people of every size, shape, and description, excepting law-abiding.

"It's good to be home," Enriquez sighed, fondly.

"Someone watches us," Marquaisa warned, removing her mask and placing it on the bench beside him.

Enriquez looked up at the ships by whom they were surrounded and between whom they were snaking and agreed, "My lady speaks the truth. Each of these vessels has posted a night watch. So, in fact, many someones are watching us."

"They all stink of grog and turn a blind eye to our passing," Marquaisa informed the captain. "The someone I speak of smells sweet, but sees red. Know you such a one?"

"I think, maybe, I might not," Enriquez replied, keeping his eyes fixed on the beach upon which they were about to run aground. Thirty yards wide and just as deep, it connected two jetties and was separated from the boardwalk by a wide strip of tall beach grass.

"So, in fact, you may," Marquaisa translated Enriquez's piratese.

His buttocks bouncing to the edge of the bench when the little boat bottomed-out, Enriquez neither confirmed, nor corrected Marquaisa's interpretation of his meaning, choosing instead to and burst over the side the dinghy. As he bounded through the shallow surf he blurted, "By the sands of Zanzibar, we are here! Vishnu, Ganesh, Yuval, you have the raft. Kill, if you must, to protect it. And be ready to leave in a hurry."

When his orders went unacknowledged he sloshed through an about turn to find out if he'd been heard. Instead, he found the launch was abandoned, rocking gently, and drifting slowly away from shore. Shouting profanities, he splashed back the way he had come and caught the craft just as his knee-high boots began to fill with silty water. After wrestling with it, briefly, he succeeded in dragging it safely out of reach of the tide.

His lieutenants were nowhere to be seen. Whatever tracks they'd left in the sand were obscured by the milky moonlight and lost among the footprints of a thousand other cut-throats. Expecting nothing less from the Maratha, he smiled, and resting his left hand on the pommel of the blade strapped to his hip swaggered towards the carnival that was Nassau, alone.

In a pool of shadow that filled a gap between blotches of torchlight cast onto the sand from one of the piers, Marquaisa watched Enriquez churn, step-by-step, up the beach. Taking her eyes off him, she inspected the packs of revelers he was about to join on the boardwalk. Reeling and staggering in time with rhythms only they could hear, they swayed side-to-side, and forward-and-back, and snapped up straight again before they fell on their faces, then started over. Steadily, she searched through them, intent on finding the one among them who did not weave or wobble and whose attention was locked on the newly arrived pirate captain.

She found no such a one. Neither did she find Enriquez tracking along the path she expected him to be following when she turned her eyes back on beach. Instead, she saw his wide-brimmed tricorn hat resting upside-down on the sand. Nearby, his sword was stabbed into the ground. Grains of sand shifted beneath its ornate guard. The swarthy buccaneer had disappeared.

Marquaisa blinked at the vacant beach knowing people were incapable of disappearing into thin air. Only witches could make themselves vanish, and only the very best witches at that. She knew, also, Enriquez was no witch. The man's idea of magic was to extract a cork, in one piece, from a bottle of wine.

Also, after a lifetime spent in the company of pirates, the captain was not the type to leave his things lying about, especially his favorite hat and beloved sword. To separate him from either required extreme amounts of alcohol or force, or a combination of the two. It held, then, if his disappearance was neither intentional, nor magical, nor voluntary, that he must have somehow been taken against his will.

"But there are no obvious signs of a struggle," Marquaisa said to herself as she crouched beside the spot occupied by Enriquez's hat and sword.

She pinched the brim of the hat between her thumb and forefinger and lifted it out of the sand. Turning it this-way-and-that, she examined it closely. It was not bent, frayed, soiled with fingerprints, stained with blood, or strung with stay lengths of his hair. The only untoward thing about it was the sand piled in its bonnet, the result, presumably, of the struggle that landed it on the beach. She dumped the sand into her palm and as it fell a mist of fine white dust separated itself from the grains, some of the particles sticking to her skin, others drifting into her nose and mouth. The grains of sand she caught in her hand, by their look and smell, gave away nothing regarding the fate of the hat's owner. So, she plunked the hat on her head and turned her attention to the sword stuck in the sand.

Buried within the arcana in the tombs of the Freemasons were their notes on an assortment of types of sand. Quarried sand of the 'sharp' variety was, they said, the type best suited for the mortar mixes that glued together the edifices humans considered great engineering achievements. Beach sand was not of the sharp variety, however Enriquez surely was going to be displeased at how jamming his sword into a bank of the grit dulled its blade.

The force with which it was rammed into the ground was evident in the effort it took to pull it out. She was able to free it with a quick tug. However, the fact she had to take it in a firm grip to do so told her an exceptionally strong human must have done the embedding. With a single blow someone that strong could have knocked Enriquez out cold, caught him before he hit the ground, slung him over their shoulder, and run off with him, thus leaving the scene devoid of any evidence of a struggle. If any of the revelers inshore saw Enriquez being spirited away they would have assumed he was just another drunk about to take a swim off the end of a pier.

"He came. He saw. He most likely is dead."

Marquaisa whirled around to face the clod who had intruded upon her processes of deductive reasoning. As she pivoted she dropped to one knee and snapped her sword arm straight, aiming the tip of Enriquez's blade at the point on the beach from whence the interruption originated. That point was a blob, crowned by a halo of fine hair, backdropped by the moonlight reflecting off the waters of the harbor. Slowly, it shuffled in her direction and took the shape of a man in his thirties, who was of average height, weight, and build. His bearing was military but was marred by a limp. He was undeterred by the dire prospects her attitude and weapon presented.

"Judging by your inspection of the evidence, I'll wager you've deduced the circumstances surrounding your man's disappearance," the intruder chatted at Marquaisa amiably as he trundled up the beach and shambled to a stop judiciously out of range of her sword. "My word, when did you last sleep? Your eyes look like hotshots."

"My man?" Marquaisa asked, ignoring the man's observations of her symptoms and what might be ailing her.

"Forgive me," the interloper apologized. "When I said, 'your man,' I meant it not in the romantic but the clinical sense. I aimed to respect the fact he is to you nothing more than a tool, given you likely would show more concern over the loss of a paint brush or watering can than you've shown over his disappearance. I would have said something like, 'your lover,' if I'd thought you were connected to him romantically. As for how I know you've misplaced a man and not a woman, the hat you wear, while it succeeds in making you look exceedingly fetching, was shaped for a man's head. Also, the sword you're pointing at me is better suited to someone who is right-handed, as well as being too heavy for a typical woman. But you're far from typical, aren't you? Guineas to green beans says you're a witch, by which I mean no offense."

Sand stirred up by a breath of wind skittered over the spot Marquaisa had vacated while the man was delivering his monologue. The windblown silt in pursuit of her, she followed a set of footprints that distinguished themselves from the many others on the beach by their enormity, the distance that separated one from the other, and the depth of their impressions, particularly those made by the left foot. Clearly, they were made by someone very big who was carrying a heavy load stacked on top of their left shoulder, and who was running away from where she hid herself under the pier. When they disappeared in the strip of long grass that separated the beach from the crowd on the boardwalk she stopped and said, loud enough for the man tailing her to hear, "I am no witch."

"Of course you aren't," he replied, masking his skepticism. "Be that as it may, we must proceed with caution. Let us not draw attention to ourselves or our investigation. Doing so will alert the kidnappers and make them act hastily. That would not bode well for your man's longevity, assuming he has any remaining. Oh dear."

Kayza was standing on the far side of the grass sniffing the air she was fanning from the crowd into her nose. As he watched, she went still and focused on the line of drunks stretching away from her left to the beach on the opposite side of the jetty. When she started marching at it he cursed and, plotting a course that would intercept her, he ran after her.

Slowed by his gimpy leg, the soft sand, and the clinging grass he could not catch her before she confronted a trio near the end of the line. Their hackles raised by her blunt intrusion they pushed back, first by arguing with her, then by crowding and shoving her. No sooner did they touch her than one fell clutching his windpipe, a second went down wailing and with blood running from his eyes, and the third crumpled, retching and holding his crotch. Roused by the altercation, the boozers nearby roared their upset at the plight of their pals, and their fury at Marquaisa for being the cause of their misery. Galvanized by their need to smash a common foe, the mob stepped on, over, and around their downed mates and rushed her, only to have its front line taken down with equally cruel efficiency.

"Enough!" a sharp command issued in a woman's rich, low register voice sent a shudder through the pack and stopped its members in their tracks. "You lot. Get back to your drinking and whoring and take with you all those sorry souls for whom the lady's attentions proved too much. She and I owe each other a conversation and I don't want the likes of you and them interrupting us with your whining."

CHAPTER 16

HOCUS-POCUS

APRIL 10TH

NASSAU, THE BAHAMAS

Forty years before Marquaisa started picking fights with Nassau's citizens, the King's Pardon was used to stop them fighting one another, as well as any outsiders who had the misfortune to cross their paths. The pardon, worded specifically for the town's pirate demographic, aimed to end the mayhem in their haven by granting swashbucklers clemency from their past transgressions and a clean slate from which to launch quiet mainstream lives, all courtesy of King George I of England. Refusal to accept the pardon equated to sentencing oneself to death. The king's henchmen, some of whom were pirates who had taken the pardon, gleefully carried out the sentence by hunting down and capturing their former brethren and consigning them to the gallows.

Unlike the king, Marquaisa did not offer the rotten apples of Nassau's population a pardon, nor did she make any of them her prisoner. What's more, while she had maimed a few of them and crippled a few more, she hadn't put any of them to death. Even more, she cared not a fig about the lives they led, law abiding or otherwise. She simply required their cooperation in ensuring the return to her of the brigand who was secreting her to Louisbourg where, for purely selfish reasons, she was going to steal a mountain of gold from the French authorities. Specifically, she needed the help of one person, preferably the master-mind behind the abduction of the aforementioned reprobate. If that meant she had to crack some skulls to draw that person out, then so be it.

"Fine, you drew me out. Why don't you tell me why you are here?" suggested the petite, deeply tanned woman, her long, wide-cuffed, brass-buttoned, black silk coat and matching damask waistcoat catching the moonlight, her contrasting white trousers and knee-high leather boots showing off her strong legs, her deep voice enchanting. Behind her, towering over her, a muscular giant, bare to the waist, the diamond studs in his ears sparkling, regarded Marquaisa with an expression that fluctuated between contempt and admiration.

"You watched us come ashore. Why?" Marquaisa asked in reply, shaking her head to try to rid herself of a compulsion to give the woman whatever she wanted.

"Whatnot," the woman heaved a sigh and teased out her long straight ashen-colored hair with both hands, then spoke to the nonde-script man who limped to Marquaisa's side. "Would you like to tell me why she is here?"

"Here, as in standing before you, Madame Emmo. Here, as in visiting our quaint little town. Or, here in a metaphysical sense, as in, why are any of us here?" Whatnot asked, seeking clarification.

"Why don't we limit ourselves to the first two, Jonah," Emmo proposed, rubbing her temples, then crossing her arms over her chest.

"She is visiting our town because, as you have just witnessed, she itches for a good scrape," Whatnot testified. "She shares a patch of dirt with you because she is searching for her man, thinks you took him, and intends to kill you for doing so."

"You said, 'her man,' as if he is something akin to a door jamb," Emmo observed.

"That is because, to her, he is but a tool. However, not so much a door jamb as a servant," Whatnot explained.

"He must be a useful one if she's willing to embark on a rescue mission to save him," Emmo surmised, then turned her attention back to Marquaisa. "Why don't you tell me why you want him back?"

"Where . . . where is he?" Marquaisa countered, wondering why her hardboiled self-possession was going mushy.

"How about I show you. Stay here, Plug," Emmo ordered the colossus guarding her, and eased her way toward Marquaisa. "By the way, nice hat. What's under the cloak?"

"A smile," Marquaisa said with a snicker and batted her eyes at the woman.

"Wicked," Emmo tsk-tsked and patted Marquaisa on the cheek. "Come, Jonah, let us reunite the little witch with her plaything."

"She says she is no witch," Whatnot informed Emmo while following her off the beach.

"Too bad," Emmo remarked and made a left turn up a narrow alley. "A bit of hocus-pocus might be entertaining. How long has it been since we've had a witch here, Jonah? It must be, what, twenty, no, thirty years."

"I haven't known there to be one here since I landed on the island," Whatnot told Emmo, looking around and not recognizing where he was. "So, it's been at least twenty years."

"That's right," Emmo agreed, making a right onto a cobbled lane peppered with horse manure. "It was before you set up shop on Bakery Street. Back when I was young. The witch was young too, when it suited her. When it did not she changed."

"So, the woman disguised herself. That doesn't mean she was a witch," Whatnot argued, dodging around horse poop. "I can disguise myself easily with a wig and a new set of clothes."

"She did not swap one costume for another, Doctor," Emmo pointed out as she bounced up the winding staircase at the end of the lane. "She shifted her bones, folded her skin, colored her hair. The only things she could not change were her eyes. They remained clear and blue."

"Médico?" Marquaisa blabbed at Whatnot, with a boff. *"Eres un médico?"* You're a doctor?

"Doctor Jonah Whatnot, Combat Surgeon, retired but at your

service," Whatnot confirmed, then reengaged with Emmo. "That cannot be true. Shapeshifting is not possible."

"I know what I saw," Emmo stopped at the top of the stairs. "But I was a child, so I told not a soul. No one would have believed me. Just as you don't believe me, Doctor. Anyway, after I watched her change, I never saw her again. That does not mean, however, that I have not seen her."

"Campfire tales," Whatnot snorted, trying to hide the shiver that rattled his spine so much he had to grab the stairway's handrail.

"Says you, Doctor," Emmo disagreed. "However, our new friend seems content to accept my story. Why don't you tell us why . . ."

"Mar . . . ummm . . . Marquaisa," with an effort Marquaisa called to mind her name and finished Emmo's sentence.

"That's a lovely name. Very regal," Emmo flattered her. "Tell us why you believe me."

"Because you are the witch!" Marquaisa cried, clapping happily and thinking how smart she must be.

"Clever," Emmo praised her and stepped down the stairs to where she stood. "How do you know?"

"Because your eyes are blue and witches kill people who know their secrets," Marquaisa said in a rush, then suddenly became very sad. "Even if those people are just little girls."

"Correct," Emmo conceded while stroking Marquaisa's hair. "And let me assure you, your and the Doctor's deaths will be just as slow and painful as that of the child who found me out. For, to be reborn in me, your unnatural deaths must be as agonizing as natural birth."

"There I was, thinking you were merely eccentric," Whatnot grumbled, his head downcast. "Well, you can count on it that Marquaisa and I will not passively go to our demise."

"Actually, you will," Emmo disagreed and detached herself from her fascination with Marquaisa. "As we speak, you and this delectable creature are following me not because you are choosing to, but because of the effects of a little 'think like me' concoction of mine that makes you very compliant. Just like the pastry you mold to suit your purposes, Doctor. The effects of the potion are temporary—they last only a few hours—but while they have hold of you, you are compelled to follow my counsel. The funny part is, you know it's happening, but you can't stop yourself. For example, Jonah, it was an excellent idea for me to have Plug hide Enriquez in your bakery, was it not?"

"Yes! Splendid!" Whatnot enthused. "Wait, why did I say that?"

"The white stuff in the sand from Enriquez's, no, *my hat!*" Marquaisa caught on, her eyes alight. *"Esto es muy bueno!" That is so cool!*

"Thank you, dear," Emmo purred and started for the top of the stairs.

"Show me. Show me, show me, show me!" Marquiasa demanded and tugged on the sleeve of Emmo's coat before she could get away.

"Show you what, sweetheart?"

"The thing. The thing, the thing, the thing!"

Thinking she pinpointed the spark firing Marquaisa's excitement, Emmo looked her full in the face. Turning her focus inward, she closed her eyes and concentrated. Slowly, her tan faded, her skin dried, deep wrinkles etched themselves into the borders of her eyes and mouth, and her hair became brittle and white. When she opened her eyes they were the same clear blue as always. Then, seeing the wonder that filled Marquaisa's face, she closed her eyes again and returned to being her more youthful self.

"Esto es increíble!" Marquaisa cried, joyfully, clapping her hands. *That is amazing!*

"Isn't it just the best?" Emmo concurred. "Now, the two of you, follow me. We have kept Enriquez waiting long enough."

"No, thank you," Whatnot refused her order while falling into step behind her as she quickstepped into a covered walkway that led further into town. "What is happening?"

"You are tasting helplessness," Emmo spoke through a giggle that echoed in the tunnel. "Delicious, is it not?"

"Yes, please make it worse," Whatnot heard himself say.

"Patience, Jonah, we are almost there," Emmo said soothingly then, after exiting the passageway, skidded down a short slippery incline to Bakery Street.

Whatnot and Marquaisa followed her without misstep.

"I should tell you why I am doing this to you, shouldn't I?" Emmo suggested and, knowing they would agree, turned to face them. Walking backwards down Bakery Street, she explained, "The answers are pleasure and personal gain. As for pleasure, it is entertaining and arousing to torture people. As for personal gain, obviously, by virtue of *being* someone I *own* their worldly goods. In your case, Doctor, the bakery you love, which will provide me a steady supply of new identities. Where Enriquez is concerned, his ship, which will allow me to take my operation global. As for you, young lady, your looks will open all kinds of doors, and in the unlikely event they do not open of their own accord you, *no I,* will be able to kick them in. In sum, your agonizing deaths will help me build an enterprise bigger than the three of you combined could imagine. The downside for you is I will be the only one who reaps the benefits. Ah, here we are at last, number one hundred twelve. Nassau's renowned bakery, famous across the length and breadth of the Spanish Main. After you, Doctor. This is, after all, your establishment. Now you, my lady. I do so love the way you move."

"Whatnot!" Enriquez exclaimed when the bell above the door rang, and the doctor entered the bakery. The pirate was walking in circles in front of the ovens at the back of the shop, a confused look on his face. When he rounded the turn and once again faced the front of the pastry emporium he asked, "Why am I not able to ask you why I want to know where I am?"

"I don't know why I don't know," Whatnot mumbled. "I think there's a witch around here, someplace, who can explain."

"Indeed, there is," Emmo said, taking Marquaisa by the hand and stepping around Whatnot. "But I won't waste my time doing so."

"Aren't you my sister from another spinster?" Enriquez rhymed, smiling at Emmo as he strode around his circuit.

"Yes, Mario, I am," Emmo answered him, smiling back at him. "I am also a witch, which accounts for how I was born of a virgin. You, on the other hand, were adopted. Now you will die. This nice young lady is here to kill you with your own sword."

"Okay," Enriquez accepted, nodding his head, puzzlement registering in his look. "I'll stop walking to make it easy for her."

"Why don't you do that," Emmo counseled the captain and joined him in front of the ovens. When Enriquez came a halt, she stood Marquaisa in front of him and took her place behind him, placing her hand on his back, behind his heart, and started chanting.

In answer to the incantation, Marquaisa raised the sword in her left hand and pressed its point against Enriquez's chest. Emmo's recitations became more urgent and Marquaisa pushed on the sword, piercing Enriquez's skin. A trickle of blood seeped from his wound and its scent, bitter and metallic compared to the sweet smells of sugar and spice that permeated the bakery, hit her like a sledgehammer, snapping her out of her trance.

"Hocus-pocus," she incanted, fiercely, and in a lightning-fast catena flung her sword to the floor, hauled Enriquez out of reach of Emmo, and punched the witch between the eyes, dropping her like a stone.

"What's going on?" Enriquez and Whatnot, instantly liberated from their funk when Emmo hit the floor, asked in unison. Seeing Emmo lying there, together they added. "How did she get there?"

"Fetch a length of rope. Bind the witch," Marquaisa instructed, rather than answered them. "Ankles, wrists, arms, legs, everything. Stick something in her mouth to stop her from talking and blindfold her so she cannot make eye contact with us. Quickly, we must finish before she wakes."

The witch's three ex-stooges worked fast. For the finishing touch, Marquaisa sat on her back and covered her eyes with a thick blindfold. No sooner was it secured than Emmo began to stir. In waking, she recognized her predicament and fought her restraints, but they held and she gave up, her chest heaving from her struggles.

Before she recovered her breath fully, Marquaisa dragged her onto her knees. Puffing deeply through her gag she twisted furiously against the ropes, so Marquaisa slapped her across the face, knocking her onto her side on the floor. She then grabbed the witch's coat and propped her up again. Once more on her knees, Emmo's shoulders shook as she cackled, but she no longer wrestled with her bonds.

Marquaisa bent at the waist, and while conducting a close-up inspection of the witch's face spoke to her, "You are not the only one who can take pleasure in the pain of others. But know this, I will be made stronger by tormenting and killing you."

"Wait," Whatnot said. Standing behind Emmo, his hand on her shoulder, he repeated his request, "Wait. Please."

"What?" Marquaisa snapped at him. "What is it?"

"I . . . I . . ." Whatnot could not finish.

"Spit it out, man," Marquaisa hissed at him, and straightening up looked him in the eye. "No," she said. "No," she repeated. "You fool!" she concluded, loudly, shaking her head.

"I cannot help it. I—"

"Do not say it!" Marquaisa cut him off and started pacing back-and-forth in front of Emmo. After a few laps she stopped before the mage and cradling her own forehead between the thumb and forefinger of her left hand summarized, for Whatnot's benefit, her grasp of their dilemma, "This is folly. She is a witch who wants to expand her crime syndicate and operate it on a global scale. Yet, even though you know what she would do to you to get what she wants, you would have me spare her."

Whatnot nodded and Emmo giggled, while Enriquez looked back-and-forth, from Marquaisa to Whatnot, and tried to figure out what was going on.

"I grant you; she is beautiful, and it is criminal to deprive the world beauty," Marquaisa nodded, and licking her lips hungrily traced the tip of her fingernail in an unbroken line along the surface of Emmo's skin from behind her ear, into the hollow at the base of her throat and ending at the cleft between her breasts.

A rash of goosebumps chased the thread-like stroke and Emmo shivered as the tingling surged across her chest. Trapped between heated urges and cold dread, the witch's heart pattered and her breathing tightened and, knowing that the bindings that were coiled around her wrists and that hobbled her ankles were inescapable, the tender sheaths of her private parts started swelling. Half-groaning, half-growling into her gag, in time with the throbbing between her legs, she tensed and relaxed her hard muscles against the ropes, for a few beats, until her tormentor clamped an unforgiving hand around her neck, just below her jaw, and started to squeeze.

"Make no mistakes, there are risks that will go with letting her live," Marquiasa warned Whatnot and grinned at the sight of Emmo writhing for air, "And it will be up to you to make sure they do not come to fruition. Are you certain you are equal to the task?"

"Madame, I was a battlefield physician," Whatnot reminded Marquaisa, shifting his eyes from her to Emmo and back again as the witch's contortions began to weaken. "I was elbows-deep in the horrors of war. I have rid myself of the demons with which it infected me. I will help her heal."

Marquaisa let the doctor's pitch sink in.

"Very well," she consented, finally, and eased her grip on Emmo, reluctantly. "You will have what you want. But there are conditions. First, I will take from the witch that which she owes me for inflicting her sorcery upon me, and for his complicity in her schemes I will teach Plug the error of his ways. Second, after I am done with her, you must keep her restrained as she is now until her magic is no more, at which point your work will truly begin."

Emmo shook her head and tried to get away when she heard the terms, but froze when Marquaisa grabbed a fistful of her hair and gave her a brusk shake.

"How will I know when her magic is gone?" Whatnot asked.

"Being a doctor, you know well the smell of foul blood," Marquaisa answered. "Let a drop of hers from time-to-time. When it no longer stinks you can free her. She is powerful, so it could take days and if it takes too long she will die. You can, however, accelerate the process."

"Yes, of course, anything," Whatnot offered, his hands upturned. "What must I do?"

"Guess," Marquaisa said, her eyes moving between his groin and Emmo's.

"I could not," Whatnot protested when he deciphered her message. "I am a gentleman."

"You will be a dead man if you free her before she is clean," Marquaisa stated, flatly. "If it makes it easier for you, I will cut the ropes that bind her thighs together. That way you can make your entry—"

"Yes, thank you!" Whatnot interjected. "I am familiar with the modus operandi. As you have just pointed out, I am a doctor after all. Suffice it to say, I will abide by your conditions and do what I must to ensure her full recovery."

"Your sacrifice is noted," Marquaisa said wryly and stiffened her grip on the witch, who started thrashing when she decoded the meaning of the workaround that might save her life. "Very well, let us begin. You two, hold her shoulders. Hold her still and look away."

Marquaisa kneeled in front of Emmo, who was breathing rapidly, and used the hold she had on her hair to tilt her head back. Emmo's pulse jumped and she flexed her wrists in the ropes that held them firmly together against the small of her back. She took a sharp, breath when Marquaisa slipped her arm around her waist and pulled her tight to her strong body. Trembling, the witch moaned when Marquaisa first kissed then licked her neck below the corner of her jaw, then squealed when she felt spikey fangs pierce her skin and plunge into her swollen vessels.

Emmo pushed and pulled her hips, stomach, and breasts into and away from Marquaisa's and tried to wriggle out of her bonds. But Marquaisa held on to her and the ropes did not slacken. Unable to break free, she continued to struggle until her body shook, uncontrollably, then contracted in rattling convulsions—once, twice, and a third time—that rolled tides of pleasure from her groin, up her spine, and down her thighs. Her chest heaving, her voice rumbling softly, she rubbed herself into Marquaisa, who giggled and continued to drink as liquid warmth spread from the witch's loins.

Hungry for more, Marquaisa let go of Emmo's hair and slid her hands over the silk that was wrapped around her bottom, feeling with her fingers for her opening, but stopped when she felt the witch begin to wilt. Rather than continue to probe, she gently ran her hands up Emmo's sides and held her by the waist while she unlocked the hold she had on her neck. She then licked the wounds she'd made, and when they started to close released the witch.

"You now can look," she told the two men, on both of whose foreheads beads of perspiration had broken out.

As Marquaisa got up from her knees they buckled, but she caught herself and straightened her quaking legs. Finding it difficult to bring the shop and her thoughts into focus, she blathered instructions for the men over a thick, pasty tongue, *"Lay . . . ummm . . . lay huh dowd add leave huh be. Theee wid cum bagh ond huh ode."* Lay her down and leave her be. She will come back on her own.

After assisting Whatnot with Emmo, Enriquez approached Marquaisa, slowly, concern on his face and in his voice, "My lady, are you alright?"

"What?" she shied, startled by his question. His worry for her irritating, she recovered herself quickly, "Of course. *Maldita brujería."* Damned sorcery.

"Indeed," Enriquez agreed, then choosing his words carefully he noted, "My lady, I cannot overstate how you understated the difference between our palates."

"You peeked," she scolded him. "We can discuss that later. Right now, your three lieutenants approach. They contemplate mutiny. They claim you abandoned them on the beach. They will kill you for your betrayal. I can deal with them as I did Emmo if you wish. I suggest, however, you serve them *Mag-Pies* instead. Sweetness soothes the savage soul, or so I've been told."

CHAPTER 17

BAZAAR

APRIL 26TH

THE BAHAMAS

Odors Enriquez referred to as "fragrances" and which he named, collectively, *Eau de Gore,* were a point of contention in the sale of the galleon *Savannah*. Garza, a pirate captain who was without a ship and so was stranded at Nassau, argued they made the ship feel cursed, and given as much Enriquez should lower his price. Enriquez insisted they gave *Savannah* an air of menace that could not be created artificially and that would definitely raise the intimidation scores of Garza and his crew, thus giving them an instant advantage over their adversaries.

Before their negotiations turned deadly, the two sides agreed their positions cancelled each other out. Enriquez got his price, which was below what Garza would have paid if he'd opted for a build-to-suit solution, and which was paid in full in gold. To assuage potential hard feelings Enriquez also threw in the uniforms his crew stripped from the bodies Marquaisa left on *Savannah*, bloodstains and all.

"The clothes were a nice touch," Marquaisa said to herself as she sat cross-legged in her dark hold onboard *Rajani* and thought back on the events at Nassau. "Perhaps the captain has some business acumen after all."

She considered the possibility for a moment, then rejected it, "More likely he added the gear to make sure Garza was distracted from blowing *Rajani* out of the water before she left port."

Whether through enterprising flare or survivalist instincts the end result was that Enriquez enriched himself and his crew and *Rajani* escaped Nassau unscathed. Shot of the semi-civilized port, they eased their way through the islands of the Bahamas and kept a lookout for Spanish treasure ships heading north on the first leg of their journey home, along the east coast of Florida. Convoys of ships, though temptingly laden with bounty, they declined to challenge. Rather, they lay in wait for the galleon that lagged behind the fleet to which it belonged and stopped to weigh anchor, with one or two of its packmates, also to lay in wait.

Prowling the ocean wore on Enriquez's crewmen, whose abilities to stay sharp while scanning empty expanses for long periods of time were tested seemingly unendingly. Seasoned though they were, their nerves were stretched to their limits by the need to see their prey before it saw them. On edge and spoiling for action, they were soothed from time to time by the soft notes Suchika coaxed from her sarod. Marquaisa, too, found comfort in the music. Alone, in the pitch darkness of her cabin, it was to her a rising and falling wave on which she could float into deep sleep.

Flipped open when *Rajani* rolled with an untimely wave that was out of rhythm with the swells, an open port invited sunlight into the gun deck and through the cracks in the hatch that barred entry into Marquaisa's blacked out cabin. In the depths of her slumber the pale, diffuse light turned opaque red as it seeped through her eyelids. Uninvited, the velvet glow filtered into the darkest recesses of her psyche and pulled within range of her mind's eye visions of a life lived not in the shadows, but under the sun.

Summer sunlight, a column of which shone on her bare skin, filled the bedchamber she shared with Augustus Caesar. At the foot of their bed he was strapping on his armor, quietly but hurriedly. He was, yet again, affecting the air of the busy yet considerate man who was late for work but who, though he was in a hurry, wished to not wake his partner. In actuality it was a day of liberty for him, which should have lifted his spirits and lightened his mood. However, the stiffness in his movements and the veins standing out at the corners of his forehead said otherwise.

"Don't worry," Augustina comforted him, "You will be fine. We will have many children."

"You assume I am the one with the problem," he snapped without looking her way. "Well, if it is my problem, Tina, then why is it I am as hard as a rock with every woman, including those tartified slave girls, but you? Even though, in all my thirty-eight years, I have never wanted anyone more than I want you. Yet, when I am with you I am as limp as a wet boot lace."

"I know and I apologize," Tina placated him. "I will talk to Char today to see if there is something more I can do to please you."

"You need not. I have spoken with Char already. We know what must be done," he told her, an unusual blend of resignation and antici-pation in his tone. "Go now and meet her at the market. She will take you to the place where you will be cured."

"Yes, my love," the emperor's chosen deferred to him, her eyes downcast as he stomped from the room.

As the echoes of his footfalls faded Tina bounced out of bed, happy to know she would be seeing Char. Spying the short toga Char liked, draped over the back of a chair, she grabbed it and slipped into it, making sure the cleavage and tush she revealed made it clear how she wished to spend their afternoon together. She then tousled her blond ringlets, feeling them cascade, cool and silky, down her back. Next came the strappy sandals Char bought for her, and with a few gold coins stuffed in the tiny satchel tied to the rope belt that loosely circled her waist she was out the door and on the road.

Skirling music piped from wooden wind instruments and the voices of a hundred hucksters flogging their wares and haggling with customers quickly grew louder as she half-walked, half-jogged the three blocks worth of narrow crowded streets that distanced Augusta

Emerita's bazaar from Caesar's villa. First to come into view as she approached the market was the forest of colorful awnings, each of which looked unique and all of which performed the same functions: provide shelter for the vendors and make it simple for marketgoers to find what they needed. Next, she saw Char standing at a row of stalls with her back turned to an old woman who was selling handwoven baskets.

Char was dressed, if anything, more revealingly than Tina, leaving little to the imagination, her auburn hair and clear skin shining in the sun. When Char saw her coming she smiled and waved and when they reached one another they hugged warmly.

Blunt as always, Char arched an eyebrow at Tina, "So, Caesar still is having trouble erecting his triumph. I keep telling him it's the wine he drinks before he sees you. But he thinks you're the problem."

"He told me you can cure me," Tina took Char's hand in her two and kissed it.

"Of course I can and it will be good not only for him, but also for us," Char promised and, keeping hold of Tina's hand, led her into the market, "Now, come with me."

Char wove through the crammed marketplace, squeezing between shifting bodies and slipping into and out of tight spaces. The deeper they pushed into the crowd, the harder it became for Tina to recognize where they were, compared to where they had come from. But Char neither slowed down, nor hesitated to shoulder people out of her way while ignoring their objections. Then, without warning she stopped in front of a tavern and gazed at the arcane engravings etched vertically into its worn wooden doors.

"We are here," she told Tina as she poured over the message inscribed on the door.

"Okay, great, let's get this done," Tina replied, and without hesitation started for the entrance.

"Wait," Char said, and holding Tina by the shoulders turned her until they faced one another. Her voice hushed, she then asked, "Do you love me?"

"Of course. With all my heart," Tina replied, quietly, thinking it odd that she had to say as much.

"As I do you. Know that will never change," Char vowed then, dodging eye contact with Tina, guided her toward the tavern door, which opened when she waved her hand at it, "After you."

Char stood in the doorway and let Tina walk into the bar alone. From her vantage, Char saw a three patrons off to one side, their hair close-cropped and their olive skin dark as tanned leather, pull clubs free from the hooks on their belts as Tina sifted through the crowded room. She saw another one, drunk and drooling, stare at Tina as she worked her way deeper into the crowd.

Suddenly, weaving and wobbling, the drunk stood up and pointed at Tina and slurred, "That's her! She's been plundering my clan for years. Now she's brought Rome's wrath down on us with her stupid rebellion. Kill her!"

Tina looked from side-to-side trying to find the person at whom the man was levelling his accusations. Instead, she saw some dark-skinned, short-haired, military-looking types heading her way with what looked like thick wooden dowels in their hands. Stuck as she was between tables, chairs, and drunkards they seized her easily, then picked her up and slammed her, face down, on top of the bar, pinning her in place.

"This is a mistake!" she cried, trying to make herself heard amid the uproar.

When the first blow landed pain exploded across her ribs. She thrashed and screamed for Char. But no aid was offered. Only more battering, until a nasal voice filled the bar from its open entrance.

"Thank you! Thank you! My fine centurions. That will be quite enough. She is quite incapacitated. However, I do require she be at least semi-conscious for this, the final stage of her Romanization. Everyone else, out!"

The muggers laughed and called back, "Hail Caesar!"

"You are too kind," Augustus thanked his soldiers and looked down his nose at the boozers filing out the door. "As for you, Char, you have served me well. So, here it is. The so-called 'Celestial Dagger' you wanted so badly. So much so you betrayed your lover to get your hands on it."

He flipped the sheathed blade to Char. The witch snatched it out of the air, drew the blade, and licked it. Satisfied with its flavor she ran the knife back into its scabbard and tucked it under her belt.

"Now, get out, witch," Caesar spat at her. "I want never to see you again. If I do you will regret it, for it will be the death of you."

Char bowed and turned her back on Tina. As the witch walked away the centurions pinning Tina to the bar released her and started toward the door to escort the witch. A step behind her comrades, one of the centurions grabbed a handful of Tina's hair, roughly cranked her head to one side, and whispered in her ear, "Hear this. I am Akuia. I command you to shed the veil cast over you by the witch, Char. Rise, Kayza of the Lugones!"

Shaken by the demand, Kayza sucked in a deep breath. The sudden, sharp intake shot a bolt of pain across her bruised ribs and she moaned.

"Save some of that for the ecstasy you are about to experience, Tina, my love," Augustus crowed as he swaggered toward the bar, "My hope was you would taste it via conventional coupling. But, you being so inadequate, I decided to take Char's advice and take you the way I do the women to whom I referred as I was getting dressed a short while ago. Namely, by using you as I would any other slave."

When he reached the bar he hauled her to its end, where she jack-knifed at the waist. Her feet on the floor, the smell of old wine wafting off the bar into her nose, she winced when Augustus's open hand smacked against her bare tush.

"Beautiful," he rasped while massaging her cheeks with one hand and loosening his woolen breeches with the other. "If you give me an heir from the blessing I am about to bestow upon you, then you will compound your good fortune. You will forever be Augustina, Empress of Rome!"

He thrust himself into her. Over excited, he entered her back door, missing her front passage completely. Surprised and fully wakened by his choice of ingress, Kayza grunted and pushed herself against him, drawing him deeper. When he was all the way home she arched her back until she was standing, clasped her hands behind his back pinning his arms to his sides, and pulled when he pushed.

"Truly, this is the essence of Romanization," she sighed, working her hips and pelvis, "Thuggery followed by buggery."

"Shit!" Augustus yelped.

"That will be difficult for me, *my lord*, given the fix we are in," she replied, holding him tight.

"Kayza! How? Release me at once!"

"I think not. I'm quite enjoying this," Kayza refused his order. "Although, you seem to be shrinking from the challenge."

"I'll call my guards," Augustus threatened, while he squirmed in her clutches. "They'll cut you down."

"Go ahead," the warrior invited him. "I'll use you as a strike dummy. Then I'll kill them, and you, and your precious empire will wilt like you've just done."

"What do you want?" the emperor changed his tone, from bullying to haggling, and stopped fidgeting.

"I would like to say, 'Finish what you started a moment ago,' but that is now clearly out of the question," she released him, spun to face him, and looked him up and down. Unimpressed, she laid out her terms, "Instead you will give me your finest horse; the gray stallion you parade around on will do. You also will grant me safe passage as 'Empress of Rome' on said stallion until I am out of your reach. Lastly, you will tell me where I can find Char. She and I have much to discuss."

"The first two are simple enough," Augustus acquiesced, grinding his teeth. He then looked Kayza in the eye and added a proviso, "But, fair warning, for as long as I live you never will be beyond my reach." The important business settled he shrugged, dismissively, and waved a off Kayza's third condition, "Regrettably, as much as I would love to facilitate, as well as be a fly on the wall for your discussion with Char, I haven't the foggiest idea where you might find her. No doubt you overheard me exile and threaten her. So, my guess is you will have to wait for her to seek you out to conclude your business."

"Fine," Kayza agreed and straightened her toga. "There is one more thing."

"Why do I doubt that's the case?"

"What of the knife the witch was so keen on obtaining?" Kayza asked.

"I don't know. She said something about it falling from the stars, and if she used the right words, then she could do things with it."

"Besides kill people?" Kayza probed.

"I don't know. I wasn't listening. She lost me at 'fell from the stars,'" Caesar floundered. "She also went on about how some obscure Egyptian pharaoh once owned it. But, as you are now painfully aware, she is a walking aqueduct of lies that never runs dry. So, as far as I know, it was just another dagger."

"We shall see," Kayza predicted, shaking out her hair and sizing him up. "Sorcery? Really? You are more pathetic than I imagined."

"Hey, a man's gotta do," Caesar shrugged.

"No matter the consequences?" Kayza dug deeper.

"What 'consequences' can ever touch me," Caesar spouted, imperiously.

"You are such an asshole," Kayza declared, turning her back on him to walk out the door. "My safe passage starts now. I'm going back to your stupid villa to grab a few things, then I'll be on my way. So, call off your dogs and keep your distance."

"Whatever," Augustus mumbled, following her to the doorway.

"By the way," Kayza stopped at the door and added, "The witch played you."

"Nonsense," Augustus sneered.

"Think you so?" Kayza questioned him, looking back at him over her shoulder, a knowing twinkle in her eye. "You can count on the fact that she spiked your wine to, shall we say, take the *bang* out of your ballista."

"What?" he replied, knitting his brow.

"You'll figure it out," she teased him and pushed open the door. "In the meantime, you might want to rethink the whole, 'I think I'll use magic to get what I want,' thing."

"If you'd been paying attention, then you'd know I don't drink wine. What's more, the magic that was in play clearly worked in the witch's favor, not mine," he countered. "So, if anyone was tricked it was you. Given time I'm sure you'll figure it out."

'I'm sure I don't know what you're talking about," Kayza shot back while walking out of the tavern. *"Vale, Octavian."* Farewell, Octavian.

"My point, exactly," he came back. *"Donec iterum conveniant, Kayza of the Lugones."* Until we meet again, Kayza of the Lugones.

The trio of guards who assaulted her were waiting in the crowd outside the door. When she appeared and Caesar did not they readied themselves to dish out another beating. But when he appeared in the doorway and to their surprise shook his head at them, they had to allow the 'empress' to walk straight through their mini phalanx.

Plebeians milling about under the frenzied canopy of awnings in the market also made way for Kayza when they saw her coming. All, that is, except one. Stiff from sitting too long in her stall and distracted by the din of barking voices and whistling music, the old woman who had been selling handwoven baskets at the entrance to the market moved too slowly to avoid blocking Kayza's path. Tears in her eyes, the old dear begged forgiveness and tried to shuffle out of the way.

"Let me help you, mother," Kayza insisted and extended her hand.

"I am not your mother, pretty thing," the elder croaked, "Even so, you make it is easy to love you as if I were."

"Thank you," Kayza replied, blushing, and balanced the old woman while she walked. "Maybe you can help me too."

"If I can," the basket weaver pledged.

"A tall fair-skinned woman with ginger hair came this way a little while ago. Did you see her?" Kayza asked, looking for hints of recollection in her face.

"I did. She ran into the sun. That way," the venerable one said, raising her hand and pointing west.

When she lifted her arm her shawl shifted. Through its fringes Kayza saw the polished nub of a dagger's hilt and she nodded appreciatively at the sight of the weapon. Then, the clamor of voices and music dwindling, the old woman's hand, withered and claw-like, came into focus. As the image became clearer in Kayza's mind the soft notes of a sarod drifted into her ears and her eyes opened.

Something had changed. Not her cabin and not the ship. *She* had changed.

She stood and flexed her arms and legs. They were strong. She combed her fingers through her hair and it was as long and thick as ever. She touched the skin on her face. It still was smooth, but one of the hands rubbing it was not. Her right hand was dry and rough. So, she opened her door a crack and slipped her hand slowly into the dim light that snuck in through the breach. It was identical, in every detail, to the claw-like hand that belonged to the old woman in August Emerita's bazaar.

"Isn't that just the best?" Emmo's voice, soft and low-pitched, tickled Marquaisa's ears, and trailing a stream of weightless giggles, skipped across the back of her mind then vanished down her spine.

CHAPTER 18

KICKOFF

MAY 10TH

HALIFAX, ACADIAN PENINSULA

Treaties promote peace and prosperity and require of participating parties they swear off greed and the atrocities it spawns. In the time-honored tradition of strategic disingenuity, however, it is understood that promises, when they no longer are convenient, will be broken. Greed will reign and brutishness will be the modus employed in the futile attempt to sate it.

In keeping with the custom of going back on your word, in 1749 the British established the fortified town of Halifax, on the Acadian Peninsula. It was more important to them to establish a base from which to threaten French shipping in the region, in the same way the French at Louisbourg bullied British ships, than to honor a treaty signed with the Mi'kmaq, the indigenous people of Acadia, a half century earlier. Their contravention sparked yet another in a string of wars with the French and their allies, the Mi'kmaq and the Acadians—French settlers who had done their best to not take sides in the conflicts —that dated back over one hundred fifty years.

Brigadier General James Peter Wolfe intended to end the drawn-out conflict within one hundred fifty days. His countdown began on the 9th of May 1758, when he cruised into Halifax harbor aboard *HMS Princess Amelia*. The kickoff of the mission was not, however, accompanied by pomp and circumstance. Rather, he touched down on shore to the voice of Agsun Swift singing, from *Amelia's* poop deck, the most current rendition of his song about sailing over the bounding mane.

Wolfe stood at attention and held a formal salute for the entire performance. When it ended he signed at Aggie rudely, to the helmsman's delight, before taking his leave of the ship once and for all. Their sea chests to follow, he and Brock then hoofed it to Hollis Street, and escorted by a flock of sea gulls found their lodgings.

Built of random rubblestone, their maisonette approximated the Georgian style of architecture and was identical to its neighbors. Its sole distinguishing feature was the number one splashed on its front door in white paint, marking it as the residence of the highest-ranking officer on the base. Its interior was utilitarian, its décor and furnishings Neo-Spartan, its ambiance cold and unrelentingly pitiless. It suited Wolfe to a tee and straight away he decided he would cram its every corner with clutter that both suited and clashed with the billet's mood.

Among the items he decided belonged in the suitable category was a wall hanging he found in the study, on which the current layout of Halifax was portrayed, to scale, from a bird's eye view. Wolfe shrugged out of his great coat, let it fall in a heap on the floor, and leaving Brock in his wake strolled across the south facing room to where the pen and ink portrait hung. Upon reaching the map he folded his arms over his chest and began absorbing its details. As he studied it he mumbled to himself, "Where to begin?"

He began by introducing himself to the officers and men under his command, later that evening, by setting fire to the ordinance store, which he emptied earlier in the day and which was situated due east of his residence on Hollis street. The fire and smoke, combined with the clanging of alarms bells and the popping of gunpowder, roused his troops from their beds and brought them running, in varying states of disarray, to the northeast corner of the base near the Landing Point. When they reached it they found Wolfe standing on a pedestal in dress uniform, flames casting him in silhouette, ready to deliver his opening address.

"I am Brigadier General James Peter Wolfe," he announced. "You are mine to do with as I see fit. I will begin by bringing all of you back to life, your chaotic response to this emergency having resulted in a fire that killed all of you and reduced the town of Halifax to a heap of ashes. I then will make you ready for war, that which we will bring to our enemies and that which they will bring to us. The former will begin tomorrow morning at seven of the clock, sharp, when you will present yourselves, looking smart and in full uniform, in formation on the parade ground where your officers will put you through your paces. The latter begins now."

Officers and men looked at him and one another with blank faces.

"Your munitions depot has been violated and set ablaze by your enemies, gentlemen," he reminded them. "Demonstrate for me how you will save it, yourselves, and the town you are sworn to defend."

Wolfe watched his officers organize their units and put them to work, some shouting orders at the top of their lungs, others quietly locating their men and using them to collect their comrades and coordinate their efforts. He also kept an eye on the rank and file, observing how they responded to their leaders. He dictated his observations to Brock, who in addition to scribbling notes tracked the time it took to extinguish the fire. When the blaze was doused and all that remained of the storehouse was charred wood, smoke, and cinders, Wolfe waited while his men, soot-stained and sweating, dragged themselves into ragtag formations and slouched before him.

"You have ten seconds to tighten your lines and stand at attention," he informed them. Five seconds later he continued, "The good news is, because of your efforts, twenty-five percent of you survived the enemy attack on the ordinance store. The bad news for the survivors is they will spend the next week burying their comrades. That is, if they live that long, munitions being in short supply and the enemy being relentless in their offensive."

Within the ranks some men tensed up, while others' mouths fell open.

"In other words, gentlemen, you are dead," he told them without flinching. "But, , this should come as no surprise to you. After all, you died the instant you enlisted in his majesty's army. As of that moment, your lives were measured in the time it takes you to draw your next breath. That is the reality all of us in the service of his majesty share. We cannot escape it and it is useless to fight it, for it is a losing battle. We must, therefore, accept it, keep breathing, and take our fight to our enemies. Speaking of which, I believe we have a fixture in our diaries for tomorrow morning. I am looking forward to fulfilling it. You may consider yourselves dismissed."

Wolfe saluted his men and held it until the last of them shuffled out of his sight. When at last he and Brock were alone he tapped his aide on his shoulder and together they jogged further east, away from the smoldering depot. At the log palisade that surrounded the camp they felt their way along the timbers, searching for the opening Wolfe found marked on the map hanging in his study. Wolfe came across the gap when his hand hit air rather than wood and he pitched headfirst through the wall onto the expanse of dirt that separated the base from the town proper.

Dark as the night was, when he got to his feet Wolfe could see Brock was about to break into one of his fits of laughter. To stifle it, he grabbed his aide by the scruff of the neck and hustled him into a sprint. In seconds they escaped the field of view available to the guards manning the nearest of the picquet forts that were built into the palisade, and disappeared into the farmland on the outskirts of town.

They reappeared the following morning on the parade ground in the middle of their base. Brock arrived early, in time to see Wolfe's officers marshal their men and get them marching through their drills precisely at the appointed hour. No sooner had they started than Wolfe made his entrance, armed with his wooden walking stick and bringing up the rear of a troop of assorted farm animals including chickens, ducks, goats, geese, and pigs, as well as their young. Without hesitation they clucked, quacked, bayed, honked, and oinked their way into the vanguard of uniformed soldiers, shattering their formations, then plowed deeper into the ranks spreading mayhem as they went. In moments, the army's discipline was in tatters and pockets of its men were being rounded up by pitchfork, broom, and shovel wielding farm families that materialized from hideouts located strategically around the parade ground.

As the rout unfolded, Wolfe toured the parade ground calming outraged officers and soldiers and thanking farmers, while bidding them to retrieve their animals and return to their farmsteads. He ended his tour at the center of the parade ground and, while the farmers went about their business, gathered his army about him.

"I am happy to report to you that I have just been admitted into the Club of Military Immortals," he reported. "Justifiably so as, armed with only this cane and supported by a squadron of barnyard critters and detachments of agricultural workers, I defeated the British Expeditionary Force sent to conquer New France. Huzzah."

His cheer was greeted with incomprehensible grumbling from among the ranks of his soldiers and the scuffing of many pairs of boots.

"If I was able to do this," he pressed on. "How will you fare against angry Mi'kmaq whom you have displaced from their ancestral homes, and Acadians, the hellcats you expelled from lands they have worked for generations, *not to mention* well-trained French troops?" he paused for a breath, then continued. "Allow me, if you will, to answer for you. You will fight them bravely like the bulldogs you are, you will lose, and in the end die shameful deaths. Not because they are your superiors, but because they know how to fight in this theater of war, whilst you do not. That must change. You must change. You will not like it. But it will make you better and you will win. This I promise you."

He allowed time for his words to sink in and for some of the fire to return to his men's eyes.

"In the meantime," he said after a moment. "As you were. Show me you can recover your wits and your discipline quickly after a surprise incursion by hostiles. Speaking of which, Thomas! I say, Farmer Thomas! That is no way to shepherd your ducks. See how the ducklings are straying? Here, let me show you."

Wolfe spent the better part of the next hour dividing his attention between critiquing the performance of his troops and reuniting chicks, ducklings, kids, goslings, and piglets with their parents. When he was satisfied training was complete and the animals and their caretakers were safely packed-off home, he summoned his officers.

"I was struck by something odd," he told them.

"*Mair (more)* so than the face that looks back at *ye (you)* from *yer (your) mirrorrr?*" one of them cut in, to the amusement of his fellows.

"*Drôle (amusing),*" Wolfe drawled, "You have me at a loss, sir."

"Lieutenant-Colonel Andrew Rollo, *surrr,*" the officer introduced himself, bowing at the waist.

"Ah, yes, late of the borough of Duncrub, if I'm not mistaken, in the great nation of Scotland. I should have known it was you from your dry wit and the wild echoes in your accent. Very well, *Rrrollie,* thank you," Wolfe threw the man a ragged salute and allowed his colleagues to tease Rollo over his new nickname, then picked up where he left off. "As I was about to say, we made a secret neither of our plan to sail for the New World, nor our purpose for doing so. Yet, oddly, we met not one challenge during our voyage. This begs the question, 'Where is the French navy?'"

"Turned tail is my guess," an officer suggested, "Soon as they saw the size of our fleet."

"Perhaps," Wolfe replied, "Then again, perhaps not. Either way, even if the French fleet fails to put in an appearance, Louisbourg will be a tough nut to crack. It is massive and lethal and the French who *are* stationed there will use every available resource to defend it. Their objective must be to hold us off until winter, on the assumption the cold will force our withdrawal. Our task is to defeat that objective. To do so we must be at our best. Which brings me to my evaluation of your performance in the drills conducted since my arrival. At worst it was abysmal, at best it was uninspired, which leaves significant room for improvement, which I expect to see in the coming days and weeks. Now it's your turn. What do you think of me?"

"You are completely insane," Rollie jumped in first.

"Crackers," one of his colleagues agreed, nodding enthusiastically.

"I would add, demented," a third threw in.

"Yes, without a doubt, totally bonkers," another piled on.

Similar descriptors were applied to his character by the rest of his officers, until all of them had their say, at which point Wolfe thanked them, "Very well, gentlemen, I appreciate your candor. You can expect we will carry this dialogue forward into our working relationship and we will see if, and to what degree, our opinions of each other evolve. For now, you may consider yourselves dismissed. If you need me at some point during the day, then you will find me out-and-about, reconnoitering our surroundings."

He returned to the base after lights out with a team of swabbies from *Princess Amelia*, volunteered by Agnus Swift, and had them raid his officers' barracks. They fired blank rounds from their pistols into the air, brandished roughhewn wooden swords, swung burning lanterns, yelled, pushed, and shoved, and goaded his executive staff into a fight. Happy to oblige, the soldiers fought back and the brawling escalated quickly, spilling into the yard outside the barracks where scores of squaddies were waiting to egg on the combatants. Wolfe stood in the open doorway of the barracks content to spectate until Rollie, who was holding his own against two sailors, was outnumbered by a third. The action prompted Wolfe to set down his cane and pounce on the swabbie who tipped the balance, to roars of approval from the audience. Giving as good as he got, the general battled beside his officers until they and the men from *Amelia* were punched out. Teetering on their feet, or flat on their backs, applause and cheers rained down on the pugilists from the crowd, some of whose members carried the fighters to the mess hall. There, Wolfe sipped tea and slapped backs before returning to Hollis Street. Well into the night, the rest dulled their aches and pains with a locally brewed, frothy brown ale they called *Sludge*, so named for the quagmire of melted snow and raw mud that filled streets, weighed down boots, and froze toes in springtime.

Up on the drumlin below which the town of Halifax was growing, hidden by brush, two men lowered their spyglasses. Fatigue wearing them thin after two days and a night spent observing the British, they rubbed their eyes. Sounds of revelry rose to them from the encampment and they exchanged looks that were at once uncertain and undoubting.

"Erieux," one of them tried to grin and, his French slanted by his Acadian upbringing, whispered to the other, *"Le nouveau général. Il est fou, non?" The new general. He's crazy, right?*

"Oui" (Yes), Erieux replied, his accent identical, anger overtaking the expression on his face, *"Et c'est très mauvais pour nous. Nous devons le render mort." And that is very bad for us. We need to make him dead.*

CHAPTER 19

SWAG

MAY 13TH

CAYO VIZCAÍNO, LA FLORIDA

G iven it was so close to the Earth's equator the hundreds of islets, islands, and cays known collectively as The Bahamas were hot. Given it was legally dead, Marquaisa's body was cold. While they were unsure of her body's legal status, *Rajani's* crew were quick to take advantage of its frigid disposition. On nights when she walked their ship's main deck they sought relief from the heat by following her and fanning themselves with the chilled air she left in her wake. When she tired of their hijinks she scattered them using her newfound shapeshifting mojo to make a terrifying change into the old woman from Augusta Emerita's market.

Suchika was spooked neither by Lady Marquaisa, nor her transformations. Her round brown eyes alight with curiosity, she carefully observed Marquaisa's changes from beginning to end. Eager, also, to learn how cold affected people, Suchika had Marquaisa apply her icy touch to her various body parts, searching for the line of demarcation between pleasure and pain. For services rendered Marquaisa was relieved of her boredom and accorded the amusement to be found in watching Suchika navigate the extremes of agony and ecstasy.

During one of their sessions, in which Marquaisa was probing Suchika's pudenda, a soft knock sounded on the door of her quarters. It was followed by Ganesh speaking quietly in the Hindi dialect Marquaisa best understood, *"Meree hamadam."* My lady.

Gently withdrawing her fingers, Marquaisa kept stroking Suchika's loins and answered, *"Pravesh karana."* Enter.

Ganesh pushed open the door, and backlit by flickering torchlight took a step into the darkened room and reported, *"Hamaare paas ek sthitihai."* We have a situation.

"Aakhirakaar" (Finally), Marquaisa welcomed the report. She retrieved Suchika's clothes and, while the girl dressed, covered her own skin with her hooded cloak. When Suchika was fully clothed, Marquaisa led the two sailors from the cabin, *"Chalo chalate hain."* Let's go.

At the hatch that opened onto the main deck she paused to make sure the sun was below the horizon before stepping into the open air. From the gun deck to the ship's castle the crew were at battle stations, while Enriquez, Vishnu, and Yuval, stood at the starboard rail of the castle, their spyglasses trained on distant targets. Marquaisa was certain she knew what they were tracking, but when she, Suchika, and Ganesh joined them at the rail she found she was only partly right.

To her west a Spanish treasure ship lay at anchor near the barrier island they called *Cayo Vizcaíno (Key Biscayne)* while two of her escorts from the fleet, one to the north and one to the south, watched over her. However, the presence of another galleon, east of the anchored vessel and directly north of *Rajani,* came as a surprise. *Savannah* was tracking steadily toward the treasure ship, her stern lantern blazing brightly, on a bearing to pluck Ferdinand's gold from under Enriquez's and Marquaisa's noses.

"Garza has changed her name," Enriquez informed Marquaisa, while keeping his eye on his plundering counterpart. "She no longer is *Savannah.* She is *Carnicera."* Butcher.

Garza, flying Spain's colors, his crew disguised in the uniforms gifted to them by Enriquez, had deceived the Spanish and outmaneu-vered Enriquez. Knowing as much, Garza kept his spyglass focused on

Rajani and signed obscenely at Enriquez with his free hand. To his irritation, Garza had to cut short his crude gesticulating when his lookout called his attention further to the north. Enriquez, and his lieutenants also heeded the call and found a French ship of the line heading, as was Garza, straight for the treasure ship.

"Here come the French," Enriquez told Marquaisa, pointing at the oncoming warship.

"Garza will attack the French to protect his claim to the treasure," she replied peeling off her cloak. "The Spanish escorts will join his attack, thinking he is one of theirs. Together they will destroy the French. Garza then will catch the Spanish off guard and turn his guns on them. With her escorts gone the treasure ship either will surrender, or it will be sunk. So, Garza must be dealt with *now* to secure our plan to make the treasure our own."

"My thoughts exact—"

Marquaisa was over the rail, in the air, and slicing through the water toward *Carnicera* before Enriquez could finish.

"—and she beat me to it," he connected his fragmented thoughts, then added, "I cannot wait to see what happens next."

A few long minutes later the pirate captain sighted Marquaisa crawling, spider-like, up *Carnicera's* port side. Next, he saw her tear open a gun port and clamber onto the gun deck, letting the port hatch slam shut behind her.

On *Carnicera's* gun deck, in response to the clatter, Garza's gunners griped about sailing on a cursed ship and argued with one another over who should check the station from whence all the noise was coming. The job fell to the man nearest the offending station who, though unhappy about being handed the short straw, completed close inspections of all the stations in his path. At one point in his tour he gasped and yelled, pretending to be shocked, and drew frightened shrieks from his mates. When he laughed at them, they first slung heated oaths at him, then laughed along with him as he picked up his inspection where he'd left off.

At the station that had caused the stir among the gun crew he checked the cannon, and finding its blocks and fuse intact moved down its length to its port. There being little light or space he moved in close to the hatch and ran his fingers around its frame, searching for its lock. When at last he found something cold and hard he pinched it with his fingers to make sure it was unbroken. When it pinched him back, then grabbed his wrist and pulled, then plunged fangs into his throat, he garbled in terror and banged his other hand and arm on the wall, and for a few short moments the rest of his body on everything within striking distance, then went still. Limp and lifeless he was lifted off the deck, and with his head battering open the hatch was shot out the gun port to slap into the surf.

Aboard *Rajani*, Enriquez and his lieutenants watched the sailor's body get chewed up in the churn. They then turned to one another and using different languages and expressions said, as one, through pitiless chuckles, "Poor Garza."

Meanwhile, onboard *Carnicera*, in good natured fashion the remaining gunners told 'short straw man' to stop messing about. With no reply forthcoming their humor turned sour and they demanded he tell them what was going on. In answer, a small flame was put to the point of a stick and was used to light the fuse of the cannon their mate was inspecting.

A single word was shouted, *"Fuego!"*

A split second later the cannon blew its payload through the hatch and it rocketed at the escort to the south. Not having been properly aimed, the round fell short. Still, the crew on the escort howled at *Carnicera*, first in surprise, then in fury. Their captain, keeping his composure, calmly issued a precautionary order to his gunners to target their sister ship, then gave her a long second look.

On *Carnicera*, Garza was in one breath screaming the order to cease fire, and in the next yelling at a pair of his men to get below and get his gunners under control. Quick to obey, they hustled for the steep staircase that led down to the gun deck. The man in the lead reached the bottom of the staircase in a hurry and was greeted by the sounds of swords ringing off one another, men crying out in pain, and the hiss of steel cutting through flesh, until all went silent.

The moment his partner joined him, shuffling footsteps started their way from the far end of the deck. In the poor light a creature with what appeared to be three heads scuffled toward them, then came to an abrupt halt at the halfway point of the deck. It was breathing heavily and chattering rhythmic prayers in multiple voices. Suddenly, between verses, it set fire to the hair of the severed head it held in one hand and dropped it on the floorboards. The fiery nut bounced on the deck and the flames leapt onto its skin. In the burst of light, the two men at the foot of the staircase recognized the dead head as belonging to one of their crewmates. They also saw two more of their mates, still living, with their heads locked in the arms of a pale-skinned, blood-spattered woman.

She was naked and muscular and the smile she flashed at them was inlaid with sharp fangs. Enraged by her taunting grin, the two men raised their swords and charged her, but she held her ground and bided her time until they came to within a few strides of where she stood. When they were within range, she snapped the spines of her captives and flung their corpses at their approaching shipmates, bowling them over. She quickly followed her shot and snatched the first of the downed men by the scruff of the neck with one hand, and his hair with her other hand. After making sure his partner had a clear view of what was happening, she tore into her victim's neck with her teeth and drank the blood that surged from his veins. As she fed, his horrified mate scrambled to escape, but without interrupting her meal she staked him to the deck by ramming a sword through his calf muscles and into the floorboards. His screams echoed around the gun deck, roared up onto the main deck, and sounded across the water to all five nearby ships.

Marquaisa first savored his pain and his fear, then drained him of his blood. Above her, on the main deck, sailors were shouting, running, and jumping overboard in panic, deserting the cursed ship. None dared descend to the gun deck, so she took her time and made sure to light the fuses of all the remaining cannons and opened fire on the Spanish escorts to the north and south. She then climbed up the staircase to the main deck, reaching the top step in time to see Garza shooting at his fleeing crewmen with his flintlock pistols.

His guns empty, when she came into view he discarded them and hurled his daggers at her. The one whose aim was true she let stab into her thigh. Then, while Garza watched, she smiled, jerked the blade free from her leg without batting an eye, and licked clean its ichor-smeared blade. Her challenge accepted, Garza drew his sword and jumped from the castle down to the main deck, bent on cutting her to ribbons.

He lunged at her but disappeared in a hail of shredded wood when the first of the rounds fired by the Spanish escorts slammed into both sides of *Carnicera's* hull. Peppered with splinters, Marquaisa kicked her way through the debris and burrowed into the pile she found at the spot where the pirate captain last stood. At the bottom of the pile she found him, still breathing and clutching his sword, and dragged him free.

With a quick twist she snapped the bones in his wrist and, screeching, he dropped his weapon. As it clattered on the deck, loud reports barked from the north and the south and a second round of shot was sent on its way to *Carnicera* by the Spanish escorts. Timing its arrival, Marquaisa lifted Garza overhead then tossed him into the path of a northbound cannonball. On impact with it the pirate burst into pieces, and while his parts splashed into the ocean the other rounds punched holes in *Carnicera's* hull and collapsed her masts.

One of the hot cannonballs ignited the ship's magazine and it exploded, breaking her in two and belching sparks, flames, ammunition, and smoke high into the sky. Stunned by the blast, Marquaisa rose into the air on its wave, then fell into the water amid the wreckage it left behind. On impact with the cold water her mind cleared enough that she knew she was sinking, along with *Carnicera's* remains. So, mustering what strength she could, she wove through the detritus that was swirling around her on its way to the ocean floor and fought her way back to the surface. Once her head was no longer submerged she spit out brackish water and, her surroundings dropping in and out of focus, searched for something that was floating that would take her weight.

Some yards away a jagged object bobbed in the soupy mix of saltwater, wood, canvas, and rope. Her limbs leaden, she pushed through the water in its direction, struggling to catch it before the current carried it out of her reach. She could see it was a section of the stair-case that once linked *Carnicera's* main deck to its castle and all she had to do was attached herself to it using her fingernails and she would no longer be in danger of sinking and being lost. But her arms and legs were no longer moving and she wanted to sleep more so than she wanted to float, so she closed her eyes and slowly slipped underwater.

She embraced the peace she found under the waves and would have been content to stay there had something warm not wrapped itself around her waist and started towing her up from the depths. Slight as she was, Suchika was a powerful swimmer and with a few kicks had Marquaisa back above water. Then, clenching her with one arm she started swimming back to *Rajani*, who Enriquez was keeping out of range of the Spanish and the French. As she swam Suchika spoke to Marquaisa and jabbed at trigger points in her neck, shoulders, and chest, trying to wake her. When she felt Marquaisa shudder she hit her again, but harder, and jolted her fully awake.

Conscious but uncomprehending, Marquaisa wrenched herself free from the grasp of her captor, then attacked it. Sensing its shock and seeing it freeze in fear she coiled an arm around it, pinning its arms to its sides, and caught its legs with hers to keep it from escaping. They sunk together and Marquaisa took a fistful of its hair in her free hand to stop its squirming, found the veins pulsing in its neck, lengthened her fangs to bite into them . . . and stopped. Her mind cleared by her rage, she recognized the light in her captive's eyes. Still burning with blood-lust, she managed to kiss Suchika, rather than kill her, then swam for the surface.

The moment they broke the waterline Suchika gulped down fresh air, then kissed her back, *"Dhanyavaad!" Thank you!*

"Sharaaratee ladakee" (Naughty girl), Marquaisa teased Suchika, then turned her back into her, and placed the girl's hands on her shoul-ders. She found *Rajani* by following the flight of the cannonballs that were falling short of her and started in her direction, but not before warning Suchika, *"Kasakar pakaden." Hold on tight.*

CHAPTER 20

PHOQ

JUNE 2ND

GABARUS BAY, ÎLE ROYALE

I n Wolfe's books all coastlines were dodgy. The rocky ones dashed
ships and landing craft to bits and the sandy ones were quagmires
that turned troops into sitting ducks. Add manmade defenses to
the mix and planning an amphibious invasion was less like courting
disaster than it was like plotting mass murder. The key to avoiding
utter catastrophe lay in finding a spot on the coast where natural
barriers weren't too bothersome and the costs to the enemy for
defending it outweighed the benefits they gained by holding it.

Wolfe, with Brock's aid, found the ideal spot at which to land the
British expeditionary force east of Lighthouse Point which, itself, overlooked the town and fortress at Louisbourg from the eastern edge of
their harbor. The location would serve as the staging area for the
army's strike against the fortifications at Lighthouse Point, as well as
the platform from which to launch the march around the harbor that
would end with the army hitting the fortress at its weakest point. In
concert, after dropping off the army, the navy would bombard Lighthouse Point, as well as the fortress, so that their French defenders

would be more concerned with finding cover and saving their skins than they were with manning their guns and fighting the British. Wolfe reckoned if his nibs, the conspicuously late to the party Commander-in-Chief Jeffrey Amherst, agreed to go ahead with his and Brock's plan, then Louisbourg would once again be in British hands inside of a week.

For his part, Amherst refused to hear any battle plans before reconnoitering the field for himself. To do so required a ship and crew, and *Amelia* having been put at his disposal he spent the day cruising from Gabarus Bay eastward, beyond Lighthouse, then back again while concocting his own plans and forcing his War Council to duck small arms fire from French infantry hunkered down behind coastal earthworks. When he was satisfied with his observations, as well as the greenish, seasickness-induced hue of Wolfe's complexion, he had *Amelia* drop her anchor in Gabarus Bay with the rest of the British fleet and retired to his quarters to complete his deliberations in seclusion.

In the warmth of his cabin, Amherst weighed his options at length. Outside on deck the War Council shivered as the raw air ignored their layers of clothes and leached through their skin to chill their bones. His quaking relieving him of his seasickness, Wolfe pulled out his pocket watch to check the time of day. As he followed the ticking of its second hand he recalled making a similar time check two weeks earlier.

For a full day he had led soldiers under his command on maneuvers in the forests that covered the drumlin that overlooked their camp and stretched beyond the northern limits of the town of Halifax. He was getting them ready for the rigors of the march on which he would lead them, from the staging point east of Lighthouse Point to the gates of Louisbourg. Their training involved learning to spot indicators of imminent ambush by Mi'kmaq warriors or Acadian guerillas, both of whom knew well how to blend in with the native foliage. At the end of the day, midway through their march south and back to camp, he called a halt to allow the troops to rest and to take water.

Accompanied by their commander, Lieutenant Bernard Birkshaw, who was a head shorter but a stone heavier than Wolfe and who waged a futile battle to keep his face clean of the shadow of his black beard,

Wolfe marched back through the ranks to check their disposition. He and the lieutenant were pleasantly surprised to find that the men had concealed themselves during their break, demonstrating a level of knowhow that was absent when he first began working with them. When they reached the end of the line he pulled out his pocket watch, the hands of which he had not adjusted since the night of his arrival, and wondered why, if it was ten o'clock at night, the sun had not set.

"Still stumped by the time, sir," Birkshaw asked, seeing him looking up-and-back from his watch to the patches of sky that were visible through the canopy of trees.

"Truth be told, I haven't given it much thought," Wolfe admitted, removing his tricorn hat and wiping the sweat from his forehead onto the sleave of his red overcoat, "Still, every so often, I do wonder."

"If I may, my lord, I think I might be able to clarify things for you," the lieutenant offered.

"By all means, please do," the general accepted.

"It has to do with the movement of the sun across the sky," Birkshaw began, glancing skyward through the trees. "Remember how it took us weeks to get here from England. Well, sir, it takes the sun just a few hours to travel the same distance. So, as of this moment, the sun has departed from the skies over England, thereby making it nighttime over there. Meanwhile, here in our neck of the woods, the sun is only part of the way through its journey across our sky, which makes it daytime here."

"How long does it take the sun to get here from England," Wolfe asked, popping his hat back onto his head.

"Four hours, sir, according to the boys in engineering," Birkshaw answered and removed his watch from his waistcoat pocket. "See how my watch says its six o'clock?"

"I suppose that makes a kind of sense," Wolfe considered the explanation and started fiddling with the dials of his timepiece, while putting together what he thought was a natural follow-on query. "When the sun finishes with us, where does it go?"

"To the westernmost edge of the world, sir," Birkshaw replied.

"Then it slips under it and goes back to its starting spot in the east to start all over again."

"I see," Wolfe hesitated, then said what was on his mind. "What about that Italian chap, Galilei, who said the world is round, not flat, and that it revolves around the sun, not the opposite? Do you think there's a chance he might be right?"

"No, sir," Birkshaw asserted, with a stern shake of his head, "The world I know is flat and the sun travels over it in a straight line from east to west."

"Okay, Birky," Wolfe concluded and punched his lieutenant lightly on the shoulder. "I'll take your word for it until I hear a better explanation. Come now and help me synchronize my watch with yours, so I no longer have to wonder why I'm being served high tea at noon."

"Aye, sir," Birkshaw obeyed and stepped in front of Wolfe so he could more easily manipulate the controls of the general's watch.

As he reached for the timepiece Birkshaw grunted once, then a second time. Swaying on his feet the lieutenant looked, wide-eyed, at Wolfe and grunted a third time then fell forward. Wolfe caught Birkshaw in his arms and, looking over his shoulder, saw three arrows protruding from him, one in his arm, one in his shoulder, and one in his back.

"To me!" Wolfe bellowed as three more arrows buried themselves in Birkshaw's back. "Enemies on my twelve! Form a line on my three and nine!"

Wolfe barked his orders just before he crumpled to the ground under Birkshaw's dead weight and more arrows whizzed over his head, some striking soldiers rushing to obey his commands. Their yelps and howls were lost in a burst of musket fire, which was cut loose by his fastest troops, that sent lead balls sizzling into the brush from whence the arrows were flying. Screams erupted from the scrub, but the people who uttered them remained hidden from view. As they wailed some of their comrades shifted their positions and fired more arrows and hit more of the British troops.

"By the big balls of the Brighton's black bull!" Wolfe fumed and wedged himself out from under Birkshaw's corpse. Standing tall, he bellowed at his soldiers and directed their movements with his cane. "Stay low, reload, and wait for my order to fire. When you do, make sure you hit them and not me!"

While his men followed his instructions arrows darted his way. Most were poorly aimed. Those that were closer to the mark he ducked, dodged, and danced away from. Amid his gyrations he checked his troops' readiness and when they were set he stood still and pointed his cane at three spots in the woods.

"There, there, and there!" he shouted, moving his cane from left to right.

Muskets cracked and more screams filled the woods accompanied, this time, by the sounds of bodies crashing through branches and thudding on the turf. A cloud of gun smoke filled the air around Wolfe and shrouded his soldiers, who were reloading and standing by for his order to fire their next volley into the enemy. Alone in front of the smoke, the tip of his cane planted in the ground, Wolfe waited for his enemy's response.

When none were forthcoming, he baited them, "You can hide well enough, I'll give you that. But you can't shoot worth a damn. So, I hope you can run as well as you can hide!"

Around him, his men chuckled, but stifled themselves when a lone man stepped out from behind the trees. He was lean and hard, with weathered skin that made him look older than a young man in his early twenties normally would, and long shaggy brown hair. His clothes were worn but they melded fluidly with the colors of the forest. In his right hand he held what Wolfe had heard the locals call a 'tomahawk' and he looked at Wolfe as if he was scat in his porridge.

"Phoq you, Général," the young man spat at Wolfe and laughter trickled from the woods behind him.

"What did he say?" Wolfe opened the question to anyone in his company who cared to respond.

"If I may, sir," one of his squaddies spoke up. "The Acadian said, *'Phoq you.'* As in *phoq,* spelled p-h-o-q. The 'p' and 'h' combine to make the 'ef' sound, like our letter 'f.' The 'o' and 'q' part sounds like 'oc,' as in octopus, with the accent on the 'o' and a hard 'q.' The word itself is derivative of our word, 'fuck,' and carries the same meaning, literally and figuratively. In this case, the Acadian is using it figuratively. So, when he says *'Phoq you,'* he means, 'Fuck you,' General."

The squaddie's explanation drew a wave of, 'Well said,' and 'Good show,' feedback from his mates.

When the rounds of congratulations subsided, Wolfe looked in the direction from which the explanation had come and offered his gratitude, "Thank you . . ."

"Private Matthew Mattheson. Double 't' in the first and last names, sir," Mattheson introduced himself and raised his hand from behind the bush that was his cover. "Under the command of Lieutenant Bernard Birkshaw, sadly deceased if I'm not mistaken. I am the son of Matthias and the grandson of Matteus, both of whom also spelled their names with a double 't.' I hail from Liverpool, via Oslo, and I am at your service, sir."

"Eh!" the Acadian snapped.

"Jolly good, Mattheson with a double 't,'" Wolfe complimented the private and ignored the Acadian. "As of now you report to me and you will continue to do so until I appoint poor Birkshaw's successor. That also goes for the rest of you lot."

"Eh!" the Acadian shouted.

"Mes excuses" (My apologies), Wolfe turned his attention to the Acadian and continued in French. "I wanted to make sure I understood you correctly. Thanks to Private Mattheson, spelled with a double 't' if you please, I do. Would you care to back it up?"

"You speak French like a girl," the Acadian snorted and took a step towards Wolfe.

"Tell that to your masters, for I learned it from their teachers," Wolfe shot back and stepped towards the Acadian.

Before the Acadian could rebut, a sharp voice called to him from the woods, *"Erieux, ça suffit! Allons-y!" Erieux, that's enough! Let's go!*

Erieux looked down at the tomahawk in his hand, then up at Wolfe, and then over his shoulder into the woods, only to have the command repeated, *"Allons-y! Maintenant!" Let's go! Now!*

Erieux raised his tomahawk and levelled it at Wolfe, then vanished into the woods as ordered. When the Acadian disappeared, Wolfe sighed and as the rush of adrenaline dissolved in his blood, lowered his head, weighed down by fatigue. On the ground at his feet, lying face up, Birkshaw's pocket watch stared back at him, its hands locked on the moment the lieutenant drew his last breath.

"Wolfe!" Amherst shouted from the entrance to his quarters on *Amelia.* "Quit your daydreaming, put your timepiece away, and get in here so I can give you your orders!"

Worn out from the day at sea, the long wait in the cold, and from wishing, fruitlessly, things had gone better for Birkshaw, Wolfe stuffed his watch in his pocket and dragged himself into Amherst's cabin. The commander-in-chief stood behind his desk, with the other members of his war council piled up around him, and eyed Wolfe as he slogged in and shut the door.

"Good of you to join us, Brigadier General," Amherst greeted Wolfe, making his rank and title sound like it was a role in a stage play, "I have decided upon our battle plan."

"We have a plan, you horse's arse," Wolfe countered, removing his hat and cradling his cane in his armpit.

"You mean the one where we land behind Lighthouse Point and have the navy bombard it and the fortress while we, the army, march around the harbor then break down the fortress gates?" Amherst completed his precis of the plan Wolfe and Brack had taken weeks to refine, in a single breath.

"That's it, in a nutshell, yes," Wolfe confirmed.

"Good plan," Amherst complimented Wolfe, "Unfortunately, I learned its details from our asset inside the fortress."

"Asset?" Wolfe asked, taken off guard.

"Good gracious, man, our *spy,*" Amherst blustered, emphasizing the last word in his reply. "Like it or not, Wolfe, espionage is a part of war—a part with which you would do well to make yourself better acquainted, I might add—and our intelligence confirms the French know all about your plan or, should I say, *all* of your plans. How do you think they knew about the training exercise that ended up costing Birkshaw his life?"

"I'm being told about this only now?" Wolfe bristled, reaching for the handle of his cane. "Why was I not informed earlier?"

"Remove your hand from your walking stick this instant, or I will have you shot," Amherst warned Wolfe and planted both of his fists on his desk. "Get this through your thick head if you can. If we told you that you'd been infiltrated you would have put all of your energy into ferreting out the rat, rather than preparing your army for war. Your doing so would have told the French we'd discovered they were spying on us. In consequence, they would have ceased to act on the information being relayed to them by their spy. However, due to your having been prevented from indulging yourself in a witch hunt, as far as the French are concerned we will proceed according to *your* plan. Hopefully, however, you have grasped that will not be the case. Rather, we will proceed according to *my* plan."

"You put my men and I in mortal danger with your pathetic subterfuges," Wolfe seethed.

"Yes, well, fortunately only a few of your men were lost during training," Amherst drawled. "Unfortunately, the same cannot be said about you. But fear not, there will be ample opportunities for you to find the death you seek and which we hope, fervently, you find in the days and weeks ahead."

"Weeks?" Wolfe blurted, "Louisbourg should be ours in under a week!"

"Oh, no," Amherst disagreed, happily, "No, sir. Knowing full well what a stubborn lot the French can be, we will lay siege to Louisbourg for as long as it takes to bring them to their knees. In so doing, we will destroy as much of the fortress and the town as possible and, also, kill as many of their inhabitants as we can manage with the tools we have at our disposal. And you, my loyal brigadier, will lead the way. Your orders are to lead the first wave of our troops that hit the coast of New France, the instant weather permits. Specifically, you will make your landing where the French least expect it, west of Louisbourg at a place called Freshwater Cove!"

Amherst's announcement was greeted with loud ballyhooing, handshakes, and slaps on the back among the war councilors surrounding the commander-in-chief.

Wolf, standing alone, added to the din by shouting a single word that got lost in the hullabaloo, *"Phoq!"*

Part 2

PROLOGUE

JUNE 7TH, 1758

GABARUS POINT, ÎLE ROYALE

L ate spring brought an icy blast of winter to Île Royale. Craggy and shaped like a heart, the chambers on whose left side were crushed, sliced, and ripped open, the rugged island was bounded on the east by the Atlantic Ocean, and on the west by the Gulf of Saint Lawrence, while its southwest tip was separated from the northeast nub of New France by the *Straits of Canseaux*. Abyssal and deathly-still, its torpid waters inky, the Vikings who squatted on Vinland in centuries past contended the straits were the realm of, *Jörmungandr,* the Midgard Serpent. As long as the serpent bit its tail, they said in their myths, the wars that would end the world would be forfended. Forerunners of the battles to come, the bone-rattling blizzards, bitter cold winds, and surging ocean swells joined forces to pry loose the serpent's clenched teeth from around its tail.

For the commanders of the British army the arrival of the foul weather meant that H-Hour for their plan to roll waves of invading troops onto the beach at *Anse de la Cormorandière (Freshwater Cove)* was put off, and then pushed back, and then delayed. To amuse themselves, they drew straws to decide who among them would deliver the

185

next update on their interrupted invasion to their bilious troops, whose agitated mood had surpassed that of Londoners waiting for an overdue stagecoach. Then, to pacify themselves, they beseeched the war gods to deliver them not favorable weather, necessarily, but only slightly less unfavorable weather. When at last their wishes were granted they instructed their charges, who were sick to their back teeth of bobbing around on the open waters of Gabarus Bay, to prepare themselves to unleash the full measure of their fury on any and every one of their French foes who stood in their way.

West of the bay, concealed from the British fleet by the black, cloud-choked night sky and sheltered from the elements by the islands off Gabarus Point, *Rajani* dropped her anchor. Her tackle well-oiled, her crew lowered a skiff smoothly and silently into a shallow. Head-to-toe clad in black, with not a word spoken between them, its crew of five cast off from the warship.

Two on the oars, one in the prow, and two on the bench facing the rowers, they made for a patch of sand hung over by the branches of trees growing out of the mainland soil. Turning the waves to their advantage, the rowers drove the little craft at their target, at speed, and beached it without easing their pace. Before it ground to a halt the rider in the prow leapt into the sand and vanished into the forest. Those left behind dragged the skiff to the edge of the woods and, after over-turning it, three of them hid it under loose brush. The tallest of them then waded ankle deep into the surf and sparked a match. As it burned down, he watched *Rajani* weigh anchor and slink out to sea.

"Suchika will return," Enriquez assured Vishnu, Ganesh, and Yuval when he returned to them and, together, they watched their ship slip out of sight. "She likes the three of you too much to strand me."

Her every stride creating greater separation between herself and the pirates, a hissing of snakes reached out to Marquaisa from the beach and curled around her ankles and the toes of her bare feet. Were the sound coming from real snakes she might have paused to bid them, *'Buenos noches' (Good evening)*. Instead, recognizing it for what it was —the hushed laughter of Enriquez's three lieutenants—she pushed deeper into the forest.

When she found a path worn into the turf by the passage of people and other animals, she turned right to follow it east along the coastline toward Louisbourg, where the treasure she was going to make her own waited to be found. At odd intervals, breaks in the tree line afforded her a view of the ocean, and where the clouds were less opaque, arrays of ships masts cast in silhouette by the glowing moon. On one occasion she tried to count the ships, and as she added up their numbers on her fingertips, nearly knocked down a sentry who was as distracted by the ships as was she.

His back was to her, and though he was carrying a military issue musket she could see he was not regular army. His pants and tunic were shaped from animal hide, his tough feet were bare, and a tomahawk and knife were tucked under the length of hide that held up his trousers. His straight black hair fell past his shoulders and the swatches of skin she was able to see were a deep shade of umber. His tunic was stretched tight across his muscular shoulders and arms. He looked tasty.

She attacked him at a sprint. Too late, he heard her charge and before he could turn to counter she tackled him. Using her left hand to clamp his mouth shut, she wrapped her right arm around his chest and, hooking her heels around his shins, pulled his feet from under him. Her bodyweight bearing him down, her palm stifling his surprised yelp, his hands still clasping his rifle, he crashed chest first on the ground with a heavy grunt when the wind burst out of his lungs and through her fingers. As he bounced off the turf she tugged his head aside to get at his neck and bit through his hair into the soft skin of his throat. He roared and twisted in her grasp, feeling his life's blood draining away, but soon went silent and still.

After she tasted his last drop she released him and rolled him over. His face told her he was in his teen years, his features handsome, almost pretty, but not yet mature. His skin was clear, his nose was straight, his lips were full, and his jawline tapered into a strong chin. She considered her kill to be of the highest quality, but as she admired it a twinge of sadness pinched her temples and a soulful, hauntingly familiar voice whispered to the boy, *"Lo siento." I am sorry.*

Startled, Marquaisa whipped her head around and peered into the wooded recesses to find who was spying on her. Unable to locate an interloper, she spit a venomous hiss into the shadows then turned her attention back to the dead youth. First she wrenched the musket out of his hands and snapped off its leather shoulder strap. She then stripped him of his remaining weapons and his clothes, bound his ankles with the strap, hauled him to the tree line, and hung him upside down from a low branch.

His body swaying, she gathered his belongings, and as waves flattened their curls on the shoreline behind her stalked back to the forest path. Warily she made her way east, planting a weapon or a piece of clothing in the undergrowth on either side of the path as she went, while also scanning the woods for more sentries and whatever it was they were guarding. She was about to lodge the boy's tomahawk in the meat of a fallen branch when snatches of quiet conversations filtered into her ears from further up the path and more inland.

Tomahawk in hand, she bent low and jogged toward the soft exchanges. After a few strides the chatter became clearer and a moment later she saw klatches of men and women huddled around a small fire. Some were dressed in hides, like the teen she had hung from the tree. Others wore wool garments cut in the style of the Old World, but dyed colors that blended with those of the forest. Their fair skin had been tanned a leathery brown by the wind and the sun, and when they spoke they blended their Acadian patois with the Mi'kmaq tongue.

Ragtag as they were, Marquaisa wondered how the catch-as-catch-can band of oddly attired and strangely spoken guerrilla-types could possibly help their French allies. Thinking it most likely the French would make use of them by turning them into cannon fodder, she shrugged and crept past their makeshift camp. When she no longer could hear them talking she walked out of her crouch and stretched her back and shoulders.

"Eh!" a man called to her from behind.

Marquaisa spun in mid-stride and cocked her left arm, making herself ready to throw the tomahawk the instant she sited her target.

She found him in the middle of the path. He was lean and hard, with weathered skin that made him look older than his years, and long shaggy brown hair. His clothes were worn but melded with the colors of the forest. In his right hand he held a tomahawk and he looked at Marquaisa as if he'd caught her pooping in his bunk.

She knew if she threw her weapon hard enough it would split his skull. But instead of killing him she stilled her arm, tripped over herself, and sprawled on the ground, her rapier rattling in its scabbard. Desperate to untangle herself, she winced as the voice that moments earlier had whispered over the dead boy's body screamed, and was joined by yet another voice that was eerily maternal and crackling with mischief. Their clamoring echoing across the length, depth, and breadth of her brain, they used their infernal energies to lock her eyes on the affronted, hatchet-wielding lookout and cantillated, *"Ayúdalo!" Help him!"*

Snarling, she scrambled to her feet and ran away from the woodsy sentry, who stood rooted to the ground wondering out loud about what had just happened. At top speed she bowled over another watchman who was hustling down the path and fretting at his comrade, *"Erieux, ne fait pas l'idiot! Gardez le silence!"* Erieux, don't be a fool! Be quiet!

A splash of red spurt from his nose when Marquaisa smashed it with her fist, but she didn't linger over him to take from him of the rest of the blood that was coursing through his veins. Rather, she kept running until the voices in her head went silent and her yearning to help the shabby, peculiarly named sentry was consigned to the abyss that was her conscience. When at last she stopped, she found herself in a stand of trees to the rear of defensive bulwarks manned by French troops, who were focused on the beach they overlooked and the ocean beyond. It was the first installation of its type she'd seen on the trail from Gabarus Point, so she knew she was about four miles west of Louisbourg, at *Anse de la Cormorandière*, where the British had made it obvious they planned to land their invading army.

Eyeing the huddling soldiers, Marquaisa relished the fear oozing from their pores and scoffed at their strutting commanding officer, whose palpable madness colored his every twitch and twitter. As he fiddled and twiddled with his gear, her scorn turned slowly inward to the voices she heard when she killed the teenager and crossed paths with Erieux. It deepened when she remembered they sprung from the one remaining speck of light that flickered in the nucleus of her wrought iron core. Vlad, fool that he was, had correctly called it a 'sliver of soul.' He had also reminded her, correctly, if the lord chancellor and those who sat at his table in the Chancery became aware of its presence they would have all the more reason to use every means at their disposal to consign her to the true death.

Damning as they were, the voices seldom spoke to Marquaisa, making themselves heard only in happenstances when the arc of her undead life intersected with the one being strung together by the ages-old wandering spirit of the fool warrior to whom she owed an eldritch debt. One of the voices, the first she heard after she took down the teenager, she knew was her own from another life. The other belonged to the witch whose spells had turned her into a deathless, night crawling blood fiend and burdened her with repaying the fool warrior for taking his love, failing to return it, and getting him killed. Where her voice was alarmingly heartfelt, the witch's was both irritatingly wise and utterly careless. Even though their tones differed, however, their message always was the same, *"Tonta. Él se para frente a ti. Paga tu deuda. Haz tu elección."* Fool. He stands in front you. Pay your debt. Make your choice.

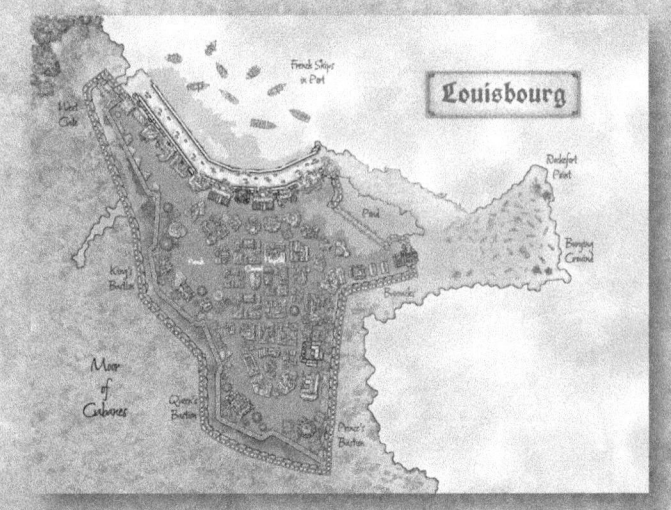

British
Camp

Freshwater
Cove

Headquarters

Stockade

Hospital

Moor
of
Cabanes

French Ships
in Port

Lighthouse
Point

Ships Sunk

Flat
Point

Louisbourg

British Ships
at Anchor

Black
Point

Atlantic
Ocean

CHAPTER 21

ADO

JUNE 8TH

ANSE DE LA CORMORANDIÈRE (FRESHWATER COVE)

As dawn broke, a biting wind ran before it out of the northeast, over the surface of the Atlantic, and down the coast of New France. Hugging the coastline, it ripped past the town and fortress of Louisbourg and banked sharply inland at Freshwater Cove. Coming out of its turn, the wind picked up speed and tore into the guts of a war, capsizing boatloads of red-coated soldiers who were scrambling for the shoreline, and throwing clouds of debris into the faces of the white-clad soldiers who were spraying the redcoats with hot lead.

"Fortess, shoot that bastard!"

"I don't take orders from bushwhacking *Acadie!*"

"Then think of it as a request, *Capitaine Parigo!*" Captain Parisian!

Fortess glowered at the red-clad Englishmen who were bent on putting Louisbourg to the torch and scattering its ashes to the wind. In growing numbers, they were piling out of their rowboats and finding their footing on the beach he and his men were defending. Sand devils, whipped up by the wind, raked across him as he dragged his eyes away from the chaos at the shoreline and glared at the Acadian.

"You are a filthy cur, Erieux." Fortess snarled. "For talking to me like that I could gut you, here and now, and no one would lift a finger to stop me. However, there is a chance you might yet help us survive this attack. So, I will spare your miserable life. On the off chance we *do* survive, however, you may rest assured our commander-in-chief, the Marquis Charry des Gouttes, will not be so considerate. Indeed, I've heard he can be most inventive when designing punishments for insubordination."

"Really?" Erieux barked at Fortess, over the thundering report of a nearby cannon, "What does he do to incompetents, like you?"

Fortess ignored Erieux's insult and squinted through billows of salt spray at the soldiers wading through the breakers, then asked, "Who is it you want me to shoot, exactly?"

Erieux grit his teeth and pointed through the haze at an officer who was slogging through the undertow and ignoring the musket balls that were whizzing past him, while bellowing at everyone who was within earshot. "The lunatic who is up to his hips in the surf and waving his cane over his head like a suicidal maniac!"

Fortess spotted the struggling Englishman, who was taking a pounding from the breakers, then looked down his nose at Erieux and snapped, "The devil take you! The tide will have that whelp! If you were so bent on killing him, then you would stop cowering behind my guns, remove yourself to the beach, and impale him on that rust-bitten potato peeler you call a knife. But you won't, will you?"

Erieux drew his knife and stood his ground, his eyes fixed on Fortess.

"So much for thinking you might help us," Fortess glanced down at the knife, then turned his back on Erieux. While his men blasted the English with more rounds of musket fire, he marched away from the Acadian and tossed a warning over his shoulder at him, "Stay out of my way or I will run *you* through!"

"Are you blind, as well as simple?" Erieux screamed and whipped tangles of long brown hair off of his face. Fuming, he chased down the Frenchman, locked an arm around his chest, and a fist around his collar, and wrestled him back to the seaward wall of their embankment.

"Look at the bars on that bloody red overcoat. See how the men rally to him. He is a senior British officer." Fortess jostled Erieux in protest, but the Acadian held him fast and growled, "He and his hordes are *not* supposed to be here. They *should* be up the coast beyond Lighthouse Point."

Erieux paused for a breath, then put the outcome of the battle in the hands of the Frenchman, "By landing here at *la Cormorandière* the British have given you a gift. Kill that officer and his men will falter and you will be remembered as the man who saved the day for *la belle France*. Let him live and we will lose the beachhead and then, in only a matter of time, all of Louisbourg."

Fortess broke out of Erieux's clutches with a loud shrug and spun away from him with a blistering curse. Then, breathing raggedly, he reached his right hand under his white overcoat and closed with the guerrilla. When they were nose-to-nose he jerked his hand from under his coattail, and in a rainbow arc brought his telescope to the *en garde* position.

As Fortess's hand shot from under his coat, Erieux raised his dagger to catch the captain's sword with its edge. When, after a moment, no blow fell Erieux dropped his arm and found himself staring at the mottled lens of a telescope. The lens winked in the daylight and when he saw it, and Fortess's droll look, he sheathed his dagger.

No longer a risk of being stabbed by the Acadian, Fortess elbowed Erieux aside and snapped open his telescope, "Let's have a closer look at this popinjay, shall we?"

While Fortess scanned the beach, zoomed in on the British commander, and hemmed and hawed, Erieux snatched glimpses of the British landing, ducked fire, and ground his teeth. Fortess looked lost in his machinations and Erieux was again reaching for his neck with clawed fingers when, suddenly, the captain snapped shut his telescope and mocked the commander and his men, "That runt actually thinks he can take the beach with that mob of drowned rats!"

Weary infantrymen within earshot of their captain interrupted their load-fire-reload routine and looked blankly at their leader. As one they bit back an assortment of profane comebacks and dragged themselves back to the business of shooting their muskets at fuzzy targets that were shifting in and out of sea spray.

For his part, Fortess searched through the haze of mist, sand, and gun smoke for the weapon he preferred to use against all of his enemies. His hunt was aided by those of his men who, while their hands were busy reloading their muskets, flicked their heads at the carriage-mounted cannon beside which Erieux was already standing.

Ignoring the Acadian, Fortess barked at the artilleryman stationed next to the iron barrel, "Brodeur, is that thing primed?" A perfunctory nod to the affirmative from the gunner was all Fortess required to leap into action, "Then stand aside, man! We can't have you hogging all of the glory!"

Marching double-time to the emplacement, Fortess snatched a burning matchstick from Brodeur and sighted down the barrel, directly at his target. Brodeur's polite suggestion that the captain raise his aim slightly to give his shot a chance of hitting his target went unheeded, and without warning Fortess fired.

The blast flattened Brodeur, Erieux, and Fortess who, from his backside, yelled in the too-loud voice of the suddenly and partially deaf, "*Mon Dieu*, that was loud!" Eager to know the results of his handiwork, he then shouted at his men, "How did we do?"

A nearby rifleman provided a recap of the action, in monotone, "You hit the sand, *mon Capitaine*. But, as you no doubt intended, the ball bounced. It missed the madman with the cane, however, and he is now on the beach with most of his host. But you did blow his flag-bearer to pieces. He was, no doubt, the more important target. *Félicitations, mon Capitaine.*" Congratulations, my Captain.

Standing upright once more, Fortess studied his polished boots for a moment, then jabbed an accusing finger at Erieux and yelled, *"Saboteur!"*

Feigning outrage, he flung his sword at the stunned Acadian. Off-target, again, he caught Brodeur full in the throat. As the blade burst through the gunner's neck, bright arterial blood sprayed out of him, soaking Erieux from the bridge of his nose to the tips of his boots.

Shocked, Erieux stared vacantly at Fortess then absently wiped his face with his hands. The blood he collected ran off his fingertips and he watched, numbly, as it dripped into the red pool in which the dead gunner lay. Shaking his head, he mouthed wordless denials at Fortess's musketeers as they forgot the beach they were guarding and took in the carnage at the smoking cannon.

Through the smoke, they saw their captain waving his fist at the blood-soaked guerrilla, at whose feet lay their dead comrade. In that instant, Erieux became not only the villain who had killed their friend, but also a traitor who had helped the British succeed in their invasion. Slowly, they raised their muskets, pointed them at Erieux, and waited for Fortess to give them the order to fire.

The sight of a dozen muzzles targeting him snapped Erieux out of his funk, and before battlefield injustice could be meted out he yanked Fortess's sword free from the dead artilleryman and flung it at the nearest of his would-be executioners. The rifleman made a fumbling attempt to block the spinning blade with his musket barrel but tracked it poorly through the haze and allowed its point to rip down his forehead and across the orbit of his eye. Yelping in pain, he jerked back the trigger of his rifle and sent a musket ball tearing into the shoulder of a squaddie down the line. The impact dropped the soldier who, while falling, cracked a shot skyward and clubbed his neighbor with the searing muzzle of his rifle.

Battle-hardened though they were, the rest of the squaddies gawped at the speed of the Acadian's attack and the chaos it spawned. In their moment of distraction, Erieux charged at Fortess, who clenched his teeth and scuttled backwards. Faster at the charge than his accuser was in retreat, Erieux overtook Fortess. In full stride, he crashed into the Frenchman and sent him airborne, only to crash land in a heap at the foot of the landward wall of the battlements. Without breaking stride, Erieux planted his boot squarely on the downed officer's chest and sprang over the wall, away from his former allies and the invading enemy.

After a jarring landing and a bone-crunching tumble to the foot of the embankment, Erieux rolled to a stop. With a groan he staggered to his feet, found his legs, and sprinted inland. He zigzagged through the grasses for long moments before he heard Fortess shout at his men to fire. Erieux took the order as his queue to dive into the vegetation, and as he flattened himself on the ground he heard hot musket balls buzz overhead. When the sizzling stopped, he resumed his flight in a thrashing crawl. Coarse grass and prickly shrubs scratched at his hands and arms, so he lurched off his hands and knees into a low crouch and careened toward the scattered, windblown trees at the forest line.

Though Erieux was clearly visible and within range, Fortess gave no more orders to his men to shoot at the Acadian's fleeing buttocks as he hightailed it toward the forest. Rather, as he took cover behind a crooked pine, the wind carried to Erieux the sounds of Fortess shrieking at his men to join in the general retreat. In counterpoint, from the beach, came cheering and chants of, "Wolfe! Wolfe! Wolfe!"

Gradually, the lyrics of victory and defeat faded with the close of the battle, and the cries of the wounded and dying rose in its aftermath. His back pressed tight to the tacky trunk of the twisted pine, the plaintive voices faded from the Acadian's hearing as he scanned the depths of the forest looking for more threats. A shadow within the shadows darkened the edges of his vision, but he did not break the rhythm of his steady sweep of the woods.

Only after he completed his survey did he take a deep breath and slump down onto his buttocks on layered beds of pine needles. As countless spines crackled under his weight, he wrapped his arms around his shins, pressed his forehead to his knees, shut his eyes tight, and squeezed himself into a ball. Breathing heavily, he rocked himself gently with tiny heel lifts, and gradually his breathing slowed. As he settled, the knots in his neck unwound and relaxation eased down through his shoulders, which first slumped, and then began to shake. In moments, the quaking escalated and spread into his arms, loosening their grip on his legs. His chest heaving, he clutched his ribs and rolled onto his side as laughter poured out of his lungs and up to the boughs high overhead.

After a few moments his belly laughs faded to hoarse snickers and he flopped onto his back. As more pine needles sprinkled down on him from the canopy, he cupped his hands around his mouth and bayed at the vacant sky, *"Phoq you, Fortess! Phoq you, Wolfe! Phoq le monde!"* *Phoq the world!*

His curses rebounded, impotently, off the indifferent foliage, and as they tumbled down over him, he flipped onto his stomach. Balling his hands into fists, he pounded on the turf and bellowed, *"Phoq you all! I will phoq, no, I will kill you all!"*

His promise delivered to a mound of loam, he sat up onto his haunches and whispered, for his ears only, "I swear to you, Raçielle, I will kill them all."

THE WEST WALL, LOUISBOURG

Louisbourg's west wall stretched from the ramparts that shielded the King's Bastion to the Dauphin Gate, which secured the northwest tip of the town. From his perch on top of the wall near the gate, Léonarre Poisson used his telescope to track the retreat of the French infantry units that had abandoned their positions on the Atlantic coast earlier in the morning. Though they were stung by their defeat and worn down by their rapid retreat, the soldiers kept up a brisk trot as they headed for the gate. They could not, however, match the pace of their captain, who charged at the gate in a hell-for-leather sprint.

"Fortess's howling would put to shame that of a banshee," Poisson drawled the leather of his tan, knee-length overcoat creaking as he adjusted his ostrich feather trimmed tricorn hat. "What's more, his pace would rival that of your prize racing pony. I do believe his coattails are level with the ground."

Trémont D'Acier laughed, and the chill wind making him shiver tried to warm himself by rubbing his arms, which were wrapped in his matte black leather overcoat, with his hands. Strands of hair from the loose tail of his top knot snagged themselves in the corner of his mouth and he as pulled them free he glanced south along the wall and added, "Indeed, my lord, he is delivering a splendid performance. He appears even to have won over our gallery mates. Look at how they are urging him on to ever greater exertions."

Poisson stayed fixated on the spectacle that was Fortess, whose pleas for sanctuary were becoming more intelligible by the second, and said offhandedly, "He truly is mad."

"Perhaps, my lord," D'Acier replied. "If, however, we are witnessing the fruits of his labors on our behalf, namely the abandonment of the defense of *la Cormorandière,* then he has proven to us he is first and foremost a fortune seeker."

"Then he and we are of like mind," Poisson affirmed. "Speaking of which, monsieur D'Acier, how fairs our coin?"

From a pocket inside his coat, D'Acier pulled out a letter written in the hand of Commandant de Chaffant and read aloud:

D'Acier, you rogue, I owe you an adventure!

Rendezvoused with a stiff lot of Spaniards off Florida and received the supplies you commissioned. They await M. Poisson's further orders, two parts in l'Arethusa for each one in Bienfaisant.

Our business with the Spanish opened in colorful enough fashion, with the Spanish sinking a pirate galleon and our helping them chase off a Mughal warship, but closed without incident. The Mughal ship dogged us through the colonies but vanished when we were joined by our escorts.

All went quietly from there, until we dropped anchor in Gabarus Bay and his lordship, Augustin de Boschenry de Drucour, Governor of Île-Royale, descended upon us. He harangued us until I had no choice but to commit a portion of our expedition to the defense of the fortress, which he has set his mind to holding.

So you, Drucour, and Poisson will bear the burden of Louisbourg. For my part I will make for Québec to deny the British the remainder of our flotilla. By now you will have found Bienfaisant sheltered in the harbor, and spotted l'Arethusa at anchor off the Barrachois Lagoon. I leave them in your capable hands, and you to the adventure I promised in my salutation.

Your servant, Chaffant

By the time D'Acier stopped reading, Poisson had lowered his spyglass and was tapping its eyepiece in his palm. "Fortune smiles upon us, Trémont, both figuratively and literally," he chimed, "By beating his hasty retreat and leaving our crates locked in steerage on those tubs, Chaffant pulled a snag out of our exit strategy. I mean, if we were seen *removing* goods from a fortress under siege, then sailing away with them our behavior would have been regarded as unseemly, at the very least, and punishable by death at the very worst."

Poisson clasped his hands at the small of his back and watched Fortess stumble to his knees and start crawling toward the gate, egged on by the ever-louder cheers of his admirers. A raised eyebrow betrayed the extent of the regent's amusement with the captain as he turned his attention to his aide. "So, my good young man, get word to Amherst, our plodding, would-be conqueror," Poisson said, his tone snide. "Tell him that his supplies are in storage. But, do not tell him where. That tidbit will remain our secret, until it is in our interest to share it."

D'Acier gave Poisson a sharp nod, then folded Chaffant's letter and returned it to his coat pocket.

"Not knowing where the treasure is stowed will force Amherst to temper his barrage," Poisson explained. "Whilst he hesitates we will fly, as did Chaffant, to Québec."

"Clearing the way for our flight will require delicacy," D'Acier said as he leaned against the stone wall and studied the veins that colored its surface.

"On our part and on the part of the British," Poisson replied. "Consider it yet another opportunity to practice diplomacy of a type opposite of the heavy-handed variety you are accustomed to practicing."

D'Acier grumbled and scratched at the veins in the stone.

"Never fear, Trémont, you will be rewarded for your restraint," Poisson chuckled at his collaborator. "Once we are settled at Québec, we will send word to Ferdinand to inform him that his payment was received. It will be his invitation to take control of the New World and quite properly, in his mind, he will dispatch his occupying forces. Naturally, Louis and Pitt will consider this an act of war and they will quite properly, in *their* minds, endeavor to throw Spain's invading forces back into the sea."

Dubious, D'Acier narrowed his eyes and shifted them toward Poisson.

"Our task then will be to manipulate events in yet another futile war, such that our profits are maximized," Poisson expanded on his vision. "Our burden will be to decide where, when, and how much of our fortunes to squander."

"Yes, my lord," D'Acier said, bowing to his patron to hide the traces of skepticism that niggled at his confidence in his and Poisson's mission. He added another layer of camouflage by gesturing rudely at Fortess.

Chuckling at D'Acier's crudity, Poisson raised his telescope to his eye for a close-up view of Fortess's agonies and got back to practicalities, "For now, however, do be a good fellow and make the necessary arrangements for us to undertake our duties as his majesty's eyes and ears here at Louisbourg. Our first duty will be to complete an inspection of Drucour's armada. But let's not do it today. After our trek from *Baie des Espangnols* with Fortess and that rabble he calls a regiment, I am in need of refreshment if not delousing. So, be a good fellow and set the appointment for tomorrow."

"Yes, my lord," D'Acier concurred and then jeered at Fortess, who narrowly avoided being trampled by the stampeding squadron of infantrymen that overtook him and poured through the Dauphin Gate.

"Speaking of rabble, what of Lady Marquaisa?" Poisson asked his aide and snapped his spyglass shut.

"Not a peep, my lord. She has not been seen," D'Acier reported as he turned and pressed his back to the wall.

Poisson mulled over the news then, rubbing his hand over his heart, pressed his associate, "She means to be seen when it suits her, D'Acier. We will not, however, afford her that luxury. Find her. She is here. I promise you."

D'Acier pursed his lips and let his eyes drift over the town that was laid out below fortress, knowing the task he'd been handed was easier given than concluded. His mind turning over the approaches he would take to solving the problem—coercion topping the list, it being the most efficient—he found himself rudely interrupted by a commotion that redirected his gaze to a point just beneath his station on the wall. A crew of squaddies had taken it upon themselves to lift Fortess onto their shoulders and cart him through the gate, amid much fraternal cheering and to the hilarity of the spectators atop the wall, some of whom passed lost wagers to their gambling mates.

As Fortess was flushed through the portal, Poisson caught D'Acier's eye and they shared an unspoken thought, which he chose to put into words, "Pay Fortess to be quiet, until we require him to be otherwise. Pay des Gouttes, as well, to make sure Fortess remains so. Tell the commodore to post him to the *Pointe du Phare*." *Lighthouse Point.*

"My lord knows the history of the *Pointe*?" D'Acier asked Poisson, already knowing how he would answer.

"If you are referring to England's use of it, in their slapdash campaign of '45, to cut the ill-conceived colossus that is Louisbourg down to size, then yes," Poisson answered as expected, then added a new twist. "It is my intention, however, that we will be well shot of said colossus before that history is repeated."

Poisson used his thumb and index finger to massage the bridge of his nose and, mimicking exhaustion, implored D'Acier, "Now,

Trémont, I truly am in need of refreshment. Please tell me that you have made arrangements for a sampling of the local fare?"

"I have not, my lord," D'Acier admitted, acting ashamed.

"Really? We have been here for one whole day," Poisson pretended to chide his attendant. "I would have thought that straightening out my kinks would have occupied the peak of your mountain of priorities." He winked at his grinning aide, "Are you becoming as shiftless as these bovine *Acadie,* about whom we've been hearing so much chit-chat?"

Freshwater Cove

Still as Death's soul and cloaked in Hell-black leather, Marquaisa stood in the forest's deepest shadows. Under a cavernous hood and behind a blood-red mask shaped in the image of a leering demon, she chuckled as Erieux's fit ran its course. Emotionally purged and physically exhausted, he pulled a wineskin from within his bloodied tunic, and between pulls alternated between a careful surveillance of the forest and a blank exploration of the pale skies beyond the treetops.

Within a few minutes, his senses muddled by wine and the stamina-draining residuals Death extracts when cheated its due, he nodded into a fitful, chattering sleep at the foot of a sheltering pine tree. Silently, she listened while he blathered in his peculiar Acadian dialect and punctuated his mutterings with loose kicks of his legs or swats with his hands. Suddenly, in the midst of his nightmares, he burst into wakefulness and gaped about in the half-light of the forest. Slowly, as he recalled the events that had cast him into the role of the pariah, the creases in his forehead deepened and his eyebrows knit together.

As his mood darkened he etched crude runes into the earth with his fingernails. Then, with a conviction that drew from Marquaisa a smile that rivaled the one carved into her mask, he struck out eastward in pursuit of the attacking British and the retreating French. As he trotted out of sight, the patter of his footfalls was replaced by the scraping of wooden arrows over rosined bows and the creaking of bowstrings as they were stretched to their extremes. When they went silent, she knew that her wait was over.

Three Mi'kmaq hunters had tracked her since her run-ins with the sentries posted on the path between Gabarus Point and Gabarus Bay. She had lost them in the twists and turns of the forest paths, but they kept up the chase and while she partook of the Acadian's performance they caught her up and surrounded her. One was positioned behind her, while the others hid themselves to her sides, one on her left and one on her right. All three were at a range short enough to guarantee any one of them a kill shot.

A sinuous *snap* behind her back was followed by a faint hissing as an arrow leapt forward. In a single, fluid movement, Marquaisa spun in a tight pirouette on the balls of her bare feet, dropped to her right knee, and snatched the shaft from mid-air. As she turned the arrow over in her hand, she coiled and allowed the bolt fired from her right to bury itself in the loam to her left. Without pause, she shot out of her crouch as the arrow shot from her left hummed through her wake.

In three powerful strides she was in her first attacker's face. With a snarl, she tackled him and staked him through his gut to the ground, burying his arrow up to its feathers. Shock at his plight was just beginning to register on the man's face when Marquaisa pushed herself away, and her hands slicing like scythes tore through the brush toward the hunter whose first shot had careened into the undergrowth.

In a hail of ripped leaves and splintered branches, she exploded through the brushwood to the spot where the Mi'kmaq was hidden. When she reached him, he was drawing his bow to kill her on site. But, stunned by the speed of her attack, his jaw slackened and he relaxed his grip on his bow. She snapped the bow in her hands, leaving him unarmed, and with her fist clenched tight hit him with a hard uppercut that slammed his jaw shut and sent shock waves into his brain that left him unconscious.

Before the killer hit the ground, Marquaisa shed her cloak and mask and dashed deeper into the woods on an encircling path that took her to a knoll behind and above the third of her assailants. After his first shot hit nothing but air, he had thumped out a volley of stone-tipped shafts that traced the path of destruction she had carved between his two associates. Barely breathing in the stillness that gripped the copse, he had stopped firing and was straining his ears for the 'all's well' from his partners. His senses preoccupied, he neither saw nor heard Marquaisa creeping naked and headlong down the trunk of the oak tree against which he was backed.

When her chin was an arm's length above his skull she halted, her taut muscles rippling smoothly beneath her alabaster skin. Her nostrils flared when she caught his scent and as her cravings surged her lips pulled back to the reaches of her wide mouth, giving full rein to gleaming fangs. Sinking the talons of her left hand through the tree bark into the rings of hardwood it encased, she reached down and plunged the claw-like fingers of her right hand, up to their knuckles, in the thick muscles that reached from the base of the man's neck to the tip of his right shoulder and lifted him off the ground. Unbridled agony roared from the man's core, but it broke silently against the sharp fangs that cut through the skin, muscles, and veins of his neck.

Feverishly, the pinioned man twisted, turned, and fought to break free from Marquaisa's clutches. His contortions futile, he pummeled her blindly, desperate to put an end to her feeding. Unable to dislodge her, his essence draining away, his flurry of blows dwindled to scattered swats, and finally to limp stillness.

No longer pestered by the dying man's thrashing, Marquaisa drank fully and finished loudly with a throaty *gulp* and satisfied *smack*. She then dropped the lifeless body and dismounted from the tree trunk. They landed together, and when the dead man bounced off the ground she kicked him into the scrub and out of sight.

When the flailing carcass reached its final resting place quiet returned to the woods. Standing statue-like on the spot formerly occupied by her aperitif, Marquaisa listened for the telltale sounds that would guide her to her entrée. Furtive rustlings and sporadic gasps drew her attention to the verdant tangle of forest overgrowth to which, earlier, she had paid a brief visit and left, staked to the ground, the most eager of her attackers.

In the amount of time a heart rests between beats, she covered the distance to the makeshift, wooded holding cell. Fast as she was, when she reached the enclosure she found it vacant, save for a broken arrow and a trail of fresh blood that pointed into the darker forest recesses. Casually, she strolled into the forest, making sure to step in the gore and grinding the mix of blood, dirt, and leaves into the crevices between her toes. *Delish.* Within a few meandering strides, she came upon the crawling man and watched as he dropped onto his stomach and dragged himself forward with his elbows, unaware that he was no longer alone.

Marquaisa announced her presence by grabbing the man by his ankle and flipping him onto his back. After a shocked squawk, the Mi'kmaq recovered, and his face set in a rictus of hate spewed out a torrent of incantations that singed Marquaisa's earlobes. Her eyebrow raised, she looked the man square in the face and replied to him with the expletive that the Acadian had coined earlier, *"Phoq you."* She then leapt onto the jabbering man, tore into his throat, and feasted on his terror, defiance, and bewilderment.

The blood lost through the hole she punched in the warrior's midriff left less of it circulating in his vessels and Marquaisa drained them quickly. At the sudden stoppage she jerked back with a growl, tearing deep gashes in the dry font. Furious at not getting all that she wanted from the man, she pounded his chest. Bone and soft tissue collapsed under the force of the blow, and a thimble of blood squirted from his open gullet, the sight of which drew from her a snort of contempt. Her eyes ruddy, she rose and grabbed the hair at the back of the corpse's head. She then stomped back the way she came, dragging the carcass down the path she cleared earlier and that led to the one surviving member of the death squad from which the dead man was now dearly departed.

The survivor lay where she left him, still was unconscious from the blow she landed on his jaw. When she reached him, Marquaisa halted and in the muted light watched his chest rise and fall. She studied the relief that his cheekbones and jawline cut against the planes of his profile, then eyed the interweaving muscles that were layered over his torso. By the time her inspection reached his hips, her blood lust had abated to the point where she was humming contemplatively like the connoisseur of the carnal arts that she was.

Quieting her tune, she crouched and softly tugged at his breeches with her left hand, while with the talons of her right hand she clipped the cord that bound them at his waist. Slowly, she peeled away the skins to reveal his fullness and nodded in approval. Then, taking care to not disturb the comatose man, she pivoted on the balls of her feet and grabbed the corpse she had hauled through the woods, stood up, and impaled it on the stump of a broken branch.

Turning her attention back to the unconscious Mi'kmaq, she noticed a break in his jawline, remnant of their earlier introduction. So, she nicked her lip with her fingernail tip and pecked him with a kiss that slid a drop of freezing ichor into his mouth. Fractured bones knit with an audible *snap* and the insentient aboriginal woke, in one piece, with a shuddering start.

Seeing his prey-turned-predator hovering over him, the warrior cried out. He fell silent, however, when her eyes locked onto his and her hand fluttered over his loins. Gently, she caressed him, slowly coaxing him to life, and in moments he was throbbing. With sure fingers she guided him easily, mounted him smoothly, and straddled him lightly.

Rolling her hips softly, Marquaisa whet his appetite while shaping and tempering his manhood, drawing more length out of him and squeezing more hardness into him with each push. As she took him in deeper, she also let her eyes wander over him. He was like the boy on whom she fed the night before, his straight hair thick and black, sharp ridges and angular planes etched into his face, his chest and shoulders broad, round muscles packed into his arms. But where the boy smelled and tasted fresh, the warrior beneath her was mature, his scent musky, fine crow's feet at the corners of his eyes, his touch gentle and knowing.

Rocking against him, she felt his strong hands tracing the sweep of her thighs, gliding over the arc of her hips, and closing around the narrows of her waist. His breathing steady, he feathered his fingers over the top of her taught cheeks and through the silken tresses of the hair that cascaded down her back to the tip of her spine. Tingling, she chuckled and, as she did, with practiced ease he quietly kneaded the muscles of her back, slowly walking his fingers up to the plates of sinew that knit her shoulder blades together and stretched across her ribs. Then, flexing his arms, he pulled her body onto his until her belly lay flat against his own and she had to brace herself on her arms, the palms of her hands pressed into the soil next to his shoulders.

He held her tight and she grinned when, rather than shying away from her cold veneer, his body warmed, and his breathing deepened. His rod swelled until it pounded on the walls of her canal, at which point he reached for her buttocks, drew her hips solidly against his own, and matched the rhythm of her movements. Sensing his excitement, Marquaisa growled huskily and pushed off the ground, and as she sat up she reached behind her back and grasped his wrists. With a tug, she pulled his hands forward, but grunted in surprise when he slipped her grip, snatched her wrists, and pinned her hands together at the small of her back, tangling them in her hair.

Marquaisa tensed her arms and jerked them from side to side, testing his grip, all the while studying his face. The Mi'kmaq fought back, tightening his hold, his expression showing his desire to not only live, but also to sing of how he trapped and made a conquest of the distaff wendigo who killed his tribesmen. Were her heart not frozen, her pulse would have spiked with craving at the thought of another taking her, bodily, for their own pleasure. Now, in place of a racing heart a gallery of titillating images flashed through her mind and kicked loose a foaming wave of abandon that rushed down the back of her neck.

Surging when shimmering bolts of her hair tumbled across her arms and eyes, the flow filled her breasts until her nipples ached, and flooded her loins. Her teeth clenched, her thighs squeezing his flanks, she writhed in his clutches as the walls of her abdomen cycled between cruel vice-like cramps and cruelly brief moments of rest. Then the warrior thrust his shaft deep, his hips driving hard until he burst in a heated eruption that filled her canal, then flowed down the length of his rod into the short hairs that warmed their groins. Liquid heat spreading, she arched her back, tilted her head back, opened her mouth wide, and screamed in delight as she was caught in a chain of convulsions that had her gushing in torrents and saturating her loins and his.

His body spent, his mind uncertain as to the consequences that might go with interrupting her as she shuddered through the after-shocks that echoed throughout her body following her momentous climactic episodes, the warrior kept his hold on Marquaisa until she went still and opened her eyes, their irises sparkling like cut, blood red diamonds. As she settled, a jumble of emotions that ricocheted between contrition, gratitude, adoration, and fear spilled out of the Mi'kmaq in a breathless monolog that Marquaisa eventually choked off by clamping her hand in an iron grip around his Adam's apple. As his lips blued and it became clear that he understood the fate that awaited him if he continued to emote, Marquaisa loosened her grip. Aided by a few breaths of air, the warrior's eyes once again sharpened into focus. As they did, she bored into them with her own, burning into his memories the story of their entanglement, particularly the slaughter of his mates, as she wished him to recite it to friend and foe alike.

Then, with a flick of her eyes and a nod of her head, Marquaisa sent the denuded and discombobulated hunter back down the trail she had laid down so carefully for him and his brothers. When he vanished, she padded to the forest edge and up to the pine tree under which the Acadian took his nap. Wisps of a warm breeze swirled around her and thickened into a milky, bitter-cold ether that drifted to the ground and melted into the soil beneath her feet. Kneeling where he made his bed she raked a sheaf of mulch into her palms and cradled it under her nose. Hovering over the loam, she sifted through the auras it captured and, as recognition dawned upon her, she began to laugh. She laughed as had the Acadian, but louder and longer, until it became a feral howl that chilled the overhead boughs to the point where they crackled with bright frost and showered her in a flurry of icy needles.

THE MOOR OF GABANES

Rough-edged and untamed the Moor of Gabanes rolled west, away from the dressed stone of Louisbourg's fortifications. His feet planted solidly on the moor, beyond the pockmarks that showed the limits of the range of the French artillery, Wolfe mulled over the challenges presented by the fortress's west wall. Flanked by the lieutenant he dragged from the surf where he made landfall, he stood well ahead of where the British brigades planned to make camp. Yawning at the potshots lobbed at him by the French, Wolfe requested a reminder from the lanky subaltern, whose wet, red coat, white pants, and black boots were stained with sea salt, sand, and blood, and whose blue-gray eyes bore the vestiges of shattered youthful illusions.

"Your name again, Lieutenant?"

"Thadan Jenkins, sir, Fraser's Highlanders," the officer announced, saluting his superior.

"That will be enough of that, young man," his eyes fixed on the wall, Wolfe reached back with his left hand and gently pulled down Jenkins's right. "Give me your account of the day's action."

"Eighth of June 1758, by Major-General Amherst's orders and under the command of Brigadier Generals Wolfe, Whitmore, and Lawrence, British brigades comprised of grenadier, infantry, and ranger companies prosecuted amphibious assaults on French positions at Freshwater Cove. General Wolfe's brigade established the beachhead at the cove and forced the French to withdraw, clearing the way for the companies of Generals Lawrence and Whitmore to come ashore. Our losses were light, considering the weight of the surf and the advantage in position owned by the enemy, and we have pushed them behind the walls of Louisbourg's fortress. We now are ready to commence siege operations, sir."

Wolfe sighed and pulled his attention off the wall, then gazed at the panorama of desolation that stretched from the fortress wall to the oceanfront. Rubbing the emptiness out of his eyes, he prodded Jenkins, "For someone so sodden that was an extraordinarily dry narrative."

Jenkins raised his eyebrows and asked, "Sir?"

"If I'd wanted the version for the mission file, then I'd have waited for Rollo's treatise," Wolfe clarified, a hint of dread at the thought of having to wade through Rollo's report coloring his explanation. "The man is nothing if not a devil for detail. So tell me, in your own words if you will, what you really thought of the day's proceedings."

"We were lucky, sir," Jenkins ventured. Then, encouraged by a crisp nod from the general, he pushed on, "If those infantry boys hadn't stumbled onto that slip of rock and shown us the way ashore, then we'd be sitting right now on *HMS Amelia* with Admiral Boscawen, out in the bay, instead of standing outside the gates of that fortress."

"Lucky, indeed," Wolfe concurred and looked to the south, away from the lieutenant, toward the ocean. "The memory of watching a cannon ball bisect the space I'd have occupied with my next step and seeing it burrow through my standard-bearer *and* your captain will be a while fading." Catching himself, he turned back to Jenkins, "Never mind, their deaths will be avenged."

"Yes, sir," Jenkins said, swallowing a tremor in his voice.

"With that having been said, I cannot help but wonder why Amherst would scupper the plans Brock and I laid down, so carefully, in favor of such a reckless assault. Audacity is not in his constitution," the general mused, an edge in his voice, as he went back to scanning the landscape. "Not only that, but the French resistance was pathetic. A circus of puffins would have put up a tougher fight."

"What are you suggesting, sir?" Jenkins asked, not entirely certain if it was his place to do so.

"Well, my good young man, I was urged by none other than Amherst, himself, to acquaint myself with the espionological aspects of war. You know, spies, subterfuge, stabs in the back, and the like," Wolfe laid the foundation for a hypothesis. "So, it seems to me that the last-minute change to a new invasion plan, together with the French army's apparent cooperation with it, smells of collaboration between British and French agents of espionology. Then again, perhaps in my zeal to become a savant in all things cloak-and-dagger, I have started to read too much into things. After all, 'ours not to wonder why,' right Jenkins?"

"Quite the opposite, if I do say, sir," Jenkins ventured, feeling a bit better about speaking freely.

"Ha! We might yet make something of you, Jenkins," Wolfe laughed then turned his attention back to Louisbourg's ramparts and thought out loud, "Now we shall see how the French bear up under the strains of *Le Siège (The Siege)*. And after they succumb, which they have done before and which they surely will do this time around, we shall deal with the real threat to the success of this expedition; the Acadian hellcats who, after generations of sweat and toil, have the audacity to consider this wind-scoured patch of nothingness their home."

Wolfe huffed at his own bluster and continued, "In the meantime, find Washington and bring him to me. Our backcountry colonel has yet to find his touch in the field. But I'm told he is a veritable maestro when it comes to turning patches of nothingness into functioning military installations of the type we will need in very short order."

"Yes, sir," Jenkins accepted his orders and stood to attention.

"Jenkins, your gravitas will be the death of me. Do please lighten up," Wolfe teased the lieutenant. "You can start by seeing to that shamefully well-endowed, naked native who is staggering around in the hummocks and making of himself a target for our hapless French gunners. Odd, do you not think it, that someone so young and robust should be so dazed and confused? See if you can't press him into some form of useful service, will you?"

Chapter 22

Toads

June 9th

Tall and pious, the spire of the King's Bastion shot skyward and jabbed the sacred, shiftless backside of the Almighty Oculus, God of Gods. All seeing, all knowing, all powerful, and to his way of thinking the creator of everything. Worshipped, despised, or ignored by everything of which he was the creator, he in turn loved, hated, or neglected all of it, depending upon how deep he was in his cups, or on the enormity of his hangover. His newly formed habit of drowning himself in oceans of grog, after having spent an eternity acting as a celestial pincushion, had made him and his ample butt-cheeks numb to the endless parades of pointed appeals for his divine intervention.

Accustomed to the Almighty's disregard of its prodding and warmed by the noonday sun, the tall, pointed spire that pierced the sky from dead center of the King's Bastion, radiated heat down its stone face and across the Bastion's broad north and south wings, which hosted the offices of Louisbourg's military, religious, and political power-elite. Largest of all of the human-built constructions in all of the New World, the King's Bastion looked proudly to the east, over Louisbourg and across the ocean toward France. At the same time it cast a watchful eye over its shoulder to the Moor of Gabanes, at the growing British encampment that had triggered the latest round of petitions to the Almighty Oculus.

Feeling neither the sun's warmth, nor a speck of faith in the Almighty's benevolence, two officers stood toe-to-toe, spewing hatred at one another, in a small briefing room at the center of the Bastion's north wing, Standing at attention in the corridor outside the meeting room, the corporal guarding its oak door grinned as Louisbourg's highest-ranking military officer lit into a junior officer.

"Fortess, you coward, I should shoot you," the squat, barrel-chested Commodore, Marquis Charry des Gouttes barked, the buttons of his uniform waistcoat straining, as he locked eyes with the haughty captain.

"On what grounds, you painted buffoon?" Fortess bit back, refusing to blink.

"At the very least for appearing late before me and for interrupting my lunch," the commodore snarled, flinging his broad hand at a rickety table behind him, upon which pastries and wine had been piled on top of notes and charts, "and for filling the King's Bastion with your stench. But most of all for failing in your duties by abandoning your position at *la Cormorandière* yesterday morning!" des Gouttes rattled off Fortess's transgressions without pausing for a breath.

"You've seen my report. We were sabotaged," Fortess disregarded the indictments.

"Yes, the Acadian. What was his name again?" des Gouttes ignored Fortess's insolence while feigning inquisitiveness.

"Erieux," Fortess reminded the commodore.

"Yes, a strange name," des Gouttes reflected, then added derisively, "Stranger still is how this lone bumpkin was able to undo a troop of seasoned infantry."

"He spoiled my shot at Wolfe," Fortess growled.

"A cannon shot, yes. I was told you nearly missed the ocean," des Gouttes scoffed.

"He killed my gunner," Fortess spat .

"With your very own sword, which I see you have since recovered. How did that peasant, Erieux, wrest it from you in the first place?" des Gouttes poked holes Fortess's case.

"He attacked my troops, then ran from his guilt," Fortess added another excuse to his catalog.

"He ran for his life," des Gouttes ripped it apart.

"He is a traitor!" Fortess yelled, stamping a foot.

"That is a myth!" des Gouttes yelled back, cutting off their quarrelling, and his eyes blazing tore into the defiant captain. "But, in choosing the lesser of two evils, I'll take the myth. Erieux will be sacrificed to help preserve our fragile morale, which I fear might weaken even more if the truth about this fiasco were known. And the truth, Fortess, is that at best you are a liar and an incompetent. At worst, you are a provocateur and a traitor and you should be slaughtered like the swine of which you reek!"

Fortess twisted away from des Gouttes's sword as, in one motion, the commodore pulled it from its scabbard and flashed it through an arc that would have cleaved him from hip to shoulder. Off balance, he crashed to the floorboards, then spun in a tight roll away from the commodore's stabbing attempt to disembowel him. In the instant it took des Gouttes to work the tip of his sword out of the wood grains, Fortess was on his feet. But as soon as he regained his balance, he had to jackknife at the hip to slip a vicious, backhanded slash that was meant to slice him through to his spine.

Momentum from cutting thin air instead of solid flesh carried des Gouttes's sword arm into a wide follow-through, so Fortess stepped into the opening and punched him square in the face. As des Gouttes's head popped back, Fortess reached up and drove the heel of his boot into his chest. The force of the kick sent the commodore crashing into his small table, which collapsed under his weight and threw up a cloud of papers and croissants, along with a shower of black ink and red wine.

While des Gouttes's stationery and victuals still were in their upward trajectory, Fortess drew his sword and pounced. Using the pommel of his sword he cracked the commodore on the wrist and broke his grip on his weapon, and as it skittered out of reach it was drenched in a syrupy mixture of spirits and inkblots. Grinning at his advantage, Fortess jammed the point of his sword into his enemy's throat and shifted his weight to drive home the killing blow. But the instant he started pushing his sword he jerked to a stop, his coat suddenly pinching his shoulders, as someone grabbed him from behind and hauled him off the commodore, then tossed him away like so much chaff.

Unable to break his fall, Fortess absorbed the full force of his landing with the back of his skull. His eyes rolling, he flung loosely balled fists at the legs that were suddenly straddling his torso and swatted lamely at the wooden musket stock that was butted into his chest.

"Thank you, Corporal Danier. That will do," Commodore des Gouttes ordered his burly young savior to stand down.

After the young man separated himself from Fortess, des Gouttes patted him on the shoulder and turned him back toward the doorway though which he had burst into the briefing room. As they began walking, the marquis took him into his confidence, "Thank you for intervening, Corporal. I'm afraid the *capitaine* and I got a bit carried away over a difference of opinion. You would be doing me a service if you kept to yourself what you witnessed within these walls."

"Yes, sir, of course," Danier said, his loyalty to des Gouttes made plain in the serious look he gave the commodore. He then turned his gaze back on Fortess, who was sitting upright with his legs splayed, rubbing the stars from his eyes.

"Excellent," des Gouttes declared and steered Danier further away from Fortess, whose sword he scooped up and handed to the corporal for safekeeping. "Now, if it is not too great an imposition, please wait outside for a moment while I finish with the *capitaine*. When I send him out, please escort him to his quarters and stand watch at his door. I will send relief for you shortly, at which time you may consider yourself on liberty for the remainder of the day. There will be a hot meal waiting for you this evening, here in the dining hall at the King's Bastion."

"Thank you, sir," Danier accepted des Gouttes's good deed, humbly, and saluted his senior officer.

"Thank *you*, Corporal," des Gouttes replied, shaking Danier's hand and guided him out the door. "The *capitaine* will join you momentarily."

Des Gouttes shut the door, about turned, and watched in silence as Fortess lurched to his feet. When he was almost upright, des Gouttes strolled up to him and drove a solid right hand into Fortess's left cheek. Fortess went down hard on his back, again, and des Gouttes took the opportunity to straddle him, as had Danier. Leaning over, he pushed his left thumb into the dazed captain's chest and growled, "You will never lay hands on me again." He then punched Fortess once more and smiled at the sight and sound of the man's head bouncing off the floor.

After a quick, final inspection of his work, des Gouttes walked away from Fortess, sidestepping the ruin that was his table and righting a chair that had been capsized during their scrape. Sitting comfortably, he stretched his legs, reached into his coat pocket and pulled out a velvet sack whose contents *chinked* and *clinked*. As he tumbled the small satchel from one hand to the other, he spoke down to Fortess, "You have been purchased a reprieve, though I am not sure why. Were you in my employ your services, such as they are, would no longer be required. Be that as it may, your benefactors have petitioned me to keep you occupied. To that end, you and your stalwarts, who defended *la Cormorandière* so gallantly, are hereby charged with the defense of the *Pointe du Phare*. Fight and, if necessary, die well."

Des Gouttes's chair protested like Oculus upon hearing, 'Last call,' as he heaved himself off its seat and slowly stood up. Taking the commodore's queue, Fortess scraped himself off the floorboards and hauled himself up into an aching slouch. After the captain steadied himself, the commodore stood nose-to-nose with him as he had at the start of their chat, jabbed one of his thick fingers into Fortess's shoulder, and dismissed him, "Remember Fortess, you are not in my employ. You are, however, under my command and if you fail in your duties again I *will* shoot you. Now, get out."

THE MAISONETTE, LOUISBOURG

Léonarre Poisson and Trémont D'Acier, decked out in their finest, Poisson bright and D'Acier black, and coiffed to perfection, Poisson powdered and D'Acier pulled tight, stilled their voices at the sight of Fortess. Rumpled and trundling along in the crowded lane in front of their maisonette, his military escort in tow, Fortess appeared to be making his way back to his lodgings in the barracks near the graveyard at the east end of the town. From their vantage point on the boardwalk before their maisonette, which next to the King's Hospital, they saw the shiner that was closing the captain's left eye and obscuring his view of his benefactors.

"Fortess has been making new friends, I see," Poisson observed as he watched the captain and his guard meld with passers-by.

"Indeed, my lord. His rendezvous with des Gouttes appears to have gone as expected," D'Acier replied. He glanced at his timepiece, and then slipped it back into his waistcoat pocket.

"Quite so," Poisson agreed, offhandedly, and shifted a small measure of his weight to the walking stick upon which his right hand was propped. "Speaking of expectations, we now have been here two nights and half of a day and my libertine cravings have yet to be satisfied. Do take time to make the arrangements, or it will be you who receives my twisted attentions." Then, arching an eyebrow, he rapped D'Acier's leg with his stick and changed his tack, "Then again, perhaps that is your desire, Trémont?"

"My lord is generous," D'Acier replied, casting his azure eyes downward artfully, "But indulging me would pale next to the amusements I have booked for him for this evening."

As the promise was delivered, it fell upon deaf ears. Poisson was busy staring up the lane along the path taken moments earlier by Fortess. Knitting his eyebrows, D'Acier followed Poisson's gaze, then rolled his eyes when he saw what had captured the regent's attention.

Guided by Governor Drucour, Lady Drucour glided along the lane in their direction. She shimmered from the strawberry blond ringlets that strayed across her smooth cheeks and fell over her shoulders and the silk of her peach blouson, to the buckles on her embroidered high heel shoes. Smiling sweetly, she chatted with some of the townies who greeted her as she and her husband steadily made their way toward the two Parisians. When the couple reached their visitors the governess stood forward, and with her right hand cupped in her husband's left curtsied. The king's men bowed formally in reply.

"Greetings, gentlemen. I am Augustin de Boschenry de Drucour, Governor of Île Royale," the governor introduced himself. Taller than both Poisson and D'Acier, the elegance of his suit was undermined by its poor fit, his already lean physique having been whittled down by worry. Like Poisson, he wore a powdered wig, in his case more so to conceal his fifty-five-year-old head, whose hair was leaving it behind, than for the sake of fashion. Drucour's pale skin was going sallow, his strong nose had turned sharp, and the light in his eyes gone rheumy. Whatever spark remained in the governor he saved for his for his spouse, upon whom it was clear he doted. His cheeks reddening in admiration of her, he presented his wife to his countrymen, "Gentlemen, I give you Marie-Anne Aubert de Courserac. The Governess. My Lady Drucour."

"You do us honor, Your Ladyship," said Poisson, stepping forward and inviting the governess to rest her right hand on his. Bowing at her touch, he announced himself, "Léonarre Poisson, Regent to His Majesty, King Louis XV, at your service."

"Thank you," Lady Drucour replied, accepting Poisson's offer and leaving no doubt she intended to take him at his word.

"My lady," the governor barged in, reclaiming the governess and whisking her past Poisson, who sniffed her perfume as she slipped past, then took a sharp breath when she brushed the back of her hand across his thighs. "Allow me to introduce to you Trémont D'Acier, aide to monsieur Poisson and by extension his majesty, the king. Monsieur D'Acier will be acting on monsieur Poisson's behalf in a business meeting we have arranged. So, monsieur Poisson will be at loose ends until dinnertime. If it is not too great an imposition, in the interim, would you be so kind as to entertain the regent?"

"As you wish, my lord," the governess consented, turning to Poisson, "What is your pleasure, *monsieur*?"

D'Acier choked and then coughed but recovered in time to click his heels and shepherd Governor Drucour into the vestibule of the maisonette. Poisson, meanwhile, waited for his aide to close the door before he replied to the governess, "If it pleases my lady, then perhaps she would show me the wonders of the town she so faithfully safeguards for the realm. If she were to do so, then in return it would be my pleasure to let her tour my battleship and share with her its payload."

The governess folded her hands at her waist, thought for a moment, then from behind shuttered eyes granted Poisson's wish, "You have a bargain, *monsieur le Conseiller*." Without another word she turned to face west, up the lane toward the King's Bastion, and waited. When Poisson joined her she raised her right hand, which he balanced on his left wrist, and walked away from the maisonette and her husband.

HMS Bienfaisant

As though he were attached to her by a length of chain, Poisson allowed Lady Drucour to march him into the expanse of Louisbourg's empty parade ground, at whose westernmost border stood King's Bastion. The state, the church, and the military coexisted peacefully in the Bastion, in part due to its mammoth dimensions. Lady Drucour, for her part, gave the grandiose edifice not a second glance; she being more interested in the gardens that lay kitty-corner to the building's southern tip. Unerringly, she led Poisson toward its trimmed hedges, while he narrowly avoided planting his face into the parade ground's cobblestones, on account of his staring at the steeple that was the bastion's centerpiece, rather than watching his step on the uneven pavers. Once they were safely in the garden, the governess expertly pointed out the rare herbs, seasonal flowers, and produce with which the plots had been planted on her direction.

Poisson was pleased to know the governess was an accomplished gardener. He was equally pleased when their travels took them out of the King's Garden. The avenue they joined led them south past the

Queen's Bastion and the Prince's Bastion, both of which were markedly smaller than the king's, then east along the fortress's ocean-facing wall. The governess chose to forgo the opportunity to mount the wall and have her coiffure and ensemble blown to bits in the breeze, but she encouraged the regent to indulge himself. Poisson made the most of it, taking in the air, the ocean vistas, and the build-out of the wall.

A few paces into his walk along the wall he stopped and looked back in the direction from which he had come. Shading his eyes, he traced the line of the ocean wall, then the fortifications that guarded the landward approaches to the town, that ran from the southeast to the northwest. He continued his inspection by turning on his heel and staring along the ocean wall. His hands on his hips, he observed how the wall angled sharply to join the fortifications that barred the occupants of the town's graveyard re-entry into the town. His inspection complete he hopped down to the embankment that was piled up to the top of wall, from the lane, and jogged down to its foot to where the governess waited.

When Poisson reached Lady Drucour he tugged his wind-blown jacket back into place before inviting her to take up his arm once more. As they made their way into the town he leaned in close to her and said, "His majesty will be pleased to know that his bastions are protected by a mountain of stonework. He will be less pleased, given the avalanche of money he has thrown into the construction of the fortress, when he is informed the ocean wall looks like it could be taken down by a clamshell lobbed at it, sternly, from the beach."

The governess chuckled at the image, then started their tour of the town proper by steering Poisson through a series of right-angle turns that made the cobblestone streets feel like a maze. As they walked the lanes that separated steepled churches, stately official residences, and brooding garrisons from one another the governess regaled Poisson with the details of their occupants' decadent lives. She then pulled him down alleyways that were bracketed by tightly packed shacks whose tenants she engaged her in a bawdy repartee. Their banter faded, however, as the governess and the regent stepped onto the wharf that was, when the port was not under military blockade, a hub for ships working the trade routes between France and its colonies in the New World.

As they roamed between the stacks of provisions and the pallets of munitions stripped from a nearby pair of men-of-war, she asked Poisson to point out the vessel he wished for her to inspect. He inclined his head toward *Bienfaisant* and without hesitation she commandeered a rowboat. The moment they boarded the tiny vessel she ordered its operators to set sail, she eyeing the massive warship, while Poisson watched the bustling port recede against her turned back.

At the challenge to their approach to *Bienfaisant*, Poisson announced himself and the governess. By way of a reply, as they pulled alongside the great ship, a windlass spun out a swing and lifted them on board, one after the other. When they both were settled on deck, the ensign on duty greeted his guests, offering himself for an escort and champagne for refreshment. Poisson politely declined the opportunity to be chaperoned, but happily accepted the bubbly. With a flourish the ensign popped the cork on the bottle and poured out three tall glasses that frothed to overflowing. The young man then toasted his guests, threw down a deep draught, and excused himself with a bow. With the formalities having been brought to a satisfactory conclusion, Poisson presented his arm, which the governess accepted, and they began their review of the ship, its crew, and its holdings.

Guiding her to the ship's stern, Poisson guarded Lady Drucour's ascent of the staircase that reached over the cabins housed under the bridge, then joined her at the helm. Standing behind the ship's wheel she surveyed the town, steering Poisson's eyes toward the places they had visited, as well as the batteries that bristled on the islands at the mouth of the harbor. Her narrative complete, Poisson complimented the ship's trim to the officer on watch and invited Lady Drucour to accompany him down the stairway to the main deck.

Steadying himself against the roll of the ship by running his hand along its gunnels, Poisson set off on a slow circuit of the ship's topside. He made a show of appreciation for the fitting-out of its riggings, and when the governess followed his gaze all the way up the main mast he preserved her dignity by placing his hand, discretely, against the middle of her back and stopping her from toppling backwards.

With a tiny nod of thanks for his consideration, Lady Drucour slipped away from Poisson into the last leg of their tour of the main deck, which took them astern. As they strolled past the cabins, Poisson nudged past his charge and hurried down the companionway that stepped below deck, to await her descent. Upon her arrival Poisson granted her a moment's pause, then continued forward along a short, cramped corridor. Pristine officer's quarters, vacant of their occupants, lined the hallway, whose end point was the entrance to the gun deck. Still and silent, the cannons hunched behind their hatches under the strict supervision of a pair of gunners who looked away from the governess. When she glided past their station the men signed themselves and whispered prayers against the bad omen that was a woman on board a ship.

Paying no attention to the guards, the governess strolled down the aisle between the rows of cannon and sniffed contemptuously. On cue Poisson perked up and inquired, "My lady is dissatisfied with the turnout of our arsenal?"

"Not at all," she replied, coming to a halt and looking back and forth along the rows. "It is impressive, but not nearly as awe inspiring as the monumental stupidity that is at the root of the defense the governor is about to mount."

"The governor believes he can hold the harbor, the town, and the fortress," Poisson noted, diplomatically.

"He is a fool," Lady Drucour told Poisson, point blank.

"He serves the king," Poisson pointed out, in return, his voice shaded more with ambivalence than patriotism.

"There is a difference?" the governess posited, taking the measure of Poisson with a hard stare. "He will fight. He will watch Louisbourg and its people turn to ash, and in the end he will fail. But you know this. So, I wonder, Léonarre Poisson, Regent to Louis XV, why are you here, really?"

"I am here to observe, to assist, and to report," Poisson looked the governess straight in the eye and spelled out his official duties.

The governess silenced the regent by inserting her gloved, right hand into the space that separated them from one another. "Do not patronize," she stated firmly. "You have an agenda of your own. Of this, I am certain. I know, also, that I will discover it. When I do you will make me a partner in it."

Poisson slowly pulled down Lady Drucour's hand, held it against her hip, and returned her stare, "My lady need only say the word and I will happily partner with her and spare her the aggravation of prying into my boring affairs."

The governess sniffed, dismissively, so Poisson sidestepped her and continued down the aisle toward the foremost companionway, whose steps reached down into the ship's holds. At the top of the stairway, he bid the lady wait for his invitation before descending. He then edged into the blackened stairwell, tapping with his walking stick as he made his way down its risers until he arrived at its foot. His stick clanged on a lantern whose glow, after he lit it, rose beyond his outstretched arm and up the staircase toward the governess. Accepting his unspoken invitation, she padded down into the hold where Poisson handed her his walking stick, then led her deeper into the darkness.

Tiptoeing in their bubble of lamplight, the two dignitaries picked their way through stacked chests, barrels, casks, and bins. Along the way Poisson interpreted for the governess the markings that were scrawled on the containers in languages both familiar and foreign. When they happened on a pile of crates whose canvas wrappings bore an inscription that included the likeness of a three-headed dog, Poisson paused. Shoulder-to-shoulder with Lady Drucour, he shuffled in close to the tarp and read aloud the *lingua franca* jottings that spoke of supplies provisioned by the kingdom of Spain. Chaffant's signature underlined the note, and on seeing it Poisson grunted and turned away to continue the investigation of the hold.

A sharp cracking sound, accompanied by a searing pain rippling across his buttocks, snapped Poisson's back into a painful arch and stopped him in his tracks. Choking back an obscenity he spun around in time to watch the governess ring another stinger off the outside of his thigh, using his very own walking stick.

"Madame!" the king's regent blurted.

"Don't *madame* me, you petty sham artist," the governess growled and rapped the tip of the stick off the back of Poisson's hand.

Acting before thinking, he seized his tormentor by the hair at the nape of her neck and spun her around. He then pulled her tight to his chest and started to speak, but stopped when her strong fingers tightened around his testicles.

"Release me," she commanded and was rewarded with instant obedience. Without returning the favor, she turned and pushed her body against Poisson's. Breathing hard, she grinned and whispered, "Actually, you may call me *madame* . . . when it pleases me."

Poisson cringed as she smacked his shins with his stick, then caught his breath as she whispered in his ear, "Amuse me. Share with me your blackest fantasies, and we shall see if we can bring them to life."

The governess punctuated her challenge by clapping a slap off Poisson's cheek that echoed though the hold and up to the gun deck. When they heard it, the guards resumed their prayers for deliverance from the misfortune the Fates surely had in store for *Bienfaisant* and her crew for allowing an accursed woman to invade the sanctity of their ship.

BLACK POINT

Offshore breezes swept the prayers of superstitious gunners and the supplications of tormented libertines out the mouth of the harbor and away to the east. On their way they tugged at the languid air hanging in the forgotten tunnels that ventilated the bedrock between Black Point and the foundations of Louisbourg. Carved by smugglers in the early years of the fortress's construction, the tunnels climbed up to the cellars of traffickers, who drove a trade in contraband that thrived for the better part of three generations. When the fortress was finally completed in 1745, the expectation within the illicit trade community was business would keep on booming. That expectation went bust, however, when in that same year the British blew up Louisbourg's newly tiled doorstep and snatched the fortress out from under France's nose. Off-the-books importing and exporting died with the regime change and the tunnels beneath Louisbourg fell from use and dropped from memory.

As tendrils of lazy currents slid over Marquaisa, they formed transparent veils that hugged the sleek curves of her breasts, belly, and thighs on their seaward journey through the cavern that was her sanctuary. Laying on a raised platform sculpted from ancient slabs of stone, their cold caresses stirred her to wakefulness. When she opened her eyes, the dreams of captive Mi'kmaq souls dissolved into the shadowy recesses of her mind and her ears pricked at the sounds of soft footsteps that halted, suddenly, at the entrance to her lair.

After a moment of silence, two voices began clicking at one another in a staccato version of the local Mi'kmaq tongue. Marquaisa lay still and listened as her visitors dove into a rapid-fire, point-counterpoint debate that was resolved in grudging compromise. Certain the squabbling was over, Marquaisa sat up slowly, slipped her bare legs over the edge of her finely dressed stone bed, dangled her feet, and waited.

Two stubby creatures were fidgeting at the mouth of her cavern. Amber light cast from the setting sun bounced off the pools that dotted the passage through which they had crept, and reflected off scales that shifted smoothly with their owners' gyrations. Their heads were broad, their noses were flat, their eyes bulged from the edges of their faces, their mouths were vast, and owing to their stumpy legs their fingertips hovered just above the smooth rock floor of the hollow.

Squirming under their host's silent scrutiny, they straightened themselves to the apex of their stunted height. Without ceremony, the monstrosity occupying the left flank of the arched entrance blurted, in a high-pitched croak, "We want them back."

"You are toads," Marquaisa countered.

A breath sharply gulped down by the pint-sized tyrant was followed by a biting retort, "We are no such thing. We are *Wiklatmu'j*. Cretins like you call us Stone Dwarves. But we are true rock spirits, born of

Tracadigash Mountain. My name is Omanahi. To my left is Shomanahi."

"She's not the first one to say we look like frogs and you know it, Omanahi. We really *do* need a fresh look," Shomanahi cut in, peevishly.

"Owe-me. Show-me," Marquaisa sneered, pointing at the sprites in succession, while butchering their names.

"The Mi'kmaq belong to us," Omanahi continued, passing on opportunities to correct Marquaisa's pronunciation of their names and rebuff Shomanahi's critique of their appearance. "You took Ulnoo and Weisis. Then you lost Neah to us. We want *all* of them back."

"By the veins in my granite garderobe, she's naked!" Shomanahi's scales jingled excitedly and he looked at Omanahi with rekindled faith. "I didn't think you had it in you anymore. You've been such a prude lately when it comes to playing pranks."

"It wasn't me!" Omanahi barked at Shomanahi. "You're the one who's always fiddling with people and their clothes. I swear, you're perverted."

Marquaisa watched the pair's fragile unity dissolve before her eyes, then stepped down from her bed, threw on her black cloak, and strapped on her jeweled rapier. Satisfied with her attire, she strode toward the rocky archway and broke off her discussion with the ghouls it sheltered, "The two I took walk with me now. The lost one wishes he did."

Wide-eyed and sputtering, the rock spirits scuttled off the path being taken by the black-clad demoness, fleeing to the moldy base of the arch in time to avoid being squashed under her bare feet. As she swept out of the cavern and was swallowed by the murky passage, Omanahi shouted a face-saving oath into her wake, "Retreat while you can, witch! But know this. We will be back! We will reclaim the souls that are rightfully ours and we will send you back to the inferno from which you were spawned!"

"Forget the souls and the inferno," Shomanahi chirped as Omanahi's threat was swallowed in the gloom. "Did you see that sword? One of those fool townies up top would pay a fortune for it. We could use the old tunnels that lead to the cellars and sneak . . ."

Ignoring Shomanahi's chatter, Omanahi watched Marquaisa disappear and sharpened his claws against the scales under his chin. As he did, a disembodied voice snaked out of the darkness into his ears and corrected him, "*I am no witch.*"

CHAPTER 23

POLITICS

JUNE 10TH

THE WHARF, LOUISBOURG

Shoved as far to the east as was possible, without its being pitched into the Atlantic, Louisbourg's cemetery straddled Rochefort Point from the seafront to the harbor front. Cast outside the protective walls of the garrison town, its occupants rattled around a landlocked purgatory that was as far away as it could be from the King's Bastion, but as close to France as the soils of the headland permitted.

His back turned to the graveyard, Trémont D'Acier squatted on the southernmost terrace of Rochefort Point and kept his eyes and his small lantern trained on an ocean that mirrored the moonlit sky. The lone living soul on the point, he fastened the top button of his overcoat and reminded himself the rustling sounds rising and falling behind him were those of the wind as it sifted through stiff, unkempt grasses, not those of the wandering departed who were trying to find their way out of the limbo in which they were trapped.

Three timed flashes from a lantern on a British cutter that was stalking the coastline pierced the disquiet that was creeping into D'Acier's bones, and informed him the message he sent earlier was received.

Released from his vigil, he doused his lamp and wrapped it in its oilskin then stowed it among the pitted rocks that were piled around the dried stems of a stand of brittle scrubs. Satisfied the bundle would not be discovered, he tucked his chin to his chest and picked his way along the roots of Louisbourg's fortifications to the beach that stretched away from the cemetery and up to and the harbor front.

Churning through the coarse footing of the beach was more taxing than anticipated, and when he at last mounted the wharf he paused to slow his breathing and steady his legs. Lean and tough as he was, he recovered quickly and stamped his heels to knock off the grit that clung to his boots. He then shaded his eyes with his wide-brimmed hat and blended in quietly with the revelers who were either ignoring, or had made themselves oblivious to the destructive British forces sitting on their doorstep.

Strolling up the quay through columns of light that shone through the windows of the buildings facing the harbor, his plan to go unnoticed was undone by his style and bearing. Shrouded in her cloak and concealed in the shadows cast from the Frédéric Gate, Marquaisa recognized the Parisian cut and quality of his suit immediately. His clothing aside, unlike the rolling sailors and stiff soldiers through whom he weaved, he moved like a predator biding its time and waiting to strike the at moment when his prey least expected it.

When he spotted his quarry, his stroll up the wharf took on a renewed purpose. Tracing his line of sight forward through the crowd, Marquaisa singled out his target; an exotic West Indian woman who was pacing quietly along a short stretch of the quay. As she walked back and forth, the bands of yellow light that streamed out of the King's Storehouse shone on her clear golden-brown skin, sparkled in her sultry brown eyes, and reflected off the layers of her thick bronze hair. Softer and more gently curved than the man, she equaled his unforced grace and tameless bearing. However, unlike the man, whose attire a shade blacker than his skin and was intended to make him next to invisible, the woman used fashion to compliment her vibrant ochre skin, accent her joyfulness, and invite attention.

As the man strode toward her, two teenaged sailors tiptoed into the pool of light she occupied, bowed to her, and introduced themselves. Greeting them like old friends, she smiled warmly at the cadets and shook their hands politely. Uncertain as to what they should do next, the youths looked at one another and started speaking over one another.

The woman watched the boys, patiently, tickled by their awkwardness, her amusement adding more light to her eyes. Before they could untangle themselves, however, the Parisian loomed up behind her and they cut short their attempts at making inquiries. Following the cadets' wide-eyed gazes over her shoulder, the woman found the man who had put an end to their advances and acknowledged him with a slight nod of her head, signaling to him to wait for her just as she had waited for him. Frozen in his tracks by her unspoken command, the grim looking man kept his eyes moving while the woman handed a small card and whispered to each of the nervous sailors. Buoyed by her goodwill and smiling broadly, the boys swaggered away down the quay. Just as satisfied with the outcome of the transaction as were the boys, the woman then went to the waiting, watching man and arm-in-arm they followed the boys down the quay, presumably toward a place both quiet and discrete.

Marquaisa tracked the couple as they wove through the crowd. When they turned right at the *Ordonnateur's* residence and headed into town, she hurried across the quay after them. From her position on the opposite side of the lane in which they were walking, Marquaisa watched as the man tried but failed to remain inconspicuous while in the company of the beguiling and, judging from the friendly greetings of passers-by, popular woman.

One of the people they met was a tall French officer whose left eye was blackened, heroically, and whose right eye was bloodshot from swilling rum. When the drunken officer made as if to stop and chat with the man, rather than the woman, the man turned him away with a tight shake of his head. Jolted by the snub, the officer reeled past the pair without saying a word and kept staggering down the lane toward the harbor.

Muddled ramblings from the slighted officer still were within earshot of Marquaisa when a soldier brushed past the couple she was following. Clad in ill-fitting kit that belonged on a low-level enlistee, at first he was a stranger to her. After a second look, however, his loose hair and limber gait struck a chord in her memory that triggered a wave of alarms that raced up and down her spine. The disheveled recruit was Erieux, the deserter whose essence had raised her hackles the day before at Freshwater Cove. Recalling his promise to, 'Kill them all,' it was clear to Marquaisa he had selected the inebriated officer for his first target. Unfortunately, by making the kill in a street full of witnesses, who either would identify him to the *gendarmes (police)* or more likely do the *gendarmes'* work for them, by hanging him from the Frédéric Gate, the Acadian was dooming to failure his grand plan for revenge.

Grinding her teeth at Erieux's stupidity, while at the same time grunting in grudging appreciation of his commitment, Marquaisa maintained a steady pace as she walked up the lane toward the Acadian and plotted her attack on him. Slowing in anticipation of his next step, which would place him into a hollow of darkness between buildings, she coiled then darted at him. Her bare feet hardly touching the paving stones as she rushed at him, she crashed her shoulder into his chest and drove him into the narrow alley and out of sight.

The shadows closed in on them quickly as she wrestled him deeper into the alleyway. When she was sure they were out of sight, with a push of her arms she straightened him up and hissed at him, "Fool!"

Her arm moving like a piston, she then hammered her fist into the middle of his forehead, knocking him out cold. His knees gave way, but she caught him by the lapels of his too large overcoat to break his fall. With a tug she stood him upright and studied the ridges that shaped his face and the creases that hid its secrets. Her mind tingling with a mix of curiosity and dread she bunched his coat in her left hand and with the other nicked his lip with her fingernail tip. She then pecked him with a kiss and slid a drop of his hot blood into her mouth.

When it hit her tongue, the chatterboxes splashing around in the solitary pin drop of water locked deep in the depthless icefield that was her core cheered and laughed, *"Told you! Told you! It's him! It's him!"*

"Maldito" (damn), Marquaisa cussed and dropped the Acadian.

She stared at him for a moment then, hearing the footsteps of the couple she was following moving further up the lane, kicked him deeper into the alley. When he flopped to a stop she warned him, "Best you be here when I get back."

Knowing her admonition fell on deaf ears, she dashed out of the alley. When she reached the lane she saw the couple make a turn in the direction of the King's Bastion. Intent on following them, she set of in pursuit, neither seeing nor sensing the man who stepped into the lane, behind her, down at the wharf.

THE MAISONETTE, LOUISBOURG

A mixed bag of merchants, soldiers, tradespeople, and civilians from a variety of close-by as well as faraway locales, all of whom had a broad range of opinions on all sorts of topics, gave the trader's wharf at Louisbourg a cosmopolitan atmosphere that was unique among the isolated outposts of the New World. As trade increased, optimism flowed inland from the wharf into the growing town, all the way to the peak of the spire of the King's Bastion.

The mood changed in 1745, when France lost Louisbourg to a mob of fishermen from New England and naval types from Merry Old England. Little by little life began to trickle out of the town, and though the fortress was returned to France, in 1748, there was no turning back the flow. The trickle became a steady stream early in 1758, when England once again set her sights on Louisbourg. By the time the British reached the garrison town in June, all but the faintest traces of the once-vibrant trade center had poured into the harbor and been washed away on the tides.

As she walked the darkened roads of the town, tracking the man and woman whose rendezvous she witnessed on the wharf, Marquaisa trekked up not only a slight incline, but also through the last dregs of hope that were being leached down the streets and out to sea by the specter of war. The couple's tour of the town ended, at last, at the door of a maisonette that stood next to the King's Hospital, and in Marquaisa's opinion dangerously close to the nunnery. She watched the man invite and then follow the woman into his vestibule and listened as he latched shut the solid wooden door. Taking care to avoid the caustic moon shadows cast from the convent, she stole across the boardwalk that fronted the house. Then, stepping down lightly from the boardwalk, she crept into the alley behind the maisonette and cracked open the shutters that covered the ground floor windows. At the third set she found the windowpanes that opened into a bedchamber and, glancing through them, witnessed the man initiating the closure of his transaction with his female companion.

Gone were the woman's clothes and undergarments. In their place she wore a golden, silk negligée that left her shoulders bare, hugged her breasts and buttocks, and hung to just below her knees. Gone also were the ties that held in place the layers of her hair, which now flowed down her back between her shoulder blades. Instead, the man was coiling bindings around her wrists to hold them together behind her back. When he finished she tested them. Satisfied they were secure, she sat on a stool while he quickly exited the chambers and sealed its door shut.

Quelling her urge to ravish the deliciously vulnerable looking feminine specimen, Marquaisa backtracked past the second set of shutters she jimmied, which hid the privy, to the first set. A quick look through the crack she made moments earlier assured her the room still was unoccupied. Moving swiftly, she pulled open the shutters one at a time and, as she did, the windowpanes creaked in their casements at the touch of cool night air. Ignoring their objections, Marquaisa unsheathed her sword and slipped its point into the crease between the window frames. Using both of her hands, she slid the blade steadily up the crevice until it was blocked by the latch that linked the frames together. With a bit of added, upward pressure the latch popped open, and when she pulled back her blade the windows turned lazily into the empty room.

Sheathing her sword, she unbuckled its scabbard from her belt and stood the weapon against the wall inside the room. She then sprung onto the windowsill, steadied herself, then dropped silently down to the rug that warmed the room's floorboards. Taking up her sword again and fastening it to her belt, she took in the contents of the spacious room. The wood cabinetry was rustic and at odds with the modern, brass, four-poster bed that butted against the exterior wall. The colors with which the walls were dressed were fresh and gave the room warmth but raised, in her mind, the question as to why it had gone unused. A locked suitcase sitting on the floor and propped against bed's footboard was the only sign a human had darkened the room's doorway which, at the moment, was wide open to the rest of the house.

She crept across the room on the balls of her bare feet. As she neared the open doorway, slim currents of warmth brushed across her cheek, pulled in from the great room at the front of the house and out through the open window of the bedchamber. Without a sound she closed the door to the point where it was open just a crack, turning away the warmth and the sounds and smells of the wood-burning stove from which it emanated. Through the slit Marquaisa could see the light that spread down the hallway from the great room and, directly opposite her, the closed door that blocked the entrance to the room holding the trussed-up damsel.

By all appearances, the man who had applied the ropes to her was more interested in feeding his stove than in stoking his escort's fires. Nevertheless, Marquaisa looked back into the bedchamber for a means of creating a diversion that would ensure she reached the girl without his detecting her. She settled on the suitcase and was about to heave it out the window, over the roof, and through the front window of the nunnery, when the sound of knuckles knocking on the front door rang throughout the maisonette. When the rapping ceased she heard an exasperated curse, then the clumping of footsteps heading for door. Upon hearing its locks being unlatched, she leapt across the hallway and slipped silently into the opposite bedroom.

"Whoever you are, do you mind?" the bound woman asked, her singsong accent taking some of the bite out of her reproach. "This is a place of business."

"Really?" Marquaisa replied, doubtful. "What is your business?"

"Why, politics of course," the entrepreneur replied, her manner suggesting there are, indeed, such things as stupid questions.

"Is that so," Marquaisa smirked, pulling off her hood. "And you are?"

"Haritha Dubusset, from *Sainte Lucie (Saint Lucia)*, by way of Paris," the woman announced herself, throwing back her strong shoulders. "Who are you?"

"Dubusset?" Marquaisa repeated the name, thoughtfully.

"Yes. Why?" Haritha barged in on Marquaisa's train of thought.

"Never mind," Marquaisa replied, then circled around behind Haritha and tested the rope that tethered her wrists. "Who did the rigging?"

"Monsieur D'Acier. Per my instructions of course," the professional boasted. "It is a specialty of mine that the regent, Monsieur Poisson, fancies."

"Poisson. Impressive," Marquaisa replied, sounding both complimentary and better informed. Then, picking up her line of inquiry, asked Haritha, "Tell me, this specialty of yours. Do you teach it to others?"

"When we were together in Paris I taught my brother, Thierry, so we could entertain ourselves. I left him to come here, but I hope to see him again soon," Haritha informed her inquisitor, while checking her bindings. "What did you do to my knots?"

"Closed a loophole I discovered in the technique, some time ago," Marquaisa said, quietly, in Haritha's ear. Then, toying with the jeweled hilt of her rapier, she walked slowly around her captive to face her. Smiling at her, she asked a different type of question, "So, this *D'Acier* works for this *Poisson*. Who do *you* work for, Haritha?"

"Donatien is my procurer. But, I work for myself," Haritha replied, trying hard to not stare at Marquaisa's fangs.

"Oh, no, you silly girl. I think not," Marquaisa tsk-tsked as she knelt in front of Haritha and slid her finger up the shallow fold in the soft fabric between her hostage's legs, from her knees to her lady parts. "Let's try again, shall we? Who do you work for?"

"I will not budge by even a fraction of a point on my percentage," Haritha countered, giving Marquaisa as hard a look as she could manage, an excited tremor in her voice.

"Done," Marquaisa agreed.

Their negotiations concluded, Marquiasa placed her hands on Haritha thighs and traced arcane patterns into her silk gown.

"I am Marquaisa," she whispered and looked deep into Haritha's eyes. "This is my promise to you: *You will live forever.* This is what you will do to help me keep it."

Marquisa was about to launch into an itemization the services Haritha would be providing, some of which were to be rendered then and there, but her newest recruit digressed, "Wait! What do you mean, *live forever?*"

"A fair question," Marquaisa replied, sliding her right leg over in Haritha's thighs and taking a seat in her lap. Once she was comfortable, while stroking Haritha's hair, caressing her skin, and kissing her lips, she clarified, "*Forever* means that for as long as I walk the Earth, so shall you."

"Meaning, also—and don't misunderstand, for you look much younger than—oh!" Haritha yipped as Marquaisa nipped at her neck, then finished her thought in a rush of words, "Meaning you have *walked the Earth* for a long time and you intend to continue to doing so for an even longer period of time, yes? For I have only just turned twenty-one and I have plans."

"Uh-huh," Marquaisa mumbled, brushing her mouth over Haritha's, then gently nibbling her ear.

"How will you do it?" Haritha whispered, pressing her crotch into Marquaisa's. "Will you cast a spell?"

"A spell? No," Marquaisa chuckled and squeezed Haritha's hips with the insides of her thighs and corrected her, "I am no witch. However, I am . . . talented; I have already done half of what I must do to keep my promise."

"What? When?"

"You might also ask, 'Where?' Marquaisa added, quietly. "The answers are *a moment ago* and *down here.*" Marquaisa kissed Haritha's neck where, earlier, she left bite marks, then explained, "I have tasted your lifeblood. It is sweet. Now, to make the bond complete, you must taste mine. It is not so sweet."

"If I do, will it make me like you?" Haritha continued to whisper, while pushing the flat of her stomach and the fullness of her breasts tight to Marquaisa's body, the silk of her gown smooth against the leather of Marquisa's cloak. "You know, all teeth, and hair, and claws?"

"Perhaps someday. But not today. Not until you are willing to die for it. Until then, you will remain young, strong, sun-kissed, and oh-so juicy, my darling. Shall we?"

Without waiting for Haritha's reply, Marquaisa nicked her lip with her fingernail tip, drawing a bead of black ichor to its surface. She then slipped one hand around Haritha's waist and another into the cool satiny hair at the back of her head and kissed her lips. Haritha shied from the taste of the cold, bitter, syrup. But Marquaisa held her tight and used her tongue to guide her essence into Harithas's mouth, blending it with hers. Their shared hunger growing, they held their kiss until the viscid mix dove down Haritha's throat. As it plunged, it changed into a swirling mist that crossed through membranes and filled tissues and fibers, repairing, rejuvenating, and strengthening them. Her body fevered, her mind enraptured, Haritha surged into Marquaisa, who, happy to accommodate, hugged her until, together, they crescen- doed in a torrid, foaming climax.

While Marquaisa and Haritha were communing, D'Acier swung open the front door of the maisonette and looked out onto an empty porch. Wise to the ways of the street he pivoted, catlike, on his left foot and backed his left shoulder into the doorframe. Neither an arrow, nor a knife, nor a musket ball flew through the open doorway, so D'Acier held his breath, listened, and waited for his attackers to make their charge. When they did not give themselves away, he poked his head through the doorway and glanced up and down the boardwalk but saw no one. Cursing softly, he was about to shut the door when a quiet cough drew his attention to the middle of the lane.

A solitary figure, backlit by the lamps of the nunnery, stood in the deserted lane waiting to be seen. Squinting against the glow cast from the lamps, D'Acier growled, "I am Trémont D'Acier. State your busi- ness or be gone."

In answer, a young French officer stepped into the light streaming from the maisonette and made his introductions, "I am Donatien Alphonse François de Sade. I believe the governor mentioned me to you during your meeting with him this afternoon." The young man paused to let the information sink in, then addressed D'Acier's demand directly, "I am here to ensure Haritha is performing to your satisfaction."

D'Acier estimated de Sade was around eighteen, but he looked younger. He noted the young man's uniform was clean and fitted to his lean physique, but his shirt was unbuttoned to his chest, his posture suggested nonchalance, and his brows arched high over bright eyes that blazed with high intelligence, bawdy humor, and genuine madness. When he moved, his carriage hinted of nobility. When he spoke, his accent was flavored with privilege and learning. Straight away D'Acier was as wary of de Sade as he was of Poisson, who not surprisingly, given the company he was last seen keeping, was late in returning to their maisonette.

Cringing, slightly, at the youngster's lack of tact D'Acier replied, "Indeed? Well then, please come inside where we can discuss our affairs in private."

With a shrug of his shoulders, de Sade accepted D'Acier's invitation and swaggered out of the lane, across the boardwalk, and into the maisonette. Bothering neither to acknowledge D'Acier nor to knock the dirt off his boots, de Sade strolled into the great room, plopped down in a lounge chair, and stretched legs to warm his feet by the stove. By the time D'Acier finished bolting the door and making his way back to the great room, de Sade was eyeing the vintage that was being allowed to breathe on a side table.

Before the young pup descended into guzzling directly from the bottle, D'Acier handed de Sade a wineglass and poured him a deep draught. D'Acier then set to pouring himself a measure but, before his cup was full, his guest was holding out his empty glass for a refill. D'Acier obliged then, bottle in hand, seated himself with his back to the wall and waited for de Sade to resume their conversation.

Blunt as a cudgel, de Sade blurted, "It has taken longer than is customary. Has Haritha fulfilled her duty to you, or are *you* having difficulties? I must know as she has other clients, as well as a timetable to observe."

"Haritha is . . . exotic. But, she is not for me. Tonight, she is for the regent, who as you can see has not returned from his visit with the governess," D'Acier explained as he pointed at a pile of memos on a side table. "In the envelope at the top of that stack you will find compensation that is more than adequate for Haritha's time, as well as your trouble. So, you may inform her other clients that their appointments are cancelled for this evening. Use whatever excuses you must, but mention neither the regent, nor myself. I am certain that you, she, and they will find the means to make amends."

Nonplussed at being dismissed, de Sade gathered his wits, threw back what remained of his wine, and picked up the envelope. After a quick inspection of its contents he stood up and sketched a bow to D'Acier, then started toward the door. Three steps into his exit, however, a familiar voice floated down the hall and into the great room, stopping him in his tracks.

"*Monsieur D'Acier,* I am cold. Can you help me?" Haritha left no doubt as to the kind of assistance she was seeking.

"She *is* good," de Sade nodded in appreciation.

"Thank you, de Sade. That will be all. You can see yourself out," D'Acier said, dismissing the young man again, then steamed down the hall and disappeared into the room from which Haritha sent her plea.

Annoyed by his abrupt dismissal, rather than heading for the door, de Sade quick-stepped back to the side table and the heap of correspondence. After a glance down the hall to make sure he would not be interrupted, he rifled through the stack of papers, finding letters from the likes of de Chaffant, the governor, someone named Fortess, and Commodore des Gouttes. Their contents gave de Sade nothing he could use against D'Acier, the regent, or any of the other dignitaries named in the messages. So, out of spite, he carried the entire set of documents to the stove and stuffed them in the fire.

When the flames began to eat into the letters, de Sade hustled for the front door. Again, he was only a couple of steps into his exit when some familiar sounds floated down the hall into the great room. Again, he stopped in his tracks. Voices and the sounds of a tussle pulled de Sade away from the front door and, grinning, he tiptoed down the hall. Looking forward to a bit of entertainment, and perhaps an opportunity to obtain some dirt he could use as leverage, he reached for the handle of the door to the room into which D'Acier had disappeared.

As de Sade was scouring his correspondence for the means to extort money, favors, or both from the highest-ranking officials in Louisbourg, D'Acier pushed open the door to Poisson's bedchamber and found, unoccupied, the stool in which he had left Haritha. Instead, she lay on her side in the four-poster bed, her bonds intact, her back facing the door. Casually, D'Acier walked to the foot of the bed and pinched the woman's ankle. The tweak returned no reaction, so he leaned in closer to her to look for other signs of life. As he placed his hand near her mouth and nose to check her breathing, he heard the bedroom door shut quietly behind him. Haritha instantly forgotten, D'Acier straightened up and pivoted slowly to find a black-clad fiend barring the exit.

It stood in profile, holding in its left hand a jewel-studded rapier whose point was set on the floor. From within the depths of the hood that concealed its face its deep voice greeted him, "She will live forever," it said, not mincing words, "You will die in one minute's time."

For the second time in the space of a few minutes, D'Acier was compelled to introduce himself, "I am Trémont D'Acier. Leave now and your life will be spared. Stay and you will perish."

By way of a reply the fiend produced in its right hand the small sword favored by Poisson, and a simple observation, "You are unarmed."

Keeping his eyes fixed on the intruder, D'Acier touched the empty space on his left hip where, normally, his own small sword hung, and shrugged, "A minor inconvenience, I assure you."

Sportingly, the intruder lobbed to D'Acier the sheathed small sword she held, along with another simple observation, "Problem solved."

D'Acier caught the scabbard with his left hand and in a fluid motion drew the sword with his right and took up his *en garde* stance. His adversary replied by pulling back its hood and freeing tresses of lustrous black hair that fell across its eyes, which were set deeply in a sharply cast oval face.

D'Acier looked at the face, picked out the accents that colored the woman's speech, and recalled his butchered pupil lying in the frozen courtyard at Versailles. "Lady Marquaisa, I presume," he said. "Enchanted to make your acquaintance."

D'Acier offered a short bow, to which Marquaisa replied by raising her left arm until her hand was level with her shoulder and the point of her rapier was aimed at D'Acier's chest.

"You are a devotee of the *Destreza* school of the art, I see," D'Acier said, sneering at her technique. "How quaint but, after all is said and done, pathetic. You, the Spanish crone, still fighting according to the obsolete rules of the defunct Spanish school of the art. Pitiful."

"While you stink of the teachings of the *esgrima vulgar,* if you can call them that, born of the cesspool as they are," Marquaisa replied, coolly, her eyebrow arched. "*Common fencing.* Is that not what they call it? How vile, and where you in particular are concerned, inadequate."

"I am among the finest duelists in France."

"Your scars say otherwise."

Weary of their repartee and fast as an adder, D'Acier lunged past Marquaisa's guard. Reading his attack easily, she parried and countered by flicking the point of her rapier at his face. D'Acier sucked in a quick breath and retreated, his left hand reaching for his chin. When it came away bloody, he winked and quipped, "Another one for the collection."

Lunging at her guard again, he disengaged when he saw her turn her wrist, as if to parry, and thrust his point at her right hip. Marquaisa dodged the speedy riposte by pivoting on her front foot and allowing D'Acier to slice through open air, rather than flesh. Then, catching him off balance, she punched his cheek with the nub of her hilt, sending him stumbling backwards into the closed bedroom door.

Angrily, D'Acier pushed himself off the door and sidestepped away from his foe. Marching after him in pursuit, Marquaisa commanded him in a grating voice, "Tell me, where is—"

Without warning the chamber's door flew open and slammed into her shoulder, cutting short her command and sending her sprawling across the floor. Momentarily dazed, by the time Marquaisa was back on her feet de Sade was through the door and into the room.

"Where is what?" de Sade asked D'Acier.

D'Acier started to reply, but de Sade cut him off when he saw Haritha on the bed and demanding, "What is going on?"

D'Acier elected to wait rather than respond to de Sade's question. He was rewarded a moment later when de Sade blinked and shook his head in confusion, asking, "Why are you bleeding?"

Choosing, again, to hold his tongue, D'Acier instead pointed at Marquaisa. Looking beyond the tip of D'Acier's finger, de Sade peered at the face that was partially hidden behind tresses of black hair. "*Well*, who is *this* beautiful creature?" he hummed. "Had I known *she* would be attending, it would be *me* who was paying *you* for—"

"She is a witch! Kill her!" D'Acier finally shouted at de Sade.

Paralyzed by terror, time slowed for de Sade as razor sharp talons reached for his jugular and behind them a pair of abyssal eyes bored into his own. Knowing only fear, his mouth burst wide open and he doused his would-be executioner in a thunderous roar that drained him of his last ounce of breath. Borrowing from his Acadian friends, he shouted their all-purpose expletive at his attacker, *"Phoq!"*

Marquaisa ground to a halt a hand-span's distance from de Sade. Snarling, she reeled away from him and covered her nose and mouth with her cloaked arm. Then, breaking into a sprint, she bounded away from him and crashed through the shuttered window in an explosion of glass shards and wood splinters.

D'Acier and de Sade scuttled after her and met at the ruined window frame. Half-heartedly, they looked after her for signs of a trail. Finding none, they turned their backs to the open air and sunk down the wall. Together, they sat on the floor under the broken window and stared vacantly at the ceiling.

After a few moments, D'Acier took a deep breath and remarked, "Congratulations on your bloodless, though no less bloodcurdling, victory."

Unsure of D'Acier and whether he was being insulting or ironic, de Sade simply accepted, saying, "Thank you."

D'Acier shook his head, then wrinkled his nose and turned to de Sade and asked, "What the devil is that stench on your breath? It can't be the wine."

Cupping his hand over his mouth, de Sade exhaled and brightened, "Oh, that's just a bit of aftertaste from dinner. An inn on the wharf slices its bread loaves then smothers the pieces in a butter that is laced with minced cloves of garlic. *Delicious*, but you're right, *very* potent."

D'Acier nodded his understanding, then pushed himself a little further out of de Sade's breathing radius. Looking at Haritha, who still slept peacefully on the bed and who remained unharmed, he asked de Sade, "What shall we do with her?

Expertly appraising the woman's generous anatomical virtues, as well as her diabolical predicament, de Sade replied with a leer, "I have a few ideas."

With an absence of restraint he considered *de rigeur (required)*, de Sade put his imagination to work to ensure he and D'Acier extracted Poisson's money's worth from Haritha, while Marquaisa put as much distance as she could between herself and garlic soaked *idiotas.*

"Ajo!" (Garlic!), Marquaisa yapped, swatting at the reeky patches of gas that clung to her. *"Ajo, ajo, ajo . . . aajjjoooo!"* she howled and stumbled, giddy from the dose of garlic-breath with which de Sade had doused her. Its effects were, to her, akin to guzzling tankards of porter.

"Mierda!" (Shit!), she cursed. Leaning against the wall of the building against which she was balancing herself, as she staggered down the lane that led back to the wharf. Using her right hand to prop herself up against a wall, she blundered on and grumbled, *"Me llaman bruja! (Call me a witch!). Ha!"* She then pointed, defiantly, at the night sky and ranted at passers-by who were walking on the opposite side of the lane, *"Les mostra una buja!" I'll show them a witch!*

Her attention divided between plotting the excruciating means by which she would set to rights the insults levied upon her, versus identifying who next would curb her suddenly voracious appetite, she failed to notice she was nearing the opening to the alley in which she left

Erieux. When she reached the break between buildings and her hand hit a pocket of air, rather than a solid stone wall, she lurched into the alley. Floundering in the dark, she bounced off the buildings that bordered it and sprawled to the ground, landing spread-eagled and staring at the stars.

As she admired the constellations, ripples of Haritha's consciousness reached out to her from the maisonette through their newly created blood bond. Connected as they were, she shared in Haritha's amusement at letting the young man with the foul breath and the duelist with the appalling technique think they were getting what they wanted, and giggled. Then, lowering her guard further, she allowed Haritha's senses to become entwined with her own. She felt the weight of the men's wants and the thrill of Haritha's needs, and as arousal jangled up and down Haritha's spine Marquaisa arched her back in unison.

When, in their turn, the men thrust deep and hard, Marquaisa grunted until, finally, she and Haritha shared another take-no-prisoners *orgasmo*. Then they slowly descended from the peak of pleasure and Haritha vacated Marquaisa's mind's eye. Her vision once again filled with a view of stars framed by rooftops, she knew, given no one had attempted either to assist her or to join her when she was in her state of euphoria, she was alone the alley. The Acadian idiot was gone. Her back flat to the ground, she kept gazing at the stars and huffed at the absent fool, "Swine."

Then, knitting her eyebrows, she turned her attention to sifting through the auras that populated the alleyway until she detected Erieux's thorny blend of courage and stupidity. Laying still, she shut her eyes and followed the signature his essence left behind to where it disappeared in the tunnels that riddled Louisbourg's foundation and reached out to the ocean. With an effort she let go of the Acadian's energy and rolled onto her knees, then stood up and chuckled, "Of course. The beaches."

With a lead on Erieux's whereabouts in hand, Marquaisa hazarded a stilted step toward the mouth of the alley. Vestiges of garlic poisoning impeded her mobility, but with each step she took she became more surefooted. When she reached the junction between the alleyway and the street her natural fluidity was largely restored and she slipped smoothly into the deserted moonlit lane.

She tracked the Acadian into the tunnels. As she descended, she called upon Oculus's sentinels to stop the fool from killing the two little *bastardo* toads if he found them lurking about the underground. That was to be her treat. She also promised herself, when she again met Erieux she would make sure she and he were properly reacquainted.

CHAPTER 24

CUTTHROAT

JUNE 11TH

THE BRITISH CAMP

West of the tunnels through which Marquaisa was stalking, at the promontory Anglos called Flat Point, a civil war was on the verge of erupting between two branches of the British expeditionary force. The navy, its landing craft battling fickle winds and waves, flung load after load of matériel at the army, which was beached and battling the same winds and waves. In the chaos, sailors ridiculed, insulted, and threatened soldiers, who responded in kind, happy to perpetuate their long-standing loathing for one another.

A mile north of Flat Point, beyond the range of the verbal fireworks, the sounds of footsteps—measured, purposeful, and beating a path into the dirt—pounded outside the entrance of the tent Brigadier General James Peter Wolfe had pitched at the heart of the British camp.

"Rollie, get in here before you grind out a ditch that will swallow my batman whole when he brings me my tea, which I expect will be at any moment!" Wolfe bellowed at the pacer, his voice warbling out through the flapping doorway of his hut.

Lieutenant-Colonel Andrew Rollo halted at the crease between the tent flaps, executed a tight turn, marched into the general's quarters, stood to attention, pinned a crisp salute above his right eyebrow, and waited.

Wolfe got up from his chair, watched the ceremony, then snarled at the immaculately attired officer, "Stand down, Rollie, damn it. If Jenkins sees you all of my efforts to corrupt him will be undone."

"Ha! Already he is beyond *rrredemption.* In just a few days, you've converted him from an embodiment of military dogma into a functioning *officerr.* Whatever will we do with him?" Rollo asked. He then placed a short stack of paper on top of the clutter that was Wolfe's desk, seated himself opposite his commanding officer, and announced, "The mission file, to date."

"Huzzah," Wolfe cheered, lamely. "What does it say?"

"In excruciating detail that you are well-meaning but incompetent and that *yer (your)* next posting ought to be to a sanatorium," Rollo summed up his accounting, a satisfied grin on his face.

"Very well, send it to Amherst. He likes a good yarn," Wolfe lifted the sheaf of paper off his desk and handed it back to the lieutenant, then seated himself. "How goes the digging in?"

"The *rrrock* begins to *rrroll* downhill thanks, in no small part, to your young Jenkins. When he takes his turn from Washington he drives the squaddies like they are a pack *o'mules,"* Rollo chuckled with Wolfe. "But, this work is tedium incarnate James. Can we not launch an impromptu raid and blow some wind up our *Frrrench brrrethren's* backsides?"

"You know I would like nothing more, but—"

"James *dinnae (don't)* be boring. Did you *ken (know)* there is a monster at large?"

"What in blazes?"

"James *dinnae (don't)* be vulgar," Rollo nagged at Wolfe. "I'll have *ye (you)* know that on the day we landed, while we were marching inland, some of the men heard an ungodly howling coming *frae (from)* the forest. Some of the pricklier ones had a look and found for themselves the remains of a slaughter. And by *rrremains* I mean *bodies,* two of them, both natives. One was hanging six feet off the ground, stuck through the chest on a broken branch. The other was broken in half and was in a tangle in the shrubbery. Both of them were *drrrained o'their blood.*"

"Campfire tales," Wolfe dismissed the gossip.

"Perhaps, but by the day the number of believers in the *Squog* multiplies," Rollo persisted.

"You did say, '*Squog?*'" Wolfe asked, wanting to be certain he had heard his lieutenant correctly.

"Aye, I did," Rollo replied. His expression assumed the aspect of someone about to explain one of life's great mysteries. "It happens to be the title the Mi'kmaq—the natives who have unwisely hitched themselves to the *Frrrench* wagon—have bestowed upon a creature that possesses the speed, agility, and cunning of a squirrel which, if you are unaware, is a tree dwelling rodent indigenous to these parts . . ."

"Thank you for elucidating."

". . . and the size, power, and savagery of a wild dog."

Wolfe looked, straight-faced, at his lieutenant and asked, "And this *Squog* has a taste for the blood of our enemy, the Mi'kmaq?"

"Quite so," Rollo congratulated Wolfe on his speedy uptake.

"Convenient for us," Wolfe mused. "But regrettable for the fellow-ship of the Mi'kmaq."

"Damned shame," Rollo drawled.

"I must remember to warn our newly minted Mi'kmaq guide," Wolfe made a note to himself.

"You did say, '*Mi'kmaq,*'" Rollo said, shooting a glance at the crease between the tent flaps.

"Indeed, I did," Wolfe's expression was that of someone about to explode one of life's great fallacies. "Jenkins rescued him on the day we landed, from the selfsame woods that shelter your *Squog*. His side of the story is he and his brothers were ambushed—his brothers were murdered, hence the carnage that was discovered by your squaddies— by a crazed Acadian who was his old friend. Oddly, monsters never entered the conversation."

"Damn it all, James! I thought I had you hornswoggled," Rollo blurted, his deceit laid bare. "Well, don't tell the men. You'll spoil their fun. By the way, what do you think of my naming their creature the *Squog*?"

"Sheer genius," Wolfe backhanded the compliment at Rollo. "It sounds like it isn't just the men who've been having fun. Speaking of which, we have our orders from Amherst."

"Splendid, when do we embark on . . . oh, bugger, you need a scribe," Rollo sagged at the prospect of more recordkeeping. "Very well, let us make a space on this wasteland you call a desk."

Rollo stood and was about to clear the mound of debris that separated him from Wolfe when the sound of someone clearing their throat drew his attention to the opening at the front of the tent.

"Excellent, come in, Brock!" Wolfe brightened and beckoned to his aide and drew the young man to his side. "Isaiah, as you can see we are fortunate to have been joined by the eminent Lieutenant-Colonel Andrew *Ramrod* Rollo, scourge of the Bay of Biscay and all things French and Spanish."

"Sir," Brock said and bowed at the waist, while balancing the dinner tray that occupied both of his hands.

"Rollie, I'm certain I need not remind you to be on your best behavior whilst you are keeping company with my *aide-de-camp*, our redoubtable Major Isaiah Brock, Esquire," Wolfe looked his young aide up down, brushed a non-existent speck of dust off his shoulder, and winked at him. "For, unlike you and I, he not only is an officer, but he is also a gentleman and, if I might be so bold as to don my soothsayer's hat for a brief moment, a future knight of the realm."

"Major," Rollo said, clicking his heels and surveying the contents of the dinner tray. "Either you've lost your appetite and found a horse's, James, or your instructions to young Brock included laying on tea for two. However, did you know you were going to have company?"

"Just a hunch," Wolfe quipped, then turned his attention to his aide. "I see you've brought the crumpets the lieutenant-colonel is so fond of. Good show. Now, off you go and see to our kit. We've a campaign to launch on the morrow and we want to be turned out in our best. Meanwhile, Rollie and I must do justice to the bounty you've supplied, as well as record, for posterity, the awesome charges bestowed upon us by the great and powerful Amherst."

"James," Rollo sighed. "You are such an ass."

THE BRITISH BEACHHEAD

Twilight shadows swarmed from Flat Point over the beach where British servicemen cursed at one another while they offloaded crates of equipment from makeshift ferries and stacked them in the sand, or piled them onto ramshackle carts that were hauled deeper into their camp. In the confusion and uproar, Erieux lost track of the sentries who were guarding the perimeter of the arms depot. Uncertain of the timing of their rounds, but eager to press forward, he was creeping amid the stacks of crates and through the shadows toward his next hiding place when a warning sounded in his mind.

"Behind you," it buzzed. Caught in a dim pool of light, Erieux spun around, ready to fend off an attack.

The British soldier spotted Erieux just as he completed his pivot. With his unkempt hair, bruised face, split lip, and battered garb, Erieux looked like spawn from Oculus's burning halls of damnation. At the sight of him, the soldier's jaw dropped and a stain spread down the inseam of his breeches.

Before he was able to cry out in fear, Erieux rushed him and tackled him to the ground. The soldier went down on his back and the momentum of the fall, combined with Erieux's weight, knocked the air from his lungs. His chest heaving, he fought for air until Erieux's fist landed between his eyes and stilled him. Erieux then pounced on him and pulled his dagger from his boot, ready to make permanent his silence, but stopped his blade short. The soldier was just a lad. Growling in disgust, Erieux pushed himself off the boy's chest and looked at him.

"Nice looking boy," he allowed, grudgingly. Then, brightening, he decided, "Let's give you some character."

Using the skills he sharpened cleaning fish and skinning hides, Erieux turned the boy's face toward the ocean and, starting behind the boy's right ear, used the point of his dagger to cut a shallow gash that traveled down the side of the boy's neck and curved to a stop in the hollow of his throat. After a moment's pause, he shrugged and pulled the point out of the hollow and ran a critical eye over his work. Satisfied, he wiped his blade on the sleeve of his overcoat and congratulated himself and the youth, "That will give you something to talk to the girls about."

Ready to move on, Erieux stood and searched for a way through the crates that would get him onto the road into the British camp and closer to Wolfe, the officer who led the assault on the beach at *Anse de la Cormorandière*. A path leading through a string of broken carts into the tree line caught his eye. But before he set foot on it he checked on the boy and found the heroically wounded young warrior still concussed and showing no signs of waking any time soon.

The sight of the boy's scattered kit made Erieux stop and think for moment longer. After a last look, from the boy up the path to the tree line, he swore, "*Phoq.*" Then, muttering oaths at his own stupidity, he acted swiftly. He peeled off the grimy *justaucorps (white overcoat)* he stole from a French infantryman in Louisbourg and shrugged into the youth's bright red overcoat. He then slung the boy's ammunition pouch over his shoulder and grabbed the musket he'd heard the British sentries refer to affectionately as their "Brown Bess." He completed his ensemble by pulling his hair back off his face and clapping on the boy's black, tricorn hat.

Pleased with his new disguise, he put his head down and marched toward the path the squaddies were tramping into the dirt to and from the beach. As he churned through the sand up to the path, in the back of his mind the voice that warned him of the youthful soldier's approach mocked him, "*Going to kill them all, were you not*"

Erieux shook off the sarcasm and, mimicking the gait of the sentries he'd seen manning the cordon around the beach, acted as if he was patrolling the pathway while he looked for an opportunity to join the traffic headed into the heart of the camp. His chance arrived a few minutes into his self-appointed sentry duty when a raucous troop came grinding up the path, towing its cannon-laden wagon while complaining loudly in course accents. Erieux fell into step behind the troop, and as he did their bellyaching stopped, much to the relief of everyone else packing along the path.

By the time the troop reached the plateau at the top of Flat Point, the troopers either were accustomed to, or were ignoring Erieux's presence. At ease with him, they once again started complaining about their plight. Topping the list of their grievances was their belief they were being picked on because they were Americans, recruits from Germany who belonged to the 60th Royal American. Topping the list of their tormentors was a *schweinehund (bastard)* officer named Vazigtonne. Apparently, because they were Americans, Vazigtonne thought they should be working harder and longer and producing better results than all the other regiments. Though he could not translate word-for-word what the Americans were saying, Erieux did cotton on to the fact that if Vazigtonne persisted in being tyrannical, then it would not bode well for him if he were in their vicinity when the musket balls started flying in earnest.

Likeminded though he was on the topic of the deserts owed to Englishmen of rank, Erieux did not descend into his own assassination fantasies. Rather, as he tagged along behind the Americans, he casually observed the goings-on in the sprawling camp, keeping a lookout for pointers that would aim him at Wolfe, and scrutinizing the men who made up the encampment, hoping to spot the frail-looking, cane-wielding madman himself.

Nearly a half-mile into their trek, just after he and the Americans passed what looked like the beginnings of a hospital station, Erieux spotted him. Wolfe, cane in hand, was standing in front of a tent whose opening faced Louisbourg and was talking to a young officer who was showing off some kit that shone brightly in the torch light. Satisfied, with the condition of the kit, Wolfe dismissed the young man and dove into his tent. Carefully concealing his identity, Erieux continued trudging along the path until he was well beyond the tent. He then quietly parted company with the Americans and circled back through the shadows to a hiding place in which he could wait for his target.

The British Camp

"Kit up to snuff, James?" Rollo asked Wolfe, offhandedly, as he rolled a set of documents into a scroll and bound it with a length of twine.

"Indeed, young Brock is quite diligent. Much more so than I was at his age," Wolfe said as he propped his cane against a side wall of the tent. Leaving it behind, he let his red overcoat fall from his shoulders to the ground as he walked toward the confusion of scrolls, pens, and ink that was his desk.

Rollo watched the coat, which caught on the heel of Wolfe's boot, drag along the ground and inquired, "Will you not reconsider and let me name these charts *The Annihilation of Louisbourg?* It's so much more compelling than your mundane title, *The Siege of Louisbourg.*

Wolfe shook the coat off his boot and looked at Rollo solemnly, "You have just completed a work that is without equal in the annals of military technical writing and cartography. Why cheapen it with a tawdry headline that would be better suited to the scandal sheets?"

Rollo looked back at Wolfe and waited. When, as expected, Wolfe's somber expression dissolved into a playful grin, the lieutenant-colonel heaved a sigh, "James, you are such an ass. Lend me your cane, will you?"

"Why?"

"For what reason other than to hammer some sense into that thick skull of yours," Rollo quipped. "Really, I could use it to help me get back to my tent, in the pitch black, without stepping on someone or in something unmentionable."

"I can have Brock accompany you if you like," Wolfe teased, but stopped when he saw his cane looking decidedly club-like in Rollo's hand. "Bring that thing back to me first thing tomorrow and be careful with that scroll. We wouldn't want our secrets falling into the wrong hands."

Rollo pushed open the tent flaps and looked left and right along the dirt path, which disappeared into the gloom in both directions, and wondered to himself, *In all of this mishmash, how are we to know whose hands are the right ones, and whose are the wrong ones?*

From his stand in the shadows a few yards down the path from Wolfe's tent, Erieux saw the crease between its flaps widen and a walking stick being used to pin the left flap to the side. Some weary squaddies blocked his view as they plodded along the path, so the next thing he saw was Wolfe striding north, away from him, and disappearing into the darkness.

Muffling a curse, Erieux eased himself out of the shadows and onto the path. When his feet hit the packed-down trail, he picked up his pace and within a few strides heard the rhythmic tapping of the cane. Within a few more strides he was catching glimpses of white braid on a red overcoat. After a quick look over his shoulder told him he was alone with his quarry, he broke into a sprint. In seconds, he was on top of his target. Wolfe was caught unawares and too late sensed the Acadian's attack, turning to face him at the last moment.

For the second time in the evening, Erieux drove an adversary backward and landed on their chest. Also, for the second time in the evening, the face that looked back at him from above the throat that he was about to cut open was not one he expected to see. Rather than the lean, pale, fiery leader he saw at *Cormorandière*, he was looking into a round face with hard eyes. Furious, he clamped his hand around the man's throat and snarled, "You are not the Wolfe!"

In answer, the officer rang the handle of his cane off Erieux's head, knocking him into the dirt path. Immediately, the officer scrambled to his feet and aimed a second blow at Erieux's ribs. The Acadian saw the handle plummeting down at him and rolled out of its arc, letting it glance off the back of his shoulder. Stung by the impact Erieux snapped onto his knees, and when the red-faced officer charged grabbed the cane with his left hand and pulled it while twisting his left shoulder away from the surprised officer and driving his right fist into his stomach. The man went down, disarmed of his walking stick and coughing, still clutching a bound-up scroll.

Erieux reached for the dagger in his boot to finish the officer, only to discover he'd lost his blade during their tussle, the sounds of which had attracted the attention of squaddies camped nearby. Snarling in frustration, he kicked the weakened officer in the gut and snatched the scroll from his hand, then bolted south. A half-dozen squaddies were running toward to the sounds of the scuffle, but when they saw Erieux sprinting at them, full speed, they slowed down.

Erieux saw them hesitate, so kept running at them but pointed back the way he'd come and yelled at them in fear and outrage, "Spy! I must tell Wolfe!"

Roaring, furiously, in reply the troops made way for Erieux and charged up the path in the direction he'd pointed. In seconds they reached Rollo, who had regained his feet and was working on regaining his breath. Recognizing his uniform as being one belonging to a senior officer, the soldiers ground to a halt and gathered around Rollo in a rough semicircle. Itching for a fight, the ruffian closest to Rollo piped up, "Sir, where is the spy?"

Rollo brushed dirt off of his lapels and looked at the man. "If I'm *no'* mistaken, you've just passed him on the path," he said flatly. He watched the men look over their shoulders, then back at him. He could see their disappointment in themselves but, determined to not let them dwell on their failure, offered them a suggestion, "If I'm *rrright,* he's just taken the piss out of you. Shall we go and kill him?"

Roaring their agreement and with Rollo in the lead the gang lit out down the path, hot on Erieux's trail. The uproar and pounding of feet caved-in the quiet evening being enjoyed by the occupants of the tents alongside the path, including that of one James Peter Wolfe, who burst out from under his canvas wrappings in his shirt sleeves, yelling above all others, "What in blazes is all this roaring about?"

All eyes followed Wolfe's as they got a fix on Rollo, who, sprinting at the head of his pack, pointed further down the path and yelled in reply, "Spy, James! Spy!"

No sooner had Rollo finished his report than an alarm sounded from the artillery landing at Flat Point, seemingly corroborating Rollo's brief report. Fully informed and motivated, Wolfe bellowed indignantly as he dug into his own sprint, "Of all the confounded cheek!"

Spurred on by the noise from the posse at his back, as well as his imaginings of the mob racing his way from the beach, Erieux flew down the path. His head on a swivel, he searched wildly for an escape.

Rounding a slight bend that pitched the path into utter blackness, he heard waves rushing onto distant beaches and, growing rapidly louder, boots thudding toward him.

Out of time and options, he veered off the path into an opening in the scrub on its border. Blindly, he pumped his legs and, shielding his face with his hands and arms, plowed over bushes and through branches, his heart and lungs bursting. Tripping, stumbling, falling, and crashing, he kept going until the only sounds he could hear over his own ragged breathing were those of the ocean. Finally, skidding to a halt at the edge of a sheer drop to the oceanfront, he dropped the scroll he'd taken from the officer, then bent over and gulped down lungful after lungful of fresh air.

When his breathing settled, he straightened up and started staggering east toward his refuge at *Cap Noire (Black Point)* chuckling, "Neah, my friend, if you could see me, then you would have to admit that under the circumstances even you could not have done better."

In reply, the voice in the back of his mind chided him, *"Fool."*

The spy's trail lost to them, Rollo and Wolfe stood on the path from which Erieux had launched himself into the scrub minutes earlier, and looked east toward Louisbourg. The mobs of soldiers from the beach and the camp had joined up. But, when it became clear the spy had escaped their adlib pincer movement, the men dispersed, grumbling at having been cheated out of a lynching.

Eyeing the stains on Rollo's otherwise immaculate uniform, Wolfe teased the lieutenant-colonel, "There you were telling me making a second copy of Amherst's magnum opus was, and I quote, 'as big a waste of time and talent as asking *the Bard (William Shakespeare)* to write usage instructions for the latrine.'"

Rollo peered up and down the path to make certain they were alone, then corrected Wolfe, "James, I called that bastard a *spy* for the benefit of the men, not because he actually was one. The plans he took *frae (from)* me? He didn't want *them.* He wanted *you,* James. He was an *assassin.*"

"Well then, Rollie," Wolfe replied. "He and his clowder of hellcats shall have me. Get back to your tent and get yourself ready. We're going on a little sortie of our own."

THE WEST WALL, LOUISBOURG

A depthless black, the still waters of the pond at the base of Louis-bourg's west wall rippled as the *Wiklatmu'j* frog-kicked along its edge, just below the surface. With each kick, sparks danced through their scales from head to toe, lighting fizzing tails of bubbles that lingered in their wake for a moment before dissolving in the murk of the pool. When they stopped suddenly and poked their heads above water, the foam followed them to the surface and popped lightly in their ears.

"Did you see that?" Owe-me, who balked at the thought of the nickname bestowed upon him by the witch, whispered as he craned his neck to see over the edge of the pool.

"I did not," Show-me, who quite liked the ring of the abbreviated version of his name, snapped. "I was too busy not ramming my head into your scaly butt to see anything."

"Over there. Look." Owe-me aimed a claw in the direction of the stone wall of the fortress.

Show-me looked to where Owe-me was pointing and his eyes bulged, "By the bark in my birchwood bedpan! Is that a pair of humans?"

"Too ugly to be anything else," Owe-me sniffed, then started paddling quietly toward the two monstrosities.

"Splendid!" Show-me chirped and splashed. "They're *sooo* afraid of the dark. Let's scare them!"

"Why not?" Owe-me said with a shrug. "Swimming in endless circles was numbing my brain. Although, I'm sure you found it stim-ulating."

As they stroked through the water, they watched one of the humans crouch down against the wall and look back in the direction from which it had come, while the other human tiptoed toward the arched stone gateway that was barred shut against the night. When it reached the base of the arch, it too crouched down. But rather than looking back at its partner, it placed a bundle on the ground at its feet. Then, with a quick snap of its wrist, it scraped the stone wall and a small flame burst open at its fingertips.

"Magic," Owe-me hissed, the tips of his claws scraping through the mud in the shallows near the edge of the pool. "Maybe they're not humans, after all."

"Maybe they know the witch we met in the caves. She was very attractive," Show-me leered.

A burst of sparks from the bundle at the feet of the human at the gate cut Show-me short, and stopped he and Owe-me in their tracks. The thick mud at the shoreline was slipping between their toes and over their feet when the human lobbed the bundle at the stone arch, then hurried back to its partner. When it finally bumped against the wooden gate, the bundle continued to hiss and fizz harmlessly.

"Pretty," Owe-me grunted, squelching through the mud. "Let's ask them what they're up to."

"Right, but only *after* we scare them," Show-me insisted.

The *Wiklatmu'j* waddled out of the water as Wolfe squatted beside Rollo. "Block your ears, Rollie," Wolfe whispered and laughed quietly, pressing his thumbs against the openings to his ears.

"James, you are such an ass," Rollo hissed and pulled Wolfe's left thumb out of the orifice into which it was inserted. "When I suggested we blow some wind up their backsides, I *didnae (didn't)* me *we,* as in *us.*"

The general studied his lieutenant, laughed again, and whispered in reply, "You wanted a bit of a lark. Well, here you have it."

Rollo unclenched his teeth to talk back, but Wolfe cut him short. "Consider it sweet revenge for the theft of your masterpiece, as well as the botched attempt on my life that nearly cost you yours. Which reminds me, be prepared to run."

Rollo grumbled again about the flaws in Wolfe's character, then closed his eyes and hunkered down against the wall. Moments later, he felt his right thumb being pulled from his ear and heard Wolfe fretting, "Something should have happened by now, Rollie. Are you certain your fuses were . . ."

Rollo caught a glimpse of what appeared to be two scaly, oversized toads waddling his way when the explosives at the gate detonated. The blast was deafening and it sent flaming debris flying high into the night sky. Then, as the thunder of the explosion faded, cinders and shrapnel poured down on the parapets, the wall, and the two-man wrecking crew at its foot. In the silence that followed, Wolfe ran from undercover to inspect the damage.

A moment later, he returned to Rollo and took him by the arm, "The gate is damaged, but it still stands. I cannot say if it is serviceable. But I *can* say that by now our French adversaries will have concluded we are in its immediate vicinity. So, what say you to our being on our way and not waiting for them to make chase?"

"Wait, James," Rollo said, squinting at the edge of the pool. "Did you see them?"

Wolfe stopped and squatted in front Rollo, glanced quickly around their position, and asked his lieutenant, "See what?"

"Just before the explosion. At the edge *o'the* pool. Two giant, hideous-looking toads," Rollo explained, pointing at the pool.

"There is no time for that right now, Rollie," Wolfe said, standing and dragging Rollo to his feet.

"Time for what?" Rollo asked, nonplussed, his eyes darting back and forth from Wolfe to the pool.

"Another one of your *Squog* tales," Wolfe teased Rollo and tugged on his arm to get him moving.

"This is no tale, James," Rollo insisted, stumbling along beside Wolfe. "I swear, one *o'them* was about *tae (to)* ask me a question."

"A giant spadefoot . . . who talks?" Wolfe put in his own words that which he was being asked to believe, tripped on an exposed root and almost took a nosedive into the dirt.

"I *rrrealize* it sounds ludicrous," Rollo confessed, catching Wolfe and helping him regain getting his footing.

"Congratulations, you have just captured the essence of what it means to make an understatement," Wolfe said, coming to a halt and saluting Rollo as alarms sounded on the opposite side of the wall. "You will forgive me, however, if I fail to celebrate your accomplishment here and now. The reason, if you hadn't noticed, is we have just upset a great many of our enemy. As such, I cannot *overstate* the importance of our being on our way. When we get back to our camp, I will be more than happy to corroborate any yarn you wish to spin for the men, no matter how bizarre it may be. But for now, we really must be going."

"Very well," Rollo grumbled, taking a last look at the pool. "But believe me, James, they *rrreally* were giant toads . . . and you *rrreally* are an ass."

As Wolfe and Rollo started loping back to their camp, Owe-me and Show-me started shaking the stars out of their eyes. Plucked from the ground and shot through the air by the wave of the blast, they had skipped like flat stones across the pond's surface and bounced to a sticky stop in a bog on the opposite side of the pool. Their scales all a muddle, they squeaked and squished themselves up to their full, if stunted, height and looked around for the two magical humans who'd given them a ride that rivaled anything they'd yet experienced at the hands of Oculus.

Turning his gaze upon the ruin that was his scaly coat, Owe-me quipped, "Well, we sure scared them."

"Well, did you get the answers you were looking for?" Show-me snorted.

"*Touché*," Owe-me said and sketched a bow to Show-me.

"Never mind *touché*," Show-me chuckled. "Let's clean up, get a bite to eat, and plan some proper tricks for some normal, stupid humans. Fancy some fish?"

BLACK POINT

Erieux deftly decapitated, gutted, and scaled the fish he caught, while whistling a tune that went best with a fiddle, spoons, and the crashing of dancers clogging their way around a crowded hall. With sure strokes he sliced the boneless flesh into fillets, then laid them across a grid of saplings that crisscrossed the smoldering remnants of burned driftwood. Heat from the glowing embers drew the oil out of the meat and turned it into a hissing mist that ran away from the

Acadian on the offshore breeze. Backed into a rocky crag at Black Point, he watched as the wisps were whisked away into the night sky.

With a shudder, Erieux pulled his eyes back to the neatly inscribed pages he had snatched from the dapper British officer he bushwhacked. He snorted in grudging admiration at the written description and the graphic illustration of the plan to annihilate Louisbourg. The most telling sketch depicted the fortress encircled by British gun emplacements, their lines of fire descending upon it from almost every direction. Shaking his head at the inevitability of the truth portrayed in the drawing, he ripped the sheets into shreds and fed them to his fire. Less concerned with the fate of nations than he was with the fatigue, hunger, and spite that wracked his bones, he yawned and watched with heavy eyes as the fragments of paper charred slowly, and the fillets sizzled softly.

Blinking his eyes into focus, he wondered how his dinner had arrived in his lap, wrapped in a rag. Glad that it had, he propped his elbows on his knees, steepled his fingers under his chin, and started into a blessing, "For what I am about to receive let me be truly . . . truly . . ." With a growl he cut himself short and concluded, bitterly, "*Mair-duuuhhhh!*" *(Shiiittt!)*

"*Thankful* is the word you have misplaced, *sí?*" The question rolled around his campfire and worked its way in coils up his torso, then down his arms into the sands in which he was seated.

"Show yourself," he challenged the disembodied voice, then started munching on his much-anticipated meal.

A rasping chuckle crackled across the beach and the embers in Erieux's fire flickered. "Who is Raçielle?"

Erieux stiffened as if he'd been stung, but continued chewing on his dinner. Between bites he shot back, "Raçielle is dead. She was swallowed in the *dérangement (deportation)*. If you had a hand in it, you soon will be joining her, witch."

"That is *how Raçielle is,* not *who Raçielle is* and, lucky for you, I am no witch. Answer the question. Ask it again, I will not."

"Show yourself and I will answer your question," he bargained.

"Here I am," velvety-smooth and razor-sharp, the reply beckoned to Erieux from the shadows that filled the rocks behind his back.

Then, a touch of ice nicked the base of his neck and goosebumps sprouted from Erieux's skin. Jerking his head around to look over his shoulder, he shrieked as his world was devoured by a nightmare of fangs, claws, and blackness that taunted him with a sarcastic reproach, "A fine answer, Erieux."

Jarred by the vision, Erieux jolted awake. The embers in his fire still were glowing, his dinner simmering above them. Chilled by his dream and the night air, he rubbed his arms with his hands to warm himself. Bone weary from the energy he spent on what was, in the end, a failed attempt at assassinating Wolfe, the Acadian massaged his temples with his fingers to help clear the fog from his brain. When he finally got round to his dinner, he was interrupted by the rumblings of an explosion that came from the fortress and that drifted over him and out into the cove. The British battle plans smoldering in his fire, Erieux started chewing his fish, knowing the blast was but the first of many yet to come.

CHAPTER 25

PALE SEEKER OF GOLD

25 BCE

LANCIA, HISPANIA

Two thousand years before Wolfe washed up on the shores of Freshwater Cove, Rome was launching its campaign to pacify the tribes of Hispania. One hundred years into the campaign, the Republic turned its attention to the northwest reaches of the region and the tribes of the Astures. Seventy-five years later Augustus, founder of the Roman Empire and its first Emperor, declared victory in the campaign after personally leading the capture of the Asturian town of Mons Medullus.

Two thousand years before Marquaisa prowled the streets of Louisbourg hunting for Spanish gold, she was Kayza of the Lugones, pride of the Astures, and pain in Augustus's imperial backside. Kayza answered Augustus's declaration of victory at Mons Medullus by having her archers send flaming arrows into his legions as he and his men hotfooted out of Astures on their way to a party in Rome. To add insult to injury, she snatched from Augustus's baggage train the gold he plundered in Mons Medullus. She and her warriors then vanished into the crevices of the Asturian sierras which, like their denizens, would not be tamed.

A few nights later, under a sliver of crescent moon, Kayza emerged from the mountain passes and steered her mare, Elazuna, into the sprawling garrison town at Lancia. As they walked between the pincers of the gateway that funneled traffic into the town the mare blew her nose and shook her head in irritation at its sounds and smells. The dust she tossed from her mane hung in the air until she marched Kayza through it, adding yet another layer of grime to the bronze scales of her mistress's cuirass and the ringlets of her waist-length flaxen hair.

The dirt put the exclamation point on the Asturcón mare's distaste for the confines of the town, which she conveyed to Kayza via choppy strides that vibrated through the four-horn saddle cinched around her belly. Mindful of Elazuna's protests, Kayza kept a firm grip on the lead rope tethered to the two geldings pulling Augustus's baggage cart and coaxed her mare forward with a gentle squeeze of her thighs. As they walked deeper into the fortress, up a paved street, she rubbed her horse's neck and complimented her, "You are brave and wise." She then chided herself, "Were I as wise, I would take that wagon and all of its treasures straight to Noega, our fearless leader Gausón be damned."

Elazuna snorted in agreement and shook more dust into the air, temporarily obscuring Kayza's view of the two figures standing in the torch-lit gateway that fronted Lancia's most imposing estate. Waving away the dust and squinting into the guttering lights, she recognized the bear-like General Gausón, as well as Kalos, his skinny lieutenant. Thinking she was tossing them an informal salutation, the two officers replied to her in kind.

Ignoring their greetings, Kayza nudged her mare into a lope and a collision course with the men, both of whom held their ground. Elazuna growled at their defiance, lowered her head, and quickened her pace, while Kayza dropped the lead rope attached to the geldings. Still, neither man flinched even as the mare broke into a gallop. A moment later, when the men were a few of Elazuna's strides away from being head-butted into their next lives, Kayza threw her right leg over the mare's neck, vaulted from the saddle, and touched down lightly on the pavers of the roadway. Her dismount was Elazuna's command to halt and, as the mare skidded to a stop beside her and the geldings pulling the cart caught up with them, Kayza continued to march toward her welcoming committee. Squaring her broad shoulders, she stopped in front of the two men at a distance that was, respectfully, beyond her sword's reach and Elazuna's bite range.

Gausón watched Kayza's theatrics with an appreciative twinkle in his eyes, while Kalos's burned into hers. Unable to wholly swallow his amusement, Gausón attempted to put a formal stamp on her entrance, "Kayza of the Lugones, lineage unknown, bloody-mindedness undeniable," he said, bowing slightly, "General, welcome to Lancia."

Unable to wholly swallow his contempt, Kalos muttered, "Welcome, General."

Marquaisa looked Gausón up and down, and returned his salutation, "Gausón of—where are you claiming to be from these days?"

"Flavionavia," Gausón chuckled.

"Very well," she agreed and pressed on. "Gausón of Flavionavia, son of—who are you now claiming for your father?"

"The purple-bearded bear," Gausón trumpeted.

"Very well, General, greetings," she returned his bow and nodded dismissively at Kalos. "The treasure of Medullus is back there." She pointed at Elazuna's posterior and changed the topic, "I need a bath."

"Agreed," Gausón wrinkled his nose, "You smell like the wolves by whom it's been said you were raised."

"I also need a drink," she added, ignoring Gausón's gibe. "I care not in what order they are provided. Kalos, see to the horses. I leave at dawn for Noega."

"And your men?" Gausón asked, his chin jutting forward.

"Camped beyond the ramparts, in full view of your sentries. That is to say, those of your sentries who are sober and awake," she watched Gausón duck her barb and Kalos's cheeks redden when it smacked him in the face. Pleased with their reactions, she walked between the two men up the path toward the massive timber dwelling.

"Thank you, General! Kalos, you have your orders and I have my instructions," Gausón called out to the night sky. "I have missed you, Kayza!"

"I have not," Kalos said as he limped away from his commanding officer and picked up the lead rope, then pointed Elazuna's nose at the stables and set off to complete his chores. "She does not respect you. She puts our cause at risk, continually. And all of the men, other than her own, are certain that she is a witch."

Ignoring Kalos' griping, Gausón nodded knowingly as a disembodied voice drifted out of the gloom toward him and his lieutenant, "*I am no witch.*"

The echoes of her denial cut through the other voices that crowded Marquaisa's dreams and she shuddered awake in her cavern under *Cap Noire (Black Point)*. Irritably, she stilled her twitching muscles and blinked away her nightmares, only to have them replaced by a whirl of half-wit plans. Erieux, the fool, was at it again.

CHAPTER 26

OMEN

JUNE 12TH

FLAT POINT

Trickles of light seeped through a curtain of slate-gray fog and slid across the British encampment on Flat Point, warning a thousand red-coated infantrymen, all of whom were half asleep on their feet, that dawn and the beginning of a long march were approaching. As they stood and stretched, several among them thickened the haze by releasing their pent-up intestinal gasses. As a result, the moisture-laden air turned into a noxious cloud of reeking toxins that triggered a chorus of bawdy curses and guttural laughter and made the soldiers more eager to be on their way.

"A moving demonstration of intestinal fortitude," Brigadier General James Wolfe, the brilliant red of his coat diluted by the fog, deadpanned for the soldiers leading the columns. He then turned to his lanky lieutenant. "Jenkins, pass the word to the men to make ready to advance . . . and no more fireworks, until I give the command."

After flashing a crisp salute, Jenkins jogged away, down the lines of men, the heels of his boots clunking in the turf. Wolfe bristled at the display of formality then bellowed, as he paced through the murk in front of his soldiers, "Where in thunder is that savage who promised, pardon the pun gentlemen, to blaze us a trail? By the infernal teachings of the divine drunkard, I can't see anything in this pea soup!"

Upon reaching the last column of soldiers, Wolfe turned on his heel, ready to carry on pacing and ranting. He was forced to check himself, however, when his about-turn brought him nose-to-nose with the painted face of his Mi'kmaq guide, who wore his red coat, which he had cut off at the waist, open over his bare chest.

"Ah, there you are, Neil. Good to see Jenkins has you kitted out presentably," Wolfe welcomed the Mi'kmaq, but checked himself when the man shook his head and angled it at the tree line north of the column.

Wolfe nodded his thanks, then ushered his guide to the leading edge of the brigade. He then squared his shoulders to the north, balled his left hand into a fist that he planted firmly on his left hip, and looked back at his men. With his right arm ramrod straight, he raised his cane to just above eye level, pointed its tip northeast, and filled his lungs with a bubble of cloying air.

The gas was meant to fuel the brigadier's explosive of *"Forward march!"* However, halfway into the first syllable of the first word of his orders, his blast was cut short by the *whirring* of a dagger that spun through the mist and split Wolfe's cane a thumb's length above his right hand. As the splintered shaft and the spinning blade pin-wheeled into the shrubbery, Wolfe blurted the expletive that was becoming fashionable among his men, *"Phoq!"*

For an instant, Wolfe blinked at the stub he still clenched in his right fist then, pinching it between his thumb and forefinger, he made a show of dropping it with utter distaste, while shooing away his subalterns and silencing their cries of alarm. To their surprise, he took several swaggering strides toward the point of origin of the attack. He then stopped, and with his hands on his hips and his eyes searching the forest shouted for his lieutenant, "Jenkins!"

From deep in the columns, the pounding beat of a single pair boots thumping on the ground rumbled around the brigade. Wolfe was on the verge of unleashing a tirade upon his unseen attacker when Jenkins came to a halt, standing at attention a respectful distance behind the brigadier. In the sudden silence, Wolfe turned and eyed his lieutenant, "Well met, Jenkins."

Reflexively, Jenkins snapped a salute that drew a shower of derision from the front ranks and a wry grin from Wolfe, who tossed the lieutenant a set of off the cuff orders, "Take three of our most despicable sorts—Dodd, Kolby, and Pilkins will do, assuming they no longer are sitting on the beach clapped in irons—and hunt down the coward skulking about our woods." Then, stepping in close to Jenkins, he lowered his voice and said, "He is an Acadian, so do not waste words on him. Wound him if necessary. Maim him if you must. But *do not* kill him. I reserve the right to take that pleasure at my leisure." Then, stepping back, he cocked an eyebrow that pinned Jenkins's right hand to his hip. He then released the lieutenant to his duty with an equally arch dismissal, "Oculus, preserve me, you're the best I've got, Jenkins. Make me look good."

With a curt nod, Jenkins was off again, loping down the lines of men. As the lieutenant disappeared, Wolfe found his Mi'kmaq guide and barked out yet more orders, "Neil, let's double-time it, shall we? The Lighthouse Point and victory beckon!"

Without waiting for acknowledgement, the general ran straight at his guide, who took to his heels with a wicked smile and a *yelp*, and with a thousand armed and agitated white-faced aliens in hot pursuit.

While Wolfe and his task force trampled the forest, Jenkins crept behind the charred husk of a lightning-shot tree that leaned perilously against one of its neighbors. Through the weave of brittle twigs that hung from the tips of a web of rotting branches, he studied his quarry. The assassin had melded with the undergrowth and was all but invisible. With enviable subtlety, he also managed to keep open his line of sight to Wolfe. But with deplorable negligence, in the span of time it took Dodd, Kolby, Pilkins, and himself to get *him* in *their* sights, he had not once paused to consider the possibility that he too was being tracked.

When Wolfe ordered a halt for water, the assassin hid. Jenkins, using rapid sign language, deployed his team in a net around him. With his eye on his target, Jenkins poked his musket barrel through the lacework of fragile tinder, zeroed in on the man's buttocks, and exhaled. As the last of his breath trickled from his nose he went still, then frowned. Locked in his stance, he slid his eyes from left-to-right, across his field of vision. The woods were as empty of movement and sound as was he.

Puzzled, but sensing no imminent threats, Jenkins relaxed the furrows in his brow and pulled the trigger of his musket. As the ball began its journey down the barrel, Jenkins's target was blocked by a pair of calloused hands descending from the branches above his position, which were followed in quick succession by Kolby's face and a gruesome explosion. Cursing, gasping, and blinking, Jenkins toppled back and scrambled on his hands, heels, and buttocks to distance himself from the ghastly maw that used to be the corporal's ugly mug.

As he crabbed-walked backwards through the detritus on the forest floor, he saw Kolby rock gently and then drop heavily out of sight. The lieutenant stopped retreating when the corporal vanished. Without letting his eyes stray from spot where the corporal had met his demise, Jenkins called out to the rest of his team, "Dodd, Pilkins, to me! Now!"

By way of reply, he heard a single set of hurried footfalls, which he assumed were those of the assassin, fading to the northeast on a course parallel to the one Wolfe and his company were pursuing. With his butt-cheeks still planted in the soil and his torso propped up on quaking arms, Jenkins drew a breath and started to repeat his command. His words stuck in his throat, however, when a black-clad wraith uncoiled and hung, bat-like, in the space through which Kolby had dropped. Kolby's blank stare was replaced by a leering, blood-red demon mask, behind which piercing ebony eyes studied him coldly.

"Demon!" the lieutenant blurted.

The crimson face cocked minutely to one side and answered him coolly, "I am no demon, sir."

The demure eloquence in the accented voice pushed deep furrows between Jenkins's eyebrows, yet he persisted, "She-devil!"

"Lieutenant Jenkins," the specter replied, calmly.

"Yes? Wait, how do you know me, fiend?"

"Kindly refrain from name-calling. It is beneath a man of your rank."

"You killed Kolby!"

"I returned him to you. You shot him."

Jenkins's sharp intake of breath and his momentary silence drew a dusky chuckle from his adversary that jarred the lieutenant from his funk, "My men will cut you down."

"Dodd and Pilkins . . . yes," the black menace said as it drew its hand slowly across the lips of its mask. It then addressed Jenkins, reprovingly, "Do not threaten. It is a declaration of weakness. You serve the Wolfe, yes?"

Jenkins flinched and then stammered, "Y—yes."

"He will die."

The omen whispered in twists and turns around Jenkins, who shivered and shot back, "Who is uttering threats now?"

"I will help him," the wraith said and went deathly still, its gaze and voice growing distant.

In the beast's moment of inattention, Jenkins reached for his musket, and summoning what remained of his strength leapt at the creature. Determined to pummel it with the butt of the weapon, he roared, "You will not harm General Wolfe!"

Jenkins slammed the brakes on his attack when the blunt end of his rifle stock was an inch from his Wolfe's forehead. His composure in tatters he raved at the general, with uncharacteristic effrontery, "Where did you come from?"

"Westerham, thank you for asking," Wolfe replied, pushing the polished wooden stock away from the tip of his nose. "There are, however, three, more important questions that require answering. First, who on earth were you quarrelling with? Second, how did one of your men finish up, over there, with a burst sausage where his head used to be? And third, where are your two other men?"

Jenkins gaped at Wolfe and sagged. He then straightened to attention and briefed the brigadier. With military precision, and without omitting a single detail, he described the pursuit and attempted apprehension of the knife-throwing assassin. When he concluded his report,

Jenkins blinked sweat from his eyes and braced himself for the rebuke his bizarre tale of ineptitude warranted. As he watched the general look him up and down, the shuffling and snickering of Wolfe's bodyguards stung his ears.

"A harrowing tale, to be sure," Wolfe began, to the further amusement of his gallery. "Invisible assassins, spectral demons, and murderous intrigue. I thought that our damnable voyage to this miserable outcrop had taken its toll on *me*. But clearly, Jenkins, it has caused you to take leave of your senses."

Wolfe then stepped in close to Jenkins and spoke to him, quietly, his voice filled with concern, "It's obvious, in your eagerness to carry out my orders, you shot your own man. A grave error, certainly, but not one to be concealed behind some fable about—"

Sodden clumping to Wolfe's right and left, like that of chopped beef bottoming out in the depths of an abattoir pit, cut short the brigadier's reprimand and stirred up a rattling commotion of profanity and clanging weaponry in Wolfe's gaggle of bodyguards. Jenkins looked warily into the overhanging branches.

Taking note of his lieutenant's reaction, Wolfe glanced at what remained of Jenkins's team members and locked eyes with him, "Dodd and Pilkins, I presume? They appear to be drained of life, most literally."

"Yes, sir," Jenkins said, dragging his eyes off the corpses.

Wolfe studied Jenkins for an instant longer, then turned to his frantic bodyguards and snapped, "You lot, return these soldiers to our camp. See to it that each of them is given a proper burial." He then invited Jenkins to accompany him as he walked back to his brigade of assault troops, "Lieutenant, walk with me. Talk to me."

CHAPTER 27

ARCHVILLAIN

JUNE 13TH

LIGHTHOUSE POINT

A brisk walk to the top of Lighthouse Point rewarded those who undertook it with a panoramic view of the ocean, as well as the town and fortress of Louisbourg and the wilderness on whose doorstep they rested. At odds with the greenery at the foot of the leeward side of the Point, a horde of red-coated Englishmen fired their muskets from behind the rocks and trees through which they were clawing toward the base of the hill. In reply, a thin line of white-coated Frenchmen returned fire from behind a rubble-stone wall at the crest of the point. Partway up the incline, cast out by the French and hunted by the British, the Acadian threw rocks and insults up and down the hill from within an outcrop.

"Shoot the assassin!" Jenkins shouted the command at the infantrymen who were starting to scrabble up the shallow slope of the escarpment. Using his saber, he directed their fire at the loose outcropping partway up the incline.

"Shoot the traitor!" Fortess called the order to the fusiliers who were hunkered down behind the rough battery that surrounded the lighthouse. Using his hands, he pointed at the same outcropping that concealed the object of Jenkins's ire.

"*Phoq le monde!*" *(Phoq the world!)* Erieux shouted from within the outcropping, to the mutual bewilderment of the redcoats and the whitecoats. He then hurled a barrage of stones at his Franco and Anglo oppressors.

Wolfe heard the muskets crackle from behind the French battery and ducked. In his crouch, he witnessed Jenkins being struck on the left cheek. On impact, the lieutenant keeled over, while the projectile that struck him ricocheted high into the air. Eyes narrowed, Wolfe scuttled to his lifeless lieutenant's side. He found Jenkins dazed and sporting a fresh wound that was swelling rapidly, but from which oozed only a trickle of blood.

In moments, Jenkins came to his senses, and seeing his commanding officer hovering over him asked, "My lord, is it mortal?"

"Hardly," Wolfe replied, squelching his lieutenant's histrionics. "You were potted by a pebble. Courtesy of our foul-mouthed assassin, I dare say. Be thankful it wasn't the knife with which he tried to skewer me. Can you stand?"

"Yes, sir," Jenkins conceded and politely declined Wolfe's offer of aid.

As Jenkins clambered to his feet, Wolfe took stock of his brigade's position and addressed the swaying officer without removing his eyes from the fusillade his soldiers unleashed at the Acadian, "Jenkins, I believe you have one properly functioning eye, yes?"

"Yes, sir," the bruised officer said, wincing as he touched his fingers to his puffy cheek.

"Splendid," the field general chirped. "Kindly draw your attention to the ragamuffin who is leeching his way up and over the rocks toward our much esteemed, but deeply detested, French adversaries. Is that the man you chased through the woods?"

"The very same," Jenkins replied with a curt nod after a moment's consideration.

"What do you suppose he is doing?" Wolfe asked his lieutenant to describe the stone pelter's actions.

"He appears to be making a frontal assault on the French position, despite the fact he is unarmed and outnumbered, sir," Jenkins reported, as objectively as he could manage after having been struck downed by the weaponless fighter.

"Precisely, and of whom does this wrong-headedness remind you?" Wolfe led Jenkins.

Lieutenant Jenkins hesitated, then answered, "With all due respect, sir, you."

"Correct yet again, Jenkins. It appears your powers of observation have not been handicapped by your impaired vision," Wolfe complimented Jenkins and clasped his hands behind his back, then began pacing back and forth across the lieutenant's slim field of vision. "And now, Jenkins, based on our non-professional diagnosis of our assassin friend's mental state, as well as the likelihood he and his French colleagues are aware of my reputation for being as wrong-headed as the assassin is pretending to be, what do you deduce are their intentions?"

The wounded lieutenant rubbed his forehead above his swelling eye and replied, "He is . . . I mean . . . *they* are baiting a trap for us. I mean, for *you*, sir."

"A truly brilliant deduction, my young brave of heart," the general praised his subaltern as he unclasped his hands and busied them with a check of his harness, while he looked eagerly up the hill at his objective. Then, wedging his tricorn hat tightly on his head, he added, "Far be it from me to undercut my reputation. Oh, by the way Jenkins, if I bite the bullet in the hairy gauntlet up yonder, you are hereby ordered to carry on and give those bastards a proper hiding."

"Yes, sir," Jenkins accepted his orders, whilst testing his own gear and bracing himself.

Wolfe gave Jenkins a snappy nod, took a deep breath, then requested a courtesy of his lieutenant, "Jenkins, we've had a hard day and night's worth of slogging getting to this point. So, do please give the order."

"*Charge!*" Jenkins bellowed, loud and clear.

Fortess heard the order shouted by the British commander and watched the rocks Erieux flung at squaddies bounce in the dirt far short of their targets. Rolling his eyes at the Acadian's feeble counterattack, he inquired of his battery gang, "Have the British found your range yet?"

"No, sir," the chorus of replies flowed down the line of men arming the battlements.

Fortess raised an eyebrow and said, "Very well, what news of the traitor, beyond his pathetic the scatterings of stones?"

A nearby rifleman answered in a dry monotone, "As we speak, he is making his way up the hill towards us. He appears to be unarmed, except for the pebbles he holds in his fists. So it is apparent, also, he wishes to be relieved of the burden of his life. Shall we grant him his wish, *mon Capitaine*?"

Fortess studied his polished boots for a moment, then straightened up and gave his squad their orders, "Make ready to kill the traitor." He then went back to pacing behind his men, while they took aim down the route Erieux would take when he stormed their battery in what would certainly be his final act of rebellion.

As anticipated, Erieux launched himself into a gallop across the plateau, straight at the lighthouse battery. Fortess's gunners tracked him as he cycled into a sprint and waited for him to come within range of their muskets. While they waited, a roar erupted from the edge of the plateau, behind the Acadian.

Fortess and his men watched the Acadian look back over his shoulder, while he continued to run at their position. Fortess followed Erieux's gaze and found himself staring into a mass of churning red tunics, screaming faces, and blazing muskets. Musket balls gouged the turf behind and in front of the Acadian like a wave of hot-lead hail that, in moments, would wash over the French position. His anxiety peaking, Fortess flicked his eyes back to the line on which the Acadian was running, only to find he had vanished.

* * *

Running hard, Erieux spotted Fortess standing behind his men and beaming back at him in smug satisfaction. Erieux returned French captain's smile, and as he raced forward shouted, *"Mange la merde, Fortess!" Eat shit, Fortess!*

A thousand voices bawling in fury drowned out his profane greeting and tore his attention away from the killers he was charging, focusing it instead on the ones who were giving him chase. Driving his legs hard, Erieux looked back at the tide of red coats then, whipping his eyes forward, smiled more broadly as Fortess's face fell.

Tingling and light-footed, Erieux ran at Fortess and curled his fingers into the claws he would use to rip into the Frenchman. After another quick check over his shoulder, he knew the British were matching his pace. He also knew they would not catch him until they all piled into the French battery up ahead.

What puzzled him was the sight of Neah, the Mi'kmaq warrior with whom he had formed a bond through years of hunting and trading, wearing a sheared off read coat and leading the posse. Stumbling slightly, he reached back to wave off his friend. But, as he did so, he lost sight of not only the Mi'kmaq, but also of the redcoats, the earth, and the sky.

Breathless, he hurtled downward, cartwheeling into blackness. As he plummeted, a ragged chain of snapping reports crackled. Sizzling musket balls ripped past him or raked at odd angles across his flailing limbs. His arms and legs scorched by hot lead, his mind stupefied by shock, Erieux opened his mouth to scream, only to have it filled with the ice-cold waters of the underground pool into which he belly flopped.

Before he could surface, swift currents dragged him down foaming rapids. Nearly senseless from being battered against smooth but unforgiving rock, he groped for handholds. When he bubbled, briefly, to the surface he coughed up icy water and gulped down wet air. Pulled under again, chilled to the bone, his strength waning, he found hope in a speck of light that appeared dead ahead and grew rapidly wider as he was swept toward it. When he finally shot into the light through a rocky aperture, he caught a glimpse of blue sky, then fell amid freezing cold sheets of water into a frothing lagoon.

* * *

Wolfe dodged boulders and soldiers in his mad dash to be the first to breach the French defenses. As he neared the front ranks, he spotted the row of enemy muskets and watched their muzzles flare. Roaring defiance, he flung his sword arm skyward and glanced side-to-side to see if the French volley claimed any of his men. Happy to see none of his men had fallen, he snapped his attention forward in time to see plumes of dirt descending around a crease in the plateau that led up to the French battery. Seconds later, Neil and a few of the men who led the charge surrounded and spent their shot into the rut. As Wolfe flashed past them, he overheard their irate cursing, first at having missed their target, then at having been left behind by their commander in the race for the French line.

Frontrunner of the pack, Wolfe had a clear view of the now-deserted lighthouse battlements. All that remained of the French were the sounds of an officer's desperate cries to retreat, uttered in panic-stricken but unmistakably courtly French, wafting over the abandoned wall.

Heady with victory, Wolfe scaled the rough-hewn stone wall, vaulted onto its topmost tier, and showered insults onto the French as they scuttled down the windward side of Lighthouse Point. Only after he exhausted his euphoria, as well as his vitriol, did he notice he was flanked by Neil and Jenkins. To his delight, his lieutenant and his guide were returning the crude gestures of those of the French troops who caught on to the meaning of Wolfe's rant.

"I shall organize the pursuit straight away, sir," Jenkins asserted, attempting to preempt Wolfe's orders, but he was brought up short by the brigadier.

His professionalism recovered, Wolfe sheathed his sword and turned to Jenkins, "To what end? To capture a few inept fusiliers? I think not. I am not in the habit of taking prisoners . . . yet another of my flaws with which the hellcats who inhabit these parts soon shall become all too familiar. I will, however, take your report, lieutenant."

"Thirteenth of June, year of our Lord 1758, by Major-General Amherst's orders . . ." Jenkins started but stopped at the sound of Wolfe's heavy sigh and the sight of Neah's puzzled expression. After an unconscious look to the skies above and a silent plea for Oculus's aide, the lieutenant shrugged and tried again, "We put our boot up their arse, sir. With just a few scratches to show for it."

"That's the spirit, Jenkins. Straight to the point. Let the poets squabble over the details." Wolfe turned his back on the Frenchmen wadding through the bogs to their skiffs, then scanned the ruins of the lighthouse battery and asked Jenkins pointedly, "What of the Acadian?"

"Disappeared, sir. Swallowed by a crevasse," Jenkins muttered angrily.

"Most interesting. Gather a retrieval party. Find a way into the caves and bring me his—" The general cut himself off and acknowledged the raised hand of his scout, "Yes, what is it, Neil?"

"Sir, our guide's name is Neah," Jenkins offered.

"Precisely. Have I said otherwise?" Wolfe replied, eyeing his lieutenant. "Now, what was it you wished to bring to my attention, Neil?"

"Name," Neah said, thinking his reply was self-explanatory.

"Why are we so suddenly preoccupied with names?" The general went hoarse as his patience reached its limits. "No, bring me his—"

"*Aluasa'sit"* *(Shadow),* Neah cut in on Wolfe's ranting without invitation, pointing in the direction of the crevasse into which Erieux vanished, "Killed my brothers." Over the ridges of his paint and grime-streaked cheekbones, Neah's eyes burned.

"Very well, Neil, the task is yours," Wolfe choked down his tirade and saluted the Mi'kmaq. He then turned to Jenkins, who once again was looking to the wide blue yonder for aid. "Well done, Jenkins, your Mi'kmaq protégé is a veritable tiger," he complimented the lieutenant then paused, letting a thought take shape before speaking it out loud, "Speaking of man-eaters, get Washington over here straight away. I've a job in mind and it will take someone with his peculiar repertoire of skills to see that it gets done properly." Then, satisfied he had adequately discharged his official duties for the day, he grinned and let his baser instincts guide him once again, "For now, let's go and fight for our share of the plunder, if there's any to be had, before the sappers get the best of it!"

Below the scuffling trio of victors, concealed in a fissure that bit into the rock foundation of the battery, Fortess smiled at what had become of Erieux. His eyes alight with newly imagined possibilities, he slid deeper into the blackened hollow and disappeared from sight.

* * *

First pushed under by sheets of water raining down on him from the waterfall, Erieux next floated to the surface in a cauldron of bubbles that churned around the spot where the falls crashed into the lagoon. Face up and splayed out, he slowly drifted to the pebbled beach that formed a crust around the edge of the pool. When he ran aground he lay still and bathed in the weak sunlight, while shallow ripples of water lapped at the studs in his pierced earlobes.

His face warmed by the sun, his body weightless in the tepid water, his consciousness partially restored, he cracked open his eyes and smiled weakly, murmuring, *"Paradis (Paradise)? Raçielle?"*

"Closer you are to Halifax," a rich voice replied, in Spanish-accented French.

Erieux opened his eyes wider, and as he did they were filled with the panels and folds that shaped a pair of weathered boots that encased a pair of crossed legs. The boots reached up the legs to just blow each of the knees, each of which was a platform for a thick forearm that widened into a knurled hand. A dagger spun in tight revolutions from one great mitt to the other. As it arced through the air, its blade reflected flashes of sunlight onto a skewed smile that split a sunbaked, sloe-eye face that studied him with amused interest.

Dazed and half submerged, Erieux blurted, *"Diabolus!"* Devil!

Tickled by the outburst, the fiend's smiled widened and he stabbed the dagger, up to its hilt, into the pebbles next to Erieux's ear and replied, "You refer to my employer, of course. You have met her, yes?"

The inquisitor paused, expectantly, and waited for Erieux's answer, then shook his head upon seeing his vacant look and concluded, "No, of course not. If you had, you would not be here."

Shrill sniggering scratched over the pebbles from further inshore. Erieux's tormentor rose and turned gracefully to face its source, with open arms and exaggerated disbelief, and inquired, "But, if that is so, then how did she know that we should meet you here?"

The sniggers dissolved into whispered prayers, to the deeper amusement of the scoundrel, who turned to Erieux and sighed, "So many questions."

Then, quickly changing tack, he apologized laughingly, "But forgotten myself, I have. Introduce myself, I shall." Posturing theatrically, he formally announced himself, "I am Mario Ortona Enriquez, grandson of Don Miguel Enriquez, the Grand Archvillain, who was among other things too numerous to mention a Royal Privateer, a Knight of the Royal Effigy of Spain, and *Capitán* of the Land and the Seas. It will be your honor to address me as *Capitán*."

The formalities having been dispensed with, the Spaniard leaned over Erieux until they were eye-to-eye, his upside down face occupying the breadth of the Acadian's field of vision, and issued his orders, "First you will tell me what is your name. Then you will speak to me of *la bello Doña Raçielle.*"

CHAPTER 28

EXPENDABLE

JUNE 20TH

THE MAISONETTE, LOUISBOURG

Commodore, Marquis Charry des Gouttes, entered the vestibule of Poisson and D'Acier's maisonette just as a carpenter was exiting at the end of his workday. After tipping his hat to the laborer in passing, he found the regent's retainer in the great room, reclining in a lounge chair and warming his feet by the woodstove. D'Acier greeted des Gouttes by pointing to an unoccupied chair and raising a half empty bottle of wine. Des Gouttes sat down, but declined the drink.

Des Gouttes watched while D'Acier poured himself another measure of wine, rekindled the fire, and ignored his presence. When at last he heard the front door click shut behind the carpenter, he began, "I wasn't aware the damages caused by the explosion at the Dauphin Gate reached so far into town. Everyone all right?"

D'Acier's eyes hardened slightly, but he did not take them off the fire as he answered his guest, "Do not patronize. On your way in, your two eyes told you the debris was outside the window, not inside, and none of the surrounding hovels sustained any damage from the blast. So, as you already know, the damages were caused by something that happened inside. Suffice it to say, that *something* involved my having to forcibly remove an uninvited guest from our humble abode." Pulling his eyes away from the flames and leveling them on des Gouttes he concluded, "At the moment, I find myself feeling similarly inclined."

"You are welcome to do your worst, *monsieur* D'Acier," des Gouttes said. He waited for signs of acceptance from D'Acier, but when none were forthcoming he dove into the business at hand. "Have you heard from Fortess?"

"Is it your habit to insult people by asking them stupid questions?" D'Acier pulled his feet away from the fire and sat forward in his chair.

"I shall take that to mean 'no,'" Des Gouttes leaned in toward D'Acier.

"Take it however you wish," D'Acier snapped at the commodore. He set aside his wine glass and scanned his surroundings for a weapon of opportunity, settling on the fireplace poker.

"Stop!" des Gouttes commanded. "I know not what has piqued your ire, but know this, I have come here to warn you."

"Did I not just tell you to *not* patronize?" D'Acier growled the reminder at the commodore.

"Very well, then allow me to *inform* you Fortess has disappeared. He was not with his men when they returned to their barracks after the British overran his command at the *Pointe du Phare*," des Gouttes relayed, looking for a reaction from D'Acier. Receiving none, he pressed on, "It has been a week since this latest debacle and there has been no sign of him. My knowledge of the man tells me he would neither sacrifice himself in the line of duty, nor would he allow himself to be taken prisoner. So, I believe him to be alive and at large."

"Well done, Fortess," D'Acier muttered, feigning admiration.

Encouraged by D'Acier's insincerity, des Gouttes continued, "I am here to inform you, also, his condition is temporary. That is to say, when last I spoke with Fortess, I promised him if he failed in his duties again, I would kill him. I intend to keep my promise."

"Suit yourself," D'Acier shrugged. "Neither I, nor the regent, will stand in your way."

"Very well," des Gouttes nodded. "If I may ask, where is the regent?"

"You may not," D'Acier snapped, returning his attention to the fire and the wine. "You may, however, walk out of here the same way you walked in. Otherwise, our carpenter will find himself redoing the job he has just completed."

THE KING'S BASTION, LOUISBOURG

Augustin de Boschenry de Drucour watched Léonarre Poisson and Lady Drucour remove themselves from his apartment in the King's Bastion. As the door closed, his view of his wife and the twilight that was fading over his Louisbourg was blocked. Alone in the spacious reception area he glanced left and right, uncertain as to where to go or what to do. He took a tentative step toward the doorway as if to follow the fashionable couple, but stopped. Head down, he took a deep breath, pivoted, and started toward his office. Not looking where he was going, he nearly knocked down Haritha.

Pulling up, abruptly, the governor squawked, "My dear, you gave me a start!" Scrambling to save face, he bobbed his head up and down and side-to-side in an attempt to see over, around, or through the silk-sheathed apparition. "Where is that boy, Opsule? He should have introduced you properly."

"Your retainer is with Clavonne, your chambermaid," Haritha replied, holding her ground and steadying him with a look.

"Who? What on earth would he be doing with her and not me?" Drucour bit his lip and bowed his head when Haritha lowered her eyes, demurely. "Oh, good gracious. Pardon my indelicacy, mademoiselle."

When Haritha accepted his apology with a bow of her own, he deflected his awkwardness smoothly, "Opsule is a fine young man with excellent prospects. However, if he wishes to avoid sabotaging his status as a gentleman, then he must learn to be more discrete."

"Other than the two principals themselves, we two are the only ones who know of the affair," Haritha assured the governor.

Drucour looked for holes in her case, and thinking he found one countered, "Ha, you found out about it!"

"No, my lord, I orchestrated it," she corrected him. "As much as I wish I could, alas, I cannot fit into my diary everyone in Louisbourg who wishes to avail themselves of my services."

Drucour raised a finger as if to protest. but taking notice of Haritha's quiet resolve let the matter drop, "Very well, my dear. What brings you my way, while you are looking so ravishing? Do I owe payment to de Sade?"

"Donatien manages his own affairs," her reply was tinged with skepticism. "I am here, my lord, because I am concerned for you."

"What? No! I mean, that is very sweet of you, my dear. But there is no cause for you to be concerned," Drucour mumbled, dodging Haritha's attempts at making eye contact.

Still and silent, she stood and watched him.

"Really, I cannot fathom your concern," Drucour insisted, coughing quietly to cover the tremor in his voice.

She waited.

"Well . . . there is this whole business of the people of Louisbourg just having survived a bitter winter, and just beginning to regain their strength, and now finding themselves surrounded by that pig Amherst's slavering brutes, whose aims are to lay siege to them and destroy their lives." The governor took a breath, then continued to spill, "The thought of negotiating with that dullard galls me to no end. So, I have chosen to compound our neighbors' misery by keeping my Louisbourg, *my Louisbourg,* out of his grasping hands for as long as I can. All for a king who cares for us not a *fig!* And, all without the help of the fleet that is at anchor in our harbor. All of the *capitaines,* with the notable exception of Jean Vauquelin, of *Arethusa,* have refused to contribute to our defense. They spite me for not letting them turn tail and run when they heard the British were coming."

Drucour had taken to pacing and gesticulating as though he were conducting an orchestral symphony, "And for standing up to the British my wife tells me I am mad, and the blood of the people of Louisbourg will be on my hands. *My hands!"*

His back turned to Haritha, Drucour's voice tailed off as he coined the name of what sounded like a new subspecies of human. "Now, she distances herself from me and humiliates me by keeping company with our visiting *Versaillien.*"

"That *is* a lot, my lord," Haritha agreed circling Drucour. When, once again, she was face-to-face with the governor, she counseled him, "However, you preoccupy yourself with problems you cannot solve: our military disadvantage and collective hardships. Difficult as you may find it, you must cast aside the worries and doubts that bind you and *act.*"

"What do you suggest?" Drucour asked, uncertainly.

"Protect your people by striking at the heart of your enemy," she proposed.

"Attack the British? You just agreed they have us at a disadvantage," the governor blurted.

"True, they are many," Haritha admitted. "However, they have but one leader. You named him," she hinted.

"Amherst, yes. What of him?" Drucour raised an eyebrow.

"He is your enemy. He would kill you without hesitation. What does that require of you?"

"That I accord him the same courtesy," Drucour snapped, without hesitation. "Which I would do, gladly, but for the fact that he cowers at sea within his fleet."

"Not so, my lord. He has been ashore for a day, or more," Haritha dropped the nugget on Drucour softly.

Drucour's eyes narrowed as he pondered, aloud, Haritha's news, "A mission requiring an expendable man or two, only, the end result of which would be the death of Amherst. If it were to succeed, then our destruction, which at the moment feels decidedly near at hand, would be forestalled, perhaps even postponed entirely."

"Whether you succeed or fail in the attempt, you will establish yourself as your people's champion, and as far as the British are concerned a force to be reckoned with," Haritha pointed out. Then she looked up at the governor and asked, "Feeling better?"

"Yes, the plan is inspired. Come to think of it, I have in mind the perfect man for the mission. The marquis, des Gouttes, will no doubt want to add a second man as a failsafe. But I will leave that to him," he decided then, in afterthought, added, "What think you of the governess? She has changed of late, has she not?"

"Indeed, but she is no longer your concern. If it becomes necessary, then I will deal with her," Haritha assured him.

"Please, be kind. I hardly know her these days. But, still, I want no harm to come to her," Drucour insisted.

"Have no fear, she will not be harmed," Haritha reassured him. "You and I know that she has the tastes of a sophisticate."

"Yes, and they appear to be taking their toll on poor Poisson," Drucour laughed.

"That is true, and just as she has made the regent a slave to her appetites, I will use her cravings against her," Haritha smiled.

"Perfect! May I watch?" Drucour asked, dropping his voice conspiratorially.

"Certainly, if you think you might find amusement in it." Then, completing her circuit of the governor, she extended him an invitation, "In the meantime, come and show me what you would like me to do with her."

Drucour smiled, and after a last look turned his back on the doorway to his apartments and all outside it.

The Wharf, Louisbourg

Léonarre Poisson made a tight left turn at the *Ordonnateur's* residence. With Lady Drucour on his arm, he made for *Bienfaisant*, which was moored to the quay, and *Prudent*, which had been run aground in the shallows beside *Bienfaisant*. As they passed through the columns of light that shone through the windows of the residence, the lady freed her arm and slapped Poisson playfully on his buttocks, just to see him wince.

"Time for another inspection of your battleship, *monsieur le Conseiller?*" her entendre was thinly veiled.

"Indeed, it is," he agreed with a low chuckle. "However, in addition, this evening I shall demonstrate for my lady the true meaning of being run aground."

"I'm guessing that a swollen payload might be at the root of the condition," she linked elbows with Poisson again as she greeted passers-by. "Will *Bienfaisant's* gunners ever recover?" She laughed, quietly, thinking of the oafs signing themselves and whispering useless prayers against evil portents.

"Given our current rate, it is my earnest belief that they have a better chance of surviving our inspections you than do I," Poisson deadpanned. "However, I intend to do my best to prove myself wrong." He freed his arm and slapped Lady Drucour playfully on her buttocks just to hear her squeak.

Shrouded in her cloak and the shadows cast from the *Fredéric* gate, Marquaisa watched the couple stroll the full length of the quay, then disappear behind the bulk of the docked man o' war. It had been days since her clash with Poisson's retainer, and since she'd made her presence known the regent had been cautious while conducting his affairs; he now ended all of his engagements before nightfall, was accompanied at all times by his armed retainer, and had posted a round-the-clock watch over his maisonette. However, it appeared as though her patience, rather than her proclivity for smashing any and all barriers that stood between her and what she wanted, had at last persuaded him to drop his guard.

Fixing her attention on the point where Poisson departed from the quay, she glided silently through the darkness. Upon reaching her objective, she picked up Lady Drucour's scent and followed it into the shadows cast from the massive ship. As she rounded its hull, she tracked the bouquet away from the wharf and down to the beach. When she stepped into the sand, loose grains swirled around her bare ankles, stirred up by the breezes that swept away the fragrant trail of her prey. Intent on reacquiring the scent, but distracted by the looming presence of a second beached ship, she failed to hear the heavy oak plank as it swung against the wind and exploded against the back of her skull.

"If only D'Acier could see me now," Poisson quipped as he stood over his downed adversary, "He might get over sulking about missing out on tonight's little adventure long enough to admit that, with a little planning, I can be as efficient a killing machine as is he. Although, I'll admit, he'd likely have chosen a better weapon. My timber shattered like glass when it struck her head."

"Shattered or not, it did its job," Lady Drucour observed as she checked Marquaisa for signs of life. "Neither a pulse, nor a breath. She is as dead as she possibly can be."

"Good riddance, I say," Poisson nodded with satisfaction. "Bind her tightly from head to toe. But leave a free strand at her ankles. We shall use it for the loops we will make around the boulder that will be her swimming mate. I shall ready the skiff."

Poisson disappeared into *Bienfaisant's* shadow and the governess roughly rolled Marquaisa onto her back. As she did she flipped open the cloak in which Marquaisa was wrapped and the governess's eyes widened at the sight of the hardened physique she exposed, "Your assassin was naked and unarmed. Perhaps she intended to sex you to death."

"I can think of no better way to meet my demise," Poisson declared as he splashed to shore, towing the small craft.

Humming, knowingly, at Poisson's admission, Lady Drucour snatched from the sand a pointed shard of oak from the plank that had laid out Marquaisa and jabbed it between the ribs over the assassin's heart, then whispered to her, "Something to discourage you if you feel inclined to seek revenge upon us any time soon."

Her notice delivered, the governess rewrapped Marquaisa in her cloak, wound a sturdy rope in tight coils around her shoulders, chest, arms, waist, and wrists, binding them behind her back. With a second line, she secured Marquaisa's legs from thigh to ankle, leaving a length for her weighty, soon-to-be companion. When she finished, she inspected her work, looking for any weak spots, and finding none turned away from Marquaisa to check on Poisson, only to find him standing directly behind her, watching her intently.

"You *are* full of surprises," he congratulated her.

"Thank you, but this is mere grunt-work. It is *much* more exciting to work on live subjects," she looked him up-and-down appraisingly and giggled when he swallowed hard.

Clearing his throat, Poisson grabbed the loose rope at Marquaisa's ankles, dragged her through the surf to the side of the skiff, and heaved her on board. He then steadied the light craft as the governess boarded and accepted the offer of her strong hand as he hopped in. Pulling smoothly on the oars, he rowed the skiff quietly into the deep, still waters of the harbor, toward the Barrachois Lagoon, while the lady attached the boulder to their dupe. In silence, they skimmed across the waters to the point where they were darkest, where *l'Arethusa* lay at anchor. In the blackness that ringed the ship they waited until they no longer heard the scuffing of the watchman's boots as he patrolled her upper deck. They then slid Marquaisa overboard, watched her vanish into the depths, and turned back for shore.

Pleased with the execution of their plan, Lady Drucour seated herself on her bench at the prow of the skiff behind Poisson and watched him strain against the oars until they neared the shoreline. Tapping her foot impatiently, the governess quipped, "I believe you promised me a lesson. Something about being run aground?"

"I was wondering for how long you might be able to hold out, sitting back there in your agitated state, watching me heaving on these infernal paddles," Poisson puffed. "Very well, come here, and be sure to not tip us over."

Easing herself past Poisson, the governess seated herself on the bench at the stern of the skiff, facing the laboring regent, who immediately launched into his tutorial. "If you would kindly open the hold," he said, nodding at his breeches, "you will find, with a little jimmying, the payload will be ready to be winched into position."

Poisson paused in his labors until his breeches hit the deck of the skiff and the governess was installed in his lap. When he pulled on the oars the governess took a sharp breath and he continued his narrative, "Now, if you would kindly place your hands over mine," he nodded at the grips he had on the oars, "and when I pull on these things, you push."

Poisson started rowing steadily toward the shoreline. while

humming an old *chant du bord (on board song)*. The governess quaked as she pushed, so locked her knees over the edge of the bench, beside Poisson's hips, to stop him from slipping away. With each stroke, the skiff sped closer to shore and the cadence of their sculling picked up. When the boat finally hit the sand and ground to a halt, Poisson pulled one last time while the governess let go in a torrent and yelled, full throat, at the sky.

Gradually, her echoes washed away on the tide of their ragged breathing and hoarse laughter. Still yearning, the governess released Poisson's hands, only to reach around his back to pull his hips tight to hers. As she breathed, Poisson sat back and stretched his arms wide across the bench. Looking to the sky, he drank her in and rasped, "That, *madame*, is what it truly means to be run aground."

BARRACHOIS LAGOON

"What was that noise?" Captain Mario Ortona Enriquez, grandson of the Grand Archvillain, asked, turning to Erieux for the answer.

For a week, Enriquez, accompanied by his three lieutenants and Erieux, had stalked the countryside surrounding the port of Louisbourg, dodging patrolling British infantrymen, and studying the French fleet. In that time, he had come to know the calls of all manner of local wildlife. However, the howl that reached out to him from the distant town, as he crouched on the knoll overlooking the mouth of the Barrachois Lagoon, was new to him, and from the looks in their widened eyes, Vishnu, Ganesh, and Yuval.

Erieux let the vestiges of the piercing wail drift overhead then, propping himself on his elbows, looked at Enriquez and smiled for the first time since he met the pirate. "That, *Capitán*, was an Acadian woman," he said.

"Doing what? Cannibalizing her young?" Enriquez inquired, amazed.

"Quite the opposite," Erieux chuckled. "That would be the sound of her taking pleasure from the rigors of trying to create more of them."

Enriquez looked at Erieux for signs of deceit, and finding none insisted, "I command you to introduce me to such a woman *this instant*."

"Gladly," Erieux consented, clearly unconvinced Enriquez was up to the challenge. "But, do we not have other business to attend to?"

"What? Oh, yes," Enriquez dragged his attention back to the ship that was lying at anchor just off the lagoon, "We have found what we have been looking for. Tell me, Rio, when you look at that ship, what do you see?"

Erieux looked at the blacked-out hulk and shrugged, "A waste of good oak."

"Again, your worldliness impresses," Enriquez shook his head and continued with his attempt to enlighten the Acadian. "Look at how she rides lower in the water than all of the other vessels we have studied. What does that tell you?"

"She is sinking," Erieux stated the obvious, to dismay of Enriquez's three lieutenants.

Undaunted, Enriquez persisted, "Imagine you are a seafaring, soldier of fortune—"

"A pirate, like you?" Erieux jabbed.

"—and you *happen* upon a ship that is in good repair, like that one, but it is *weighed down*. Other than your fear for the welfare of its crew, what would be your first thought?"

"Too . . . much . . . cargo?" Erieux guessed.

"Precisely, and being the pirate you are, what type of cargo do you think would weigh so heavily on such sturdy a ship?" Enriquez held his breath.

"Gold?" Erieux peeked at Vishnu, Ganesh, and Yuval, all of whom clapped quietly for him.

"Yes!" Enriquez cheered and slapped Erieux on the shoulder. "Let us now go and see if we are deceived." Turning to his lieutenants, he rattled off his orders, "Vishnu, Ganesh, cover the flanks. Yuval, take up the rear. Kill anything that looks or smells odd, except for Rio." He then trotted off down the shallow slope of the dune, peeling off his clothes as he went.

Erieux stood and watched the Spaniard for a moment, then turned to look at how the other crew were positioning themselves, only to find that they had faded out of sight. Awkward and exposed, he set out in the pirate's wake, glancing left and right as he pulled himself out of his clothes. In a few strides he was fully naked, but far away from the water. So he hurried to its edge and joined Enriquez, who had taken a knee in the ebb and flow and was eyeing the ship.

"Have a care, Rio," the buccaneer warned his apprentice. "She looks deserted. But, if it is gold she carries, a watch there will be. Kill anything on board that lives, except for me, of course." Without another word he waded into the chill surf, with Erieux at his side, until they were forced to swim. As they stroked toward the ship, they kept their heads above water and their eyes on her main deck.

Calm waters and a friendly undercurrent hastened their approach to the ship. Even so, by the time they reached its hull their teeth were chattering and their lips were bluing. Swimming in the blackness that ringed the ship, they spluttered and searched for handholds they could use to pull themselves out of the brine. Finally, on the seaward facing side of the ship, Enriquez found a set of scars in the timbers and hauled himself up the gently rocking wall. Fully removed from water, he looked back for Erieux. But, rather than follow his lead, Erieux had gone completely still and was on the verge of sinking.

"Rio!" Enriquez called to the Acadian, whose eyes had gone as dark as the waters in which he was, for the moment, suspended. When the Acadian failed to answer him, the pirate tagged him with yet another new moniker, hissing at Erieux, *"Stupido!"* His fledgling free-booter still deaf to his summons, Enriquez eased himself down the wall of the ship and kicked water at the neophyte, "Follow me now, Rio, or die!"

"Someone is here," Erieux mumbled, trying to see into the depths of the lagoon.

Enriquez shot a glance up to the ship's rail and barked at Erieux, "Yes, all the more reason for us to be up and over the rail, quickly, so that we can fight the watchman properly. Move yourself!"

Shaken from his reverie by the gruff command, Erieux dragged himself up the wall and clambered over the railing. Enriquez steadied him when his wet feet slipped on the deck, then pulled Erieux into a low crouch and snuck toward the ship's stern. When they reached the cabins below the bridge, the Spaniard found the companionway easily and went below deck, quickly, with Erieux on his heels.

Moving instinctively, Enriquez whisked past the officer's quarters and through the gunnery to the foremost companionway, whose steps reached down into the ship's holds. Slowing to a stop at the top of the stairway, he held his breath and signaled Erieux to do the same. For a full minute they stood still and silent then, satisfied they hadn't attracted unwanted attention, they edged down the blackened stairwell.

When they hit the landing, Enriquez bid Erieux stand watch while he slipped deeper into the hold and started rummaging around in the dark. Erieux had taken to looking back and forth, from the gray-black opening at the top of the stairs to the pitch black of the hold, when a flame in a boxed lantern flickered, then began to burn evenly. Hastily, Enriquez hoisted the lantern to shoulder height, beckoned at Erieux to follow, and set off into the maze of stacked provisions. Carefully, the Spaniard inspected the markings that were scrawled on the containers, moving from one pile to the next, until he found one whose canvas wrappings were stamped with a seal that included the likeness of a three-headed dog. Exhaling, audibly, the pirate captain ran his hand gently over the tarpaulin and then turned away from it abruptly and rushed past Erieux, back through the maze.

Erieux hustled after Enriquez so as to not lose himself in the maze, and when he drew level with the him at the foot of the companionway, he found the pirate sweating, despite the chill. Without a word, Enriquez doused the flame and put the lantern down quietly on the landing. Staying silent, he then led the way up the companionway, through the gunnery, and up through the doorway that opened onto the main deck. After cracking the door open and taking a quick peek past it, he turned and grinned at Erieux. Then, without warning, Enriquez threw the door open, sprinted at the ship's landward facing rail, dove over it, and arced gracefully into the water.

Awkward and exposed yet again, and recalling how a similar plunge had ended with his introduction to the pirate captain, the

Acadian grinned, as had the Spaniard, and took off after him. As he flew over the rail, Erieux expected a voice to crackle in the back of his mind, mocking him for being a fool. Instead, as he knifed through the air, he heard only the curses of the watchman and, when he resurfaced, Enriquez laughing at him and daring him to try to keep up.

* * *

Above a knoll and beyond the hearing range of the three scouts, Fortess peered through his spyglass and watched Erieux and his associate return to shore empty-handed. Grunting in amusement at the failure of their mission, he slid backwards, on his stomach, down and away from his lookout in the dunes, then rolled over and sat up, cross-legged. It had been a week since he had let the British take Lighthouse Point and then disappeared. By now, des Gouttes would have concluded his least favorite captain was lost, either killed or captured. Knowing what des Gouttes thought of him, Fortess was certain the commodore would go out of his way to do nothing whatsoever to confirm his suspicions.

Fortess chuckled at the thought of being made a ghost by the marquis's foolish assumptions and willful negligence. Determined to use it to his advantage he capered away, kicking at the sand and swatting at the long grass, toward the town and a happy reunion with Poisson and D'Acier, during which he would take his next steps toward securing his personal fortune. Killing the Acadian would have to wait.

CHAPTER 29

SKULLDUGGERY

JUNE 21ST

LIGHTHOUSE POINT

After they routed the French at Lighthouse Point the British busied themselves with building a ring of gun emplacements around the harbor for the express purpose of blowing Louisbourg to bits. For his part, in the days that followed his victory at the point, Wolfe had his men transform its dilapidated fortifications into a functioning military installation, complete with a new road that connected the point with the harbor and that eased the process of bringing in the tools he would use to contribute to the destruction of the town.

The order and discipline with which Wolfe infused his battery stood in stark contrast to the chaos that reigned over his makeshift office, which lay in the ruins of the lighthouse that gave the point its name. In the midst of broken crates, tipped stools, and crumpled papers he slouched behind a set of loose planks that were stretched between a pair of shaky, A-frame legs to form a facsimile of a work bench. With a grunt, he sat up and reached into the papers that were strewn across the bench and rummaged through them until he found the to-do list he'd created for himself. Slouching back on his stool, he ran his eyes down the items it contained and groused about not being able to include a check mark next to the one entitled, 'Capture that dastardly Acadian assassin.'

With a snort, Wolfe crumpled the list and tossed it over his shoulder. As is rolled to a stop at the foot of a pile, Neah walked into the office, unannounced, wearing his hacked off red coat, layers of dirt on his body, and a weary expression on his face. Brightening at the prospect of good news, Wolfe spun a biscuit through the air at the Mi'kmaq's head and asked, "Have you found him?"

Neah snatched the stale rusk before it gashed his prominent forehead and whirred it back at Wolfe, who barked out a laugh and blocked it with the leather bindings of the journal into which he was scrawling his musings. The brittle cookie exploded in a starburst over the general and, as the kiln-baked shrapnel ricocheted off his rickety table, he peeked over his diary, ready to deflect any following barrage. When none arrived, he breathed a contented chuckle, tossed his leather-bound shield onto the confusion of papers on his bench, and settled back on his stool in anticipation of his sparring partner's report.

"Found him, yes. Killed him, no. *Kajuewj (Demons)* with him," Neah said, grinding the Mi'kmaq word through his teeth as he stalked across Wolfe's hovel and sat on a stool opposite the general. He then proceeded to start flicking random crumbs off the tabletop at the Englishman.

Wolfe watched a few of the missiles bounce off his jerkin, then pointed at his diary, "I will be sure to add *kajuewj* to my rapidly growing list of colorful, local profanities."

Neah looked at Wolfe blankly, then clarified, "*Aluasa'sit* with a *Spanush.*" Spanish.

"Splendid," Wolfe nodded. "You're certain they were Spanish? How can you be sure?"

"Smell," the hunter replied, simply.

"I wonder what those hellions are up to," he muttered to himself, then shook himself from his reverie. "So, murderer to your kin, assassin to me, and now traitor to his people. Our Canadian is building an impressive set of credentials, is he not?"

299

"Acadian," Neah correct the general.

"Precisely," Wolfe agreed. He then assured the Mi'kmaq, "Not to worry, Neil, there will be a reckoning. In the meantime, while you've been out sightseeing, Jenkins and I have been slaving away."

At that moment, Jenkins poked his head into the doorway, ducked, and scanned the air for projectiles. Satisfied no flying objects were soaring his way, he stood to his full height and stepped into the shelter.

Wolfe watched his subaltern materialize and sat up, wariness and wonder coloring his expression, "Jenkins! Do you have the second sight? How did you know I wanted to speak with you? What . . . whatever are you looking at?"

"Your jerkin, sir," the lieutenant replied, grinning.

"What of it?" the general asked, slightly confused and glancing down his tunic. "Ah, yes, friend Neil here has very kindly been bombarding me with breadcrumbs." He scrubbed his hands quickly over the supple leather of the sleeveless jacket.

"It's not that, sir," Jenkins smirked.

"Well, for pity's sake, what is it?" Wolfe demanded, his eyes boring into Jenkins.

"It's rather seventeenth century, don't you think?" Jenkins suggested, with a snicker.

Wolfe blinked and shot back, "I hadn't any notion you'd such finely honed fashion sensibilities, Jenkins. Now that I do, I'll make it a point to consult you on my seasonal wardrobe, as well as on my choice of attire prior to my appearances at court. In the meantime, I hope you'll forgive my lack of style and allow us all to get on with this next bit of business."

"It will be my pleasure to serve the general in whatever way he sees fit, and yes, let's move along, shall we," the lieutenant replied, all Wolfe-like.

Wolfe clenched his jaw, swallowed hard, and looked his next-in-command up and down, "Well met, Jenkins, you idiot."

"Id-eee-ut," (Idiot) Neah deadpanned for Jenkins, who was searching for something to sit on to which he would not stick.

"Quite," Wolfe agreed with Neah, then stood and bowed from the waist at the Mi'kmaq. "As I was about to say, before the regimental clothes horse landed in our laps, our newly acquired battery has been a hive of activity in the week since we last had the pleasure of your company, Neil. After chasing out the French, we secured the perimeter of our position and, aided by our odd friend Washington, built the roadway up which our cannon will be delivered." He abruptly halted his narrative and peered down at Neah, "By the way, how is it you were able to pass through my sentries and invade my quarters without their raising an alarm, or my being warned in advance?"

The Mi'kmaq shrugged.

Wolfe awaited a further, more detailed explanation. When none was offered, he turned his attention to his deputy, "Right, Jenkins, make a note of it. Neil is to provide skulking instructions to those worthless sappers of yours." The general then continued reporting to the Mi'kmaq, "Amherst, our chief, finally sent us our guns which, I am expecting Jenkins is about to report, we have finished installing in their emplacements."

"Quite so, sir," Jenkins reported, happily.

"Thank you, Jenkins. We shall commence our bombardment straightaway. Our targets are the battery on the island to our west, the town, and the fortress. Everything but the boats. Neither theirs, nor ours, tempting as it might be to pot a few of the latter," Wolfe grinned at Jenkins. He then offered Neah a theory, "I suspect it is those very boats, or more precisely their cargo, that have drawn the Spanish into the fray and enticed your *Aluasa'sit* to take up their cause. But, fear not, neither the Spanish, nor their newest recruit will see profit in this. Like the French, they will know naught but wrack and ruin."

Jenkins waited a moment before intruding upon the general's gravitas, then piped up, "There is one more thing, sir."

Wolfe shook himself and nodded at Jenkins, "Very well. What is it?"

"It's Washington, sir," the lieutenant started. "He's been riding his Americans hard and they're saying that when the musket balls start flying an errant one or two of theirs might 'accidentally' find the back of his skull. Could just be wild talk, sir, but I suggest we defuse the situation by rewarding the colonel for his hard work by posting him to a place that takes him out of their musket range."

Wolfe cocked an eyebrow and said, "Good for you for keeping your finger on the pulse of the battalion, Jenkins." He thought for a moment and then decided, "Let us add some breadth to our colonel's qualifications. Yes, we shall put him to sea. Give him to George Balfour, on *HMS Aetna*, if for no other reason than they've a first name in common. Have Balfour assign him to salvage duty. That will keep him out of harm's way and Balfour's crew might find it entertaining to watch the landlubber find his sea legs."

Wolfe then scoured the morass that was his writing table, and having found the letter for which he was searching, waved the tattered sheet of paper as if it were a flag, "I've been summoned by Amherst. In my absence, Jenkins, you will take command of the battery. See to it Neil properly drills the men in skullduggery and get our twenty-four pounders humming. Keep them blazing away until someone like me tells you to stop."

His orders made clear, Wolfe stepped back half a step from his table, tossed a ragged salute at his lieutenant and their guide, and released them to their duties, "Oculus preserve me. You two are the best I've got. Make me look good."

CHAPTER 30

UNDERBELLIES

JULY 9TH

THE MOOR OF GABANES

June twenty-first, the first day of summer, was the longest day in the year 1758. The citizens of Louisbourg celebrated the solstice by seeking shelter, not from the rays of the sun, but from the ravages of siege warfare. Beginning that day, and for weeks to come, no matter whether the summer sky beamed with sunshine or poured down rain, the forecast for Louisbourg always was the same; days filled with the thunder of cannons, lightning of explosions, and hailstorms of lead. The nights were absent of gunfire, but were lit by a halo of campfires that burned in the surrounding countryside, reminding all in Louisbourg of what would follow come sunrise.

The French and British leaders attempted to gloss over the carnage with a pasty civility whose glue was a periodic exchange of gifts. Drucour sent Amherst rancid butter that was intended to poison anyone who tasted it. Amherst reciprocated with rotten fruit. No sooner were the gifts received, however, than pretenses were kicked aside and the savagery was renewed.

The ugliness and barbarism in which they were embroiled was bludgeoned into the people of Louisbourg in the first week of July, when their hospital, patients included, was obliterated by the British shelling. Drucour's objections over the incident elicited little more than a shrug from Amherst, provoking the governor, at last, to hit back.

It was no secret the British advanced on Louisbourg by moving their earthworks and artillery on the Moor of Gabanes a few feet to the east each night. Knowing this, and still in a rage a few nights after the atrocity at the hospital, Drucour sent seven hundred of his French regulars over Louisbourg's ramparts, onto the moor, and into the British front lines.

In the wee hours of the morning, while they had their heads down and their backs into driving forward their creeping assault, the British squaddies were caught off guard by the surprise attack of the French. Battle hardened and prideful, the squaddies rallied quickly and the hand-to-hand fighting that followed was vicious, bloody, and exhausting. When both sides had their fill, the French pulled back from the moor and behind their walls with a score of British prisoners in tow.

As false dawn edged over the moor, both sides could clearly see the raid by the French had cost the British little more than the few men taken captive. Wounds would heal, broken earthworks would be rebuilt, and artillery would be repositioned. What went unseen by both sides, however, were the two black-clad figures who, one-by-one, slipped away from the French ranks. Once detached, they each wove through their own separate way through the battle and then stole away west, over the moor, and into the heart of the British encampment.

CHAPTER 31

RAJANI

JULY 12TH

GABARUS POINT

Tucked behind the islands that acted as a breakwater for Gabarus Point, *Rajani*, the Mughal warship that was the apple of Enriquez's weather eye, rode the shallow swells, hidden from the British fleet that crowded Gabarus Bay to the north. His back turned to the fleet, Erieux leaned against *Rajani's* rail and studied his likeness as it had been sketched onto the poster Vishnu tore from the trunk of a tree at the southernmost tip of the British encampment.

For three days, the cannon fire of the British had been furious and relentless. On the fourth day, Enriquez sent Vishnu, Ganesh, and Yuval on a mission to discover the reasons behind the escalation in hostilities. At the end of the day, when the trio dragged themselves back to *Rajani*, they reported they'd been allowed to drift into the British camp unchallenged, the British rank and file assuming they were brokers of trade who worked for the English East India Company.

Difficult as the idea had been to swallow, Vishnu, Ganesh, and Yuval took the insult in stride and added intrigue to it by suggesting their affiliation with the company allowed them to traffic in all manner of contraband, like the vials of liquid opium they happened to have in their pockets and which they handed out to the squaddies for sampling. The lie and its associated freebies earned Vishnu, Ganesh, and Yuval access to every available measure of hospitality and they spent the balance of the day touring the camp, talking, and boozing with the British. As the day wound down and the stories started to repeat over one another the three pirates slipped out of the British camp burdened with much information, as well as an interesting portrait of their newest shipmate.

Not yet completely attuned to their language, Erieux pieced together from their report the British were punishing the French for an attack a few days earlier, while at the same time tightening the noose around Louisbourg. Enriquez soaked in the tale, but was particularly delighted with the poster depicting a fearsome-looking Erieux with the word *"SPY"* scrawled above his head and the word *"KILL"* under-scoring his chin. Less amused than Enriquez, Erieux handed the poster back to Vishnu, who immediately nailed it to the mizzen, and along with Ganesh and Yuval began using it as the target in a knife-throwing game.

Erieux watched as his face was punctured by the points of an assortment of blades, until Enriquez joined him at the ship's rail and chuckled, "You are growing on them. Were you not, it would be you nailed to the mast, not your portrait."

"Heartwarming," Erieux grumbled as the threesome shredded his likeness. "Do I want to know how you came to be their *capitán?*"

"Most definitely," Enriquez nodded with each word. "They are Maratha warriors from Bombay, which is a place, I am certain, that you have never heard of. But, picture it this way. If we are this close to Louisbourg—" he held up his right hand with his thumb and forefinger pressed together, "—then we are this far distant from Bombay and the Arabian Sea that feeds it." He spread his arms as wide as he could. "I fished those three out of that same sea. Their *capitán* had thrown them overboard for failing to capture a prize from an East India Company merchant ship, and the man-eaters of the deep had turned up their noses at them for being too bony."

"Noble of you," Erieux said, arching an eyebrow. "And you gained?"

"As you said, a warmed heart," the pirate's sincerity splattered all over the deck. "As well as their knowledge of *Rajani* and her *capitán*. His name was Akella. A pirate of the Corsair persuasion. Utterly merciless. If you think me harsh in my judgment of the man, then you may ask his three castaways, over there."

"Far be it from me to doubt you."

Erieux's derisive tone made the pirate laugh, "Good!"

He looked at Vishnu, Ganesh, and Yuval and continued his story, "Those three led us to Akella's favorite hideaway; a quiet cove carved into the landward side of the Elephant Island, which is in Bombay Harbor, just east of Bombay itself. As quick as we could, we steered *Letizia*, my ship at the time, to the northern tip of the island and anchored her off the point out of sight. I set a watch over the cove, and two days later, when they brought word they'd sighted *Rajani,* we made our next move." Eager for audience participation he asked Erieux, "What do you think that was?"

"You weighed anchor and got out of there as fast as you could," Erieux deliberately selected the most incorrect answer to Enriquez's question.

"A *lesser* man would have," Enriquez blustered. "But no, the grandson of the Grand Archvillain, his best fighting men, and his three new friends, braved the jungle, which is like your forest but hotter, wetter, and infinitely more dangerous, and *trapped* his prey. My three friends informed me that Akella liked to set some of his men ashore to gather water and fruit, and sure enough, he did. So, like the man-eating jungle cats, we *pounced* on them when they crossed from the beach into our domain, silencing all of them and killing the ones who needed it . . . but eating none."

"What fascination does cannibalism hold for you?" Erieux frowned, recalling Enriquez's first impression of the sexual expressiveness of Acadian women.

"None, I assure you," the pirate hurried on. "Next, we dressed in the pajamas we took from Akella's men, which were much like the ones the men and I are wearing today, and after a little while rowed out to *Rajani*. Yuval, Vishnu, and Ganesh talked us on board, and then surprised their old shipmates with their reappearance. Some of them collapsed with fright, taking the three of them for ghosts, I presume. Some others jumped overboard in a panic at the sight of a band of macho Spaniards. A few others drew their swords. The ones who stood and fought were given honorable deaths, except for Akella. He was given, in partial payment of their share of the booty, to the three men whom he'd punished for his own failures."

"So, you were left with two ships and two crews," Erieux itemized Enriquez and Company's bottom line for the takeover.

"Correct, which was one too many of each," the pirate assured his audience. "So, I gave *Letizia* to Fonterro, my second-in-command, as part of *his* share of the prize, and let the crew decide who they wanted to follow for their *capitán*. To a man they chose Fonterro, which was not surprising; the first mate is always the most popular man on the ship. So I cut them loose, and with my three new friends' help, gathered what remained of *Rajani's* crew and got underway."

"A happy ending?" Erieux asked the question Enriquez was hoping to hear.

"Most definitely not," Enriquez shook his head with each word. "No sooner were we underway than Fonterro attacked us. Apparently, he and the crew had been plotting against me for some time. Apparently, also, it was not enough that I gave them *Letizia* and their freedom. No, they were greedy for more, and in *Rajani* they saw a plump prize for the taking, as well as a *capitán* ripe for overthrow."

"Shocking," Erieux reacted to the twist in the tale, not surprised in the least,

"Not at all," Enriquez shook his head again. "I would have done the same thing . . . and I would have been disappointed had Fonterro done anything less. What they failed to consider, however, was the quality of *Rajani* and her crew. She'd been crafted in Bombay's shipyard from the hardest teak, and her crew were yet harder still."

Enriquez grew more animated, tracing the ships' movements in the air with his hands. "Fonterro turned on me, sharply, and fired *Letizia's* sixteen pounders. But they bounced off *Rajani's* flanks with no harm done. So, we hit back at him with a broadside. We sheered *Letizia's* masts and holed her at the waterline. She nosed down and went under in a blink, with all her hands."

Erieux said nothing, waiting while Enriquez drifted with his memories. Then, clearing his throat, the captain wrapped up his story, "Since then, *Rajani* has made her *capitán* and crew rich and famous, or infamous depending on your allegiance."

"Which does your current employer consider you?" Erieux asked, a hint of real interest in his voice.

"Neither," the Spaniard said abruptly. "She is not bound by allegiance."

"The men fear her. I see you tormenting them about it from time-to-time," Erieux kidded Enriquez.

"No, Rio, they do not fear her," the Spaniard muttered. "Unlike the sailors of the Old World, they do not think she brings bad luck on board. They believe she is a guardian. They *worship* her."

"Is that why we have been waiting for so long to hear from her?" Erieux asked as if he were beginning to understand the *capitán* and his crew.

"That, and I do not get paid until the job is done," Enriquez stated what he thought was the obvious.

"So, we wait," Erieux reverted to grumbling.

"So, we wait," Enriquez decreed. Then, while stretching his arms overhead, tossed Erieux a piece of advice, "While we wait, continue endearing yourself to the men. If you do, then you will know that if they kill you, then it is because it is the best thing for you. You must trust them in this."

The booming of more volleys from the British gun emplacements ringing the harbor, town, and fortress smothered Erieux's declaration that he would never rest his fate in anyone's hands other than his own.

CHAPTER 32

IMPERATOR NUMERUS UNUS

JULY 12TH

BARRACHOIS LAGOON

Roaring cannonades shook the air over Louisbourg's harbor and pounded the swells that rolled along *l'Arethusa's* hull. Dampened slightly by the water's surface, the booming reverberated into the depths of Barrachois Lagoon and buffeted Marquaisa, making her sway in the currents at the end of the tether that held her to a weed-swathed boulder.

Around her, two clouds of luminous shards swam through the currents and swirled around her. Within the clouds a pair of voices clicked at one another in a staccato version of the local Mi'kmaq tongue. Hovering close enough to Marquaisa that its chattering plumbed the depths of her comatose mind, one of the clouds trilled, "You see, Shomanahi, she's dead. I knew it! I knew it!"

The proclamation burrowed into her repository of memories and wrapped itself around a claim, equivalent in pomposity and inaccuracy, made centuries earlier in a place far different from the cloud-cuckoo-land occupied by the splintered rock spirit.

"I knew it! Did I not say she had a pet?" Augustus Caesar, Emperor

310

of Rome, chirped as thunder rolled away from the town of Noega, over the *Cantabrorum (the Bay of Biscay)* and off the northern coast of Hispania.

His sharp voice sliced through the splashing of rainwater gushing off the roof of the villa owned by Kayza of the Lugones, General in the army of the rebel Gausón. Fully wakened by his caustic tone of voice, tingling with rage, and moving like quicksilver, she slid over Ryhu's prone, naked body. In a fluid movement, she snatched her knife from the belt that was tangled amongst her clothes and snapped it at the figures who crowded the entrance to her bedchamber.

Caesar stood aside and let the blade whirl past his throat to stab through the jugular of the centurion guarding his back. As the soldier crumpled, the emperor looked at the guard who was next in line behind the corpse and warned him, "Did I not say, also, she is as deadly as a viper and so be on your guard?"

The soldier and the two who flanked him thumped their fists against their cuirasses. After a curt nod at the castigated men, Caesar returned his attention to naked woman, "Kayza of the Lugones, *General*, you were expecting me."

"Your vanity surpasses your intelligence, as well as your other, lesser attributes," she said, looking pointedly at his manhood as she swept a pelt of blond locks off her face and over her back. "So, yes."

"Good," the emperor nodded, again. "We can spare ourselves the whole, 'you did this to me, so now I must do this to you, your family, your entire tribe, and all of your allies' back-and-forth and get on with things."

Ryhu, now fully awake, butted in, "I am Ryhu of the Penios, son of Sekilos. Leave now, *Roman*, or die."

"Fool," Kayza whispered to herself, shaking her head in annoyance at the boy's bravado.

"Correction, you are a toy, young man," Caesar sneered at Ryhu. "The general's plaything."

His eyes sparkled as Ryhu glanced at Kayza, who would not look back at him.

"I know. The truth hurts," Caesar mocked the slumping youth and wagged his finger at him. "But, it appears you already have the measure of the general's heart. Let me guess, you thought with time you could change it and she would love you." His voice suddenly took on a rough edge, "You were wrong. She *cannot* love. I know this as well as I know the curve of her hips, the smell of her skin, and the sounds of her lies." The emperor took a breath and composed himself before continuing, "True, there is little comfort in knowing you are not the only one to have been deceived. But, have no fear, your pain will be short-lived." He turned to the three centurions and stood aside to allow them through the doorway, "Kill them."

Seasoned by years of campaigning, they surged into the room and surrounded their naked and unarmed foes, blocking the doorway as well as the window that framed a vista of heavy rain clouds that were in the process of breaking up. Her back to the wall, Kayza glared at Caesar and her lip curled at the sight of his bristling cropped hair, and his close-set eyes peering down the length of his nose at his fingernails. Fired by hate, she launched herself at the soldier to her left, ducking his sword arm as he swung at her throat. In a heartbeat, she was behind him clenching his neck in an iron lock formed by the crook of her right elbow, then wrenching his head until his bones *crunched* and he crumpled.

Barely blinking at his comrade's plight, the soldier who was blocking the door, as well as Caesar's view of the action, aimed a cleaving hack at Kayza's exposed back. Knowing the attack would come, she pivoted hard and the dead man she was gripping took the force of the blow with his helmeted head. Blood and brains sprayed as the sword lodged itself in the corpse's head and, pushing the body to the floor, she pulled her second attacker off balance. Kayza stepped behind the man as he was dragged forward by the weight of his dead friend, and kicked him twice in the groin, as hard as she could. The soldier's knees buckled, and without pause she turned for the third centurion. As she spun, she saw the soldier catch Ryhu between the eyes with the heel of his left hand, straightening him up, then run him through, driving his blade into the flesh between Ryhu's right shoulder and chest.

Howling in fury, Kayza charged the centurion, crashing into him and sending him sprawling to the floor. Then, hurrying to Ryhu, she jerked the blade free from his shoulder and flung it at the head of the downed soldier. As the sword rang off the soldier's helmet, she hauled Ryhu to his feet and dove with him through the window.

Rolling to her feet, she scrambled back to Ryhu, who was flat on his back, reached under his arms, and wrestled him to his feet. His legs uncertain, she threw his left arm around her neck and dragged him away from her villa into the forest. As she turned away from her home, she saw Caesar standing at the window, staring at her, and heard his taunts, "Kalos, the cripple, was right after all. I should have brought more men to deal with you. Oh well, never mind, we shall very quickly *pacify* Noega. After we do, I will have men to spare to hunt you down. So, one way or another, dead or alive, *I shall see you soon, Kayza!*"

Caesar's scratchy giggles scraped over the low-hanging branches through which Kayza and Ryhu crashed. Patches of gray light filtered down through the leaves and flashed off their skin as they ran deeper into the woods and pusher higher up the mountain, which before Kalos' betrayal, hid Noega in the ranges that lined the northern border of the Iberian Peninsula.

The further they ran and the higher they climbed, the weaker Ryhu became. When, finally, they reached a ridge above the tree line, she dropped to her knees and sat him against a moss-grown standing stone. Her chest heaving, she blinked her eyes against the sunlight and her exhaustion.

Straining her vision, she searched the network of trails that scored the hillside above her for markers that would guide her to the caves she hoped truly were carved in the mountains, not just etched in the lore of Noega. Finding nothing, she sat back on her heels and looked at the young man who was slowly bleeding out in front of her. Handsome, strong, brave, and infatuated with her as he was, she shuddered at the sight of him and, in her mind, turned Caesar's heated accusation into a question, "She *cannot* love?"

As if seeking the inspiration she needed to answer the question, she looked up the slope that angled steeply up the mountain, behind the standing stone. Partway up the slope, a rock whose crimson-tinted veins were at odds with those of its neighbors caught her eye. Fixing her gaze on the spot, she grabbed Ryhu and stepped him up the slope toward the outcrop into which the stone was wedged.

When they reached the crag she paused and, carrying yet more of the Ryhu's weight, scanned further upwards for another marker. Higher up the mountainside, she picked out a sliver of red in the grasses, and with no path to guide her plodded on.

Two more markers, each more difficult to find than its forerunner, pulled her higher up the mountain, her strength fading, his lifeblood trickling into the grass. The second of the two sat on a plateau that ran to the foot of a sheer rock face that reached skywards, marking the end of her climb and, it appeared, Ryhu's life.

Groaning at the futility of having chased what had turned out to be a fable, she collapsed, taking Ryhu with her. Unconscious, he planted his face into the turf, while she rolled onto her back and wheezed in the thin air. Naked, cold, and spent, she lay still and waited for her breathing to slow and for his to stop. As her panting quieted, his ragged puffing sped up sharply, and then suddenly went still. Sighing, she opened her eyes and turned her head to look at him, but he had vanished.

Puzzled, but too drained to investigate, she closed her eyes and searched inside herself for whatever remnants remained of her strength. When she found what little was left of it, she opened her eyes, but rather than seeing the sky, she found herself looking into an oval face and a pair of deep-set, ice-blue eyes, one of which winked at her from behind loose strands of blond ringlets.

"Hello, Kayza of the Lugones," a rich, elusively familiar, and disturbingly maternal voice reached out to her. "I am Akuia. We don't have much time, so hurry. *Hurry!*"

Distant thunder punctuated the enjoinder but, her will wrung dry, Kayza lay still and let her eyes slowly close. As her world went black, streams of insistent chittering nibbled at the crust that had formed around her and that was sandwiched in the ether that separated wakefulness from unconsciousness.

"Hurry! Hurry! Hurry, Omanahi!" she heard someone jabbering. "We have to get back to the cave and find her sword before some fool townie does."

after days spent dodging British patrols and stealing their guns and ammunition, less than twenty-four hours earlier an opportunity to kill Amherst and finish the mission had slipped by.

Out of the blue, the general had appeared on the road that marked the western boundary of the British encampment. Marching in front of his lieutenants, the general was exposed, unarmed, and off guard. But, unfocused and equally off guard, the agent failed to strike. Consolation for the failure, small though it was, came from following the general to his headquarters, which were located roughly one mile north of Flat Point, just off the edge of the roadway.

Opposite the headquarters building, on the other side of the road, the agent dug into a hideout and observed the general for two days. Amherst worked, ate, and slept in the squat structure, leaving it only rarely. When he did come out, he did so accompanied by a cadre of officers who, whether they intended to or not, blocked a clear shot at him. On the morning of the third day, however, the general let his guard down. On horseback, at the head of a column of his subalterns, he trotted away from his headquarters, north along the makeshift road.

Tracking the mounted detail, while staying undercover and searching for an open shot at the general, proved taxing for the operative. So, it came as a relief when Amherst stopped to inspect the light infantry stationed at the northernmost tip of the encampment. The inspection, apparently, went well; none of the floggings for which the British military was notorious were doled out. However, throughout the inspection, Amherst's officers maintained a defensive ring around the general, once more blocking a clear shot.

The journey back to Amherst's headquarters was equally challenging for the field agent. It also was uneventful, until the British neared their headquarters and a crackling report split the air from the woods west of the roadway. Every head in the detail, save one, turned to find the white puff of smoke that would give away the shooter's position. The one head that did not turn belonged to a subaltern whose blood was leaking through his shirt onto his trousers and who slumped, slack-jawed, against the officer to his left.

CHAPTER 33

POACHER

JULY 13TH

THE MAISONETTE

C ompared to other structures in its vicinity, the maisonette occupied by Poisson and D'Acier was unscathed after almost three weeks of constant bombardment. Poisson attributed their luck to the maisonette's proximity to the nunnery, which went untouched by the shelling until Drucour sent out a task force to attack the British. Enraged by the assault, the British bombarded the harbor, fortress, and town with renewed ferocity for days, toppling buildings in every quarter. The nunnery was spared until late in the afternoon of the fourth day, when Oculus abandoned his adoptive daughters and allowed a burst of shots to make Swiss cheese of the hallowed halls of his convent. The cloister was reduced to a heap of rubble, under which half of the sisters were entombed.

Poisson cited this latest atrocity as yet further evidence of Oculus's flippant nature, and yet another fingerpost pointing him at the exit from Louisbourg. His resolve renewed, he briefed D'Acier on the contents of their final communiqué to the British, which included new information, as well as the terms by which they would conclude their partnership. Then, after dispatching D'Acier, he wrapped himself in his tan leather coat, took a stool and his pair of matching flintlock pistols out to the boardwalk that fronted their maisonette, and settled in for another evening of poaching would-be looters.

Hours elapsed, but unlike previous evenings Poisson shot not a single looter. When at last he set his sights on a target it turned into D'Acier, who was ambling up the debris-strewn lane in his matte black leather duster as though he were enjoying an evening stroll on the *Champs-Élysées*. Declining the opportunity to plug his retainer, Poisson allowed D'Acier to reach the boardwalk unharmed, then led him through their vestibule into their great room. After they settled in front of their barren fireplace, the regent debriefed his retainer.

"I take it, from your casual manner, our message was well received," Poisson observed.

"Indeed it was, my lord," D'Acier confirmed. "The British were appreciative of the information, and agreeable to the date and terms of our departure."

"Splendid," Poisson replied, guardedly. "However, I sense there is a '*but*' to which you were required to acquiesce."

"My lord is perceptive," D'Acier nodded.

"Well, let's have it then," Poisson said and sat forward in his chair.

"As you expected, the British—" D'Acier's report was interrupted by a commotion on the boardwalk.

Poisson rolled his eyes and sighed impatiently, while D'Acier cocked one of his pistols and, raising it to the ready position, stalked toward the front door. Once at the door, he bent his ear toward it for a moment, then flung it open and leveled his pistol.

Faced with the business end of D'Acier's barrel, Fortess shied away and shielded himself with his prisoner, a ragged, gangling, adolescent boy, and yelped, "Shoot him! I caught him trying to break in!"

D'Acier looked at the starving youth and said, "More likely you caught him when he tried to take a bite out of your leg. Let him go, you idiot."

Fortess shoved the youth up the boardwalk and shouted after him as he ran, "Do not come back! Next time, I will not be so merciful!"

D'Acier watched Fortess's performance, then stood aside for the tall, out of uniform, former French officer, saying mockingly, "Please, *mon Capitaine*, do come in."

Failing to catch D'Acier's sarcasm, Fortess thanked him and marched past him into the vestibule, then waited to be announced. D'Acier obliged by sidestepping Fortess, who was standing as near to attention as he was capable, and sitting down in his chair opposite Poisson. Once seated D'Acier flicked his head towards the vestibule, "Fortess is back from running his errand."

"Well, don't just stand there, Fortess," Poisson chided the ex-officer, who was looking decidedly awkward in his stolen, ill-fitting, worse for wear civilian garb, "Fetch the stool from the porch, then seat yourself and give us good news." Poisson's invitation had the ring of an ultimatum.

Stiffly, Fortess retrieved the stool, strode back into the great room, and placed himself between D'Acier and Poisson. Before taking his seat, however, he presented the regent with a dusty, but full magnum of wine.

"Ah, that is good news. Well done, Fortess," Poisson commended his operative as he inspected the bottle before setting it aside. "You have proven yourself to be most resourceful in your service to us. Count on it that your rewards will be commensurate with your actions," Poisson looked away from Fortess and into the empty fireplace as he made this promise. "I have, however, one more challenge to lay at your feet, and I fear it will be the most difficult one that you have yet faced. But, if you succeed there will be a bonus in it for you."

Fortess gulped and asked, "What must I do?"

Poisson looked hard at Fortess and said, "Your ready procurement of this bottle suggests you have, as I suspected, cultivated some *connections*. So, if you are up to it, then you will handle for us the sticky business of removing provisions from our beloved, but besieged Louisbourg and delivering them to the *l'Arethusa*."

Fortess looked at Poisson blankly.

"She is a ship," Poisson clarified. "She is at anchor in Barrachois Lagoon."

Recognition dawned on Fortess, "Ah, yes, I know her. What provisions do you need?"

"We are not embarking on an ocean voyage. So, foodstuffs enough to sustain a skeleton crew and four passengers for, what say you D'Acier, a week?" Poisson looked to his retainer, who nodded in agreement.

"I am assuming I am one of the four passengers, and said passage is the bonus to which you referred," Fortess clarified, a blend of nervousness and hopefulness swirling in his voice.

"Very astute of you, Fortess," Poisson again commended his operative.

"When do you plan on leaving?" Fortess inquired, his eyes shifting as the gears in his gray matter started grinding.

"The fifteenth," Poisson replied, definitely, but keeping to himself the 'no matter what' qualifier, "That gives you two days."

Fortess mulled over the variables, then declared, "It can be done. I know people in . . ."

Poisson's upraised hand silenced Fortess. "Your agreement will suffice," the regent said. "I have no desire to know the details. They will remain in your capable hands." Poisson then clasped Fortess's extended right hand with his own to seal their pact. His plan set in motion, Poisson picked up the bottle proffered earlier by Fortess, "Now, let us enjoy this vintage and toast Oculus, wherever he may be, by wishing an everlasting plague upon his misbegotten soul."

Chapter 34

Damnation

July 14th

M uck oozed from heaps of garbage piled on top of Flat Point, down its ridge and into fires on the beach that belched clouds of acrid smoke over Gabarus Bay. Pressed into a gap between munitions crates stacked, haphazardly, on the beach, a black-clad figure watched the clouds drift away to the south. Thinking it likely they would burn in the same fires, the thief scooped an armful of muskets from a cracked open box and snorted in amusement at the thought.

The sniff caught the attention of a young British sentry passing by the crates and, the hairs on the back of his neck rising, he scuffled to a stop in the sand. Slowly, he bent at the waist and took a tentative step towards the opening between the stacked crates. Squinting his eyes against the shadows and leading with the barrel of his musket, he duck walked into the crevice. After a few shuffling steps into the opening, he stopped. Eyes wide, he reached for a crate that looked like it had been forced open.

When he touched the rim of the crate, a sudden succession of loud *knocks* rang off the containers behind his back. Frightened by the racket, he yelped then scuttled backwards out of the crack between the stacks. When he reached open air, he raised his musket to his shoulder and, twitching uncontrollably, aimed it every which way. As he jerked from side to side, moonlight highlighted a nasty scar that ran from behind his right ear, down the side of his neck, and under the collar of his red overcoat which, compared to the threadbare one worn by the sergeant at whom he ended up pointing his rifle, looked new.

"Well met, Private Bridge. Now, lower your weapon," the sergeant ordered the sentry in a gruff voice. He then asked him a question, "What day is it?"

Bridge obeyed the sergeant's order immediately, but was flustered by his question and blurted out the first answer that came to mind, "Fourteenth of July, Sergeant!"

"Very good," the sergeant's voice became sterner as he approached the sentry. "Thought you could hide it from me, did you?"

"No, sir!" Bridge, appalled by the notion of concealing anything from the man to whom he reported, was confused, "Hide what, sir?"

"Your birthday, you great oaf," the sergeant chuckled. "How old are you, boy?"

The private relaxed slightly, then puffed up his chest, "I'm nineteen, sir."

"A man, then," the sergeant acknowledged the youth's ascension and shook his hand. "Old enough for a man's drink."

From nowhere, a silver flask appeared in the sergeant's hand and glinted in the moonlight. "Here's to you," the sergeant toasted Private Bridge and took a swig, then handed the flask to the teenager. The young man mimicked his superior's every move, then added his own touch with a choking cough when the liquor hit the back of his throat.

The sergeant laughed and took back the flask, which Bridge happily returned to him. He then reached out and turned the teenager's head to the side. "Your wound's knitting well, I see. It'll give you something to talk to the girls about when you get home," he teased the youth and looked him up and down with a playfully critical eye and sent him on his way, "Well, carry on young *man*."

"Yes, sir!" Bridge dropped the butt of his rifle into the sand and snapped a salute. He then propped the barrel of the musket on his shoulder, in the carry position, and pivoted away from the sergeant. As the young private strode away towards the surf his sergeant, still chuckling, trudged back up the beach.

Low-key though the celebration was, the black-clad bandit, who listened to it from among the munitions crates, breathed a sigh of relief when, at its conclusion, the sentry continued on his rounds, rather than his inspection of the open crate. Worn down after days of playing cat-and-mouse with General Amherst, the interruption caused by the simple recognition of a birthday chaffed the raw nerve endings of the assassin to the point where they were ready to howl in exasperation at the desperation of their mission, the glacial pace of its progress, and the increasing odds against its ending successfully.

Though it had been just five days since the French sortie into the British lines on the Moor of Gabanes, to the agent it felt like it had been a lifetime since Drucour, in a brief meeting in his office in the King's Bastion, issued his orders, "You will act independent of the other agent who is working on this assignment. Use all of the guile and cunning you have at your disposal and, at all costs, kill General Amherst." With a dismissive wave, Drucour concluded their meeting, saying, "France and His Majesty, King Louis XV, will not forget your service."

Dimly, the agent recalled accepting the governor's razor-thin reassurance with an equally thin salute, then marching out of the Bastion. Outfitted in black coveralls, identity unknown either to the governor or the soldiers on the parade ground, the assassin made ready, quickly, and rushed over the ramparts with the squaddies. Then came the chaos of battle, hammering on every inch of everyone within reach, using fists, elbows, knees, and feet. Then, suddenly, the rear of the British line was in the background and the clangor of the fight faded as quickly from hearing as the operative faded from view.

More so than images of fighting, the French agent remembered the stench of the ruptured, rotting bodies that littered the terrain behind the battlefield. Haunted by the stomach-turning memory and exhausted

The officer recoiled from the injured man at first, then grabbed his left arm. Reacting quickly, a second officer offered aid, skittering up to the right of the wounded man and grabbing him by his belt to keep him mounted on his horse. Then, amid much shouting and arm-waving, two other riders peeled away from the detail and galloped west towards the wood stand from which the offending puff of smoke was seen floating into space. The remaining members of the detail, including Amherst, high-tailed it to their headquarters.

In hiding further up the road, the operative watched a trio of British officers lug their wounded comrade into the command post, while two more kept galloping south to the hospital to fetch a surgeon, raising alarms as they went. Their cries succeeded in putting the camp into a state of high alert, but the commotion they caused served only to slow down their return to base. When they finally reached its door the two men who had ridden off in pursuit of the shooter arrived, coincidentally, dragging a bruised and muddied man who was attached by a length of rope to one of their saddles.

The surgeon and the two officers escorting him were seen by the agent as entering the building first, followed by the shooter and his captors. A few minutes later, the surgeon emerged from the building, his hands and his smock smattered with fresh blood. His escort hard on his heels, the doctor took the brunt of their frustrations as they railed at him for failing to save their comrade.

Moments later, the French operative witnessed the shooter being tossed outside through the open door of the squat building. His hands still bound, he ran away blindly and was shot in the back instantly by one of the officer's escorting the doctor. Face down in the dirt, the assassin writhed in pain until the doctor's second escort pinned him to the ground under the heel of his boot, then shot him in the back of the head.

While the doctor retched, his officer escorts nudged the murderer with the toes of their boots. Satisfied he was dead, they then straightened up the doctor and hustled him back down the road toward the hospital. The body of the man they'd shot was left face down in the mud on the side of the road, for passers-by to admire.

By lunchtime Amherst's would be assassin's corpse no longer was an object of interest, so the garbage wagon was summoned to take it away. When the cart arrived, its two-man crew tossed the carcass onto its bed as if they were collecting a sack of table scraps from the canteen. They then steered their wagon back onto the roadway and pointed it in the direction of the rubbish tip on Flat Point.

Later, still numbed by the failure of Drucour's other agent and the brutality of the British backlash, the surviving agent stumbled back to the hideout opposite the headquarters building. Upon reaching the den, however, the cite of their weapons cache, emptied, apparently while the pursuit of Amherst was afoot, shook the malaise from their bones. Rankled by having been robbed of their stolen weapons, the operative coaxed a slow burn from their dampened enthusiasm and stomped away from the hideout in the direction of the weapons depot at Flat Point.

Now, with the anxiety of the close encounter with the scarred sentry waning, Drucour's surviving agent looked at broken munitions crates scattered about in the sand, all as empty as the consciences of the British officers who murdered the defenseless man earlier in the day. Armed to gritted teeth with more stolen weaponry and hardened with resolve, the operative watched smoke float from Flat Point over Gabarus Bay, knowing whose ashes seeded the clouds. Walking up the beach, away from the crates, the assassin vowed Amherst would meet a similar fate in Oculus's burning halls of damnation.

BARRACHOIS LAGOON

Fine grains of sand whisked over the ridge of the dune overlooking Barrachois Lagoon. Their flight obscured by darkness, they stung Erieux's eyes and slipped under the collar of his shirt and down his back as, flat on his stomach, he peered over the lip of the dune. Taking care to brush more of the grains off his hands before rubbing his eyes, Erieux scowled at Enriquez, who was watching *l'Arethusa* like a hawk.

"What in the name of Oculus are we doing here?" Erieux asked Enriquez, who was decked out in his skintight black raiding gear, and had his wavy hair pulled into in a ponytail. When the Spaniard, who also was laying on his stomach but was bent at the waist, ignored him, Erieux added, "And what is that bulge in your pants?"

"It is the happy side effect of my piratical instincts telling me there is treasure to be had," Enriquez replied, straight-faced. Then, sensing the Acadian was about to request clarification, cut him short, "The second part answers the first."

Erieux blinked sand from his eyes until he filtered out the meaning in Enriquez's abstraction. He then shook his head in disbelief, "Treasure? On that ship? The one we snuck onto, then jumped off of? What makes you think so?"

"The three-headed dog told me," Enriquez informed the Acadian, straight-faced.

Erieux looked to Vishnu, Ganesh, and Yuval for translation. None of the three Maratha obliged. So, his blood warming, the Acadian turned back to the Spaniard and asked Enriquez to confirm the absurd, "Tell me if I've misunderstood. We are again spying on a ship we searched, *and ran away from not that long ago,* because a three-headed dog spoke to you, and during the conversation, it told you the ship in question is loaded with treasure?"

Without waiting for Enriquez to reply, he then rolled onto his back and asked, "How did you make it from there," he spread his arms wide to represent the distance from Bombay to Louisbourg, then pulled his right hand in front of his nose and pressed his thumb and forefinger together to represent the distance from *Rajani* to Louisbourg, "to here without your three friends doing you and the world a favor by ending your madcap existence?"

Enriquez propped himself on his left elbow and needled the Acadian, "Such passion, Rio. I do believe the bulge in my pants is growing." Then, keeping half an eye on the bustle of activity on and around the ship, he clarified, "We are here because I am your *capitán* and I decided here is where we need to be."

Erieux's eyes sparked with irritation, but he bit his tongue to allow the pecking order of the crew to be restored and for Enriquez to continue, which he did, "Three-headed or not, everyone knows dogs are not gifted with speech . . . as you and I know it. But, if you pay attention, they tell you many things: a wagging tail for *happiness*, a curled lip for *anger*, and so on. You will agree?"

Erieux shrugged his shoulders, agreeing with the obvious, and Enriquez pressed on, "Sometimes, just the image of a dog can have meaning; a three-headed dog on a crate full of gold, for instance."

"That's stretching it a bit, don't you think?" Erieux rolled his eyes at Enriquez.

"Not if you were told by your mysterious employer to look for such an image in the hold of a ship weighed down with, you said it yourself not long ago, *gold*," The pirate's teeth gleamed within the borders of the black goatee that framed his mouth.

Searching for an escape from the pirate's logic, as well as the path down which it appeared to be heading, Erieux asked, "Speaking of your employer, are we not supposed to be waiting on *Rajani* for word from her?"

"I *am* waiting. I am waiting *here*. The others can wait on *Rajani*," he said and smiled again. Then, when a movement caught the corner of his eye, Enriquez grabbed Erieux and started crawling on his elbows toward the ship, while keeping his weight off of the bulge in his pants pocket. "Quickly," he whispered to Erieux, "The crewmen are leaving! You must be on board before they return!"

"Wait! What? Why me?" Erieux spluttered as he scurried to catch up with Enriquez.

"So you can prove to me you are right. That there is, in fact, gold on that ship," the pirate replied and gave Erieux a hard look. "And, also, so I can await word from my employer. After all, as you know, I will not get paid until the job is done. Now hurry, you are putting all of us at risk!"

Erieux tried to assemble a rebuttal as he slithered through the sand, but swallowed his words when he felt first his boots, then his trousers being tugged off, and then his buttocks being prodded forward by the daggers of the trailing Maratha. Cursing as the points nicked his butt-cheeks, he scuttled onward until he was in the water next to Enriquez, brine lapping against his chin.

"When you reach the ship do not delay in boarding her as you did last time. Remember, also, a guard stands watch," Enriquez rattled off his instructions while searching Erieux's eyes for signs of comprehension. Happy to find none, he carried on, "Hide in the hold. You know where it is. Find the gold if it is there. Find out where it is being taken, and then return to us. We will be here, on shore, waiting for you."

"Hide? For how long?"

"Until tomorrow. They will leave tomorrow, at the latest. Of this I am sure."

"Find out where they are going? How?"

"You will find a way, Rio. You are clever. After all, it was you who deduced the ship is laden with gold," Enriquez flattered the Acadian. He then clapped Erieux on the shoulder and sent him on his way, "Now go! Do not fail!"

Three well placed jabs in the buttocks sent Erieux doggy-paddling into the surf toward the ship, his shirt blooming out and away from his body. As he distanced himself from the shoreline and rode the swells, he spat out salty water with every stroke, and heaped curses on Enriquez and the Maratha, as well as Oculus and all his creations.

Weighed down by his shirt and wrestling with the undercurrents, Erieux inched toward the ship. As he neared its hull he stopped his cursing, but could not still his chattering teeth as icy fingers of the water reached into his flesh and gripped his bones. Shivering, his breathing becoming more rapid and shallow, he edged out of the swells and into the oily, black pool that slithered around the ship.

The inky pool reflected no light, and as he slid into it, he fought the urge to let himself be dragged to its bottom by the unseen leviathan that once more numbed his mind. Sputtering, he splashed his face with water to shake off his fatigue-induced fantasies. As he shook his head, he shed his shirt, surrendering it to the monsters of his imagination, and swam for the webbing that hung from the ship's rail. Grasping the soggy ropes with his deadened fingers, he pulled himself free from the water to the faint sounds of applause coming from the scoundrels on the beach.

While scaling the webbing, Erieux also heard footfalls clacking steadily along the deck overhead, but he kept climbing. When he reached to top of the meshwork, he peered over the rail, and as the watchman walked to the fore of the ship, Erieux eased himself over the guardrail and onto the deck. Then, after a last glance at the watchman, he crouched low and padded in the opposite direction, toward the ship's stern.

Familiar with the layout of the ship from his previous stop on board, Erieux found the companionway below the bridge and between the cabins, easily, and stepped quickly below deck. When he hit the foot of the companionway, muffled voices drifted back to him from further up the aisle that ran through the middle of the gun deck. Freezing in place, he listened to their tone, and when they remained quiet and unalarmed, crept down the aisle towards them, while checking, carefully, the officers' quarters on each side.

When he saw all of the rooms were unoccupied, he retreated into the first room at the foot of the companionway and backed into it silently. Once inside, he latched the door shut and started his search for clothes that would warm him, and when the time came conceal him among the crew, as well as for information that would tell him where Enriquez's gold was to be taken. One-by-one, over the next few hours, he searched the officers' rooms, thanked them for contributing to his disguise, and fussed at them for failing to leave behind a memo or a map that would point out the treasure's destination.

As he rummaged through the last room, he bit back his hisses of frustration when two sets of footsteps, growing steadily louder, thumped up the aisle from the depths of the gun deck. Pressing his back to the wall next to the door hinges, he held his breath as the two guards thudded past the room and then clumped up the companionway. As they marched away on the main deck, Erieux slowly let go of his breath, and after stepping to the opposite side of the door, cracked it open.

Stillness and silence greeted Erieux when he looked and listened through the slim opening in the doorway. Warily, he opened the door wider and poked his head into the aisle. Certain it was empty, he slipped out of the room and between the cannons to the foremost companionway. When he reached the top of the stairway, as Enriquez had done on their last visit, Erieux stood still and listened for unwelcome noises. Hearing none, he edged his way down into the hold.

When he reached the bottom of the stairs, he glanced up at the opening at the top of the stairs. When neither sight nor sound of activity reached down to him, he stepped into the blackness of the hold. After giving his eyes a moment to adjust to the deeper darkness of the storage cell, he set off into the maze of stacked provisions. Carefully, he inspected the stacks, moving from one pile to the next, until he found one whose canvas wrappings were stamped with a seal that included the likeness of a three-headed dog.

Exhaling audibly, the Acadian ran his hand down the tarpaulin until it reached the floor of the hold. When his fingers touched the solid wood of the deck, he pinched the canvas between his fingers and pulled it up and back, over the lowest of the crates it covered. Shifting his weight and bracing one knee on the floor, Erieux pulled out the dagger he'd lifted from one of the French officer's rooms and jammed it between the lid and the lip of the crate. As he levered the dagger around the rim, the lid gradually loosened until it popped up and away from the blade.

With his free hand, Erieux shifted the lid further out of the way, then reached into the wooden box. Near the lip of the box, the tips of his fingers touched the surface of a smooth, warm, metal bar. After rubbing its surface with the palm of his hand, he wrapped his fingers around the bar and pulled it from the crate. For its size, which was a bit longer than his dagger and about the thickness of a wooden plank, it was heavy. Then, as he lifted it into the early morning light creeping down the companionway it threw golden rays back at him.

Gold, lots and lots of gold, was packed in the hold. Thrilled as he was by the discovery, Erieux's excitement was tempered by the knowledge he still had no idea where it was going to be taken. That bit of information would have to come from the crew while they made ready to depart, if Enriquez was to be believed, later in the day. Once he had it, Erieux's only remaining challenge would be to get himself off the ship and back to shore without getting himself killed.

"Child's play," he sighed and, exhausted, crawled under the canvas cloaking the stash of gold. Then, lulled by the gentle rocking of the ship and the drone of the cannons as they started their daily barrage, he drifted into a fitful sleep under the watchful eyes of a pack of three-headed dogs.

CHAPTER 35

UNDONE

JULY 15TH

BRITISH HEADQUARTERS

As twilight hovered over the British encampment, Governor Drucour's surviving assassin looked back and forth from the replenished weapons cache to the British headquarters. General Amherst had emerged from the squat building earlier in the afternoon to continue his inspections, which were so rudely interrupted the previous day by the Drucour's other, now dead, assassin. Electing to not follow the general on his tour, the operative chose, instead, to stake out the cache. If whoever emptied it the day before returned, then they would die. Amherst's consignment to eternal torment could wait until he returned from his inspections.

Stiff to the point of seizing up from perching above the cache all afternoon, the agent was stretching a leg over a nearby branch when the hollow rasp of worn leather brushing through scrub rose up from the forest floor. Keeping the extended leg on the branch, the operative pressed back into the trunk of the tree and looked down into the undergrowth, straining for a glimpse of the thief. Camouflaged by the tones of his leathers and the tints of his body paint, the burglar remained concealed until he emerged from the shrubbery at the base of the tree. From his outward appearance, he looked like a Mi'kmaq warrior. Given, also, he showed up just as Amherst returned to his headquarters, it was likely he also was a member of the general's bodyguard.

When the Mi'kmaq spotted the cache, he froze at the sight of the newly arrayed foliage that was being used to conceal its presence. Placing his feet carefully, he edged toward the cache for a couple of steps, and then crept on his hands and knees to its rim. He ran his hands around the pit, gently, testing it for traps. Finding none, he cleared away the branches and leaves that covered the store of weapons. As he had done with the pit, he cleared the weapons for traps, and again found none. Grunting either in satisfaction or out of arrogance, he reached into the shallow pit and grabbed one of the muskets.

With his head down and his eyes on the rifle, and with the rumble of cannons washing out most of the sounds from the forest, the Mi'kmaq neither saw nor heard the black-clad bomb that was dropping toward him from the branches above. The missile exploded on the warrior's exposed back with a hard elbow that slammed his chest to the ground. Squashed between the heavy blow and the hard ground his lungs blasted out all of the air the held. His arms flailing, he flipped onto his back, gasping for air and throwing off his attacker.

Recovering quickly, the French operative straddled the Mi'kmaq, sat on his chest, and clamped a hand around his throat to further thwart his efforts to regain his breath. A confused, *not again* expression flitted over the warrior's purpling face, and he frothed at the mouth as he tried to speak.

But the assassin cut him off and asked, harshly, "*Neah?* What are you doing?"

His eyes tearing up with the strain of trying to breathe through the combination of a chokehold and a collapsed diaphragm, the Mi'kmaq gurgled a one-word question in reply, "*Aluasa'sit?*"

The masked agent drew the flintlock pistol pilfered from a crate on Flat Point and pressed the open end of its barrel between the warrior's eyes. Thumb inching toward the hammer, the assassin stopped suddenly and growled at the Mi'kmaq, "I am not your *phoqing* friend." Then, doing the opposite of what the British had shown they would do, the operative flipped the pistol over and smashed its butt, rather than a lead ball, into the Mi'kmaq's skull.

Satisfied Neah would not be raising any alarms anytime soon, the assassin shoved as much of him into the pit as would fit, tossed some foliage over him, and loped away toward the seat of the British high command. Squat and solid, the building's heavy timbers soaked up the ink of the night sky and, with no lanterns lighting its walls, gave the appearance of being deserted.

Running low and smooth, the French agent glided across the road toward the blacked-out building, but veered away from it when a column yellow light shot out from its doorway. Crouching in the shadows, the operative watched an officer's aide pop through the doorway, his red waistcoat shining, and march crisply south, away from the command post.

In contrast to the aide's rapid footfalls, the lobster box's door shut slowly. When it was fully closed, Drucour's agent raced to the side of the building. Back pressed to the north-facing wall, pistol cocked, the agent peaked around the corner of the building. All was clear, so the assassin sidestepped along the dirt porch at the front of the building, while keeping an eye on the roadway it faced.

Upon reaching the front door, the agent took a quick breath and pivoted sharply to kick it open, only to be rammed by someone equally black-clad who was coming at the door from the opposite direction, but who was using identical tactics. Stunned, Drucour's two agents pointed their pistols at one another for an instant, then yelled in unison, *"Je pensais que tu étais mort!"* I thought you were dead!

Almost immediately their shared disbelief turned into fury, and in concert they cursed, *"Merde!"* Shit!

With not another word spoken they threw glances left and right, looking for the soldiers who would close the trap into which they'd been lured. Unwilling to wait for their arrival, they aimed the heels of their boots at the door and kicked it in.

THE KING'S BASTION, LOUISBOURG

Open to the night air, the open doorway to the entrance hall of the King's Bastion looked in on Augustin de Boschenry de Drucour. Alone, his elegant suit sullied, he sat cross-legged, hunched over a flickering candle whose puddle of light lapped up against the pile of rubble that was stacked up against his back.

Tendrils of air, rank with the smell of burned wood and scorched flesh, slid through the doorway. As the rank wisps curled around the governor's stooped frame, they stretched his candle's light over the graffiti scratched into the largest of the chunks of rubble. From beneath a layer of fine dust, a single word, *"Follie!,"* screamed at the governor in mute outrage over his decision to force a siege upon the town.

Starting, as if stung by the rebuke, Drucour snapped his eyes anxiously toward the entrance to the Bastion. Bracing himself for yet more criticism, he squinted through the dust that hovered over the smashed masonry, looking for Lady Drucour, the most ardent opponent of his holdout against the British. Seeing only the splintered and vacant door casement, he shrugged and slumped closer to his sputtering flame.

Earlier in the day, in an unexpected display of heroic defiance, the governess made a tour of Louisbourg's ramparts. Staring down the cannons of both sides, she succeeded in silencing them for the duration of her circuit, then descended into the ruins of the town, followed by the awestruck, '*Hoorahs,*' of its surviving citizenry. She had not been seen since.

Less awed by her than he was ambivalent about her disappearance, Drucour glanced at the block onto which his legacy was scratched, under which lay his aide, Opsule's, crushed body. Heaving a deep sigh, he assured his retainer, "Small comfort though it may be to you, my young friend, know this; Clavonne will be welcome in my household for as long as she wishes to be part of it." Having favored his aide for the last time, he offhandedly requested insight in return, "By the way, what do you think her ladyship, the governess, is up to?"

HMS L'ARETHUSA

Blacker than the night sky whose currents rustled her sails, the ebon waters clinging to *l'Arethusa* churned as Lady Drucour was lifted out of their reach and onto the deck of the great ship. As she swung in the windlass carrying her, she was greeted by a barrel-chested sailor who showed her a deference more suited to a courtier than a deckhand. As he guided the governess on board, another deckhand steered the basket away from the rail and let it out to the skiff that was riding the murky waters and thumping against the tall ship's hull.

As it spun down to the skiff Fortess, who was straddling one of the rowboat's slippery benches, grabbed the basket. Thrown off balance by its weight, he pitched toward the ship's hull. Wrenching himself backwards to avoid pounding his forehead into the heavy timbers, he bounced the side of the skiff off the hull and forced up a shower of frigid water that sprayed D'Acier and Poisson.

The two Parisians ducked their heads under the shower and clung to the bench on which they were seated. When the little craft finally settled and Fortess wrestled the whirling windlass into submission, they brushed the salt spray off of their coats and applauded the acrobatics of the tall officer. Then Poisson, who was next in line, climbed into the basket, waved at the two seamen at the rail, and began his ascent.

As Poisson was lifted up to the top deck, deep in the dark hold of the ship, nestled under the canvas that concealed the stash of gold, Erieux mumbled incoherently at the thumping on the ship's hull that was intruding upon his dreamy interlude with Raçielle. When, finally, his imaginings succumbed to the constant pounding, he juddered awake, bounced the back of his head off a wooden crate, and flailed in the canvas in which he'd entangled himself.

Unable to free himself from the tarp, Erieux forced himself to relax, and as his breathing slowed he remembered his mission, as well as the fact it was unfinished. He had yet to find out where the gold, next to which he'd curled up for his nap, was to be taken. Only after he had the gold's destination would he be able to beat his hasty retreat to Enriquez and relative safety. If he was discovered on board the French ship, then his death would certainly be instantaneous. If, on the other hand, he was able to tell Enriquez where the gold was going, then the pirate might have Vishnu, Ganesh, and Yuval refrain from killing him, at least for the time being.

The sound of many pairs of feet scurrying every which way on the ship told the Acadian he had to act quickly if he wanted to avoid becoming a stowaway on a ship bound for points unknown. Careful to not trigger an avalanche of gold ingots, he bid farewell to his gang of three-headed watchdogs and wiggled out from between the folds of the heavy tarpaulin. A dim halo of light floating in the abysmal blackness of the hold guided Erieux to the foot of the companionway that led up to the shadowy gun deck.

Peeking over the lip of the stairwell, Erieux could see the gun ports had been opened to the night sky, but the gunners had yet to be posted. The weak light filtering through the gunnery was seeping from a small lantern hanging above the stairway to the main deck. Keeping his eyes fixed on the light, he sprinted past the cannons and then slid to a stop at the end of the short corridor on either side of which were the officers' quarters he'd ransacked. Certain that the rooms were deserted, he crept up the sharply inclined stairs to the threshold of the main deck, which was alive with activity.

Taking on the attitude of one of the crew, he swaggered out of the doorway and merged with the traffic on deck. Elbowing his way to the starboard rail, he glanced over the harbor at the campfires that lined the hillside all the way up to Lighthouse Point. He then grabbed a brush and followed other crewmen around the deck, looking for a mess to clean up or an officer to eavesdrop upon.

Head down and brush in hand he worked his way aft along the port rail, snatching glances at the shoreline and looking for clues as to where Enriquez might be hiding. None were being given away, so he went back to his job, but froze in his tracks when a familiar voice trickled through the mix of accents that were buzzing around the ship.

Slowly, he lifted his eyes up from the deck and found a knot of people, dressed in their finery, strolling along beside the ship's rail on a collision course with him. In the middle of the troupe, smiling sweetly behind the blond ringlets that blew across her cheeks and over her shoulders, walked the woman about whom he'd been dreaming just a few short minutes before.

"Raçielle? You're alive?" the stunned Acadian cried.

"Erieux? What are you doing here?" the governess fumed.

"Fortess, at your service," the former captain's flintlock pistol barked and the lead ball crashed into the Acadian's chest, just below his right shoulder, and out his back, sending him cartwheeling over the rail towards the darkness that ringed the ship.

D'Acier had the point of his sword at Fortess's throat at the crack of his pistol's report, but he stayed his hand when Poisson grabbed him by his wrist and hissed at the governess and the deserter, "What is the meaning of this?"

"Ex-boyfriend," the governess snapped.

"Old score," Fortess shrugged.

Poisson weighed the replies against the actions taken, and then nodded at D'Acier to sheath his sword. With a tip of his hat to the governess and the madman, he saluted them, "Well then, I congratulate you both."

With the momentary inconvenience of Erieux's sudden appearance having been dealt with, Poisson waved at the crew, some of whom hit the deck when the pistol was fired, others of whom were searching the water for their mate, to carry on with their duties and called over his shoulder, "*Capitaine Vauquelin*, let us get underway, if you please. Oh, and *Capitaine*, let's not shoot back at the British tonight shall we. Do try, however, to avoid the shipwrecks in the channel." He then invited Lady Drucour to again take his arm and resume their conversation at the point where it had been interrupted, "Now, what *were* we talking about?"

As the governess took up the regent on his invitation, Erieux saw swarms of lights circling in the depths of the lagoon before he blacked out. As he sank towards the multicolored clouds they whirled in agitation. From within their billows, two chattering voices clicked at one another. Omanahi's, the shriller of the two, held the floor.

"She moved! Look she's moving! She's alive, I tell you, Shomanahi! *She's alive!*

CHAPTER 36

UNPACIFIED

25 BC

NOEGA, HISPANIA

K ayza's head swam with watery images of a desperate climb up a mountain and flowed into a vision of an ashen-faced young warrior whose eyes turned into a reflection of her own. As she fought to uncover the secrets the eyes hid, a rich, irritatingly maternal voice breathed into her right ear, "I told you, Kayza, we don't have much time and there are things you must know. Wake up. *Wake up!*"

Grumbling, the warrior dragged her mind out of its torpor and cracked open her eyes. Dapples of muted light, trapped in the pockmarks that pitted the rough-hewn walls of a cavern, made a halo of the ringlets that tumbled around the oval face that was smiling over her own. Her arms stretched above her head, her legs fully straightened, her wrists and ankles were tightly bound to stakes that were embedded in the smooth pedestal on which she lay.

"Ageless, you will be. Strength, you will have. Eat what you must. Out of the sunlight, you must stay. Pay your debt, then make your choice. Know these things," Akuia hummed in her ear.

"Ryhu," Kayza rasped and flexed against the ropes, but stayed stretched across the pedestal.

"Feel love for him, you think?" in the manner in which Kayza's captor asked the question, it could just as easily have been an accusation.

When Kayza said nothing in reply, a low chuckle rumbled deep within Akuia, who winked at her. She then reached between Kayza's thighs, and rubbed her crevice with the palm of her hand. Her eyes twinkling at the shock in Kayza's, after a few sure strokes she gently pulled her hand from between the general's clamped legs and sniffed her palm. Savoring the essences, she tilted her head back and *harrumphed,* then rested her chin on the pedestal next to Kayza.

"You do not," she whispered, "But took from him love, you did. Now, owe him love, you do. So, find him love, you will. That is your debt. Pay it you will, then your choice you will make."

"You are a witch," Kayza shot back.

"I am, indeed," Akuia agreed, then stood over Kayza and looked her over, approvingly. "You have strength. You will need all of it and more." Without another word she flipped Kayza onto her stomach, twisting and tightening the knots at her wrists and ankles.

Prone, her chin hovering over a deep bowl carved into the pedestal, Kayza saw Ryhu slumped against the cavern wall. Pale and shivering, his eyes were shut and she could see the wound in his chest was festering.

"He is nearly gone," Akuia answered Kayza's unspoken question matter-of-factly. "But, bring him back, you will. Now, and again, and again, and yet again. Until your debt is paid."

Without another word, Akuia ran the long fingers of her right hand into Kayza's hair and clenched a fistful of the blond ringlets. Powerful beyond definition, she tilted Kayza's head back until the artery throbbing in her throat was centered over the bowl in the pedestal. With a sharp downward stroke of the nail on her left thumb, Akuia sliced cleanly through the vessel.

Hot red blood leapt from the warrior and into the bowl. As it filled, the witch chanted an archaic incantation, and as the verses lengthened,

Kayza watched, through clouding eyes, as her blood turned to cold, black ichor. Suddenly, the witch cut off her chanting, dipped a finger in the ichor, and with a swift upward stroke swiped it across the cut she'd opened in Kayza's throat, staunching her bleeding.

Moving quickly, the witch reached under Kayza into the bowl and filled her cupped hands with ichor. Her hands dripping, she glided to Ryhu and spoke to him as she poured the foul broth over his lips and into his mouth, "Live a little bit longer, you must."

When the steady stream slowed to infrequent droplets, she tended to his wound using her ichor-stained fingers, rubbing patterns over and into the gash. The instant she removed her hands his sliced skin began to knit together and, satisfied with her work, the witch returned to Kayza, who was sagging in her bonds.

Once more at her place beside the pedestal, she took a deep breath then slapped the naked warrior's bare buttocks to wake her. Kayza strained against her bonds and the witch again grabbed a fistful of her hair, this time to still her, then leaned in close to the warrior and whispered reminders into her ear. "Ageless, you will be. Strength, you will have. When they come, eat what you must. Do not let the sun look upon you. Pay your debt. Make your choice. Remember these things, my sweet little Kayza."

Without another word, she pressed her right hand between Kayza's shoulder blades and pushed her chest tight to the pedestal. Then, with the fistful of Kayza's hair still clenched in her left hand, she pushed her face into the black ichor. The warrior recoiled, but the witch pinned her, and the ropes wound around her wrists and ankles held her fast.

Desperate for air, Kayza sucked in a mouthful of black ichor and convulsed in agony as the cold, syrupy fluid saturated her lungs. Frantic, she gasped, and as her cursed, black blood blocked her mouth and nose, she weakened. When she finally went limp, the witch pushed her head deep into the bowl and held it there until she inhaled the last of the foul ooze.

When at last she passed, Akuia released Kayza and waited silently by the pedestal, until the moon peeked into the entrance to her cavern and Kayza began to change. Slowly, as the moon crept across the mouth of the cave and its gray-blue light slid up the pedestal and onto Kayza's body, webs of black veins reached out of her heart, wound around her torso, and stretched over the length of her arms and legs to the tips of her fingers and toes. When her nails hardened into razor talons, the network of veins retreated to her core, then shot up her throat and poured through her scalp into her hair. Blond ringlets straightened and blackened into glossy raven tresses that swept down to the small of her bare back and spilled onto the pedestal. Her skin glowed as if it was sculpted from the purest white alabaster.

"Not a bad look," Akuia whistled. "You are welcome, my dear."

Then, after a quick look at Ryhu, who was pasty and listless, the witch sighed, "Time for us to go, fool. We do not want to make things easy for this exquisite creature. Nor do we want to spoil the surprise she has in store for her guests, who if I'm not mistaken will be arriving shortly."

Deaf as she had been to Akuia's parting words, the six heartbeats that surrounded her, not long after the witch vacated the cavern, rang in Kayza's ears. Their cadences told her two of them fluttered with fright, two hammered with rage, one lagged out of boredom, and one pattered with arousal. Seeping through the pores in the bodies through which they coursed, the hodgepodge of emotions cut through the shell of the deathly sleep in which she was encased. Slowly, Kayza cracked open her eyes to a world that was shrouded in a red haze and in which she knew only ravening hunger.

"That's not her," one of the Romans snapped. "The one who cracked my nuts had yellow hair."

"Well, the blood trail led us here," another bit back impatiently. "So, who else can it be? The face looks the same as the one I saw."

"Just cut off her head," drawled another. "We'll bring it back to camp and let Caesar decide if it's her."

At the sound of the name, a shiver ran down the length of the body around which the centurions were gathered.

"She moved! She moved!" someone squealed and retreated away from the body.

"Death throes," a voice thick with lust rasped in reply. "She's pale.

Bloodless, but fresh. Not long dead. I can stick a little something in her to make sure if you like."

"*Little* is right," the crabby Roman scoffed, kicking off a round of bawdy taunts. When the banter abated, he decided for the rest of the troop, "Tiro's right. We'll cut off the head and bring it back to Caesar."

When Caesar's name dropped a second time, the body on the pedestal began to quake, and what remained of the Romans' good humor was sucked out of them into the cavern walls.

"*Some throes, Numa,*" the testy Roman chided the lecher, having had enough of the chit-chat. "All of you, hold her! I'll take her head."

Five pairs of hands grabbed Kayza. She went still and the soldiers held their breath while their companion drew his sword from its scabbard. Four of them watched, eyes wide, as the sword arced to the limits of the man's backswing.

The fifth man, Numa, who was fixated on the woman's curves, licked his lips at the sight of them, then frowned at them, and then screamed. Cable-like muscles, riddled with a network of black veins, bulged and writhed along the length of the woman's body, and with a twist of her wrists and ankles, she burst her bonds and was free. Jack-knifing into a low crouch in the middle of the pedestal, she swatted off the centurions' grips, and watched as the sword that was aimed at her neck hacked a chip from the lip of the pedestal's empty bowl.

Hands flat on the pedestal, Kayza pivoted slowly on the balls of her feet, took the measure of her foes, and planned her attack. Her intentions clear, some of the centurions drew their swords and slashed at her, while others took to their heels and dashed for the exit. All of them died, throats torn, lifeblood drained, their shrieks shredded by the ice in Kayza's howl.

CHAPTER 37

LIGHT OF DEATH

JULY 15TH

BARRACHOIS LAGOON

A breeze slipped over Enriquez as, chin planted in the sand, limp hands hanging over the edge of the dune, his eyelids slid down over his eyes. Hours ago, weary of watching Vishnu, Ganesh, and Yuval dodge the knives they threw at one another, he returned to his vigil over *l'Arethusa*. Deliveries of matériel to the ship had ceased at sundown, and as the twilight faded into night, its crew settled into its routines and made ready to depart. Soothed by the rhythm of their preparations, Enriquez's resolve to keep watch for Erieux gradually weakened.

The shutters had nearly slammed shut on the pirate's view of the world when a flash lit up the ship's rail, and the crack of a flintlock skipped over the water to the beach. In the flare that burst from the gun, Enriquez saw a body topple backwards off the ship. A moment later, when the body cut the surface, a muffled roar erupted from the depths of the lagoon. Enriquez jolted awake, and distracted by the pirate's sudden move, Yuval squawked as Vishnu's dagger nicked his cheek.

"Boys, did you hear that?" Enriquez called to his lieutenants, straining his eyes against the darkness while thrashing around in the sand as he tried to get to his knees. "Again, while we are at this lagoon, I am hearing the sounds of a woman cannibalizing her young, and this time she sounds truly hungry. I wonder if it was Rio who went over the side and whet her appetite."

White-hot hunger fueling her rage, Marquaisa's howling ruptured the undercurrents that buffeted her. Caught in the blasts, the thousand, luminous shards that swirled around her exploded into a million particles that shrieked as they flared, then fizzled out as they rained down into the mud that caked the floor of the bay. The coils of sturdy rope in which she was entwined popped in rapid-fire succession and the oak shard that weakened her burst from her chest. Unfettered, she surged at the slack body that was sinking towards her and streaming tantalizing blood. With her left hand she caught it by the hair at the back of its head, then kicked against the weight of the water until she broke from underneath it. Her head finally above water, she found the shoreline, wrapped her arm around the chest of the body, and drove toward the shallows, leaving a frothing trail in her wake.

When her feet struck bottom, she hitched the body up under her arm and sprinted onto the beach. She ran until the sand between her toes went dry, and then heaved the body into the wall of a low dune that was crested with reedy beach grasses. Snarling at the defenseless man, her fangs gleaming, she found a sluggish pulse in his neck and pounced on him.

Poised to bite, she caught a glimpse of the wound in his chest and the blood in the sand behind his back, and hesitated. Shaking her head in confusion, she halted her attack. Curious, she took his scent and looked closely at the ridges and lines of his face. Pulling back, startled, she poked his chest and waited. When he did not respond, she nicked her lip with her fingernail tip and dabbed freezing ichor into and around his wound.

Fascinated, she watched in silence as the bloody holes in the man's chest and back bubbled and hissed as they closed. But when the sounds of boot heels scuffing through the sand reached her ears, she snarled and spun away from the unconscious man to face her attackers. A man, showing off gleaming white teeth and a bulge in his pocket, was walking toward her, leading three others whose dark skin was accented by their bright, colorful clothing. The smiling man raised his hand as if to greet her, but he and the others froze when they saw her; the ropes of her tangled hair slashing through the air and slapping against her sodden black cloak, while her ruddy eyes drilled hungrily into them.

"My lady?" Enriquez sought her recognition as he slowly lowered his right hand and found the bulge in his pocket. Marquaisa ignored his salutation and squared her hips at him, ready to spring. Abandoning caution, Enriquez shoved his hand into his pocket and yanked out a silver chain at the end of which dangled a crystal sphere roughly the size and shape of a chicken's egg.

Its chain wrapped tightly around his fist, the pirate jerked the talisman to chest height and thrust it at Marquaisa as she hurtled at him. Wrestling his eyes off her, Enriquez focused on the pendant and flicked the crystal with a finger on his left hand. As it spun, the crystal began to glow with the Light of Death. Mortals, deemed worthy by Oculus, were welcomed by its glow when they passed from the world of the living. It was less receptive to the ranks of the undead.

A handful of talismans like Enriquez's were scattered around the globe and they could be put to a variety of uses, including saving their wielder's lives. Enriquez had *inherited* his talisman while *inspecting* his grandfather's collection of ill-gotten goods, knowing it would be handy for extracting himself from sticky situations, such as the one in which he was mired with his current employer.

After a few calamitous experiments—people turned to dust, buildings reduced to rubble, natural disasters triggered—Enriquez became a passable, but shaky, user of the talisman. His skills graduated from apocalyptic to wobbly when, in the aftermath of one of his failed experiments, he discovered the secret incantation that allowed him to lasso the unearthly power that was pent-up within the crystal. Now, as his employer bore down on him the pirate bellowed his rendition of the sacred words, handed down from time immemorial, that were guaranteed to unleash the light and stop the demon in her tracks, "*Holy shiiitt!*"

Marquaisa froze when she hit the globe of silver light that burst from the crystal and surrounded the four men. In the split second she stood motionless, Enriquez saw through her veil of tangled black hair into her carnal soul. Her cheeks were hollow, her skin was taut, and her eyes, sunken in a pitiless scowl, knew only a blind rage that was stoked by deprivation and abyssal craving. His eyes wide, he blinked in shock, but by the time he opened them again, she had vanished.

Enriquez repeated the words of his incantation, this time not intending to conjure forth supernatural energies, and as the glow from the crystal faded he gulped down a stilted breath of air. When he was sure Marquaisa's departure was permanent, he relaxed and began to lower his arm, but stopped when the points of three knives nipped at the base of his spine, the back of his ribcage, and beside his left shoulder blade, behind his heart. Their warnings received, Enriquez pocketed his pendant and faced the three Maratha, whose knives traced lines on his skintight shirt as he turned.

Unblinking, the captain looked into the eyes of his three crewmen and made clear to them what had just transpired, "I *did not* harm her. I *could not* harm her, even if I wanted to. I *would not* harm her for all of the gold in the Grand Archvillain's treasure vault. But, she is lost to herself, and she would have harmed all of you finding her way back. That is something I *will not* allow. So, I sent her on her way. But, have no fear, she *will* return to us."

Without another word, he brushed aside all three blades and strode away from the Maratha, over to where Erieux still lay flattened in the sand. Upon reaching the Acadian, Enriquez gleefully noted his disguise, as well as how rapidly the hole in his chest, which peeked through the rip in his shirt, was healing. He was less pleased that the Acadian insisted upon acting as if he was unconscious, so he nudged his buttocks with the toe of his boot. Erieux rewarded him with a stream of groggy obscenities, as well as a familiar refrain, *"Paradis (Paradise)? Raçielle?"*

"No, Rio, still you are closer to Halifax," Enriquez shook his head and informed the Acadian as to his whereabouts.

Erieux thumped the back of his skull in the sand, in dismay, and girned, "Raçielle. She is alive. I saw her on the ship."

"Happy she was to see you, I can tell," Enriquez said, arching an eyebrow at the scar on Erieux's chest. "You may now forget the order I gave to you some days ago—which you have ignored most despicably —that you introduce me to one of your Acadian women."

"I found her. After all this time," Erieux fretted and sunk deeper into the sand, not hearing Enriquez. "She hated me for it."

"Shocking. Charmer that you are," Enriquez exaggerated his disbelief for the benefit of the Vishnu, Ganesh, and Yuval who, along with Enriquez, formed a rough semicircle around their semiconscious crewmate. His patience eroding rapidly, the captain got down to the business of addressing what was most important, asking Erieux, "Did you find the gold?"

"Tons and tons of gold," the Acadian murmured in a faraway voice.

"Did I not tell you?" Enriquez smiled and slapped Vishnu on the shoulder then, obliged to maintain the pretense of the mission, booted Erieux again, "I mean, well done Rio. You were right! Now, did you find out where it is being taken?"

"No," Erieux eked out the one-word answer, then passed out.

The streams of deflated sighs from Enriquez and the Maratha turned into a haze of robust curses that blew away down the beach. As their swearing faded from earshot they scanned the black waters of the harbor for sights of, or sounds from, the ship that got away. Stubbornly, the silent harbor returned none. Instead, they were treated to Erieux's sleeptalking ramblings about a betrayal perpetrated by a traitor named Kalos, and a rescue fashioned by an angel named Akuia.

HMS L'ARETHUSA

Shrouded by the moonless sky, but guided by the lights from the camp-fires that lined the eastern rim of the harbor and extended up to Light-house Point, *l'Arethusa* eased by the wrecks of the ships Drucour had scuttled at the mouth of the port. As the frigate slipped past the sunken hulks, two of her crew slipped over the rail and went about their duties, silently, unnoticed by all but a few of their mates. The barrel-chested seaman and his shipmate, who earlier in the evening winched the four passengers onto *l'Arethusa*, clambered down her webbing to the skiff she was towing and from which the passengers had been delivered.

At the ship's rail, behind the helm, the passengers watched the fires that burned Louisbourg, while casting wary eyes at the British battery that loomed silently over them from the top of Lighthouse Point. Without warning, the captain shattered the hush gripping the ship with a harsh command to come to a full stop. Hustling to carry out the order, the crew reined in the ship, which rumbled and shook as it struggled to do their bidding. When the ship finally heaved to, the captain lit a lantern, placed it on the rail by the passengers, left the helm under the watchful eye of an ensign, and went below deck.

"Lighting a candle for Louisbourg's deliverance?" Fortess ventured.

"Louisbourg, such as it is, will be delivered. But not by appealing to the whims of Oculus," Poisson replied. "Rather, ruin that she is, Louisbourg will be saved according to the terms of a business agreement that I, as Regent to His Majesty, King Louis XV, have struck with the British."

"What 'business agreement?'" Fortess bristled.

Poisson pivoted and took a step away from the rail, then pivoted, once more, in order to face the ex-captain, "Did I not mention to you, Fortess, on the evening you agreed to make arrangements for *l'Arethusa* to be stocked for our voyage, that it was a voyage to which the British had consented, and that there were conditions attached to their consent?"

"You did not," Fortess growled through clenched teeth, scowling at Poisson.

"Do forgive me," Poisson sneered back Fortess, neither wanting nor needing absolution from anyone. "Well, here it is. In exchange for my safe passage, as well my word that I will not return with a fleet to destroy them, I agreed to relinquish to the British a hostage of value. As an aside, they agreed that upon our delivery of said hostage, they would temper their bombardment of Louisbourg, somewhat, and repatriate the hostage after the siege has run its course. Any questions?"

"I have done all that you have asked of me!" Fortess snapped at the regent.

"Two things, Fortess," Poisson cut off the madman, "First, that is not a question. Second, kindly refrain from flattering yourself."

"What do you mean?" Fortess demanded, shocked at the possibility he might not be considered valuable.

"It means, my good man, that the British consider you worthless," Poisson confirmed Fortess's fear. He then turned to D'Acier, gave him an appraising once over and informed him, "It means, also, the British demanded the opportunity to extend their hospitality to the governess."

"What! What have you done?" the governess barked. "I refuse! I will not go! Send him," she pointed at D'Acier.

"You may refuse. But you will go either as a willing participant, or in a burlap sack towed behind a rowboat. It makes no difference to me. The British did not specify the condition in which you are to be delivered," Poisson gave the governess a hard look. "Now, be a good girl and run along. A pair of stalwarts await you, below, in the skiff that will transport you to your salvation. You may thank me properly when next we meet."

The regent dismissed the governess with a backhanded wave, and watched her clomp down to the main deck to be plopped into a basket and winched over the side. As the governess disappeared, Poisson spied a grin spreading across Fortess's face, the mirth in which he immediately quashed, "By the way, Fortess, you are not entirely off the hook."

"What do you mean?" Fortess asked warily.

"There's that question again. Fortess, you really do need to learn to anticipate me," Poisson taunted the angular Frenchman. "What it means is you will be my representative in delivering to the British two things: first, her ladyship, and second, this message." Poisson pulled a damp, sealed page from his breast pocket and handed it and his orders to Fortess, "See to it that it is delivered to Admiral Boscawen on *HMS Amelia*, which if I am not mistaken approaches us as we speak."

Fortess and D'Acier followed Poisson's gaze beyond *l'Arethusa's* prow and found a man o' war approaching from the southeast. When the admiral showed himself at the ship's helm, the Parisians were satisfied the British intended to act in good faith, insofar as they would not risk shelling the French vessel while the British vessel was in such close proximity. Determined not to delay their transaction, Poisson pointed Fortess at the basket that was waiting to carry him from the main deck, down to the skiff and sent him on his way.

After Fortess dropped out of sight, Poisson approached the ensign at the helm, and imposed on him, "Young man, would you be so kind as to track down the *capitaine* and tell him we are again ready to 'make sail?' I believe that is the correct nautical term, is it not?"

HMS Amelia

A stony silence gripped the four occupants of the skiff as it splashed through the swells toward *HMS Amelia*. The two seamen, wrapped up and hooded to keep out the wet and the chill, worked their oars. Lady Drucour and Fortess kept watch as they drew closer to the British warship, while trying to avoid eye contact with the pale faces peering at them over its rail. When the skiff bumped against the ship's hull, a swing was rolled down, and knowing the drill the governess installed herself in its seat and rode it over the rail without a word.

Matters went less smoothly for Fortess, who first had to get the attention of the deckhand in charge of the winch, then convince him that he too needed to be brought up top. After an animated discussion involving much arm waving, some off-color sign language, and the use of the increasingly sodden, sealed letter as a prop, Fortess's request to come aboard finally was understood and the swing was let out.

Unlike the governess's smooth ascent, Fortess's ride was bumpy. Some inexplicable malfunctions in the winch caused him to be bounced off the ship's hull, then without warning to be dropped a few feet, and finally to come to a stop an arm's length below the rail. He had barely handed his dripping letter to the deckhand in charge when the swing let go again, and he plummeted toward the skiff.

Fortess and the oarsmen were bracing for his crash landing when he jolted to a stop, a few feet above the skiff's deck. Unable to obtain a toehold on the little boat, Fortess had to squirm out of the swing and throw himself down to the skiff. When his boots hit its slick deck, his feet shot out from underneath him, his legs cycled through the air, and he slammed flat on his back in the skiff, facing up into the grinning faces of the audience that had congregated at the rail to watch his pratfall. Straight-faced, the oarsmen collected him off the deck, installed him on his bench, pushed off from the ship's hull, and got underway in the direction of *l'Arethusa.*

On the main deck of *HMS Amelia,* while Fortess was enduring his humiliations, Admiral Boscawen, with the governess at his side, took delivery of the tattered letter the Frenchman had delivered and carefully broke its seal. A single word, penned in elaborate script, was inscribed on the linen. A few of the characters were legible, but the remainder either were smeared or completely erased as a result of the soaking the letter received during it journey.

Squinting at the message, the admiral apologized to the governess, "Please, bear with me my lady. This will take but a moment, after which I shall escort you to your quarters." He then scanned the deck, and spotting his aide at the rail called to him, "Oswald, if you find you are able to pry yourself away from the entertainment being provided by our French messenger, then I would like for you to join me for a moment."

His cheeks reddening, the junior officer hurried to where the admiral was waiting to introduce him. "Lady Drucour," Boscawen began. "I give you Major Noel Oswald, lionheart and protector of the empire. He is yours to abuse as you see fit. However, before I release him to do your every bidding, I require his assistance in deciphering this confounded message. Have a look at this will you, Oswald, and tell me what you see."

The aide accepted the page from the admiral, looked at the inscription carefully, and conveyed his understandings to his commanding officer, "Sir, I see the letters *B—i—e—n—and—v.* The rest of the inscription is a blur that is beyond fathoming."

"Well done, Oswald," the admiral congratulated his aide. "But, not to put too fine a point on it, what the deuce does it mean?"

"Well, sir, given the circumstances, I'd say they were bidding you *'Bienvenue.'* As in, *'Good day to you, sir.'*

"Damned polite of them," the admiral huffed, and then crumpled the message in his hand. "Let's return the compliment, shall we? Oswald, if you would be so kind, please throw your lantern overboard."

Oswald's lamp glowed through a wide arc, away from *HMS Amelia*, then drowned the instant it plunged into the dark waters of the channel. Its blaze of glory went unseen by Fortess, who watched, puzzled, as a lantern thrown from the deck of *l'Arethusa* met the exact same fate. Even more mystifying was the fact the skiff on which he was a passenger seemed to be gaining no ground on the French warship, no matter how hard his oarsmen pulled.

"Why are we not catching up to them?" Fortess asked, craning his neck at the ship that was disappearing into the night. "Is it the tides? Could something be wrong with the ship?"

"Perhaps it is because they have left you behind," the barrel-chested oarsman stated.

"That is not possible. I have a deal with . . ." Fortess stopped himself and looked at the oarsman, who had pulled back his hood, "des Gouttes!"

"At your service," the commodore greeted Fortess, then drew a flintlock pistol and shot the other oarsman in the head, killing him instantly.

As the dead man slid to the floor of the skiff, his hood slipped back and Fortess recognized him as Corporal Danier, the young soldier who had pulled him off des Gouttes and put a stop to their fight in the King's Bastion. "What have you done?" Fortess shouted.

"No, Fortess. The question is, 'What have *you* done?'" des Gouttes drew a second pistol from beneath his cloak. "The answer, I'm afraid, is you murdered poor Danier in your attempt to escape apprehension for the crimes you have committed against France. Fortunately, you were killed by *me* as you fled. Goodbye, Fortess."

The commodore leveled his pistol at Fortess, but as he cocked the hammer the battery on Lighthouse Point boomed out a salvo. A split second later, whistles filled the night air as a handful of twenty-four pounders descended on the point in the channel where the flying lanterns last were seen. The cannons' roars still were echoing around the harbor when the sounds of wood shearing off *l'Arethusa* reached the skiff. An instant later, the skiff blew apart when it too was clipped by one of the huge cannon balls.

Danier was tossed into the frothing waves like a ragdoll, impaled by wood shards ripped out of boards blasted from the floor of the skiff. Tensing his body the moment the little craft shattered, without willing it des Gouttes squeezed the trigger of his pistol as he was thrown into the air. The lead ball from his pistol tore through the skin over Fortess's ribs and knocked the captain into a dizzying spin in which he lost his bearings, as well as his sight of the briny water, until he smacked against it and disappeared beneath its surface.

In the hush that followed the thunder of the volley, Poisson studied the stern of *l'Arethusa* and sniffed at the damage that had been inflicted upon it, "From what we have witnessed in town over the past weeks, it's hard to know if what I'm looking at is the product of good shooting, or bad."

"Agreed," D'Acier said, ambling up beside the regent. "How do you think Fortess faired? I believe I heard a bit of a commotion out on the water, just before the cannons went to work."

"Fortess's fortunes are no longer are our concern. They belong to des Gouttes," Poisson locked arms with D'Acier. "I did warn the idiot to better anticipate me. You heard me."

"Indeed, I did," D'Acier said, trying to break free from Poisson.

"Oh, tut-tut Trémont. We have done what we set out to do. Just as we envisioned we would so long ago. Our only burden now is to decide where, when, and how much of our loot to squander," Poisson said, holding D'Acier tight as they descended to the main deck. "Speaking of which, now that your pockets are full and you are a gentleman I suppose I shall be left to my own devices when it comes to arranging my diversions. In that regard, there is a chance I might actually miss the governess. She was singularly entertaining."

On *HMS Amelia*, Boscawen watched *l'Arethusa* slink off into the night and echoed Poisson's sentiment, "That was amusing."

Profoundly unamused by her predicament, Lady Drucour stiffened and, frowning, asked the admiral to explain himself, *"Excusez-moi?" Pardon me?*

"Pardon me, my lady," Boscawen replied, his attitude devoid of contrition. "I was simply expressing my satisfaction with our parting gift to your countrymen. After all, what more than fair warning of the consequences of breaking his word could a fighting man, such as your *Capitaine Vauquelin*, ask for. Now, there is someone who would like to make your acquaintance. If you would be so kind as to accompany me?"

With Oswald in tow and the governess on his arm, the admiral strolled to the stern of the ship and the quarters housed below the helm. When he reached the door, he rapped on it sharply, then turned to Oswald and gave him his instructions, "Bide here a moment and do not let anyone disturb us." Without waiting for acknowledgment from his aide, the admiral opened the door and stood aside to allow the governess to precede him into the dimly lit room.

A lone man stood behind a bureau with his back facing the door, looking through the windows at the fires of Louisbourg. At the sound of the cabin door closing, he turned and faced his two visitors and waited, a smirk tugging at the corners of his mouth. The man's amusement was not lost on Boscawen, who sighed and waded into another round of introductions, "Lady Drucour, I give you Major General Jeffrey Amherst, Commander-in-Chief of the British forces here at Louisbourg. General Amherst, Lady Drucour."

The general bowed while the governess curtsied.

The formalities taken care of, Amherst complimented Boscawen, "Well done, Eddie. Sending the twenty-four pounders up their back-sides was a nice touch." The two men chuckled amongst themselves. To the side, her cheeks coloring, the lady cleared her throat and

Amherst moved the conversation forward quickly, "Any messages from the French?"

"They bid us 'good day,' is all," Boscawen answered, paraphrasing his aide's interpretations of the message delivered by Fortess.

Amherst raised an eyebrow, and with a hint of irritation in his voice pressed the admiral, "Just, 'Good day?' Nothing else?"

"That was it," the admiral matched the general's tone. "I had Oswald do the translation, and my lady witnessed it."

"Very well, very well, understood. Sorry, Eddie, I'm a bit testy these days," the general said, excusing himself. "Now, if you wouldn't mind, would you give the governess and I the room for the few minutes? I would like to make the lady's acquaintance."

"Good enough, Jeff," the admiral snorted. "Oswald will be waiting outside for her ladyship, when she is ready."

When the cabin door closed behind the admiral, Amherst shot the governess a judgmental glare and she flinched when he scowled, "Your romp around the ramparts, this morning, caused quite the sensation up and down our ranks, my lady. Personally, it reminded me of an outrageous plan my most talented captain brought to me, months ago, when we started planning this expedition. The plan involved infiltrating Louisbourg's political inner circle and convincing its members to give up the town without a fight."

The general turned his back on the governess, to once again watch Louisbourg burn, and continued, "It was absurd to think the French would do such a thing. But, I consented to the plan, nonetheless. The slim chance it might help us avoid yet another battle in this endless war was enough to sway me."

Amherst walked around the bureau, sat on its edge, and looked the governess in the eye, "By some miracle of ingenuity, my captain penetrated said inner circle and persuaded most of the captains of the French ships to stand down from fighting. However, by looking through the windows behind me, and by recalling your own experiences ducking our flying cannonballs, you will know that ultimately my cunning young protégé failed."

The governess winced at the general's harshness.

"With that said, were it not for Drucour's refusal to let go of his lunatic plan to hold the town until the weather forced us to withdraw, the plan might very well have succeeded. And so, my good, young, Captain Race, allow me to be the first to congratulate you on a job well done."

Amherst extended his right hand and shook his captain's. Race eased out a breath and the general continued, "A pity Drucour didn't heed your counsel and avoid all of this ugliness. But, he is nothing if not stubborn, and I know that you did your best to change his mind. As for that peacock of a regent, Poisson, were you able to get to the bottom of whatever it is he was up to?"

"No, sir," Race admitted. "But there was something on that ship, '*l'Arethusa*, which had his interest."

"I'll bet there was," Amherst said, covering up a cough. "Anyway, I suppose, eventually, we will have to make Admiral Boscawen wise to our little secret. For the time being, however, let's have a bit fun with him and have you stay in your disguise. You've earned whatever luxuries he and Oswald intend shower upon you."

"Yes, sir," the captain said, her eyes twinkling.

"By the way, that recent bit of news you had Poisson share with us, about the plot to assassinate me, was much appreciated," Amherst thanked Race, smiling brightly, "Got me out of harm's way and gave me a reason to free myself from the rigors of camp life for a few days."

"Glad to be of service, sir," Race accepted the general's gratitude. "Sir, if I may ask. Who is standing in for you at camp in your absence?"

By way of a reply, the general allowed his grin to widen. He then laughed as he hadn't since he left the secret meeting with Pitt, in which the *Great Commoner* informed him, in all seriousness, about Poisson's scheme.

BRITISH HEADQUARTERS

The door of British command post burst open under the boot heels of the two black-clad assassins and they marched through the opening with their pistols leveled at the general, who was sitting behind his desk. At the sight of him, they pulled their triggers. As they did, the barrels of their weapons were slapped upwards from below, and their shots went high and wide of their target.

Rather than plugging their target with lead, making him dead, and ending their mission in triumph, their bullets succeeded only in causing a shower of wood chips. When the rain of shavings stopped, the general, who had not moved a muscle, kept the barrels of his two pistols aimed at their chests, while yet more pistols were pressed to their heads and their backs.

"James Wolfe, Brigadier General, at your service," Wolfe said, then stood up from his chair and bowed. "Allow me to introduce my associates. To my left, your right, Lieutenant-Colonel Andrew Rollo. To my right, your left, Lieutenant Thadan Jenkins. To your rear, Major Isaiah Brock. Somewhere in the woods a Mi'kmaq named Neil is skulking about."

The assassin to Wolfe's left started at the mention of Neah's name, prompting Wolfe to kick off his inquiries, "I see you've already met my stealthy friend. Tell me, does he still live?"

The assassin nodded, then blurted, "You are Amherst!"

Wolfe parried, "I most certainly am not, and have a care, for you risk adding insult to my reputation, on top of the injury you planned to inflict on our commander-in-chief. Besides that, everyone knows that I am the more handsome."

"Squids!" the assassin to Wolfe's right squeaked, as if he'd pinched his pecker in the buttonhole of his flannels.

"Brock, add that one to our list of colorful local profanities," Wolfe cocked an eyebrow as he instructed the young, pistol-totting major.

"*Phoq*," the assassin to Wolfe's left muttered.

"That one I've heard, thank you." Wolfe paused, and thinking himself inspired asked the assassins, "By chance, are either of you Acadian?"

The masked killers looked at one another, then back at Wolfe and shook their heads.

"I see," the general said to himself and paused, again. Then, thinking himself truly inspired, he lent his voice to a stream of consciousness as he paced back and forth behind his desk, "So, you do not know one another's identity. I'll wager, also, you worked independently to increase the odds of your mission succeeding; you know, one of you gets caught or killed, and oblivious to that fact the other carries on. That sort of thing. Deuced clever, wouldn't you say Rollo?"

"Underhanded, *mair (more)* like," Rollo huffed. His arm tiring, he lowered his pistol.

"Don't be such a spoilsport, Rollie. After all, we played a bit of a game ourselves to entice these people to join us, and you didn't judge Amherst so harshly on the deception," Wolfe teased the lieutenant-colonel. "By the way, for the benefit of our new friends, the players in the comedy were as follows: Rollie played the mortally wounded officer, and splendidly, I might add; and I played his captured killer. Amherst then jumped into the role of the assassin and allowed himself to be killed and then carted off to the trash heap. I expect, by now, he is well into his cups with Boscawen out on *Amelia*. They're quite a pair, you know."

The two assassins sagged, beaten and exhausted. Seeing them waning, Wolfe engaged them more directly, "Well, now you know us and our story. So, let's hear yours, shall we? If you would kindly remove your masks, then all of us can get properly acquainted."

The assassins pulled off their masks simultaneously. To Wolfe's right a young man whose carriage hinted of nobility, but whose eyes blazed with palpable madness, revealed himself and made his introduction, "I am Donatien Alphonse François de Sade, officer in training."

To Wolfe's left, a Venus of West Indian extraction, with golden brown skin and layers of bronze hair, unveiled herself and lifted her chin, "I am Haritha."

"Egads, Rollie," Wolfe drawled. "Fancy Drucour sending in a woman."

"It was my idea. The governor does not know I am here," Haritha clarified, her accent lilting. "Commodore des Gouttes wanted to send a young corporal he wanted rid of. Danier, I think was his name. But, I had Clavonne distract him and took his place."

To her left, de Sade choked, "'Rid of?' You mean they expected all along we would . . ."

Wolfe watched de Sade unravel, pitying ever so briefly the young man's delusions, then refocused on Haritha, "Distracted Danier, so you say. With Clavonne, am I right? Exactly what do you mean by 'distracted?'"

The mixture of coughing, choking, and throat clearing that erupted from Rollo, Jenkins, and Brock told Wolfe that either there was a rapidly spreading epidemic in the camp, or he had been colossally inappropriate. Not having received any reports from the hospital concerning the former, he had no choice but to concede the latter was the case, so he backtracked rapidly, "Pardon me, *mademoiselle,* you need not answer that question. I assume it is '*mademoiselle?*'"

"You are correct, *monsieur,* and please, call me Haritha."

"Haritha," Wolfe softened his voice as he let the name roll off his tongue. "Tell me, Haritha, when you are not taking on assignments to assassinate military leaders, what do you do for a living?"

"I genuflect," Haritha replied, proudly, looking Wolfe in the eye, while another round of expectorations burst from his associates.

"I assure you, Haritha, there is no need," Wolfe was magnanimous.

"Indeed, there is a need, *monsieur.* A *great* need," Haritha insisted. "I know this to be true because I genuflect every day. For men, for women, sometimes for men and women at the same time. I am the very best and I can barely keep up with the need."

"Of that, there is no doubt," de Sade rediscovered his voice.

"James, when Lady *Harrritha* says 'genuflect,' she is using it idiomatically," Rollo cut in, as discretely as possible.

"On the contrary, Rollie, Haritha strikes me as being someone who is the very opposite of an idiot," Wolfe contended.

"That is *no'what* I meant, James," Rollo replied, urgently.

"Very well, Rollie. In plain English, tell me what you mean."

"I will show *monsieur*," Haritha interjected.

Before either Rollo, Jenkins, or Brock could stop her, Haritha was over the desk and standing in front of Wolfe. When she arrived, he pressed the muzzles of his pistols against her belly, but she put her hands on top of their barrels and pushed them gently aside. She then looked up at Wolfe and kissed him, softly, on the lips while cupping his jewels in her two hands and kneading him expertly.

Slack-jawed, Rollo and Jenkins watched. Brock closed the door quietly as he hurried out. Wolfe froze and de Sade nodded in appreciation, "She *is* good."

CHAPTER 38

ESCAPADES

JULY 16TH

HMS AETNA

HMS *Aetna* coasted in the channel below Lighthouse Point, her masters carefully avoiding the vessels that had been scuttled at the mouth of the harbor. Earlier in the morning, she'd been tasked with searching the channel for bodies, or items of value, on the advice of the gunners who lobbed some twenty-four pounders at two flashes of light the night before.

Dutifully, *Aetna* trolled the area, with nothing to show for her efforts, waiting for word she could desist. Likewise resolved to persist in his duties until he was instructed to do otherwise, one of *Aetna's* officers remained fixed to his post at the stern rail, his spyglass pinned to his eye, scanning the surroundings for anything untoward. He finally was rewarded for his persistence when he spotted movement on the shoreline of Battery Island. Through his spyglass, he watched a sailor drag himself out of the surf and flop onto his back. After a few minutes, it was clear the exhausted man was content to lay still, and encouraged by his discovery, the officer panned across the harbor looking for more unusual activity.

His first pass, which covered the area from Battery Island to the mouth of the small northeast harbor, yielded no returns. On his return pass, however, when his line of sight crossed the three ships that were anchored off the wharf, he saw the crew of one of the ships fish from the water the body of a tall man dressed in fine, but too small civilian clothing. Judging from the frantic reactions of the seamen who hauled the body on board it appeared, as was the case with the beached sailor, the sodden citizen was showing signs of life.

Snapping shut his spyglass, the young officer began to piece together the scenarios that might link together the twin flashes, a beached sailor, and a half-drowned private citizen, but was interrupted by a belligerent voice that roared up at him from the main deck, "Washington, stop acting like Sam Holland on one of his damned cartographical escapades!" George Balfour, Captain of the *Aetna,* kept shouting, "Come and make yourself useful and help me get the navy out of mop-up duty and into the fight. I've a plan in mind, and I'll have your opinion of it before I take it to Boscawen. Now, get down here, you great lummox!"

The British Camp - North Flank

By sundown, *HMS Aetna* was resting safely at anchor in Gabarus Bay. Her bowels, however, roiled loudly in concert with the planning session that was taking place in Captain Balfour's quarters. Tactics and logistics had been put to bed. Politics, however, were proving to be a more colicky proposition. Washington, as the army's representative, wanted full participation in the action. Balfour wanted Washington to take a long walk off a short pier, and the rest of the army with him. Neither considered the possibility that they might be dooming the mission to failure by shouting its details across the bay.

Had their voices been loud enough to reach Enriquez, his would have drowned theirs out as he bellowed at Erieux to be quieter, and to stop crashing through the forest like a blind, three-legged bull. When Marquaisa vanished the previous evening, she had done so heading in a southerly direction, towards the town of Louisbourg. Eager to create as much space as possible between himself and his employer, Enriquez headed north on a roundabout route to Gabarus Point. He and his three lieutenants and Erieux, if he still was alive, were to rendezvous with *Rajani* at the point, assuming Suchika still was waiting for them. Traveling at night to avoid capture, the Spaniard lost his way, and the Acadian was bearing the brunt of his frustration.

"*Phoq you!*" Erieux shouted back. "I told you to let me lead. But *nooo*, the grandson of the Grand Archvillain knew better. And where are we now, eh? Where are we now? Lost, that's where. So, what do we do now, *Capitán?*"

Erieux waited for a reply. When none came, he continued to rant, "What, nothing to say, oh wisest of the wise? Probably fell into a trap, or something. Dumb shit that you are. Don't be thinking I'll be crawling in to pull the stakes out of your ass. You're so smart, get them out yourself!"

Erieux continued tromping through the undergrowth, cursing every step of the way, until he blundered into a small clearing. Stumbling forward for a few steps, his every move no longer blocked by branches or roots, he lurched to a stop at the sight of a nearby campfire, as well as the sound of a handful of muskets being cocked. Knowing, from prior experience, how to escape such predicaments, he spun, crouched, and ran back the way he'd come and slammed his forehead straight into the rifle butt of the British Marine who had circled around behind him. Concussed instantly, he backflipped and landed face first in the dirt. A few well-placed jabs of the ends of musket barrels confirmed he was out cold, and he was dragged by his heels to the campsite.

A bucket of icy water dumped on his head shocked Erieux into semiconsciousness, and as his eyes opened he strained to make sense of where he was and who he was with. Backlit by a campfire, a man in a red coat confronted him, growling in English-accented French, "Where is he?"

"What? Who?" Erieux spluttered, his eyes blinking, his head lolling.

The man smacked Erieux across the face with an open hand, to the amusement of his comrades, and pressed the Acadian, "You were talking to someone, out there. Where is he? Where is the grandson of the Grand Archvillain?"

"Enriquez?" the Acadian deciphered his inquisitor's query and braced himself for another crack in the skull

"That'll be him. Where . . .," the soldier stopped his interrogation and barked at some new arrivals to the camp. "You three, never mind what's going on here. Get back on patrol before—"

Cut off by the knife that thudded through his throat, the inquisitor's eyes bulged and his tongue lolled over his lips. Choking and quivering, he toppled into the dirt beside Erieux, who scrambled away from the rush of blood that poured from the man's neck and mouth.

Erieux heard two more *thuds* and saw two more bodies hit the dirt before the four surviving members of the squad recognized the danger and sprang at their attackers. The Acadian watched three colorful figures shed too big red coats and sidle into the firelight to circle their quarry. A fourth raider strode forward, and before his enemy could counter, slashed him from hip to throat with the tip of his sword, and then decapitated him as he fell backwards. In quick succession, the three remaining squaddies also fell, the arteries in their necks spewing blood.

When all of their victims were still, the four raiders paused and listened carefully for the sounds of alarms. When none were heard, they crouched next to the bodies of the soldiers they had slain. Knives were reclaimed and the red coats in which the corpses were dressed were used as rags to clean their blades. Pockets, fingers, ears, and teeth were searched, and anything that gleamed was claimed as a prize. Last of all, pistols were yanked out of dead hands, and pouches of ammunition were pulled free and strapped to the bodies of their new owners. Their ransacking complete, the raiders turned their attention to Erieux, who was on his hands and knees, crawling aimlessly and dangerously close to the campfire.

Before the dazed Acadian stuck his hands into the embers, the swordsman who decapitated his opponent, moments earlier, grabbed him and dragged him back to the body of the soldier who, moments earlier, was his interrogator. Enriquez then sat Erieux beside the body, steadied him, and smiled, "Good boy, Rio. Now watch."

Whistling, softly, Enriquez jerked the knife from the man's throat and tossed it to the three Maratha. He then flipped the body onto its back and searched it for valuables. He was rewarded with a few coins that he dropped deftly into a leather pouch. The dead soldier's pistol was unkempt, so the pirate ignored it and pressed the leather pouch into Erieux's hand, then hauled him to his feet.

Chuckling, Enriquez looked into Erieux's glassy eyes and explained, "That is your prize for playing your role so well. Hold onto it, because you know what these British say; 'Take care of the pennies, and the farthings and shillings will take care of themselves!'" He wrapped Erieux's fingers around the pouch, and his own arm around the Acadian's shoulders, and while hauling him to his feet critiqued his performance, "Just so you know, *my* favorite part was when you threatened to leave me stuck in a pit. *The boys* liked it best when you called me a 'dumb shit.' Now, find your feet and let's go. We must keep moving. There are many more British about, and not all of them are as stupid as me."

BRITISH HEADQUARTERS

"Don't be an idiot, Jenkins," Wolfe said as he swept woodchips, remnants of the previous evening's excitement, off his desk, "I can manage the interrogation of Lady Haritha on my own, without your protection. She is properly restrained, yes?"

"Shackled, hand and foot," Jenkins nodded. "She is an assassin, after all."

"Then neither my life, nor my virtue should be at risk. Although, to be truthful, I am not entirely certain whether the restraints will make Lady Haritha more or less dangerous." Wolfe blew the sawdust off the desk. He then stood out of his chair and bellowed, "Show in the prisoner!"

Jenkins rolled his eyes and opened the command post door, the front of which still bore imprints left by a pair of boots. Her black costume long since replaced with a standard issue, loose-fitting shirt than hung over snug breeches and boots, Haritha was engaging her guards and a handful of their mates in a bit of chitchat that had them all blushing from their collars to the brims of their tricorns. When Jenkins approached the crowd, the soldiers eyed him jealously and reluctantly released Haritha into his custody.

After prying her loose from her admirers, Jenkins steered Haritha toward the command post. As they walked toward to the open door he was surprised at the solid constitution of the arm that he held in his hand, as well as the firmness of the hip that accidentally swayed into his. He attributed the bead of sweat that trickled from behind her ear, down her neck, and into the gap between her breasts to the heat of the night, the thickness of the mane of bronze hair that fell down her back, and her nervous anticipation of the interview with the general. Still, he stubbed his toe as he took a step into the office and watched her walk toward Wolfe.

"I'll be just outside if you need me," Jenkins, his voice cracking, reminded Wolfe and closed the door.

"You look hot, *mademoiselle,*" Wolfe observed as Haritha approached his desk.

"Thank you, *monsieur,*" Haritha smiled, warmly.

Puzzled by her reply to what he hadn't intended to be a compliment, Wolfe pointed at the chair beside which Haritha stood, "Please, sit down."

"Actually, I was hoping you would tell me to kneel," Haritha suggested, her dulcet voice saturated with anticipation and excitement.

"I'm sorry, what?" Wolfe asked, caught off his guard.

Without a word, and before Wolfe could utter another one, Haritha made her way around Wolfe's desk. The only sound she made was to scuff the chain links that ran between the shackles on her ankles across the floor planks. When she reached him, she bumped her chest into his and pinned him to the wall. Her warm breath brushing his cheeks, she lifted her chin and when her lips were a hairsbreadth away from his, ran the tip of her tongue softly across them.

"*Mademoiselle,* you mustn't," Wolfe whispered, sensing the futility of his resistance.

"Yes, I must," Haritha insisted, pressing her hips against his. "But, *monsieur* must help a little. As he can see, my jailors very kindly fit my manacles very snuggly around my wrists and used a very short chain to join them together behind my back."

"The key is in my desk drawer," Wolfe told her then, unsure as to where his actions would fall on the chivalry scale, he added, "I will free you."

"I think not," Haritha whispered. "There are many who would appreciate your kind offer. However, I am more the risqué type. I find it arousing to be restrained."

"Truly?" Wolfe intoned huskily, telling her, though not in so many words, how arousing it was to have her in restraints.

"Oh, yes," she said softly, reading his thoughts, "It presents thrilling challenges."

"Such as?" Wolfe invited her to share, guessing she and he were alike of mind.

"Such as, how to unsheathe *Sexcalibur?*" Haritha divulged, proving him right. "I could use my teeth to peel away your breeches and your briefs. But, I assure you, the sensations my doing so would evoke in you would trigger your early release. That being the way of things, if you wish to avoid the blue wave, then you must help us both and free yourself."

"Very well. If I must," Wolfe surrendered, willingly, unbuckled his belt, and unbuttoned his trousers.

"Yes, you must," Haritha insisted, giving him room to extract himself. "I will do the rest."

Wolfe kicked off his boots, then let his trousers slip down around his ankles. Next, he stretched his skivvies over his swelling package and let them join his trousers. He then punted his suddenly inessential apparel off to one side.

"You have been thinking of me," Haritha hummed at the sight of him.

"Hardly a little. Almost a lot," Wolfe confessed, craving her touch.

falls told her blocks of stone crowded the waterfront, though frantic to feed, she slowed to a walk. Feeling her way quietly through the rocks, she sorted through the sounds and smells that hung over them or clung to them, scanning for the markers that would steer her to the souls whose lifeblood she would seize to regain her strength.

Hushed voices and shuffling footsteps drew her attention to a section of stonework near the base of which water was lapping. Soft and quavering, the voices were weighed down with fears born of distant muzzle flashes and the hot iron hailstorms that followed that, sooner or later, would obliterate them. To quell their fears, they whispered to one another of how the tall ships moored nearby soon would spirit them away to safety. Preoccupied as they were with nurturing their hopes, no matter how false, they were oblivious to the menace, close at hand, who was aching to rid them of their petty woes by replacing them with torments that surpassed their worst nightmares.

Sharply focused and pleasingly sadistic, Marquaisa licked her lips and set her plan in motion. No sooner had her tongue slithered back into her mouth, than four unfortunates separated themselves from the herd, shambling away from their mates, through the sand, to dip their toes in the water. Her ears attuned first to the scraping of sand, then the puddling of water, she skipped down the beach and slid to a stop between the dabbling foursome and their amigos in the dunes. Some of the sand she kicked up sprayed into the shallows, but the pattering sounds it made on contact with the surface went unheard or unheeded; the voices, male and guttural, continued to carry away from her and out over the harbor.

A wispy offshore breeze slipped through her ropey black tresses and the tatters of her cloak and she chased it into the water, churning up a crashing, foaming train that splatted against the backsides of her prey. Startled by the sudden noise and shocked by the smacking of the cold water on their behinds, all four spun around in the knee-deep water to find out who from among their klatch was thinking they were being funny and to rip into them with salty rebukes. But, before a word was uttered, their windpipes were sliced open by razor-sharp talons wielded with surgical precision by a snarling fiend whose tangled black hair hid most of its ashen face and sinewy body, and covered over some of the many rips its shredded black cloak.

Gagging and pawing at their throats they went down in the water, on their knees or on their buttocks. Working by feel, Marquaisa groped around until she found one of the kneeling men, who at her touch flung himself backwards and underwater. Clawing at him, she grabbed a handful of his hair, pulled him up, and tore into his jugular with her fangs. As she drank from him, she closed her mouth tighter and tighter until she ripped a chunk of muscle and skin out of his neck. A wash of blood poured out of the gash and pooled around the dying man and she spit his flesh from her mouth into the spreading gore, laughed, and then pounced on another man who, in his throes, unwittingly kicked her in the shin.

He saw her coming and tried to scream, but wheezed dryly while wallowing in a feeble attempt dodge her attack. In a fury, Marquaisa snatched his shirtfront in her fists and hauled him out of the water as she stood up straight. When she reached her full height she flipped her hair off her face, giving the man a closeup view of the ravages that went along with being tethered to a hunk of stone at the bottom of a lagoon for a month. Her skin was a translucent film that was stretched across and torn apart by the sharp bones of her brow, nose, cheeks, and jaw. Tracks of black veins threaded from her temples over her forehead and into the hollows of her eyes and cheeks. Her lips were split and peeling and her ears were frayed. Her eyes were coated over with shiny metal, the chips in which showed her orbs were a depthless black, and were shifting, stopping, then shifting again as she searched for the sweet spot in his neck. When she found it, she opened her mouth wide, then plunged her fangs into the veins that ran through it and drank hungrily while he gibbered and pissed himself.

When he ran dry, Marquaisa dropped him on the corpse of one of the men whose throat she had cut but whose blood she had not tasted. The last man in the foursome no longer stirred in the water, so he too was off her menu. His four beachcombing friends, however, who were milling about and calling out to their now deceased companions, were ripe for the taking. By way of a reply, the stern lantern on one of the tall ships sparked to life and, the light from the lamp showing flashes of a solitary figure wadding out of the water toward shore, the sailor on watch called back asking if there was cause for alarm.

Marquaisa snickered, hoarsely, and strolled onto the beach seeking out the mewling vagrants, who on seeing her rising from the harbor had closed ranks and huddled together, silently, inside a henge-like stand of boulders. Relishing the gnawing dread that emanated from the group, she drifted into its midst and let its members watch the blood of their friends stream from her face and drip off the tips of her talons. Numbed to their cores and paralyzed with terror, they gawped at her, so she grabbed two of them, one in each of her hands, and fed on them, moving from one to the other and back again, until their knees buckled. Before their carcasses hit the ground, she was hot on the heels of the two survivors who, having seen more than enough of her, had taken flight.

She caught the slower of the two within a few strides and silenced his screams by pinning him to the ground, sinking her teeth into his throat, and gulping down his essence. When she finished with him, her cravings still were aching so she listened for the footfalls of the other escapee. None were to be heard. Not because the woman was being stealthy, but because she was screaming bloody murder at the top of her lungs. Her cries caused an uproar in a much larger group of stragglers loitering around the waterfront, who ran toward her, then past her when she pointed at where she last saw the 'monstre.' Snarling, Marquaisa stalked toward the horde, but sensing its overwhelming numbers, veered away from it and the beach and disappeared into the bombed-out shells of the buildings on the wharf.

Moving on a path that ran in the direction opposite to that in which the mob was headed, she picked her way through the ruins of Louisbourg. Fortified by her meal, the brittleness in her bones began to ease, her vision began to clear, and kernels of knowledge started to pop open in her brain. Hard-won lessons on survival jumped to the forefront of her mind, steering her along a trail that took her underground and into the tunnels that aerated the bedrock from the town all the way out to Black Point. Still partially blind, she felt her way along the pitch-black

tunnels to the cavern that was her sanctuary, and the raised stone platform at its center that was her cot. As she dragged herself onto it, her
talons pinged off a long, hard, slender thing that ran to a point at one
end. Attached to its opposite end was a familiar, studded handle.

Wrapping herself contentedly around her rapier, Marquaisa fell
instantly into a dreamless sleep. She lay deathly still while her body
used the fuel she seized during the slaughter at the waterfront to repair
itself. Fast asleep until sunset on the following day, she wakened in as
ravenous a state as she had been the night before. Her body restored,
her eyesight recovered, her strength growing, her hair and cloak still a
shambles, she strapped her rapier to her back and loped out of her lair.
Tracking west along the coastline, she headed for the source of the
reeking smoke that was a sure sign of the presence of people.

When she reached the beach below the smoldering pile of refuse,
Marquaisa found the hunting to be good. She notched three kills
quickly, all sentries patrolling the stockpiles of crates stacked haphazardly in the sands. Straddling her fourth, she was about to finish him
when she shivered, not from the coolness of the breeze that swept
across the hot blood on her face, but from the fragrance it lifted from
the crates that sent a tingling up her spine to the base of her skull.
When it hit her brain it cracked open memories of a woman with
bronze hair, golden brown skin, and insatiable, infectious sensuality. A
second later, when the vision disappeared, her attention caved in on the
youth whose throat and fate she held in her clenched fist.

In the blink of an eye she drove down to tear into his neck, but
stopped at the sight of a scar that ran from behind his right ear, down
the side of his neck, and curved under the collar of his red overcoat.
While the youth watched, wide-eyed, she traced the line of the scar
with the talon on her left thumb, and then pressed her nose against the
wound, sniffing it deeply. As she snuffled along its length, memories of
a faraway land, a small bedchamber, a rainstorm, and thrusting hips
filled her mind's eye and jolted her upright in the youth's lap.

As quickly as she had decided to eat him, a moment earlier,
Marquaisa changed her mind and ripped off what was left of her cloak
and tore away the young man's trousers. Using the tips of her talons,

she teased him until he was ready, and then eased herself onto him. Her legs locked with his, she flipped onto her back, and when she was certain he was well in she grabbed his buttocks and pulled him deeper, released him, then pulled him in again. Her instructions well received, the youth surged into her until, with a cry, he dug his fingers into the sand and pushed one last time. Then, empty but intoxicated, he cupped her face in his hands and kissed her, slowly and sweetly.

"Private Bridge!" a gruff voice called, punctuating his moment of lost virginity. "Why in the name of the cursed three-headed hound is your bare arse hangin' out all over my beach?"

Startled by the intrusion, Marquaisa pushed the youth away with her left hand and punched him in the face with her right, knocking him out cold. As he crumpled into the sand, she leapt to her feet and charged the man who had so rudely interrupted her pleasure. As she ran she drew, with her left hand, the rapier that was strapped to her back. On top of him before he could react, she stabbed the point of her blade into his right eye and out the back of his skull. Catching him by the back of his head with her right hand, she bit into his carotid and hurried him on his way to oblivion.

When he was drained, Marquaisa released him, and as he sank to the ground and her rapier slid out of his skull, she let loose a feral howl that ripped into the wooden crates surrounding her and nipped at the earlobes of the groggy youth whose virginity she had just appropriated. Roused to waking, he rolled onto his back and lay perfectly still while she walked back to him, looking him over and licking her lips.

"I am Bridge. Shanklin Bridge," he introduced himself when she stopped and stood over him.

Marquaisa bent at the waist and looked in his eyes and her face, body, and rapier streaked with blood, rasped, *"Estas asustado, Shanklin Bridge?"* Are you afraid, Shanklin Bridge?

His knowledge of Spanish was sketchy, but Bridge could tell from her body language she was testing him on a subject he knew all too well, fear. It being his constant companion, he gave her his most honest answer in as steady a voice as he could muster, "Of most things, yes. Of you, no."

Concealing her surprise behind a scowl, Marquaisa kept her eyes locked on his and wondered to herself, *What does he mean he's not afraid of me?* Unable to answer her own question and unwilling to ask the boy for an explanation of his reply, she snorted dismissively and moved the point of her rapier over his chest.

Bridge tracked it until it was over his heart, then closed his eyes. A second later he flinched as she raked the blade across his chest. He felt no pain, neither did his lungs stop working, nor did his heart stop beating, and it occurred to him that being killed wasn't as bad as he thought it would be. But when the feeling that he was being sawn in half persisted, though he wished not to see the mutilations she had inflicted upon his body, he snapped open his eyes and blenched.

Marquaisa ignored him and finished wiping her blade free of blood on his red overcoat. When it gleamed to her satisfaction she sheathed it in its scabbard and trotted away from Bridge before he could say anything else that would confuse her. To her it was enough that she knew neither who the bronze-haired sex goddess was, nor why the kiss with Bridge tasted so sweet, nor where she was going to get a new suit of clothes.

CHAPTER 39

SEPSIS

JULY 17TH

HMS CAPRICIEUX

Since her christening *Capricieux* had served the French navy faithfully, as a weapon of war. Since the previous morning she also had provided sanctuary for the wounded French civilian her crew had scooped out of the harbor. Sprawled over the cot that was jammed against the wall of the tiny cabin into which he'd been thrown, Fortess cracked his eyes open and hissed in pain; the sunlight that was angling through the porthole of the cabin burned through his eyeballs and slammed into the back of his skull. Shutting his eyes tight, he rolled onto his right side and retched emptily over the edge of his cot until his gut ached. When he flopped back in exhaustion, he slapped his left side against the timber wall, screamed, and blacked out.

Fortess still was out for the count when, a little while later, a duty officer named Auzire Duros poked his scar-faced and patch-eyed head into the make-do sickbay to check on his condition. Glad to find Fortess unconscious, Duros shuffled to his side and pulled back the dressing that clung to the wound over the left side of his ribcage. The dressing parted from Fortess's skin stickily, and as it did the smell of infectious decay filled the small cabin.

With a sigh, Duros replaced the dressing and yelled tiredly out the open door of the cabin, "This one's rotting! Someone bring me a hot iron!"

Looking back at Fortess, he pulled out his dagger with his left hand. Squaring his shoulders to Fortess, he aimed the point of the blade below and to the left of his sternum. Poised to strike, instead he paused and confided in the unconscious man, "I should let you die, or better yet, kill you and call it a mercy, *monsieur* Fortess. The sepsis has poisoned your brain. Since they hauled you on board *Capricieux,* your lunatic ravings have said as much."

Rather than drive the point of the dagger up into Fortess's heart, Duros used its keen edge to severe the wrappings around the wounded man's ribs. When he was finished, he cleaned his blade on a loose fold in the wrappings, sheathed it, and sat back. Looking blankly through the open doorway of the cabin, he picked up where he had left off in his one-sided conversation with his unconscious patient. "But, who am I to stand in the way of vengeance? I will cut out and burn the root of the infection. Maybe I will stop it before it kills you. If, by some miracle, you live, then you can seek your revenge as you see fit. Who knows? You may even succeed."

Duros looked doubtfully at Fortess's limp body and continued, "If you *do* succeed, then it will please me to know that I had a small hand in it. I never did like that pig des Gouttes. If you send him to an early grave, then it will be just desserts, not only for what he did to you, but also for taking my eye over that bronze-haired nymph."

ROCHEFORT POINT

Grave mold, churned up by stray French and British shells, clung to the tattered cuffs of des Gouttes' trousers as he hobbled through the cemetery that funneled down from the harbor front to the battery on Rochefort Point. After an eternity of negotiating tides and shoals and ducking errant cannonballs, as well as the plumes of shrapnel they spawned, he was near exhaustion when he clambered onto the battered fortifications that looked down on the graveyard. When he reached the parapets, he stopped and watched as, with unrelenting regularity, cannonballs launched from the Lighthouse Point battery soared over the harbor and crashed into the ruins of the town. With a sniff and a shake of his head, he made his way onto what was left of the bridge that led to the Maurepas Gate, and was greeted from within the ruins of the guardhouse that stood beside it by a harsh demand that he identify himself.

"It's me, des Gouttes," the commodore growled. "What day is it, you fool?"

"Excuse me, *monsieur le Marquis*. I did not recognize you," the guard apologized. "It is the seventeenth of July."

"*Phoq*," des Gouttes cursed. "Do you have any wine?"

"There is *always* wine," the guard joked, slinging his wineskin off his shoulder and handing it to des Gouttes. "*Monsieur* le Marquis, how is it that you were not certain of the date?"

"I apprehended a traitor who was attempting to escape on *l'Arethusa*. But the skiff we were on was destroyed by cannon fire. I washed up on that island, out there. I think it was the next morning. I've been making my way back here ever since and I've lost track of time," des Gouttes explained, and then pulled a mouthful from the wineskin. "Have you heard tell of, or seen any other bodies washing up nearby?"

"I have not, *monsieur le Marquis*," the guard replied, shaking his head.

"A shame," des Gouttes said, handing the wineskin back to the guard. "Would you mind if I had a look at your musket? It looks as though you have kept it in excellent repair."

"Of course, *monsieur le Marquis*," the guard allowed and proudly handed the commodore his musket, then ducked his head to sling his wineskin over his shoulder. When he looked up, he was looking down the barrel of his weapon, which des Gouttes was cocking. A cannon on Lighthouse Point boomed, and an instant later des Gouttes pulled the trigger of the musket, shattering the guard's forehead.

"Thank you for the wine and the weaponry, Corporal," des Gouttes said. He grabbed back the wineskin and yanked free the guard's ammunition pouch. "You can rest assured I will put them to good use, and that I will bury that traitor, Fortess, once and for all."

THE BRITISH CAMP - SOUTH FLANK

"Parksie, it's good and dark. Time for us to dig ourselves some new holes, just a little closer to our French friends. The Brass still thinks we need to make better targets of ourselves," the trooper said. He tossed his gallows humor to his battery mate, who was lying face down at the end of an earthworks on the Moor of Gabanes.

When Parksie neither spoke nor moved in reply his mate slid over to him. Irritated at being ignored, he gave him a shove and whispered harshly, "Parksie, wake up! Time to go!"

When Parksie replied by rolling over into his slit trench and turning up his pallid face, his eyes vacant and his neck gashed, his mate scrambled away from him. Without taking his eyes off Parksie's, he scuttled back to his own trench and slid awkwardly into it. Thrashing and squirming across the shallow ditch, his retreat ended abruptly, when his buttocks thumped into a pair of legs. Fevered with panic, he twisted around to see who was blocking his path and found himself staring up into Marquaisa's blood-smeared face and predatory eyes. He managed a single syllable of a scream before she cut it off by slamming his jaw shut and tearing into his throat.

"Wills, what's going on?" a third trooper, further up the line, called to Parksie's mate, Wills.

Marquaisa could hear the soldier crawling in her direction, but did not interrupt her enjoyment of her second course. Holding onto Wills with her right hand, she reached back with her left hand to the rapier that was strapped to her back, and without looking drew it and hurled it, end-over-end, at the advancing trooper. The point of the blade hammered into the soldier's forehead, and as his head jerked back his joints locked and his tricorn hat flew back over the heels of his boots.

Ready for her third course, Marquaisa dropped Wills into his trench and lunged for the third trooper, who was stuck on all fours and whose jaw was silently flapping. Seizing him by the scruff of the neck, she wrapped her right fist around a chunk of his red coat and hauled him to his feet. With a tug, she pulled her rapier out of his skull, sampling the sweet blood that flowed from the split in his forehead as it came free. Her eyes flaring in anticipation of tasting more of the same, she tightened her grip on his neck, dipped him back and bit into his throat. No sooner had she locked on than a fourth soldier stumbled on to the scene.

"Davey, is that you?" the soldier asked, then caught a glimpse of Davey's plight and Marquaisa's role in it. His question answered, he leveled his musket at Marquaisa and yelled at her, "Stop what you're doing! Tell me who you are!"

When she ignored his command, the soldier fired his Brown Bess. When Marquaisa caught the lead ball with Davey's back and carried on with what she was doing, the soldier drew his flintlock pistol and cracked off a second shot. When Marquaisa caught the second shot with Davey's head, the soldier drew his sword and charged Marquaisa. When Marquaisa dropped Davey to the ground, the soldier slashed at her neck. When Marquaisa's rapier flashed upwards and caught him at the wrist, his hand, still clenching his sword, spun away harmlessly over the earthworks.

The soldier cut loose an ear-splitting scream, which Marquasia cut off by tackling him and draining him before all of his lifeblood poured out of the stump at the end of his right arm. When he'd given her all he had, she arched her neck and howled into the night sky. Her wail was met with a crackle of musketry from the trenches to the north and the south, and the sizzle of lead balls flying in every direction, none of which hit anything of consequence. In the quiet that followed the volley, she wiped the blade of her rapier on the now handless soldier's trousers, then relieved Davey of his coat and pants, clapped his hat on her head, and strolled away into the darkness. As she vanished over the earthworks, a second volley erupted, finding their marks in the bodies she left behind.

THE BRITISH CAMP – NORTH FLANK

The Light Infantry squaddies thought they'd found their marks in the three East India traffickers who were making a return visit to the British encampment. Earlier in the evening, quite by chance, the dealers crossed paths with the squaddies, who invited them back to their campsite for a friendly round of dice—hospitable sorts that they were. It was clear the three suppliers knew nothing of the game of chance, but were enticed by the thought of taking some winnings off their hosts.

Vishnu had quickly become addicted to the game, and he had just as quickly been bankrupted by the squaddies, who had manipulated the rules of the game on the fly in order to filch their colorfully attired chumps. When the newly penniless Maratha appealed to Ganesh and Yuval, they, having taken heavy losses of their own, declined. The three nearly came to blows on the matter, and the prospect of a dust-up between three members of a people fabled for their savagery attracted a small audience of off-duty soldiers looking for an evening's entertainment.

Bloodshed was avoided, however, when Vishnu persuaded Ganesh and Yuval he could and would repay them if any losses were taken, or give them equal shares of the winnings if any were realized. After a round of bobbing heads, backslapping, and smiling assurances to the audience that all was well, Ganesh and Yuval pitched what was left of their loot into the ring and readied themselves for the final roll of the dice.

Vishnu was about to toss the dice when the sounds of an unearthly howl, followed by a string of musket pops, reached the campsite from the southern tip of the front line. Not one of the soldiers gathered around the fire showed the slightest concern for what might be happening at the far end of the line. Their only interest was in the Maratha, and what they would do to one another when they lost. Aware of their eagerness, Vishnu shook the dice in his fist and cocked his wrist to roll them, but jolted to a stop just before he released them.

Full of suspicion, he slowly stood and stared at the faces that surrounded him. He sniffed the air, and then riveted his eyes on a patch of undergrowth that was off in the shadows on the opposite side of the campsite. Suddenly, he pointed at the clump of vegetation and shrieked in his accented English, "*Assa-seeen!*"

Two of the squaddies ran and leapt into the bushes, while the rest of the onlookers crowded in front of Vishnu, Ganesh, and Yuval to get a good look at what their brethren might dredge out of the woods. After a brief scuffle that was punctuated by a *thud*, the two squaddies emerged from the shadows. Between them, a woozy Erieux stumbled, squinting in the light and then staring blankly at the mouths of the musket barrels that were pointed at him.

While the crowd stared back at Erieux, Enriquez joined Vishnu, Ganesh, and Yuval. A moment later, when a few of the squaddies in the crowd pulled back the hammers of their muskets, intent on killing Erieux, the pirate captain and the three Maratha sliced into them with their knives and swords. Their attack was so sudden that most of the British were dead before they were aware it had been launched. The few that recognized the danger were alerted when their dying comrades fired their muskets reflexively as they fell. Even with the warning, those left standing were unprepared for the speed and savagery of the four man crew's assault, which left them with their hearts and lungs punctured and their throats slit.

The soldiers dropped as if scythed and, mesmerized by the sight, the two troopers who plucked Erieux out of the woods froze. Light-headed, but not so far gone that he didn't recognize an opportunity to increase his chances of survival, Erieux stepped back and kicked the soldier on his right in the crotch as hard as he could. When his partner jerked his head around to see what had happened, Erieux wrestled him to the ground and pounded him into submission with his fists. When he stopped and came to his senses, Erieux saw Yuval standing over the corpse of the soldier whose nuts he cracked a second earlier. Ganesh joined him and watched, for a moment, while Yuval stripped the man of his valuables. He then stepped around Erieux and cut the throat of the soldier the Acadian beat down.

In instants, alarms began to sound along the length of the British encampment. Still, without urgency and while chatting quietly amongst themselves, Enriquez and the three Maratha methodically liberated the valuables from all the soldiers they killed. Copying their method, Erieux did the same with the soldier whose throat Ganesh slashed, and then waited for the Spaniard and the three Maratha to finish gathering their prizes. When they were done, Vishnu handed Enriquez a pouch then, with Ganesh and Yuval, made his way back into the shadows and away from the alarms. Enriquez weighed the pouch in his hand. Satisfied with its heft, he tossed it to Erieux.

"That is a gift from the boys for agreeing to act as a target," Enriquez said, smiling. "You will find in that pouch a coin from each of the soldiers who aimed his musket at you. Well done!"

"I agreed to no such thing!" Erieux fumed. "Last night, you told me you wouldn't use me as bait ever again. Tonight, you told me all I had to do was, 'watch and learn,' and I almost got killed for it. You have to stop treating me like a pawn!"

"First, I will tell the boys how much you appreciate their consideration," Enriquez said. He paced back and forth in front of Erieux, and as he made his points he counted them off on his fingers. "Second, you are not a 'pawn.' You are my apprentice. And third, my young apprentice, you were not bait. You were a distraction. Think on the difference, and prepare yourself for your next lesson, which could take place in the next few moments if we don't follow those three devils into the woods right now."

"I swear, I will kill you," Erieux threatened Enriquez, half snarling at him, half laughing with him.

"You are not the first to make me such a promise, nor will you be the last. For, as the Grand Archvillain is known to have said, 'You can't kill a bad weed,'" the Spaniard quoted his grandfather and bowed theatrically to the Acadian. He then wrapped his arm around Erieux's shoulders and hustled him toward the darkness of the forest, adding, "By the way, did you hear her? She is getting stronger, yes? She will return to us soon, I think."

CHAPTER 40

DEDUCTIONS

JULY 18TH

THE BRITISH CAMP - SOUTH FLANK

"This is not the kind of decision upon which one rolls the dice, Rollie," Wolfe declared. He squinted into the darkness, trying to avoid falling into another crater as he and Rollo picked their way over the Moor of Gabanes toward the front line.

"We're talking about your new walking stick, James, no the conquest o'*this* wasteland," Rollo countered as he stumbled across the tundra.

"You have forgotten how instrumental my *stick* was at Freshwater Cove. Why, it was a veritable *beacon*," Wolfe stopped and scanned the terrain. "Its successor must be sculpted by the finest of craftsmen—a person I will identify only after I conduct an exhaustive search. I believe I shall start in Halifax." He moved as if to take a step and march on, but pulled up and made an observation, "I say, Rollie, speaking of searches, I do believe we have found what we were hoping we would not. Come have a look."

"Bugger!" Rollo blasted, trudging up to Wolfe's side and spewing a stream of obscenities at the sight of the corpse that was lying face down. "That's *thrrree* nights running! I thought we'd posted extra guards!"

"We did," Wolfe confirmed his lieutenant's recollections, taking his eyes off the dead man and scanning the surrounding terrain. "Hard to tell in this murk, I know, but we are still some ways away from the front. So, I believe this unfortunate soul *was* one of our guards, and since none of his comrades challenged us as we clatter-banged our way over the moor, I suspect they too have found their peace."

"Damn it all," Rollo swore, crouching next to the corpse. "Well, let's have a look at you." He rolled the dead soldier onto his back and cursed again. "Look, James," he pointed at the soldier's neck, "See these gashes? The same kinds o'wounds were found on the other victims of these attacks . . . as well as the same absence of blood in, on, or around the victim."

"Are you suggesting these killings are related, and that somehow they are connected to the ones our sappers reported on the day that we landed?" Wolfe anticipated what Rollo was implying, while casting sidelong glance at the wounds inflicted on the body they had discovered.

"The similarities are undeniable," Rollo observed, no longer implying anything.

"I'll grant you that. But, if you start blathering about some half-squirrel, half-dog monstrosity, then I shall have no choice but to recommend to Amherst that your next post be to a sanatorium," Wolfe conceded a point to his lieutenant in one breath, while in the next censoring him.

Rollo grunted at Wolfe, then stood up. He and the general then shuffled around the dead man, searching for clues as to who, or what killed him. As they did, a shadow within the shadows darkened the edges of their vision and started shuffling toward them. The two officers went still and silently watched it's approach. As it neared them, its contours showed the familiar shapes of a tricorn hat and a bulky red overcoat. Five or six paces from the officers it halted, its face obscured by the hat.

"Well, I'll be damned! You've some nerve, soldier, sashaying up *t'us* without so much as a 'by-your-leave.' Show some damned *rrre-spect* for your betters," Rollo said, taking a step toward what he assumed was a sentry.

"Hold, Rollie," Wolfe said slowly, placing a hand on his friend's shoulder.

Marquaisa studied the officers for a long moment, then grated, "Wolfe."

Rollo growled, and Wolfe steadied him again, but flashed his eyes at the lieutenant-colonel's flintlock pistol as he stepped in front of him and replied, "Indeed, it is I, and I am at your service. But, you have me at a disadvantage. Whom do I have the pleasure of addressing?"

Marquaisa considered the question for another long moment, then growled, "Death."

Rollo sidestepped to Wolfe's right and fired his pistol at their would-be assassin. The sparks off Rollo's flint were still spreading when Wolfe followed suit by cracking off a shot of his own. Neither men hit their target as, pivoting smoothly on her left foot, Marquaisa watched the lead balls sail past her chest. Squaring her broad shoulders to the two officers she chuckled, long and low.

"Poser," Wolfe muttered.

In reply, Marquaisa reached back and over her shoulder with her left hand and drew a jewel-studded rapier. When her arm was straight, she swept the blade in a wide arc that ended when its point was level with her shoulder and Wolfe's chest. With a flick of her wrist, she snapped the point of the rapier up, inviting Wolfe and Rollo to indulge themselves.

The two officers obliged by drawing their swords and advancing on their enemy. As they moved forward they separated, Wolfe moving to her left, Rollo to her right. When they split apart, Marquaisa dropped her arm to her side, rested the point of her sword in the ground and waited. When they lunged, she stepped back and, her blade a blur, slapped Wolfe's sword out of his hand. She then grabbed the general's sword arm and flung him at Rollo. The lieutenant-colonel could not avoid crashing into the reeling general, and on impact the two officers tangled their arms and legs and went down in a heap, in the mud, cursing.

Before the two men could scramble to their feet, Marquaisa was over top them, her rapier pressed against the middle of Wolfe's back. With a slap of the flat of her blade against Wolfe's buttocks, she ordered the general to roll over onto his back. As he moved, Rollo shifted as if to attack, but she pushed the point of her blade tight to Wolfe's chest. Rollo went still and Marquaisa rolled her wrist, preparing to run her blade through Wolfe if necessary. She then squatted next to the general.

Wolfe lay still as Marquaisa pulled off her borrowed hat and tossed it out of sight. Tresses of lustrous black hair fell across her sharply cast face. Ignoring the strands that flitted around her eyes, she looked steadily into Wolfe's. After yet another long moment, in a deep, pitiless voice, she stated flatly, "Expected me, you did."

"Strictly speaking, no I did not," Wolfe replied. He let the back of his head hit the ground as he looked into the night sky. "I was expecting some men who, between them, could string together more than three words in a sentence. Not some taciturn witch."

"Witch?" Marquaisa exploded. Snarling, with one hand she grabbed Wolfe by the lapels of his overcoat, stood up, and dragged him off the ground toward her gleaming fangs. Wolfe was about to invoke the incantation, handed down from time immemorial, which was guaranteed to put the kibosh on demonic intentions, when a familiar scent wafting off his person flooded Marquaisa's nasal passages and she stopped her attack.

Shivering, not from exposure to the acid in Wolfe's insult, but from scenting the gentle fragrance that emanated from him, Marquaisa kissed Wolfe full on the mouth. As their lips pressed together, Marquaisa's mind filled with memories of a bronze-haired beauty and a tingling raced up her spine to the base of her skull. Hungry for more, she was on the verge of devouring Wolfe's tongue when the sounds of Rollo scrambling in the dirt and struggling to get to his feet forced her to break her lip lock with the general. With a shove of her two arms, she threw Wolfe at Rollo and they again went down in a pile.

Marquaisa watched the two officers flounder, backing away from them until she noticed the handle of the dagger Wolfe had stabbed under her ribs on her left side. Cocking her head at the two men, who had wiggled up to their knees, she pulled the dagger from her side. Inch-by-inch, as it emerged, she let a trickle of black ichor run out of the wound, down the blade, and over her fist. When it was free, she hurled it at Rollo, catching him in the cheek with its knob, then disappeared into the gloom.

Wolfe looked back and forth, from the path down which the woman vanished, to Rollo, whose cheek was sprouting an impressive welt. When it was apparent she would not be returning, and that Rollo had exhausted his repertoire of expletives, Wolfe sat back on his heels. Pointing after her, he looked at his friend and made an introduction, "Rollie, I give you the *Squog*."

Rollo blinked at Wolfe and, vexation overtaking him, asked, "Do you mean to tell me you *drrragged* me out here just so you could put my little myth to the test?"

"Not *just* that," Wolfe chuckled, "I had a genuine interest in getting to the bottom of these killings which, by the way, I have satisfied. For you to be able to see with your own eyes the perpetrator of the crimes is no monster but a human, albeit a monstrous human, was shall we call it, a happy coincidence."

"James, you are such an ass!" Rollo hollered at Wolfe, pounding the turf with his fist.

"There can be no denying it," Wolfe agreed, offering his friend a helping hand and pulling him up off the ground. "Just as there can be no denying there was neither squirrel, nor dog in our killer's breeding. Just an unhealthy dose of bloodlust."

"That, and a healthy dose *o'carrrnal* lust," Rollo huffed, brushing loose dirt of his coat and trousers.

"There can be no denying that either," Wolfe concurred. Reminded of the kiss he shared with the *Squog,* he spit out its bitter aftertaste. "So, my young stalwart, I hope you have learned your lesson, and there will be no more making up fairy tales. It's getting hard enough to convince the men to take the field, what with these massacres taking place on a nightly basis, without *also* having to convince them the moors and the forests are not crawling with demons. The splits in the seams of our army's aura of invincibility are growing by the day, whilst the morale of our troops shrivels. We must stem both of those tides if we hope to make a success of this campaign."

"And *nearrrly* getting both of us killed was part of your plan to stem those tides, I suppose?" Rollo knew his conjecture was as much a statement of fact as it was a question.

"There is risk in every plan, Rollie," Wolfe said, slapping his comrade on the back. "At least we now know that our killer is of flesh and blood. Cunning, ruthless, and hard as iron. But flesh and blood, nonetheless. So, that means she's beatable. And *that,* oh spinner of tales, is the message you will take back to the men. You can leave out the bits where she made mincemeat of us. But do play up the part where I got my knife in her."

"Of course, Sir Knight," Rollo hailed the hero of the hour with a mocking bow.

"That's the spirit, Rollie," Wolfe smiled. "Now, I'll bet you're wondering what else, beyond propagandizing, we're going to do to eradicate this menace?"

"Do enlighten me," Rollo bid Wolfe elucidate, expecting to regret it.

"With pleasure. Follow me," Wolfe urged Rollo and started marching back towards their headquarters. "In a couple of days, Amherst will be lending me Race."

"Rrrace? Rrreally?" Rollo stammered, and cleared his throat.

"What's that, Rollie?" Wolfe asked, raising an eyebrow. "Am I detecting an interest in our Captain Race that is something more than professional? Perhaps, even verging on the romantic?"

Rollo busied himself with brushing more dirt off of his overcoat, trousers, and now his boots.

"I see. Well, since you've come face-to-face with our killer, perhaps I'll have you team up with the good captain, so you can assist her with her investigation," Wolfe said, checking Rollo's expression for hints of un-Rollo-like interest. "Apparently, she's something of an expert when it comes to tracking down and putting a stop to people who murder others in their masses."

The British Camp - North Flank

"How many do you count?" Jenkins asked Neah, who was crouched over a body on the side of the campsite opposite to where the lieutenant stood.

The Mi'kmaq held up both of his hands and extended all of his fingers and both of his thumbs.

"Right. Thanks," the lieutenant said, and then waved to his partner, "That's upwards of forty men in three nights, and that's not including however many General Wolfe and Lieutenant-Colonel Rollo may have found at the front. If the French keep holding out, and we keep losing men at this rate, then it will take a miracle for us to close out the siege before the bad weather closes in."

As he listened to Jenkins, Neah moved carefully around the campsite, studying the positions of the bodies and the manner in which they'd been killed. Eventually, he made it to Jenkins, and after a quick glance at the man over whom the lieutenant was standing reported, in a single word, the findings of his investigation, "*Kajuewj.*"

"Demons, indeed," Jenkins agreed, nodding his head, "I thought as much. But we can't be telling that to the men. They're already on edge, what with Lieutenant-Colonel Rollo's stories about the *Squog.*"

Neah shook his head, and clarified, "Not real *kajuewj*. Men *like kajuewj*." He held up the brightly colored piece of fabric he had picked up in his search of the campsite.

Jenkins looked at the swatch, and furrowing his brows reflected on it, "I've seen something like that before." He tilted his tricorn hat back and scratched his head until his eyes lit up with recognition, "Hang on just a minute. All of these men, as well as the men at the sites of the other massacres, had their valuables taken, yes?"

Neah growled in confirmation.

"Shameful, I agree," Jenkins shook his head. "And the wounds you've seen are not the type you or I or any Frenchman—ordinary soldiers I mean—would inflict, right?"

"Most," Neah hedged.

"Very well. But it would be fair to say our comrades were victimized by a gang that includes a mix of ordinary men and extraordinary men. Men who are like *kajuewj*, yes?" Jenkins put forth his theory with growing conviction.

Neah snapped his head forward, definitively.

"Quite so," Jenkins imitated Neha's head nod. "And the most extraordinary men we have seen traipsing around camp, recently, were the three, colorfully attired, East India traffickers! Well done, Neah. That really is a solid bit of detecting work."

"At your service," Neah said, mimicking Wolfe.

"Well said," Jenkins congratulated Neah. "Here is what I think is happening. The attacks to the south are a diversion and, to a lesser degree, so are the massacres that have taken place here in the north. What I mean is, the attacks at the opposite ends of our line have us running every which way. But the ransacking that has taken place in the north has disguised a higher purpose. These northern devils mean for us to think they are simple raiders, pirates if you will. In fact, however, they are slowly and methodically working their way south. So, I believe this is yet another attempt to eliminate our senior commanders and prolong the siege."

Neah looked back at the slaughterhouse that was once a campsite, thought about what Jenkins was proposing, and shook his head in disagreement. But before he could voice his objections, Jenkins started on his way back to their command post with a bit of a spring in his step.

"These are good beginnings for us, Neah," Jenkins called back over his shoulder, his spirits uplifted by the headway they'd made. "We have suspects and we have a theory, which is more than what we started with. So, we'll report our findings to the general and put in place a plan to stop the shenanigans of these blackguards."

Neah took a last look at a familiar set of footprints, bottled up his suspicions as they related to *Aluasa'sit*, and joined Jenkins on the road.

CHAPTER 41

FABLES

JULY 19TH

HMS CAPRICIEUX

When it was not under siege, Louisbourg was a booming commercial port. Merchant ships passed through it regularly as they worked the trade routes between the Caribbean and Québec. Their comings and goings came to a screeching halt, however, with the arrival of the British fleet, and Drucour's subsequent decree that no shipping was allowed either to enter, or to leave the port.

Peeved with the governor, the commanders of the French naval vessels that were confined to port thumbed their noses at his dictates. They did not defy Drucour's mandate by deserting Louisbourg. But, neither did they support him by aggressively defending the fortress town.

Choosing to not shoot back in order to not make targets of themselves, the guns of the French warships stayed silent while the British blew Louisbourg into pieces. Due either to the fact it was harder to hit them than it was to hit a town, or to the possibility they might take possession of them after the siege, good sports that they were, the British spared the French ships.

Hoping the tactic might also help protect the town, the captains of

Entreprenant, *Calabre*, and *Capricieux* gathered their vessels near the wharf and set up a defensive shield. The British responded by lobbing their bombs higher, overtop the ships, and into the sitting rooms of the beleaguered citizens of Louisbourg.

Well-intentioned though the commanders of the three ships may have been, with just his one good eye Auzire Duros recognized the risks that came with keeping the three warships so close together. If a single shot, errant or well-aimed, hit any one of the ship's ammunition stores the results would be catastrophic for all three of the vessels. If the exploding munitions of the one didn't detonate the others, then its flames would be sure to spread to them and burn them to the waterline.

No fool, Duros intended to be well clear of all three ships not if, but when the chain reaction was triggered. It was debatable as to whether the same could be said for Fortess. Weakened by his prolonged exposure to the cold waters of the harbor and from fighting off infection, even after cauterization the wound to his ribs still was inflamed. For Fortess, every waking breath was an agony, so his convalescence consisted primarily of remaining in a stupefied state that lent itself well to long periods of sleep.

When his shift coincided with Fortess's moments of wakefulness, Duros listened to the former captain's ravings about the people and events that had conspired against him and contributed to his fall from grace, an eventuality Fortess found increasingly amusing as the days went on. Commodore Marquis Charry des Gouttes occupied the eye of the storm that was Fortess's life and the one-eyed duty officer gradually extracted from him more information on the commodore's role in his downfall. Sensing there remained only a couple of holes in Fortess's story that required filling, Duros poked his head into his patient's cabin and was pleased to find him awake.

"Give it to me," Fortess croaked when he saw the duty officer.

"I grow concerned for you, *Capitaine*," Duros lied. "Your body is weak, and your mind is telling you that you need more of my medicine, but it appears to be helping you less. Let us chat for a while, and afterwards, if you still think that you need it, then I will give you another dose of the drug. How does that sound?"

Fortess pouted, wincing at the effort it took to do so, but agreed, "Very well. What shall we talk about?"

"Why don't you tell me about the monster, des Gouttes?" Duros suggested.

"Oh, yes, des Gouttes!" Fortess cackled. "He thinks he has killed me, you know."

With his one good eye, Duros checked the vile containing the tincture Haritha had provided him to assist with his healing, after des Gouttes disfigured him. Certain he had quantity enough to keep Fortess subdued for as long as would be necessary, he feigned concern for his patient and encouraged him to give up more of the information that would help him take his own revenge, "Really? Why would he think such an awful thing?"

THE BRITISH STOCKADE

The British army and navy detested one another, and their prolonged exposure to one another during the siege of Louisbourg intensified their mutual loathing. Were it not for the presence of the French, whom they hated more than they hated each other, and the waters of Gabarus Bay, which separated the sailors from the soldiers, the expeditionary force might have torn itself apart from the inside as the siege wore on into the summer of 1758.

When coincidence put seamen and troopers in the same place at the same time, the trading of insults inevitably bubbled over into exchanges of punches. The casualties of these brawls were carted to the hospital station for rough treatment and quick release back into the ranks. The instigators, as well as the liveliest participants in the festivities, were hauled off to the stockade, which was situated north of the hospital and close to the headquarters building in which they were judged for their transgressions.

Like the command center, the stockade occupied a roughed-out compound west of the road, and was backdropped by the forest that shielded the encampment's rear. Also, like the command center, it was squat, solid, and built of local hardwoods. *Unlike* the blockish headquarters building, which was built around a single office, the stockade was rectangular and built to accommodate a row of three sturdy cells whose iron grillwork was embedded in the prison's floors, walls, and ceiling.

A single heavy door posted with guards, inside and out, barred entry to the dreary building, making it almost as difficult to get into as out of. A few days earlier, the door had been heaved open and the occupants of the cells had been dragged out, so as to complete their punishments doing menial, degrading tasks. Their evictions were enforced as a result of the arrival of two new tenants, who were thought to be of higher value. For her part, one of the inmates would have preferred accommodations more akin to those offered by the Spanish Inquisition.

"James, I am so glad you have come to visit me!" Haritha called to Wolfe from her cell. "It has been awful in here without you. There is a wall between Donatien and I, and the two strong, young men who are guarding us have blinded themselves with illusions about celibacy and virtuousness that would be humorous, were they not so tragic."

"Well done, gentlemen," General Wolfe congratulated the two guards who were stationed at opposite ends of the narrow corridor that fronted the three cells in the stockade. "You may go and seek, what I am certain, is some well-needed relief and refreshment. I will call for you when I again have need of you."

The guards saluted the general and marched out through the doorway that stood open in front of de Sade's cell. As he shut the door behind them and watched them march hurriedly in the direction of the canteen, Wolfe could not help but notice the patches of sweat that darkened the backs of their red coats and that seemed to be symptomatic of prolonged exposure to the occupant of the middle cell in the block. Taking a deep breath, he braced himself for an assault on his notions of propriety, only to be interrupted by the self-confessed Lord of Impropriety.

"General Wolfe," de Sade whined. "I have told you everything I know about Drucour and his plans to hold on to Louisbourg, misguided though they may be. I have told you, also, that I will help you in any way I can to bring about a speedy end to your campaign. Yet you insist on keeping me confined in this cage. Am I, therefore, to understand you have found little use for my information, and you have rejected my offer?"

"On the contrary, de Sade," Wolfe replied, closing the doorlatch. Then, leaning his back against wooden door, he crossed his arms over his chest and spoke directly to de Sade, his manner casual, his tone and conversational, "Your information, though worthless in terms of strategic value, was ranked very highly by my peers for its entertainment value. As for your offer, we are considering its merits as we speak, and will inform you of our decision in due time. In the meantime, keep quiet and mind your manners. Am I understood?"

"Yes," de Sade sulked, slinking to the back of his cell.

"Excellent." Wolfe gave a short bow to the prisoner, took another breath, and prepared to confront she who was beyond restraint.

"James, you were so stern with Donatien," Haritha giggled. "You will be the same way with me, yes?"

"Haritha, do put on your clothes, please," Wolfe sighed when he reached the point in the corridor that provided him an unhindered view of the interior of Haritha's prison cell.

"The sight of me displeases you?" Haritha joked as she prowled around her cell in patterns that combined circles with figure eights and that guaranteed Wolfe could see every inch of her body.

"No. I mean, yes," Wolfe tripped over himself, then tried to recover. "What I mean is, I will not talk to you until you are dressed."

"Come in here and I will dress while we talk," Haritha bargained, coming to a standstill at the center point of her cell with her back turned to Wolfe, her skin glowing in the diffused light of the stockade.

"That would be dangerous," Wolfe attempted to reason with her . . . and himself.

"You are *afraid* of me," Haritha goaded Wolfe. She then tiptoed through a half turn to face him and began taking small, slow steps toward him, taunting him with soft clucking noises.

"I most certainly am not!" Wolfe squawked.

"Are too," more clucking sounds accompanied Haritha's rebuttal and continued when she reached the iron grillwork at the front of her cage.

"Am not," Wolfe stuck out his chin.

"Prove it," she challenged him.

"Very well," he accepted. "But, the instant I step into that cell you will put on your shirt. Am I understood?"

"*Chick–ken!*" she clucked as he unlocked the padlock that held together the chain links that locked the gate to her cell.

Wolfe stepped past the gate and shut it behind himself without taking his eyes off Haritha. The instant the door clanged shut, she pounced, tackling Wolfe onto her straw bedding.

"*Ahhh*, it is good to be able to lay down without those little prickly things sticking into me," Haritha purred and snuggled into his arms.

"Haritha, you said you would dress while we spoke," Wolfe reminded her.

"And you told me to start with my shirt, which I shall do," she pushed off his chest, sat across his hips and tugged on her loose-fitting white shirt. Without pausing to button up she unbuttoned Wolfe's trousers. When he started to protest, she silenced him with a look, then straddle him and slowly took him in.

Closing her eyes contentedly, she rolled her hips against his, and in a faraway voice asked, "You wished to speak?"

"I have told you that some of my men . . . some of my men . . . have been murdered," Wolfe spoke, his voice strained, his thought processes taxed.

"You are at war, James. You cannot make accusations of murder without incriminating yourself," she crooned.

"Be that as it may, the manner in which they have been killed . . . the way . . . my soldiers . . . the killing has been most unnatural!" Wolfe blurted, the tension in his loins building.

"More unnatural than being blown to bits by cannon balls, crushed to death by falling bricks and stones, or burned alive in a building?" Haritha challenged him, slowing her undulating hips to prolong his pleasure.

"How does being completely drained of blood sound?" Wolfe countered, a spark of mental acuity burst from the flames of his ardor.

Haritha stopped churning her pelvis, grabbed Wolfe by his wrists and pinned them above his head, then surged into him and whispered into his mouth, "You speak of the *Squog*."

Wolfe caught his breath, for a couple of reasons, and rasped, "You know of it?"

"Half squirrel, half wild dog. Speed of one, strength of the other," she chanted in time with the push and pull of their hips.

"How can this be?" Wolfe heaved.

"It is simple. I am a professional," Haritha ground her teeth.

"No, I mean . . ." Wolfe thumped the back of his head through the straw bedding and onto the floor of the cell.

"Yes, I know," Haritha held Wolfe down, pushed off his chest, arched her back and thrust her hips until he emptied himself into her and she flooded him. Her muscles near cramping at the height of her climax, when it ended they went limp and she collapsed on top of him.

Haritha did not move until they both were breathing quietly. She then rolled off Wolfe and slipped into her trousers, fulfilling her clothing obligations, and waited for him to reassemble himself and recommence their conversation.

"Where were we?" he began.

"The *Squog*," she reminded him.

"Ah, yes, did you say that the thing is real?" Wolfe asked, knowing he was neither thinking nor hearing clearly when their earlier conversation broached the topic of monsters of the non-human variety.

"I did not. It is a fable invented by your friend, Rollick," she corrected him.

"Well, I suppose that's welcome news," Wolfe frowned. "Although, in some ways it might have been easier to stick with the story that a monster was to blame. It might even have helped to sharpen up the men. I've noticed they've been getting a bit complacent lately."

"Be truthful with your men," she suggested. "And the truth is that you do not yet have a reasonable explanation for the killings, and that they must remain vigilant."

"I suppose you're right. Honesty being the best policy and all," Wolfe quoted the old axiom whose openness to interpretation he and others routinely abused, truth being relative and all. "Besides, I've got someone coming in tomorrow morning who may be able to help get us to the bottom of these mysteries. One Captain Race. Have you heard of her?"

"I have not," Haritha admitted. "But, please ask her to come and see me. I do so enjoy speaking with you and I would like to find out if speaking with her is just as enjoyable."

"I would pay good money to see that," de Sade called over the wall that separated his cell from Haritha's.

Chapter 42

Race

July 20th

D ue to the passage of time and the steady consumption of matériel the chaos that gripped Flat Point during the early days of the siege, when men and supplies were being rushed ashore, had subsided to near non-existence. Reminders of the tumult of the first landings were scattered across the beach in the form of shattered crates, discarded weaponry, and occasionally a bloated washed-up corpse. But the tension that went with digging in a foothold had eased to the level of the everyday, organized confusion that is a military beachhead.

Ignoring the banter of the working squaddies, while soaking in the morning sun that warmed the beach, Wolfe teased Rollo, "Rollie, you are priceless. There you are, the *'here's blood in your eye'* commander who has faced down man and monster alike, fidgeting like a schoolboy."

"I'm no' fidgeting," Rollo snarled as he tugged out the wrinkles in his coat and straightened his hat. "Unlike you, I take *prrride* in my *prrresentation* of self, particularly when I am greeting a fellow officer."

"Have no fear, Rollie, you look very dashing. In fact, if you've got nothing planned later on, would you mind accompanying me to dinner," Rollo cut off Wolfe's invitation with a look, but the general persisted. "What? Is that cologne you're wearing? I do believe I recognize the fragrance from my time in Paris." Wolfe dodged the kick Rollo attempted to land on his backside.

"Enough, James, she is here," Rollo said, pointing discretely at the pinnace carrying their guest as it was beached at the waterline.

"Excellent," Wolfe said, then swaggered off toward the small vessel. "Don't worry, Rollie, I'll be on my best behavior. And I promise, I will make it my mission to ensure your many shining virtues are extoled before your Captain Race."

"Oculus help me," Rollo appealed to the Almighty as he hurried to catch up with Wolfe.

The heels of the general's boots were sinking slowly into the soft sand at the waterline when Race hopped out of the pinnace into the shallow surf. As she splashed ashore, some of the spray from her boots splattered onto Wolfe, who sketched her a ragged salute, "Well met, Race. You know Rollo, I believe."

"Indeed, I do. A pleasure to see you again, Lieutenant-Colonel," Race smiled brightly at Rollo and shook his hand warmly.

"Shall we?" Wolfe invited his two subalterns to follow him up the beach.

"Actually, sir," Race stood still, "General Amherst has requested you join him on *Amelia*. He and Admiral Boscawen require your assistance in the planning of the next stage of the expedition."

"Ha! I doubt they'll like hearing what I have to say," Wolfe blustered and started slogging through the surf toward the small boat, but stopped to harangue his audience. "Mark my words, we should right now be advancing on Québec to finish off these Canadian hellcats. We have the initiative, and to delay the operation will only cost us time, and ultimately lives."

"Sir," Race and Rollo acknowledged Wolfe, saluting in unison.

Wolfe narrowed his eyes at the two officers, then turned away from them and took up his march toward the waiting vessel, admonishing them as he went, "Behave yourselves, you two, and catch yourselves some killers! Now, men of the good ship *Pinnace*, hide your valuables. You are about to be boarded!"

Race and Rollo watched Wolfe shoo an oarsman out of his seat and into the one reserved for him, then take up the man's oar, and without waiting for the other oarsmen, start heaving on it to get the boat moving. His thrashing threw the vessel onto a course that would have taken it out to the open ocean rather than to *Amelia*, and nearly caused a mutiny on the pinnace. But after a bit of shouting and waving of oars the crew righted the boat. Until they were out of earshot, Wolfe could be heard chatting them up as he tugged on his oar.

"He *is* a handful," Race chose understatement in deference to Rollo's relationship with Wolfe.

"Aye, he's that, and *mair (more),* sod him," Rollo chuckled. "But, enough of that madman. How can I be of assistance to you, Captain *Rrrace?"*

"Well, first, let's have a look at what's been going on in the south," Race suggested. "Then, we'll focus on what's happened up north. The south is more puzzling, to be sure, but the greater threat is in the north."

"Agreed," Rollo said, then started up the beach with Race. "In the south, we are dealing with a single deranged individual. While, according to Jenkins, in the north we are dealing with a highly sophisticated task force."

"So I heard," Race acknowledged. "I also heard where you and General Wolfe met our southern friend, face-to-face."

"Aye," Rollo nodded. "She made fools *o 'us* both. James managed a strike with his dagger. But she shrugged it off as though it were no more than a flea's bite. I've not before seen the like of it."

"Nor have I," Race replied, looking away from Rollo. "But, I have heard there are warriors who can put themselves into a trance and render themselves oblivious to pain, as well as reason. Perhaps that is what we are dealing with in the south. If so, then we must catch her when she is in her more human, vulnerable state, if she has one."

"Well, it's a better theory than mine," Rollo complimented Race, while shaking his head.

"The *Squog*!" Race clapped. "I thought it a very creative hypothesis. However, did you come up the idea?"

Rollo explained to Race the circumstances surrounding his invention of the monster, then guided her on a morbid tour of the massacre sites that dotted the southern margin of the British encampment. They began by inspecting the arms depot on the beach, then made their way up to the earthworks at the front, and finished with the hospital just south of the stockade, which had been devastated during the previous evening.

"The two ends do look as though they wish to meet at the middle," Race observed as they trudged up the road past the stockade. "However, I'm wondering where that middle might be. Your Jenkins thinks the real target is our headquarters, does he not?"

"Aye, he does," Rollo confirmed. "You can ask him for yourself when we reach headquarters. I've asked him to meet us there to discuss his findings and his theories."

"Thank you," Race replied and looked at Rollo. "May I call you Andrew?"

"I would welcome it," Rollo tipped his hat. "How does my lady prefer to be addressed?"

"Truth be told, I like the simplicity of *Race*," she grinned.

"Well then, *Rrrace* it shall be, my lady," Rollo granted and tipped his tricorn hat again. "Ah, here we are, *central command*. You will find its splendor to be overwhelming," Rollo hyperbolized, bowing Race down the beaten dirt path that twisted its way to the building's broken front door.

"I must say, Andrew," Race whispered to Rollo. "Jenkins's theory is looking a tab bit thin, at the moment. This place looks more like our gunners' practice target than our command post."

Rollo chuckled and shifted the door out of their way so they could enter the building. As they walked through the doorway, Jenkins stood to attention and saluted the two officers. Neah stuffed the knife he'd been sharpening through a loop in his pants and shuffled his feet.

"Captain *Rrrace,* this is Lieutenant Jenkins. Jenkins, *Rrrace,*" Rollo announced, hustling through the introductions.

"And who might this be?" Race smiled at Neah.

"This is my good friend Neah," Jenkins introduced the Mi'kmaq. "Neah has been helping us find our way through these parts since he joined our unit at the beginning of the campaign. Say hello to the captain, Neah."

Jenkins elbowed Neah.

"Heh-low," Neah croaked.

"Pleased to make your acquaintance, Neah," Race replied, smiling again. "If I'm not mistaken, you are of the Mi'kmaq, are you not?"

Neah looked at Jenkins.

"Very perceptive of you, Captain," Jenkins replied on behalf of his friend.

"And, if I'm not mistaken, the Mi'kmaq are allied with the French, are they not?" Race pressed.

"You are correct again, Captain," Jenkins nodded. "However, an Acadian killed Neah's two brothers and attempted to kill him on the very day we landed. We rescued him, and since then he has been as loyal to our cause as he has been a good friend to myself and General Wolfe."

"Good enough for me," Race said, then sat on the edge of the desk that took up the middle of the room. "So, let's hear what you have to say about these attacks."

"They are bloody massacres. Not to put too fine a point on it," Jenkins started. "From what Neah and I have pieced together, the perpetrators are cunning, well-coordinated and, obviously, deadly. Their attacks follow a pattern of deception, or distraction, followed by lightning-quick strikes. We know this not from eyewitness accounts, for they leave no survivors, but from the nature of the wounds they inflict. In most cases, they originate from behind the victims—cut throats, caved-in skulls, punctured hearts and lungs—the kinds of things you'd expect to see from brigands, or pirates. So, first they preoccupy our men, then they sneak up on them from behind and kill them."

"And they have been steadily working their way south?" Race asked Jenkins.

"Indeed, Captain," Jenkins confirmed. "I believe they intend to attack the very same headquarters in which we are standing."

Race looked pointedly around the interior of the structure, then back at Jenkins and asked, "To what end?"

"To kill as many senior officers as they can, and to atone for their past failures," Jenkins replied.

"Very well," Race nodded. "We shall test your theory tonight, Lieutenant, and we shall use our friends' very own tactics against them."

Race turned to Rollo and inquired, "General Wolfe acted as the bait during the last invasion of these premises, did he not?"

"Aye, he did," Rollo confirmed.

"Well, congratulations, *General Rrrollo*, you have just been promoted to the rank of *Carrot*."

British Headquarters

General Rollo arrived at headquarters at mid-afternoon in full regalia, mounted on a white horse and accompanied by the company's treasurer, as well as two body guards whose saddle bags were bursting with coin. He promptly installed himself inside the command post and spent the remainder of the day, then into the evening, dispensing wages to a steady stream of soldiers. As evening ran into night, Race and Jenkins watched the procession of troopers from their hideout east of the headquarters building, which was last occupied by one of Amherst's would-be assassins.

"Tommy. Rudy. Come up here," Jenkins whispered to two young privates.

When the boys reached his side, Jenkins gave them their orders, "Tommy, go to the right. Rudy, go to the left. Tell the men they are to remain quiet and out of sight until they hear my whistle. Understood?" Jenkins looked at the young men, each of whom replied with a quick salute. "Good boys. Off you go. Report back to the captain and me when you've finished."

Jenkins watched the boys disappear noiselessly into the trees and down the line of men that had been placed along the road. He was about to praise them to Race, but stopped when she pressed her finger to her lips, then pointed at the command post. His back pressed to its north-facing wall, flintlock pistol drawn, a man was sidestepping toward its corner. When he reached the turn, he raked tangles of long hair off his face and peeked around the timbers. Satisfied he'd gone undetected, he jogged across the front face of the building, then stopped beside the doorway and whistled, twice, back down the path he'd taken.

"We've got him," Jenkins whispered to Race.

"Wait," Race cautioned the lieutenant. "Remember, he is just the decoy."

Jenkins sunk back into the undergrowth and watched the raider, who was crouching beside the door and looking around anxiously for his comrades.

"Come on. Come on," Jenkins rumbled, but stopped when he felt a tap on his right arm. Pulling his eyes off of the command post, he looked over his shoulder and saw Tommy, his face drained of color, lying in the grass beside him.

"What is it, lad? What's happened?" he asked the boy.

"Dead, sir. All dead. The men are all dead," Tommy mumbled.

No sooner had Tommy finished his report than Jenkins heard Race swear softly. Rudy was sitting beside her, pallid like Tommy. Jenkins guessed he was delivering to her the same unwelcome news he had just received.

"Shit, we're made!" Jenkins cursed.

A crash of splintered wood reached the two officers and the two enlistees from the command post.

"Shit! Rollo!" Race swore.

"We need to go!" Jenkins snapped. "Tommy, Rudy, stay close to the captain and I."

As they sprinted across the road they saw the longhaired raider lurch into the building through the open doorway, then disappear as he was taken down from his right.

"Got you!" Rollo cheered. "Well done, Neah! Now, bundle him up and let's be off. We've no time to lose."

Neah and Rollo were dragging their hooded prisoner through the doorway when Jenkins landed on the command post, nearly knocking the three of them back into the room.

"By the six balls of Cerberus, you're a load Jenkins!" Rollo yelped in surprise. Then, refocusing, he told the lieutenant what to do, "Get this thing to the stockade, quick as you can. *Rrrace* and I will hold back his friends for as long as we can, then we'll join you."

"You two!" Jenkins yelled at Tommy and Rudy as he pushed away from the doorway with Neah and the prisoner. "Run! That way!" He jerked his left thumb over his shoulder to the west, away from the command post. "Stop when you drop!"

"But—" the boys started to object.

"That is an order, gentlemen," Jenkins bellowed. "Now go!"

"Rio!"

The accented voice rolled over the compound that hosted the headquarters building and down the moonlit road of the British encampment.

"Shut up!" Jenkins punched his hooded prisoner in the head before he could answer.

"*Rrrun,* Jenkins!" Rollo shouted at Jenkins, before firing a shot into the spot in the shadows from which the voice originated.

Second, third, and fourth shots followed as Rollo and Race mounted their rear guard. No cries of pain were returned to them from the darkness. But, satisfied they had created a bit of space between themselves and their attackers, Rollo and Race tossed aside their pistols and joined in the race to the stockade.

As they approached the staggering, six-legged beast that was Jenkins, Neah, and the prisoner, Neah stumbled and went down. Before the other two toppled over, Race rammed into the prisoner's left shoulder and grabbed him roughly around the waist.

"Congratulations, Jenkins," Race huffed, as she helped the lieutenant drag the prisoner toward the stockade, "Your theory proved out. Too bad we caught only this fool and not the brains of their operation."

"Wait!" Rollo barked. "Look."

He pointed out at a solitary figure standing over a pair of dead sentries, in the middle of the road near the stockade.

"Her!" Jenkins gasped.

"I'll wager that's your *Squog*, Andrew," Race guessed. "Am I right?"

"Aye, *y'are,*" Rollo growled. "It appears your theory about the two ends meeting in the middle also has proven out, Jenkins."

"Phoq!" Race cursed.

"Jenkins," Rollo snapped. "Take Neah and get this bastard into the stockade. Bar the door. *Rrrace, wi'me.* Time to kill a monster!"

Jenkins and Neah hiked off the road with their prisoner, toward the jailhouse, while Rollo and Race charged the killer in the road.

Stock-still, Marquaisa watched the approaching group split apart. Calmly, she stepped over the bodies lying at her feet in the road, then exploded into a sprint that put her on a collision course with the two charging officers. Too fast for either Rollo or Race, Marquaisa crashed headlong into Rollo, carrying him ten yards up the road before pile driving down on top of him on the hard, packed dirt.

Under the force of the impact, Rollo's lungs collapsed, his ribs buckled, and his eyes welled up with tears. Through the pain and the haze he saw a sculpted, oval face set with a pair of sanguine eyes. He tried to cry out at the nightmare of fangs that flashed toward his neck, but neither his flattened lungs, nor the teeth that dug into his throat allowed it.

Rollo was fading when Marquaisa jerked back suddenly and looked down at the point of the sword that momentarily stuck out of her chest, then disappeared. With a growl, she spun and reached for the throat of her attacker, who tried without luck to avoid her lunge. Clenching her fingers tight, Marquaisa stood up, pulling her attacker's feet off the ground. When she reached her full height, she pulled the choking woman in close.

When they were chest-to-chest, Marquaisa angled her mouth at the woman's throat, but as she touched it with her lips a familiar smell wafted up to her from her victim's red coat. Still holding the struggling woman, she sniffed the air and found the same scent trail leading into the building that squatted in the shadows off the road. With a snort, she turned her attention back to the woman dangling in her fist and looked into her icy blue eyes, one of which winked at her.

"Witch!" Marquaisa howled and threw Race on top of Rollo, who screamed in pain when she landed.

Race rolled off Rollo and onto her knees, but by the time she regained her balance, Marquaisa had disappeared.

"Help!" Race called in the direction of the stockade.

Jenkins, Neah, and a guard rushed out of the stockade, brandishing their swords. In an instant, they recognized the threat had vanished, but one of their officers was in danger.

"Get him to the hospital, quickly!" Race ordered Neah and the guard. "His ribs are damaged, and he is having trouble breathing. Hurry!"

Neah and the young guard grabbed Rollo, who moaned as they lifted him, draped his arms over their shoulders, and dragged him further down the road toward the hospital station. As they disappeared, Jenkins offered a hand to Race, who grabbed his wrist and pulled herself to her feet.

"Are you injured?" Jenkins asked Race, checking her for open wounds.

"Just my pride," Race shrugged him off. "Damn, she's fast."

"Not fast enough, though," Jenkins shook his head. "You saw her off, from the looks of things."

"Luck, I assure you," she looked down the road in the direction in which Rollo was being dragged. "But, that is something that we cannot be assured will last."

Race looked at the black fluid that stained the blade of her sword, then turned to Jenkins and asked, "Would you mind securing the prisoner? We need to be ready if his friends come for him."

"Certainly," Jenkins nodded.

"Thank you," Race shook Jenkins' hand. "If you need me, you will find me at the hospital. I will be tending to Rollo."

CHAPTER 43

BLACK PUDDING

JULY 21ST

Warm rays of early morning sunlight did little to cheer up the surgeon who had been doctoring Rollo through the night. As he leaned against the wall of the hospital and let the light wash over him, he watched Race march toward him across the compound and returned her hopeful expression with a bleak one of his own.

"Good morning, Captain," the doctor greeted the officer and furrowed his brow, concerned at the shadows under her eyes and the bruises that ringed her neck. "I wish I had better news for you. However, I'm afraid I must inform you the lieutenant-colonel's condition is grave, and is worsening rapidly. His breathing is shallow and labored, and a froth of blood has appeared at the corners of his mouth. There is little doubt his lungs have been ruptured. As we speak, blood leaks into them and I cannot reverse the flow. I have done all I can to ease his pain. But, it is only a matter of time before he passes from us."

"Very well, Doctor," Race answered, her body stiffening at the news. "Hand me whatever it is you've been giving the lieutenant-colonel, and I will watch over him. Go and rest. I will find you if I need you."

The surgeon looked at Race uncertainly, but relented when she gave him a steely look, "Very well. The medicine in these vials is for pain. Give it to him as he requires it."

Race accepted the handful of little bottles from the doctor and then waved him up the road. When he disappeared, she uncorked the bottles and poured their contents into the dirt. She then spat into them and swirled her phlegm into a film that coated their insides. Squatting down, she pulled a handful of her own vials from within her ammunition pouch and dumped their contents into the vials from which she'd emptied the doctor's prescription. Before sealing them, she whispered an incantation over them, and when they replied by releasing wisps of vapor she plugged their openings.

Snatching up the vials, Race stuffed all but one of them back into her pouch and strode into the small dimly lit hospital. Rollo, pale and sweating, lay on the floor in the darkest corner of the room, his eyes shut, trembling with each breath that rattled through his failing lungs. Quickly, she popped the cork of the bottle she held in her hand and crouched next to the dying man. Tilting his head up using her right hand, she shoved the neck of the bottle into his mouth with her left and emptied its contents down his throat. She then clamped her left hand under his chin to keep his mouth shut, and to stop him from spitting out the fluid.

Rollo choked, blew a breath through his nose, and rocked weakly, but Race held him tight. When he relaxed, she whispered into his ear the incantation with which she'd imbued her medicine. When the words ran out she took off her red overcoat, rolled it up, and slid it under his head. She then lay down next to him, watched the sun rise through the hospital's open doorway, and listened as his breathing eased.

Fatigue was stinging her eyes and tugging at their lids when Rollo stirred an hour later, struggling for air. Without hesitation, Race rolled quickly onto her knees, reached for her ammunition pouch, and repeated her treatments. When he lay still, she stretched out on the floor next to him, and with her back pressed against him hummed softly to herself until she drifted into a soothing trance.

Rollo puffed again at midday, but less strenuously. With a bit of an effort, he steadied himself and cracked open his eyes.

"Hello, Andrew," Race greeted Rollo, hovering over him. "You are not going to like this."

Sure handed, she dosed him and resisted his protests, until he collapsed, exhausted.

"Better," Race said, casting a clinical eye over her patient. "But you're not there quite yet. Sorry, old sport, but you've got a long afternoon ahead of you."

Stiff from resting on the cold floor, Race stood up and walked out of the hospital, into the afternoon sun. As she basked in the warming rays she felt eyes upon her and turned to see the surgeon, whom she'd relieved in the morning, walking down the road toward her.

"Doctor," Race greeted the man. "You underestimated yourself. The lieutenant-colonel is improving."

"What?" the doctor sputtered. "Let me see."

Race led the doctor into the hospital and back to where Rollo was sleeping and breathing easily.

"This is impossible!" the doctor put his open palm across Rollo's forehead, then pulled it back. "This man should be dead!" he caught himself and softened his manner, "I mean, as I was saying this morning, his prognosis was terminal."

"Apparently, the lieutenant-colonel disagreed," Race suggested and turned the doctor away from Rollo. "And now, since he is on the mend, why don't you see to your other patients? I will continue to watch over the lieutenant-colonel."

After a bewildered shake of his head, the doctor started making his rounds of the other casualties on the ward. Race sat down next to Rollo, her back against the wall, shut her eyes, and counted the minutes until it would be necessary to wake him for his next round of therapy.

At the appointed hour, near teatime, she shook him until he woke. When he blinked his eyes open, she waited for him to recognize where he was, then nudged his backside with the toe of her boot.

"Hello again, Andrew," she greeted him pleasantly. "Feeling better?"

Rollo thought for a moment, then rolled his eyes and croaked, "No."

"I thought so," Race heaved a sigh. "But, believe it or not, thanks to the doctor, you are much better now than you were this morning. He says you need just a couple of more doses of his medicine, and then you will be home free. So, open up."

Before Rollo could object, Race had the vial in his mouth and was pouring the fluid down his throat. His strength returning, she had to lock his chin in the crook of her elbow to make him swallow. Only after it went down did she release him.

"This is not how I imagined we would come to know one another," Rollo gurgled.

"Thought you'd sweep me off my feet, did you?" Race teased him.

"Kind of hoped we'd . . ." he yawned. "Pardon me, lassie. Actually, I kind of hoped we'd take in a show. James fancies himself something of an actor and a poet. It's quite comical."

Race laughed softly, leaning back against the wall as Rollo passed out under the influence of her medicine. One more vial remained, and as she pulled it from the bottom of her ammunition pouch, she scraped up black grit with her fingernails. Carefully, she scrubbed the fine dirt from under her hard cuticles into the palm of her hand. With the tip of her tongue, she wet the end of one of her fingers, which she dipped into the grains, then rubbed over the flat of her tongue.

As she expected, the black residue did not give back the sulfur essence of gun powder. Rather, she recognized the coppery taste of blood. Her own, very old blood. Slowly, the taste dissolved in her mouth and as it did the scar on the cut that ran across her palm, through which she'd bled herself, vanished, as did the bruises on her throat.

Rested and fully healed, she waited until the sun set before rousing Rollo for his final dose of medicine. When he woke he tried to sit up, but fell back in dizziness and breathed deeply to recover from the exertion.

"That stuff smells and tastes like the blood pudding my gran' crammed into me when I holidayed with her as a wee boy," Rollo complained. "It nearly killed me."

"Well, Andrew," Race said, pretending to scold. "You are a grown man at war, and this is not poison. It is the tincture that has been easing your pain, helping you sleep, and speeding your healing. So, show us a good boy and open up. Or, do I again need to put you in a headlock?"

"You have my permission to headlock me any time you feel so inclined," Rollo granted. "However, I'll not make it a prerequisite to the taking of your medicine. Do your worst."

Race dumped the contents of her vial into Rollo, who gagged at the taste, but swallowed it anyway, then shivered from head to toe.

"Good boy. Here's some sugar," Race praised him like an obedient puppy, then gave him a peck on the cheek. "Now, get some more sleep. I'm off to see what Jenkins has in store for the nasty devils who have made of themselves a thorn in our collective sides. I'll tell you all about it in the morning."

"Aye, see that you do," Rollo mumbled as he dropped into dreamless sleep.

The British Stockade

Vishnu dashed between Ganesh and Yuval toward the stockade as they dragged the bodies of the two dead British sentries away from it and into the forest's shadows. Sacrificing stealth for speed, he sprinted straight at the back wall of the squat building. When he was a stride away, he hurdled off his left leg, pushed himself higher up the wall with his right, spun to face back the way he'd come, jackknifed both legs up and over the lip of the roof, and used their momentum to carry his chest and shoulders onto its shallow incline. Immediately, he slithered backwards up the incline so his head no longer would hang over the edge of the roof.

Two more soldiers making their rounds of the stockade turned a corner of the building and walked below him along the back wall of the prison. His eyes riveted on the guards, he reached into the folds of his pajamas, drew a dagger, and clenched it between his teeth. Grinning at the prospect of two more kills, but wary of the uproar his fight with the guards might cause, he watched the men pass beneath him and looked for signs they were aware of his presence. Without breaking stride, the two men walked on, chatting quietly while keeping their eyes open for anything out of the ordinary that might emerge from the trees.

When they disappeared around the next corner of the building, Vishnu sheathed his blade and clicked his tongue twice at the spot from which he'd burst from the woods. He then sidled to his left, moving toward a small, barred window that sat just below the roofline. When he was above the window, he wiggled forward carefully and hung his face over the opening. His view into the cell was limited mainly to the piles of straw that were banked up against the grillwork of iron bars at its front. But he also caught glimpses of the black leather boots of guard who was standing at attention outside the cell, as well as the stock of his musket, whose butt he was resting on the floor of the stockade next to the heel of his left boot.

Without making a sound, Vishnu slid back from the window and along the roof, back to where he'd started. When he was sure the guards patrolling the outside of the building would not hear him, he clicked his tongue one more time at the shadows. Then, the first part of his mission complete, Vishnu took a deep breath. As he exhaled he relaxed, but caught his breath when, behind him, the sounds of rhythmic tapping pecked at this ears. He angled his hand toward his blade, but stilled his hand when a voice growled at him.

"No, Vish . . . nu," the low voice warned him.

Showing both of his hands, Vishnu rolled over onto his back. Near his feet Marquaisa squatted on her haunches with her chin cupped in her left hand and the talons of her right hand drumming across her right knee. Vishnu recoiled, but she stilled him by dropping her left hand to the surface of the roof, pressing her right forefinger against her lips, and smiling at him, showing off her fangs, somewhat unnervingly. When he calmed she nodded at him, and using her fingers signed to him their situation, some of which he knew, some of which to him was new.

He knew there were soldiers in the shadows, watching the stockade. He did not know there were so many as Marquaisa had counted. They agreed there had been four, but were now only two soldiers stationed outside the stockade. However, she found it necessary to correct him on his understandings of the number of guards on duty inside the building; there were at least two. She confirmed for him, also, their visit to the stockade not only was expected, but also most certainly had been detected. To Vishnu, the former was a given, while the latter was more hurtful to his pride than fearsome in its portents.

On receiving the last bit of news, Vishnu rolled onto his stomach and hissed twice into the shadows. For a brief moment, furtive rustlings rose from the shadows, some heading north, others heading south along the darkened perimeter of the compound. Vishnu sighed and shook his head at the clumsiness of his comrades, then turned his attention back to Marquaisa to collaborate on their next steps.

Marquaisa pointed at Vishnu, then at the two guards who continued to march around the stockade, and drew a short stroke across her throat with the talon on her left thumb. She then pointed at herself, signaling her intention to invade the building. Vishnu nodded, and without a backward glance crept to the edge of the roof, pulled a pair of daggers out of his pajamas, and waited for the soldiers to return to the back wall of the building.

Marquaisa watched Vishnu prepare to strike, and when the sounds of hand-to-hand fighting erupted from the shadows north and south of the stockade, saw him leap over the edge of the roof. Before he disappeared, she followed suit, leaping off the roof and down to the front of the stockade. When she landed she saw a broken line of soldiers in red coats inching from the shadows across the road. She heard the heartbeats pounding beneath the coats, and felt the fear and hate that drove the men wearing them.

Pivoting on her right foot, she kicked in the door to the stockade with her left foot, and waited while the panic-stricken guard at the far end of the corridor shot the stunned guard who stood at its near end. Before the shooter could recover, she jumped through the doorway and raced down the corridor at him. Shots from the soldiers who were advancing on the stockade followed her through the door and rang off the iron grillwork of the first cell, drawing an alarmed yelp from its inmate.

Sparks from the grillwork and the hot musket balls that ricocheted off the bars started to smolder in the bedding of the cell, and the man who occupied it could be heard stamping frantically on the smoking straw. As frantic as the prisoner was to put out the fires, the guard at the end of the corridor was desperate to fire his pistol at his attacker, and when she was at point-blank range, he pulled the trigger.

Marquaisa winced as the ball punched through her throat, but did not waver in her attack. With a last push, she crashed into the soldier, pinned him to the wall, and ripped into his neck. As his lifeblood coursed into her, the wound he'd opened in her neck sealed itself from the inside out. When it snapped shut and the soldier was empty, she dropped him and looked at the man in the cell he'd been guarding.

Erieux looked back and forth between Marquaisa and the dead guard, and as she stepped up to his gate he retreated to the back of his cell. When she reached the gate and shook it the iron screeched and the chain locking it shut rattled. Snarling, she tore away the padlock that linked the ends of the chain together, and as it slid to the floor, the gate swung lazily into the cell.

Erieux's back was pressed to the timbers. At the sight of his futile search for a way around her, Marquaisa snorted, "Fool."

Anger flared in his eyes, but before he could act on it, she grabbed him by his shirtsleeve and the scruff of his neck. She then dragged him out of his cell into the narrow corridor that was filled with the sounds of the skirmish raging outside the stockade. As they passed the jail cell occupied by Erieux's neighbor, Marquaisa saw a pair of light brown hands wrapped around the iron grillwork, and heard the voice of their owner float through the bars.

"Kayza?" Haritha looked in wonder at the hard-bitten beast who was manhandling one of her block mates.

Marquaisa jerked to a halt and Erieux tried to off-balance her when she turned to look through the bars. In response, she punched him in the face and shook him by the neck, and when he settled into a more cooperative state she peered between the bars. When the person behind them came into focus she joggled her head to break up the fog clouding her memory. Then, deciding a closer look might help, she pinned Erieux to the wall using her right hand, while with her left hand she tore open the padlock sealing Haritha's cell.

With a shove she flung open the gate, and with Erieux in tow walked into the cage. With a push, she tossed him at a back corner of the cell and pointed a stern warning finger at him to stay put. When he nodded understanding, she turned her attention to Haritha, who stood in the middle of the cell, her white shirt loose-fitting, beads of sweat glistening as they trickled down the dark skin of her neck, thick bronze hair falling over her shoulders and down her back.

"Te conozco," Marquaisa rasped, advancing on the girl. *I know you.*

"I am Haritha," the girl said, retreating to the back wall.

"You have a brother," Marquaisa recalled, advancing on the beauty until she stood nose-to-nose with her.

"Thierry," Haritha spoke his name and tried to smile.

"He is dead. Killed in Paris by a Spanish *bastardo*," Marquaisa told her without either hesitation, or sympathy.

Haritha gasped and, tears welling up in her eyes, pushed Marquaisa away towards the bars at the front of the cell asking, "Why did you not tell me this before?"

Confused, Marquaisa backed up and in reply asked Haritha, "Before?"

"When first we met, at Poisson's house," Haritha reminded her, and when she had her pinned against the bars slapped her across the face. "You made a promise to me."

"You will live forever," Marquaisa recited. Then, her memories peeking through the haze in her brain, offered an excuse, "It was not the time, I think."

"What do you mean?" Haritha demanded, taking Marquaisa's face in her two hands and staring into her eyes.

"You were busy," Marquaisa explained, returning her glare.

"Busy with what?" Haritha insisted on knowing more.

"Politics," Marquaisa added and took Haritha by the shoulders, then spun her around and pinned her back to the bars.

"Yes, but the news about Thierry was important," Haritha protested, squirming in Marquaisa's grip.

"You are angry," Marquaisa guessed, her hold on Haritha unbreakable.

"No," Haritha staked a claim to having been misread.

"You are sad," Marquaisa guessed again, while trying to regain eye contact with Haritha.

"A little," Haritha admitted she was feeling slightly vulnerable.

"Do not be," Marquaisa ordered Haritha, then kissed her softly on the lips.

"I will try," Haritha pouted, and tasted Marquaisa's kiss with the tip of her tongue. "But next time, if something is important, then let me know right away."

"Okay," Marquaisa agreed, then bit Haritha's neck, gently, while unfastening the buttons of her shirt.

"This is not the time," Haritha tried to protest.

"This is important," Marquaisa disagreed, then slowly worked her lips and hands downward from Haritha's neck to her breasts, and over the flat of her belly, while sliding her breeches over her buttocks.

"Time to go, don't you think?" Erieux suggested as he dashed past the girls.

Champing at the bit to leave Haritha's cell behind, Erieux rushed through its open gate and smashed face first into a the red-coated soldier shot, earlier, by his comrade. Now he was furious and was charging up the corridor outside Haritha's cell. Screaming wildly, the soldier slammed Erieux into the outside of the cell's iron grillwork, behind Haritha.

"Yes!" Haritha exclaimed, feeling the bars shudder.

"I mean, we really need to get going!" Erieux implored her, while grabbing the soldier's wrist to avoid being skewered by the dagger that was arcing up towards his ribs. The Acadian succeeded in slowing it down, but the soldier was strong and the point of his blade kept inching upwards. Frantic to avoid being stabbed, the Acadian twisted away from the dagger and drove his knee into the soldier's groin.

"Okay! Okay!" Haritha cried out, her fingers wrapped tightly around the grillwork over her head.

"Great, let's go!" Erieux urged her as he pounded his elbow into the back of the retching soldier's skull.

"Oh yes! Yes! Yes!" Haritha exulted, arched her back, pushed her shoulder blades into the grillwork, and convulsed.

Erieux dropped his left knee into the middle of the soldier's back and snatched the man's dagger from the floor beside his right knee. Grabbing a handful of the soldier's hair with his left hand, he pulled the man's head back and stabbed at his throat. But before he delivered the blow, his arm locked.

When he looked back to see what was wrong, he saw that the demoness who had dragged him out of his stall had taken his arm in an iron grip. Ignoring the fiend, he turned back to the soldier and tried to finish him, but was yanked off the man. As he fell back into the stockade wall, Marquaisa lunged past him and pounced on the soldier, who shrieked when she landed on him and twitched under her attack, but quickly went silent.

Finished with the soldier, Marquaisa leapt to her feet and shoved Erieux at the open doorway of the stockade, while getting in front of Haritha and leading her past the first cell in the block. A pall of smoke lingered in the cell, and when they passed in front of its grillwork, its occupant rushed at the bars.

"Haritha, my love, free me!" de Sade cried.

Marquaisa hurled herself at the bars and snarled at de Sade, who fell onto his backside and scrabbled to the back wall of the cell.

"You again!" he wailed. "Stay away from me, or I shall breathe on you!"

"Goodbye, Donatien," Haritha dismissed de Sade. "I will be expecting a share of the profits you accrue from publishing your notes on the things I have taught you. Be advised, if you cheat me, then Kayza and I will be obliged to visit you to collect from you that which is owed."

"Say what you will, Haritha," de Sade shrieked. "But it was *I* who taught *you. I made you!*"

De Sade's hysterics were all but lost in the clamor of the alarms that were blaring throughout the British camp. The uproar lost on them, crumpled, lifeless bodies in red coats made a ruddy ring around the stockade. In its center Vishnu, Ganesh, and Yuval, each of whom was leaking blood from an assortment of gashes, finished off the soldiers who hadn't had the good sense to flee.

Race stood to the rear of her squaddies, watching the last of them fall before the wounded and tiring Maratha. Burning with rage, she yanked her sword from its scabbard and took a quick first step toward them, lusting for their blood. No sooner did she start her charge, however, than a scruffy-looking rogue materialized in the open doorway of the stockade, angling to make an escape. Her fury searing away her hesitation, she stopped in her tracks and swept her blade back, pointing it at the spot where her reserves were positioned, then forward at the doorway. At her signal, Jenkins and Neah stood up from their trenches, raised their muskets, and aimed them at the escapee.

Following their aim, she turned to face the stockade. As though in a dream, she saw Erieux, his face peeking out from behind his shaggy locks, come into focus in the open doorway.

"What?" she frowned. "No!" she shouted.

Careless of the toll taken on her battle-hardened squaddies by the Martha, Race dashed at them and in desperation slashed through and past them.

"Get down!" she screamed at the stunned Acadian, just as Neah cracked off his shot.

The ball smashed into her back, below her left shoulder blade.

"Race?" Jenkins mumbled to himself, peering through gun smoke. "Stop!" he yelled at the captain and his musket ball, both.

"Raçielle?" Erieux stammered as Race knocked him back into the stockade and Jenkins's shot rang off the grillwork of de Sade's cell.

"Madame Drucour?" Haritha looked around Marquaisa at the wounded soldier.

"Who is Madame Drucour?" Erieux asked Haritha.

"Who is Raçielle?" Haritha asked him in return.

Erieux clamped his hand over the hole in Raçielle's back. As her blood began to seep through his fingers, he heard a growl and felt the monster who freed him explode past him and out through the doorway. At the same instant, a musket shot snapped outside the open door and sent hot lead at Jenkins and Neah.

"*Holy shiiittt!*" Neah hollered a tick before the shot reached his and Jenkins's post. His demon repelling countermeasure too late, he grunted when Marquaisa crashed into him and drove him heavily into the ground behind Jenkins.

"*Phoq!*" Jenkins cursed as a musket ball buried itself in the dirt at his feet. He flinched as tiny pebbles and grains of earth flew up at his face and two bodies thudded to the ground a few feet behind where he stood.

On instinct, Jenkins drew his sword and swept it above his head, just in time to block the powerful chopping slash of the blade held by the raider who fired the shot at him. Staggered by the force of the blow, Jenkins dropped to one knee. Second, third, and fourth blows followed in merciless succession, and before he knew it Jenkins was on his back, helpless and looking up into a swarthy, goateed face.

"I am Mario Ortona Enriquez, grandson of Don Miguel Enriquez, the Grand Archvillain, and it will be your honor to die by my hand," the pirate said, then reached up to deliver the deathblow.

"Kayza!" Haritha shouted from the doorway of the stockade.

Marquaisa pulled herself off Neah's corpse, whirled, and sprinted for Haritha. On her way she grabbed Enriquez, whose two hands were above his head, wrapped around the handle of the sword whose point he was aiming at a downed soldier's heart, and dragged him back toward the stockade. When she reached the knot of people that crowded the doorway, Marquaisa dropped Enriquez and kneeled next to Haritha.

"This one *was* a friend," Haritha jerked her thumb at Race, whose blood was running freely over Erieux's fingers.

"Witch," Marquaisa jabbed Race's buttocks with one of her talons.

"I agree, but she is important to this one, who *is* a friend," Haritha put her hand on Erieux's shoulder.

"Fool," Marquaisa snorted at Erieux.

"Perhaps he is. But, she is dying. For his sake, will you help her?" Haritha asked Marquaisa.

Marquaisa bore her fangs and leaned in toward the neck of the bleeding soldier.

"No! No, Kayza," Haritha stopped Marquaisa. "Much as she may deserve to have her lifeblood taken from her, I mean, 'will you help her in the same way you helped me.'"

Marquaisa shrugged and ran her fingers between Race's legs.

"No, Kayza," Haritha chuckled and stopped Marquaisa, again. "The *other* way."

Marquaisa raised an eyebrow. Then, understanding dawning upon her, nicked her lip with her fingernail tip and squeezed a drop of freezing ichor into the wound in Race's back. Sitting back on her heels, she then watched, intently, as the hole bubbled, hissed, and constricted from the inside. When it snapped shut a bloody, red musket ball rolled out of the wound. Marquaisa snatched up the gory projectile and looked at it closely, then popped it into her mouth and crunched on it happily. When it was gone, she smiled at Haritha, her teeth and fangs gleaming in the shadows of the doorway.

Haritha, the pirates, and Erieux watched the otherworldly display, speechless. Then they looked on in wonder as the British officer, who seconds earlier was rattling the rusty gates outside Oculus's burning halls of damnation, showed signs of life.

"I will stay with her," Erieux held on to Raçielle.

"Fool," Marquaisa bristled and punched Erieux in the head, knocking him unconscious.

"Problem solved," Enriquez beamed. "Shall we take our leave of this place? In one ear, I hear the approach of British reinforcements. In the other, I hear the call of *Rajani*. Of the two, I find the latter to be more agreeable. Any votes to the contrary? Rio?"

Enriquez cautiously edged close to Marquaisa, over whose shoulder Erieux was slung. When she did not try to kill him, the pirate captain grabbed a handful of the Acadian's hair and looked into his drooping face.

"I thought not," he said. "I shall bring up the rear."

Enriquez then dropped Erieux's head, bowed to Haritha and Marquaisa, and let them and the three limping Maratha precede him out of the stockade and into the shadows.

As they disappeared, de Sade's voice reached out to them through the smoke that seeped out the window of his cell, "Remember, Haritha, you are mine! I made you and someday I will find you and reclaim you!"

THE KING'S BASTION, LOUISBOURG

Scar-faced and patch-eyed, Auzire Duros made his way across the parade ground that stood in front of the King's Bastion, weaving through the people whom Drucour had evicted from its casemates so they could take in some fresh air and walk along the waterfront. Damaged though the Bastion was after weeks of bombardment, its spire still pointed defiantly at the divine void, and reminded Duros of who he was looking for, and where he would find him.

Narrowing his good left eye to shield it from the dust that hovered in the stale air, Duros trod through the remains of the entrance hall of the Bastion, past chunks of rubble into which angry messages had been scratched for the governor, and over which hung the stench of decaying flesh. Covering his nose with his hand, he turned right and picked his way along the debris-strewn corridor to the doorway he was seeking. The oaken door, long since displaced from its hinges, was propped at an angle against its casement. A feeble light, which flickered when a body passed it by, shone through the crack. Squaring his shoulders to the door, he raised his left foot, kicked it down with the heel of his boot, and followed the flattened door into the room.

"Duros!" des Gouttes shouted. "I should have killed you when I had the chance. Haritha was mine!"

Duros spat on the floor and corrected the commodore, heatedly, "Haritha is for everyone, except the likes of you, you swine."

Des Gouttes made a move to rush the one-eyed man, but stopped when Duros aimed his pistol at him. "So, you've come to take your revenge," the commodore said, ignoring the pistol and showing his empty hands, "On an unarmed man, no less."

"Ha!" Duros barked, coarsely, "For one thing, you never are unarmed. For another, do not presume to know what I want."

"I do not. Nor do I care. Get out," des Gouttes growled, oozing contempt for the sailor.

"Come down from your high horse, des Gouttes," Duros derided the marquis, refusing either to back down or lower his gun, "I am here to help you. Believe me, or don't, it is up to you."

"What makes you think I need any help?" des Gouttes sniffed, imperiously. Peering down his nose at Duros, he threw in, "Even if I did, how could a one-eyed jack like you possibly help me?"

"By helping you to finish off a mutual acquaintance of ours," Duros explained. Then, turning his head and aiming his left eye at des Gouttes, to clearly see the marquis's reaction, the one-eyed man clarified, "A certain *monsieur* Fortess."

Des Gouttes bristled, "He is a traitor and I will see him hang. He allowed the British to overrun his position at *la Cormorandière.*"

"He fell back on the orders of Commander St. Julhien and ensured the safe return of his men to the city," Duros countered.

"He failed in his duty," des Gouttes stated, unequivocally. "Furthermore, I told him he would be executed if he abandoned the *Pointe du Phare.* He did and I intend to keep my word on the matter."

"He was overrun by superior numbers," Duros argued. "But he somehow saved the lives of the men in his unit. He then spent a week behind enemy lines, alone."

"He is a deserter and he will be punished," des Gouttes contended, adding, "He tried to flee Louisbourg on *l'Arethusa.*"

"He is a hero, who helped the king's regent remove himself from harm's way," Duros rejoined, unruffled by the commodore's accusations.

"Are you his *avocat*?" (*Lawyer*) des Gouttes asked, waving his arms, exasperated.

"No, but I have been acting as his physician for the past week," Duros informed the commodore as he passed his pistol from his right hand to his left, but kept it levelled at des Gouttes. "He has told me many things while he has been in my care."

"What things?" des Gouttes asked, warily.

"Many things," Duros deflected. "The most important of which, where you are concerned, would be your cold-blooded murder of a certain Corporal Danier on the night Fortess aided the regent. There also is the small matter of your attempted murder of Fortess himself, subsequent to the murder of Danier. I think you'll agree that the former offence supersedes the latter in terms of gravity, and that taken together they prove you have a homicidal streak that needs to be locked away or, better yet, put to rest."

"And you believe him?" des Gouttes sputtered, his eyes bulging, "The word of a man who is a traitor, a coward, and a deserter?"

"I just now made the case for his heroism," Duros reminded the commodore, coolly. "Be that as it may, the fact is Fortess is a danger to us all. The man's brain is poisoned and he will not hesitate to share his stories about you with anyone who is within earshot. If he does, then it will be a matter of time, only, before someone actually listens. It will be your downfall and how, I ask, will the rest of us benefit from the undoing of a man of your, shall we call it, stature?"

Duros paused to let des Gouttes squirm in the corner into which he'd been painted. He then provided a glimpse into an opening through which the commodore could choose to escape, "By rights, Fortess should already be dead. Unfortunately, he is not. As you have just pointed out, however, you have reasons aplenty for seeing to it that he actually meets his demise, and quickly. If you were to succeed, then you would be doing all of us a great favor, believe me."

"What are you proposing?" des Gouttes asked, still wary.

"Fortess is bedridden on *Capricieux*. The British, as you know, have damaged the ship with their cannon fire," Duros began. "Find a gun and shoot back. If your aim is off and your shot lands on *Capricieux,* then at worst it will be deemed a heroic action gone wrong. At best, the destruction of *Capricieux* will be thought of as nothing more than a misfortune of war. You cannot lose. Or, you could let Fortess live to tell his tale"

"Her crew is ashore?" des Gouttes inquired, not caring one way or the other.

"Indeed they are," Duros reported, not knowing one way or the other.

"Very well," des Gouttes said, throwing on his overcoat. "By the way, why are you helping me?"

"I am not," Duros redressed the commodore's assumption, cagily, while backing out through the shattered doorway, "I am helping myself. I will make that clear to you in due time."

Des Gouttes let the man slink away, then and hustled after him. But, by the time he reached the corridor, Duros had disappeared. With a snarl the commodore lowered the pistol with which he'd intended to kill the conniver. Then, his mind racing, he turned left and marched up the corridor, toward the doorway that faced the Dauphin Gate.

After he shoved aside the remnants of the double doors, des Gouttes jogged along the base of the fortress's fortifications, searching for a ramp he could use to mount the wall. When, at last, he found one that was more intact than not, he bounded up to the top of the wall and looked out over the harbor. Three ships at anchor near the quay were burning, but it was clear the smoldering fires required encouragement if they were to be made into something catastrophic. He could not single out *Capricieux*. However, the three ships were grouped so tightly it was a given that a shot that landed somewhere in the vicinity of one of their ammunition stores would start a destructive chain reaction.

"You!" he yelled at a sentry patrolling the rampart. "Find me some shot, and be quick about it!"

The soldier looked at des Gouttes dully, but leapt into action when he recognized the commodore.

"And you!" he shouted at a second sentry. "Don't just stand there. Get over here and help me with this gun. We're not going to let those British bastards sink our ships without a fight!"

With a wave, the second sentry recruited a third, and the two young men joined des Gouttes, who was tugging on the big gun. Together, the three men pushed and pulled on the cannon until its barrel pointed over the harbor.

"Do either of you know how to sight this thing?" des Gouttes asked the two sentries, who were trying to regain their breath after wrestling the cannon into position. Both of the men shook their heads. Pleased with their replies, des Gouttes shrugged, "Very well, I shall do my best."

The commodore was fiddling with the aim of the barrel when his first recruit returned from his errand with a bag of powder, some wadding, and a used cannon ball. Des Gouttes nodded his thanks, "Very good. Go and collect as many cannon balls as you can find. We're going to show the British what we're made of."

As the young sentry loped away, des Gouttes poured what he thought was a pound of powder into the bore of the cannon. He then stuffed wadding down the barrel and packed it with the butt end of a musket that belonged to one of the two remaining sentries. With a grunt, he picked up the pockmarked cannon ball, tipped it over the lip of the barrel, and let it roll into place. Finally, he snapped his fingers at the ammunition pouch of one of the sentries, who handed it over without question, and filled the ignition port with gunpowder.

"We need to light this somehow," des Gouttes said, looking at the sentries for suggestions.

The sentries looked at one another, then reluctantly dug into the pockets of their great coats and pulled out their pipes, tobacco, and strikers.

Des Gouttes snatched one of the strikers and ordered the men, "Stand back."

With practiced ease, he scraped the flint across the steel and sent a stream of sparks into the ignition port of the big gun. A plume of sizzling smoke puffed out of the port, and a moment later the powder in the cannon exploded. The hot shot screamed over the ruins of the town and into the water of the harbor, short of the burning ships.

"Phoq!" des Gouttes's profanity drowned the chorus of protests that drifted up from the quay to his position on the wall.

"Help me," the commodore growled at his two battery mates, and together they raised the aim of the cannon. He then repeated the priming ritual. When he was finished, he drummed his fingers impatiently on the barrel and looked for the boy who would, he hoped, supply him with more ammunition.

Des Gouttes was pacing the wall behind his cannon when the lad returned with another used ball. With a cursory nod, he accepted the shot and rolled it down the barrel of the gun. With a perfunctory wave, he backed off the three sentries, who blocked their ears, and fired the ignition port. The cannon erupted and the shot ripped through the air and tore into *Entreprenant*. In every direction, thick splinters spiraled upward and outward from the section of the ship's hull the ball punctured. Before the jagged shards could begin their descent into the harbor, a blast from the ship's ammunition room sent a tower of flame skyward, and a shockwave landward, and rocked the ship and it two neighbors.

Des Gouttes exulted as an inferno engulfed the three great ships. *"Mange la merde, Fortess!"* Eat shit, Fortess!

Puzzled by the commodore's celebration, the three sentries looked at one another. The uncertainty they saw in one another evaporated a moment later, when a roaring, disjointed volley from the gun decks of the three blazing ships hurled a maelstrom of red hot shot at the quay, spawning a rolling wave of thunder that swept over the ruins of the town and shook the parapets on which they stood.

The fires from the ships lit up the rim of the harbor, and a string of random explosions chased the blast wave into the town. But the detonations were only a background to the keening wail that was rising up from the people whom Drucour had encouraged to walk along the waterfront, and who had just watched as their friends, neighbors, and loved ones were shredded before their eyes.

"What have you done?" Drucour roared at des Gouttes from the broken doorway to the King's Bastion.

"I have fought back. Which is more that can be said for you, cowering in your casemates!" des Gouttes shot back.

"You have done no such thing! You have put your thirst for blood above the needs of everyone else. And, en masse, they have paid the price!" Drucour raged at des Gouttes.

"You're mad!" des Gouttes screamed, pointing an accusing finger the governor.

"No, des Gouttes, it is you who has lost his mind," Drucour replied, lowering his voice and shaking his head. Then, ignoring des Gouttes, he focused his attention on the three sentries who stood next to the marquis and gave them a choice, "Seize him or join him on the gallows."

Their uncertainties resolved, the three soldiers grabbed des Gouttes and started dragging him roughly toward the ramp at the base of which Drucour stood. When they reached the top of the ramp, des Gouttes watched Auzire Duros, scar-faced and patch-eyed, slip from behind Drucour, salute him, then disappear in the rubble of the King's Bastion.

HMS CAPRICIEUX

The explosion that rocked *Capricieux* tossed Fortess out of his billet and onto the floor of his cabin. Moaning at the agony that were his ribs, he staggered to his feet and groped his way through thickening smoke, up to the main deck. He was greeted not by fresh air, as he'd hoped, but by walls of flame that were chewing rapidly into the heavy timbers of the ship's hull, while belching out billows of smoke that chaffed his lungs.

Alone and encircled by fire, he watched his too small clothes smolder and winced as his hair began to singe. Knowing neither where he was, nor what to do, his shoulders slumped and he started to laugh. He pointed at the flames and laughed. He looked at the blisters that were rising off his skin and laughed. He laughed at the sounds of his own hacking guffaws, and when the explosion tore through the ship and peeled back the main deck he laughed as he flew through the air, until he crashed into the freezing waters of the harbor.

When he surfaced, he hooked his arm around a piece of charred decking and let himself drift. While he floated in the wreckage, he hummed along with the discordant wailing that rose and fell, in choppy waves, from the tormented souls that were hidden behind the flames, smoke, and ashes that were spewing from the burning ships. In-between the bars of his crude tune, he cackled at the whirlwind of fractured thoughts and images that spun between his ears and rattled off nonsense rhymes.

"Fortess is a man in the drink. He is *dead*, he is *gone*, so they think. But when he rises once more, they'll know they thought wrong, and their lives he will end in a blink."

CHAPTER 44

QUICKSILVER AND THE BAIT

JULY 23RD

Ripples of the blast wave that shredded Louisbourg's harbor front had raked through the tunnels that were threaded into the bedrock that lay between the town and the coast at *Cap Noir (Black Point)*. Razor-edged, they had slashed at the sediments that were hardpacked into the curves of the caverns' crusty walls. Now, days removed from their scathing sweep, glittering particulates torn loose by their passing still hung in the torpid underground air that continued to echo with the cries of the doomed souls who were sacrificed *en masse* to pestilential mammonism.

A film of the powdered, orange sandstone clinging to the tatters of her untucked woolen shirt and threadbare ankle-length skirt, Clavonne shuffled through the twists and turns of the maze-like warren of tunnels. Her bare feet scuffing the rocky floor of the path, with each step she kicked up swirls of silt that clouded her view of what was before her and blacked out what lay behind. Caught in the moments that spanned each of her strides, she trod onward, leaning on a lifetime of memories of the caves' contours and hoping her recollections would not be toppled over and buried beneath the images, fresh in her mind, of the carnage at the harbor.

In her mind's eye, she saw Governor Drucour sitting alone on the floor at the far end of a casemate below the ruins of the King's Bastion. With her help, during a pause in the bombardment being levied by the British, he had cleared all the casemates of the townsfolk who sought from them what little refuge they offered, but who needed a reprieve from their stale air. Now, filthy, careworn, and numb, he met the resonating *boom* of a solitary cannon fired from the fortress's ramparts with a blank expression that was at odds with the howls thrown back at the ramparts by the folk milling about the harbor.

As their voices shrilled, unbidden and unannounced a scar-faced, patch-eyed man scrabbled into the casemate. His back turned to her, he delivered to Drucour what was, based on the shock that registered on the governor's face, unwelcome news. Cursing in outrage, Drucour leapt to his feet and stormed out of the casemate, nearly knocking down the myopic messenger who, smirking and sniggering, hobbled after the governor.

As she dragged herself out of the casemate after them, she heard the solitary cannon on the ramparts roar again. Its muzzle flash flickered in the corner of her eye and its shot streaked through her field of vision. Tracking its wisping tail of smoke, she traced the arc the sizzling cannonball etched across the sky and frowned; it was headed not for the British positions at the *Pointe du Phare (Lighthouse Point)* on the opposite side of the harbor. Rather it was on a collision course with the three tall ships that were docked in the harbor that were shielding the town from British shells fired from the point.

When the shot hit one of the ships, splintered chunks of its deck and hull sprayed high into the air and far out into the water. A second later, the stricken ship exploded, bursting its seams from the inside-out and triggering on its two neighbors a string of rapid-fire detonations that forged themselves into a wall of superheated flame, ordinance, armaments, and debris that slammed into the harbor front like a lightning bolt and, in and eye blink, reduced people and the buildings in which they lived, loved, and laughed to burning ash. A fizzing reddish-pink mist at the leading edge of the wall, that vaporized as quickly as it bubbled up, showed when and where, like grime before a bristle brush, the people were scrubbed off the face of the earth.

The wailing surge of wind they whipped up in their passing bowled over Clavonne, flattening her on the floor of the casemate under billows of sparking embers. The gassy pall they threw off reeked of scorched flesh, and in the days following the blast the stench leeched into Clavonne's every pore. Seeking an escape from the noxious fumes, as well as the crushing guilt she felt for driving her friends out of the casemates to their deaths, she wandered into the tunnels. Lonesome for her mistress, Haritha, who had vanished, as well as for the boy, Opsule, who lay dead under a pile of rubble in the King's Bastion, and hoping to dull her pinings with the help of some cool untainted air she felt her way along the labyrinthian underground trails, angling for the *Cap Noire (Black Point)*.

A sudden, downward spiraling incline and the faint hissing of surf on sand told Clavonne she had reached the grotto in which, when she was a little girl, she and her playmates had made all of their childhood dreams come true. The wide, raised platform sculpted from ancient slabs of stone that sat in the center of its floor was the throne from which they ruled their fabulous earthly domains, while the vaulted ceiling that arched into abyssal blackness high over their heads was their bridge to happier, less frightening worlds. As she walked beside the platform on her way to the archway that marked the exit from the grotto to the beach, she ran her fingertips along the edge of its top surface and paused. Smooth as polished glass, unlike everything else in the tunnels it was not marred by either a speck of dust or a grain of sand. She imagined, if she had a torch, she would be able to see her reflection on the stone. Thankful she did not have one, and so could not see it, she let the sounds of the waves pull her out of the cavern toward the beach.

Behind her, at the back of the platform, Marquaisa stretched out from under lengths of her jet black hair and rolled from her left side

onto her right. Propping her head on her right hand, she stroked the
ends of the tresses of her hair that lay on her left hip and watched the
girl traipse out of her lair.

"So soft are you, Clavonne. Sweet as wine you would taste," she
said to herself, licking her lips and listening to the quiet ticking of
Clavonne's heart. "But, tougher and saltier have I been told you must
become. Or, die you will. Watch you, I shall."

Giggling, Marquaisa sat up slowly, slipped her bare legs over the
edge of her pedestal, dangled her feet, and waited for Clavonne's
silhouette to dissolve. When it was gone, she stepped down from her
dais, threw on the red greatcoat she'd peeled off the back of a squaddie
she'd made a meal of, and strapped on her jeweled rapier. Satisfied
with her attire, she strode toward the rocky archway, looking forward
to witnessing what the evening held in store for Clavonne.

Clavonne looked back over her shoulder when she heard what
sounded a little bit like laughter, but more like the grating of a minia-
ture rockslide, follow her out of the grotto. No plume of dust puffed out
through the gouge in the rockface that was the entrance to the cavern,
so she shrugged and turned to face the calm, moonlit waters of the
cape. As her head came around it was knocked back the way it had
come by the fist that crashed into her cheek. She went down like a ton
of bricks, only to have a rough hand grab a fistful of the hair at the
back of her head and haul her back onto her feet. Once she was upright
she was released and, swaying on her feet, she took a bootheel to the
gut that drove the air out of her lungs and landed her on her back in the
shallow surf. Wheezing, her hands clawing at the wet sand, through
blurred vision she watched a ragged man, whose clothes were shorn,
whose hair was singed, and whose skin was scalded straddle her at the
waist, water lapping over his bare feet up to his knobby ankles.

"Vous avez tué ma famille" (You killed my family), he grated,
peering down at her, his voice crackling over his scorched windpipe.
Coughing, he croaked, "We were safe. Under the bastion. Then you
and that pig, Drucour, threw us out, and everything blew up, and they
were gone. Just . . . gone."

He reached down and gripped Clavonne by her shirt, below her chin, and yanked on her, pulling her out of the shallow water, from her shoulders to her hips. Brine flooded out of her hair and off her back. Shaking her head, she blinked her eyes, furiously, trying to bring them back into focus as she recaptured her wind.

"Now, you'll be gone too," the man growled, bending over and huffing fetid breath in her face. "But not before you do a little something for me and the boys to help ease our suffering, if you know what I mean. Talk has it you're good at it, what with the smiles you've been putting on the faces of that *putain (whore)* Haritha, and that pretty boy, Opsule."

Clavonne stiffened and seized the man's forearm in both of her hands, and sneered in his face, *"Je te connais, Tardiff (I know you, Tardiff).* Don't give me that shit about *family.* You suck British cock. So, the only family you have left are the rats who drop scraps on the dock when they jump off their ships. Them, I will miss. You, I will not."

"Maybe not," Tardiff, seethed through what few teeth still were attached to his rotting gums, and wound up to punch Clavonne one more time, "But you will remember me, in your next life, for the way I ended you in this one. Boys! Come grab a hold of—"

Tardiff dropped Clavonne and grabbed at his groin, sucking in air and pawing at the imprint left by her foot after it pounded his testicles into his pelvis. In a full body cramp, his eyes crossed, he crash landed on his side with his head half submerged and blowing sticky bubbles with his nose and mouth. Their wet popping pinging in her ears, Clavonne jumped to her feet and splashed around, pivoting left and right and looking, wide-eyed, for Tardiff's "boys." None were to be seen, so she kicked Tardif until he turned, turtle-like, onto this back. His knees tucked tight to his chest, his hands searching for his balls, his face was exposed. So, she scooped up handfuls of waterlogged sand and stuffed his mouth full. When his eyes were bugging out of the sockets, she jammed her hands into his armpits and, her fingernails digging into his flesh, towed him into deeper water.

At knee depth, with one hand Clavonne shoved Tardiff's head under water and pushed it into the shifting sand. She used her other hand to pin down his body while he fought her through his death throes. When they petered out and he went still, she kicked him once more, sending him on his way toward the British ships that were scattered off the point of the cape.

Her eyes fixed on the drifting corpse, she knelt down in the soft swells and rubbed the lump on her cheek with cold water. Long minutes later, cooled and calmed, she stood and turned for shore and froze. Standing in dry sand, just beyond the waterline, bloody sword in hand, a grizzled man in a battered, blood and dirt-stained, white greatcoat was observing her.

"Je m'appelle Constantin Bonfils" (I am Constantin Bonfils), he introduced himself, his voice steady and just loud enough to be heard over the rustling of the water.

Clavonne looked him up and down and, hands on her hips, said knowingly, "You are the one the British call *Quicksilver*."

"And you are the one I called *Bait* . . . for that one," Bonfils flicked sand at Tardiff's bobbing carcass with the point of his sword, "and his gang of traitors. But, I believe your real name is Clavonne. My apologies for underestimating you."

"Thank you for the assist," Clavonne replied, nodding at the gore on Bonfils's blade, then hiking up her skirt and wading for shore.

"De riens" (You're welcome), Bonfils bowed politely, but kept a wary eye on the girl as she sloshed out of the water. When she reached dry land he added, "Times being what they are, *mademoiselle,* I'm wondering if you might be willing to return the favor?"

Clavonne slowed to a stop before Bonfils, clasped her hands at her waist and, her demeanor businesslike, replied, "I can grant many kinds of favors. What does *monsieur* desire?"

Encouraged by Clavonne's willingness, Bonfils began feeling her out, "How old are you Clavonne?"

"Seventeen," Clavonne replied, without hesitation. Then, eager to make a favorable impression, gave him a taste of her ware, "I know that sounds young, but I have received instruction from my mistress, Haritha, and I have had made any clients very happy."

"Good. You have experience," Bonfils scratched a checkmark in a big mental box. Impressed with the girl, he propositioned her, "I could use someone with your skills."

"My skills," Clavonne handed Bonfils's words back to him, hoping he would be more specific.

"Yes," Bonfils confirmed she had heard him correctly, "The skills you learned from your mistress. But, full disclosure, you would be providing them on a strictly volunteer basis."

"Volunteer," as though it were rancid, Clavonne wrinkled her nose as she repeated the word. Then, shaking her head regretfully, she rejected the opportunity Bonfils was pitching, "My mistress would not approve."

"I'm sure, in this case, she would make an exception," Bonfils persisted, determined to not let a talent like Clavonne slip through his fingers. "After all, we are at war. People kill other people every day without expecting to be paid for doing so."

"Kill people," Clavonne echoed Bonfils, staring wide-eyed at him as she struggled to understand the turn their negotiations had taken.

"Yes, the way you did Tardiff. That was magnificent! Your mistress would be very proud of you, I have no doubt," Bonfils was effusive in his praise. He then attempted to close the deal, As I was saying, I could use someone with your skills. We have not lost the war yet, and until we do my guerrillas and I will kill as many British as we can. I would like you to help us do that."

"Kill British. Like the ones who killed Opsule?" her voice small and sad, Clavonne put the pieces of Bonfils's tender together, while hiding her tears by looking down into the sand.

"Yes, like those ones," Bonfils answered, gently, not having any clue as to who or what Opsule might be.

"Very well, *Monsieur Quicksilver,* if that is your desire," Clavonne swallowed her tears and met the guerilla-fighter's gaze, "I will join you and your pack and kill British. Happily, and for free. But, I will not fight like a monkey."

"Caramba!" Marquaisa rumbled, sinking deeper into the shadows that crowded the split in the rockface. "Amusing are you, Clavonne. Strong and *so spicy.* Like the *pimienta de cayena (cayenne pepper).* Live forever, you might."

CHAPTER 45

ALL IS FAIR

JULY 25TH

THE RUINS OF LOUISBOURG

T he rumble of drumbeats rolling over Louisbourg's west wall, from the Moor of Gabanes, brought to an abrupt end the incarceration of Commodore Marquis Charry des Gouttes. Abandoned to his own devices by the guards who unlocked the cell he occupied in the Queen's Bastion, he walked out of the ruins of her majesty's stronghold, through the remains of his majesty's gardens, and lost himself in the chaos of a town full of hunger-crazed siege victims trying to salvage what remained of their ruined homes and lives. Careless of their plight, he immediately began stalking through the town with the sole intent of finding and killing the one remaining witness who, with Fortess having been blown to bits, could speak against him and bring him down.

Once vibrant, the Louisbourg into which des Gouttes emerged was an apocalyptic, dog-eat-dog wasteland. As he prowled its ruins hunting for the man who betrayed him to Drucour, des Gouttes stole scraps of food and beat back emaciated townies who, in turn, tried to pound him into submission and take what little he had. Finally, with a charred bone of dubious origin in his clutches, he found a perch on top of a broken section of crenellated oceanfront wall that provided him a high point from which to view the goings on in the decimated town. At times squatting, at other times standing, he gnawed the bone constantly while keeping his eyes peeled, and soon was rewarded with a glimpse of Auzire Duros, the scar-faced, patch-eyed sailor for whom he was hunting, scrounging for crumbs in the burned out husks of warehouses that fronted the wharf.

Desperate to keep the sailor in sight, while not drawing attention to himself, des Gouttes descended from his perch. Ducking and diving between piles of rubble, he followed the scuffling man through the fog that was seeping into the harbor until he holed up in *Prudent.* A grimace hardening his look, des Gouttes cast away what was left of the bone he'd ground down in his teeth and looked for a quiet way onto the great ship, which still lay hard aground in the shallows beside *Bien-faisant.*

LOUISBOURG HARBOR

"Washington, get down from the prow!" Captain George Balfour barked while waving his open hand down toward the deck of the pinnace, repeatedly, as if he was trying to squash the tall colonel. "It's hard enough to see in this fog without that great gourd of yours getting in the way!"

The men who were crowded into the small boat chuckled as Washington plunked himself down on a bench. When he was seated, Balfour continued hazing him asking, with exaggerated incredulity, a nearby sailor, "Young man, why is the army involved in a naval exercise?"

"I don't know, sir," the sailor huffed as he heaved on his oar. "Maybe they think we need a nanny to wipe our arses."

"Young man, your answer presumes that by being here the army might actually perform some useful service. Regrettably, you are wrong," Balfour shook his head and smiled at the oarsman, while the rest of the crew laughed. "With that having been said, the correct answer smells just as bad. In fact, the army wishes to steal our thunder, after we pull their arses out of the fire, so their blundering of the siege will be glossed over in the record books."

Balfour paused to let his message sink into his like-minded audience, then pressed on, "But, mark my words boys, this is the action that will end the French and this Oculus-forsaken siege. And *you,* the men of the navy, are the ones who will do it. That will be the way of it, no matter what the books say." He snorted and removed his watch from a pocket in his vest, then looked to where he thought the town was situated, "Now, if my timepiece is accurate, which it is, and assuming our army comrades know the big hand from the little hand on *their* watches, we should be hearing from them at any moment."

For long minutes the only sounds the sailors in the pinnace heard were the dips and scoops of their oars and, occasionally, those of the two dozen other boats in the task force. Balfour checked his watch for the fourth time, and as he looked up from replacing it in his pocket, he caught his first glimpse of the tips of the masts of a tall ship looming over the blanket of fog. He cursed softly, and as if in reply a voice reached out to him from the ship, through the fog.

"*Qui va là?*" *Who is there?*

Balfour's face went blank, and when he looked around the boat he saw his expression mirrored in the faces of his crew. Then, from the prow, he heard a caustic reply bark at the French sailor.

"*Qui pensez-vous que c'est, vous jeune choit?*" Washington growled. *Who do you think it is, you young pup?*

"*Désolé, Monsieur le Marquis,*" the disembodied voice apologized. "*S'il vous plaît venir à bord.*" *Sorry, Marquis. Please come on board.*

"Well, blow me down," Balfour exhaled as Washington plunked himself back in his seat. "The army did something right. Boscawen will never hear the end of it."

HMS PRUDENT

As he skirted the hull of *Prudent*, des Gouttes heard snippets of an exchange between a young ensign on *Bienfaisant* and a gruff officer who wanted to board the great ship. The dampening effects of the fog did nothing to mask the officer's impatience, and he chuckled at how like himself the man sounded. Whatever humor he may have found in the encounter was lost, however, when cannon fire erupted from beyond Louisbourg's west-facing walls.

Des Gouttes heard, more than he saw, the reactions of *Prudent's* men to the cannonade. Dozens of pairs of footfalls thudded forward on the main deck of the ship, and shortly thereafter, *'Oohs'* and *'Ahhs'* filled the gaps between detonations. Seasoned opportunist that he was, des Gouttes used the distraction provided by the barrage to scale the ship's webbing and slip over her rail, unseen by her crew. Without a backward glance, he sprinted at the cabins that were housed at the ship's stern, under the bridge.

As he ran, des Gouttes saw soldiers of the British task force, muskets strapped to their backs, clambering up the side and over the rail of *Bienfaisant,* and heard stirrings of the same type of activity taking place on *Prudent*. Ducking inside the cabins just before the first group of British raiders hopped over *Prudent's* rail, he peeked back through the doorway in time to see the first of the ship's crew recognize the threat, raise an alarm for his crewmates, and then fall to a musket ball. As he turned to bolt deeper into the ship, the two sides charged one another, and ringing clashes of steel followed him below deck.

Concealed by the shadows that surrounded him, and the furor on the main deck above, des Gouttes padded forward through the gun deck, waiting for the proverbial rat to desert the ill-fated ship. The ruckus up top was so loud he nearly missed the tapping feet of someone climbing the ladder between the gun deck and the ship's hold. Des Gouttes went still and strained his ears, desperate to be certain of what he'd heard. When the footfalls continued, he smiled hungrily and shifted his eyes from side to side scouring the deck for a spot from which to pounce. He found his solution in the light thrown from *Bienfaisant* through the gun ports of *Prudent*. Catlike, he used the shadows it cast to conceal himself in the middle of the aisle that ran between the rows of cannons. He used the light to find the opening to the companionway that housed the ladder.

Scar-faced, one-eyed, gaunt, and oblivious to des Gouttes's presence, Duros popped out of the hole and started limping along the aisle toward the ship's stern. As he hobbled across the planks, he watched the action on board *Bienfaisant*, but stopped abruptly when he heard a man clear his throat further up the aisle. Shrinking back a step, he squinted and then recoiled even further when he recognized who he was looking at.

"You!" Duros shouted at des Gouttes. "I should have killed you when I had the chance!"

"Funny, I made the same mistake with you," des Gouttes shot back. "Neither of us will be making it again."

Des Gouttes charged Duros, who turned and scrabbled toward the companionway. He was two steps into his flight when the side of *Prudent* nearest *Bienfaisant* exploded. Thick oak splinters, blown out of the hull, sliced across the aisle and ripped into what was left of the crippled man after the cannon ball ruptured his torso.

Stunned by the explosion, des Gouttes landed heavily on the barrel of a cannon and was buried under a pile of oak shards. His head thick as the fog that shrouded the ships, he fought back lamely, a few minutes later, when rough hands grabbed him and dragged him through the gun deck and up to the main deck. When he tripped over the mutilated body of a French sailor he was allowed to fall. As his head bounced off the deck he buckled at the waist and retched as a series of blasts rocked *Prudent's* gun deck.

The heat pouring up from the gun deck through the heavy planks of the main deck got des Gouttes up and onto his feet and into the horde of bodies flooding over the ship's rail. Weakened and dazed, he bumped down the webbing until he was jarred loose from it by a sailor overhead, who fell with him as he tumbled into the sand. Kicked, kneed, and elbowed into moving, he joined the crowd of his countrymen who were fleeing up the beach, away from *Prudent,* while flames climbed out of her gun ports, through her riggings, and up her masts.

Cool, damp air cycling up his legs and around his arms and face, finally brought des Gouttes to a standstill. Fleeing sailors crashed into him where he stood, cursing and pummeling him as they trampled him in their haste to distance themselves from *Prudent* and the British. When the last wave of survivors rolled over or around him, he pushed himself onto his knees in the churned up soil.

Bright firelight from *Prudent* forced des Gouttes to shade his eyes for long minutes, with his dirt-encrusted hands, until his eyes got used to the glare. When at last he was able to lower his hands, he saw *Bienfaisant* disappear into the mist and gloom of the harbor, as the British tugged her away and deprived Louisbourg of its last shred of defense. While *Bienfaisant* faded out of sight, some final fitful blasts collapsed what remained of *Prudent* and turned her into a pyre. Careless of the ship's destruction, des Gouttes grit his teeth and watched her turn to ash, just as he would the life of any man or woman who spoke against him or tried to bring him down.

The Moor of Gabanes

True to their word, after reaching their agreement with Poisson at mid-July, the British tempered their bombardment of Louisbourg. However, whether by accident or design, the contract language was left open to interpretation. Opting for the most liberal understanding of the verbiage, rather than shelling the town indiscriminately and causing random destruction, the British selected their targets systematically and ruthlessly destroyed them using an array of imaginative explosive devices.

With Poisson well rid of, the British used a deadly raid on their stockade as an excuse to pour an unrelenting, night and day barrage on Louisbourg. The sadistic onslaught was, for the British, their nadir. The maelstrom interminable, the people yet living in Louisbourg chucked hope into the midden heap that was their ruined town and filled the hollow in their soul with a deep-rooted, hate-fueled, hard-bitten defiance.

They put their scorn on display whenever the soldiers stationed on the Moor of Gabanes lit their torches and sounded their drums before bombarding the town. Rather than sit in their casemates and await obliteration, the citizenry of Louisbourg climbed to the top of what was left of its west wall and jeered at the British, daring them to try to knock them off of it. While keeping their distance, the British obliged by firing volley after volley at them, crushing the wall and the people manning it, and pitting the ruins of the town.

One of their salvos smashed into the wall, just north of the King's Bastion. On impact, rock, mortar, dust, and body parts were hurled into the air. On the town side of the wall, below the point of impact, the men and women in a pack of French militia curled up against its base and covered their heads with their hands as the debris rained down on and around them.

Huddled next to the pack leader, sixteen-year-old Adélard Arquette shut his eyes tight and tried to stop the shaking in his bones that was burning through what little life was left in his body. Breathing fast to keep pace with his racing heart, he choked on a cloud of dust and convulsed in a coughing fit that did little to clear his lungs, but did keep him from fainting. Hacking hard enough that he brought tears to the corners of his eyes, he rubbed them away as soon as he felt their dampness he rubbed them away, determined no one would know how truly terrified he really was.

After his coughing subsided, spasms racked his lean chest and shoulders and shot along his arms in fits and starts. The tremors buzzed into his hands and numbed his fingers to his fumbling attempts to lift his empty musket out of the dirt. He knew neither how to load, nor fire the weapon, as powder and shot both were critically short in supply. He had, however, been shown how to turn it into a spear, by strapping a knife to the end of its muzzle, and how to use it to defend himself or attack someone else.

"Remember," Constantin Bonfils, his leader, said to him quietly while wrapping his arm around the boy's shoulders and touching foreheads with him, "if you manage to stick that thing into someone and you can't get it out, then let it go and get out the sword the *capitaine* gave you. Then cut to pieces everything you see."

Adélard nodded wordlessly, his brown bloodshot eyes bulging, and wiped his nose on the sleave of his ragged shirt.

Bonfils read the fear in the lad and, grinning, ruffled his matted black hair and gave him his final instructions, "Stay behind me and watch my back. I won't let anything happen to you. Not because I give a damn about you, mind. But, if you go home with so much as a scratch your mother, rest her soul, will have my arse in a sling when I meet her in the next life."

Adélard bobbed his head again, and his voice cracking eked out a one word reply, "Okay."

"Good boy," Bonfils praised him, and the grin on his grizzled face fading kissed the boy on the forehead. "Now, pinch Clavonne on the bum so she'll stop moping about Opsule, may he rest in peace, and we can get on our way!"

Adélard did as he was told, and when Bonfils heard Clavonne squeak and then land a slap on Adélard, he set out. Running low, the tails of his threadbare, blood and dirt-stained white greatcoat trailing behind him in the grime, he led his dozen militia along the base of the west wall, weaving between stacks of rubble as he went. As they ran, the overlapping sounds of drums thudding, harsh orders barked in English, voices chanting in French, and cannons booming beat down on them. The flashes of light that went with the roar of the cannons were followed, seconds later, by rending crashes as the cannonballs pummeled the length of the wall, piercing whistles as they hurtled overhead then pounded into the town, and the screams of shredded townsfolk. Wincing against the racket and stumbling in the rubble, the troop scrambled to its objective; a crumbling section of wall from which massive chunks of stone had been blown away. Without pause, Bonfils scaled the rocks piled up against the wall and onto the wide ledge of the shot through section.

"No one is watching," he called to Adélard over the din. "When you get up here you will need to jump down to the other side, but it is not high. Pass the word back. Now, come quickly!"

When he reached the ledge, Adélard scanned the whole of the panoramic view it provided of the British lines that stretched as far as he could see southwards, to his left, and ended a little further north, to his right. Paralyzed by the show of firepower, his feet stayed rooted to the broken wall until Clavonne shoved him from behind and he pitched forward off the ledge. When he hit the ground he tumbled awkwardly, but kept his grip on his musket. Clutching it tight to his body, he logrolled to a stop a few feet from where he landed, facing up into the smoke-filled night sky.

"Very graceful," Bonfils teased Adélard and, chuckling, hauled him to his feet. Then, when his entire team was on the ground, he gathered them together and reminded them what to do, "Follow me until we reach the British. Then go north and south with your partners and attack them as you see fit. Kill as many as you can. Stop when you must. Then get back over the wall, or disappear into the forest. *Au revoir mes amis, et bonne chance!" Goodbye my friends, and good luck!*

After a last look at each of them, Bonfils grabbed Adélard, and staying low dashed west from one patch of shadow to the next, snaking toward the British lines. When he neared their earthworks, he signed with his hand for his pack to stop and wait. He then crawled on his belly to the closest mound. When he reached it, he pulled a dagger from his boot and peeked into where the two men defending it were crouched side-by-side. Both soldiers were fixated on the demolition of Louisbourg's west wall so they neither saw, nor heard Bonfils coming at them from their left, the knife strapped to his musket aimed at the heart of the first soldier, his dagger clenched between his teeth and ready for the second. Using all the strength he could summon, Bonfils plunged the knife on his musket into his first target and drove him into his mate. As they toppled, he snatched his dagger out of his mouth and drove it into their necks and guts, over and over, until they lay still on the ground. Splashed by their blood and breathing heavily, he kicked the dead men, then waved his hand in circles over the top of the earthworks, signaling the rest of his pack to get to work. Adélard joined Bonfils in time to see him cleaning his dagger on the dirt-stained white trousers of one of his victims, his musket laying across their backs.

"How?" Adélard whispered while dropping to one knee and staring at the corpses.

"Quickly and quietly as you can," Bonfils explained. "Just know, it will get noisier and messier the deeper we push into their lines. Speaking of which, our next target is over there, to our left, behind the most forward dugout in their line. Are you ready?"

"Yes," Adélard tried to sound convincing.

"No, you are not," Bonfils disagreed, then reached out and smeared fresh blood across the boy's face. "Now you are ready. Follow me."

With Adélard mimicking his every move, Bonfils crept up on their next target. When they were a few feet from the little bunker, he sat on his haunches and signed to the boy to circle around behind the two British soldiers. He then counted down from ten. When he reached zero, he sprang from his squat and sprinted across the front of the earthworks, raking his sword across two soldiers' eyes. Their shrieks drew Adélard out of the shadows, on the run, and he reached the soldiers just as Bonfils cut one's throat. Hot blood shot out of the gash and the soldier fell to his knees, then lurched face first into the packed dirt when Bonfils slammed his boot into the middle of his back.

With his third kill pinned and bleeding out, Bonfils waved Adélard forward. Hesitant, the teenager inched forward to where he was close enough that Bonfils could reach out and grab him. Adélard tried to escape, but Bonfils wrestled with him until the boy's back was tight to his chest. He then grabbed Adélard's wrists and forced him to turn over his musket so the point of the knife strapped to its muzzle was aimed down. Knowing what was about to happen, Adélard fought back harder, but could not stop his hands from being stretched over his head. Nor, could he keep them from being yanked down, hard, only to jolt to a sudden stop when the hilt of the knife rammed against the back of the second, blinded soldier.

Bonfils guided Adélard through the stroke a second time. He then released the boy and prodded him to do it on his own for a third and fourth time, reminding him it was men like the one he was killing who were responsible for the death of his mother. After the fourth stroke, Adélard needed no more prodding and kept stabbing until he was dead to the soldier's agonies and the horror he felt at inflicting them. Bonfils brought the initiation to a close by bearhugging the boy and backing him away from the riddled and bleeding carcass.

"Enough, enough, enough," he whispered into Adélard's ear. "Now you know what to do and how to do it. So, thank the man properly for supporting your education, so we can move on to your next lesson."

He let go of Adélard, but watched him carefully, uncertain as to who he might *thank* for the terrible tutorial. When he kicked the dead man, Bonfils breathed a bit easier. Still, he chose to be cautious, and rather than take the lead pointed Adélard at their next objective and kept his hand on the boy's hip as he followed him deeper into the British lines.

Adélard and Bonfils stalked further south, toward an artillery crew that was merrily blasting away at the fortress. To the west of the happy battery, Marquaisa hopped onto the roof of the British stockade. Still sporting the red greatcoat she stripped off a squaddie she slaughtered in a slit trench, she had added to her ensemble the newly polished riding boots she had yanked off an officer she exsanguinated after vaulting onto his horse's back and pitching him out of the saddle. She also had on his gold-trimmed tricorn hat which, for fun, she chose to wear backwards. Roused by the drums and the cannon fire, she strolled to the edge of the stockade's roof, sat down cross-legged, and took in the fireworks.

Picking her teeth, absently, with a shoeing nail crafted by the blacksmith she ate on the way to the stockade, she returned the waves sent to her, in greeting, by soldiers who saw only the red of her coat as they walked the road that bypassed the jailhouse. To the east, at the front, the King's Bastion succumbed to the incendiaries with which the British peppered it and bloomed into a raging inferno. Marquaisa was impressed when the Queen's Bastion took the same turn, but yawned when the Prince's Bastion finally got round to copying its predecessors.

Bored with the lightshow, she was about to break into the stockade to kill de Sade when the flash of a flintlock, out of place among the big gun emplacements positioned before the King's Bastion, caught her eye. Intrigued, she tossed aside her toothpick and waited to see if it was a chance occurrence—some nervous squaddie firing his weapon at something imagined—or part of something bigger that she might find amusing. Within moments, she saw a second, then a third flash spark at the same spot on the battlefield. Her curiosity peaked, she decided a closer look was in order, leapt down from the roof, and struck out for the front.

The Moor of Gabanes was pockmarked with craters punched into the turf by cannonballs, as well as dugouts gouged into the ground and then abandoned by soldiers who moved their earthworks forward by a few feet each night. It also was scarred by shallow trenches that allowed the British to move north and south along their lines without making themselves easy targets for French snipers. While negotiating the obstacles, Marquaisa saw soldiers who had rotated off the front lines sheltering in the trenches, some snoring, some smoking their pipes, and some shaking, their wide eyes and searching for something to which they could not attach a name. None of the smokers or searchers so much as glanced at her as she marched past. The nearer she got to the spot where crackling musket fire popped in counterpoint to the thunder of cannons, however, the more questioning looks were cast her way.

A few yards and a knot of earthworks separated her from the small arms skirmish when a squaddie sprang up in front of her and blocked her way, demanding she identify herself and state her business. She answered him by snapping her rapier out of the scabbard strapped across her back and cutting the head off the jabbering soldier, in between the syllables of the word whose pronunciation he was butchering. Dead before he knew it, his jaw continued to chew on the word as his head spun to the ground, stopping only when his body crashed down on top of it.

Her audacity and his disgorging blood diverted the attention of a handful of gunners away from their artillery stations, and along with a few infantrymen they wandered her way. A few of the soldiers reckoned the beheading of their comrade was punishment for some transgression or other, which they wanted to know about so as to avoid committing it. A couple of others decided Marquaisa was a murderer and tightened their grips on their weapons, readying themselves to offer her *a Roland for an Oliver*. One of them, pointing at the bare skin peeking out from behind the hem of her overcoat, spoke out loud the question that was on all of their minds, "Where are his trousers?"

Standing in a semi-circle before Marquaisa, they waited for their question to be answered. "Move aside, or die," she replied, going off on what was, to some of the soldiers, a not entirely unexpected tangent.

"How about, instead, we kill *you,*" one of the gunners countered.

"That was not one of your choices," Marquaisa informed the group, during a pause in the cannon fire.

"Well, it's the one that works best for me," an infantryman to her right declared, raising his sword and swinging a heavy downstroke at her head.

Marquaisa whirled and slashed her rapier upward in an arc that sliced through the soldier's descending sword arm, above his elbow. Before he could scream at the sight of his arm flopping in the dirt she turned over her forearm, and using an underhand grip ripped him open with the point of her blade, from his right hip to his left shoulder. His eyes wide, he dropped to his knees, then fell forward as his innards pushed through the tear in his torso and waistcoat.

A decapitation and a disembowelment proof enough of what she was capable, two of the gunners scuttled back to the relative safety of their battery. The five who chose to test themselves against her clustered around her and started hacking at her with their swords. Slow and predictable, their strikes were better suited to chopping wood than winning at swordplay. But their numbers compensated for their ineptitude and they managed to sneak past her lightning fast parries to score a few hits. Barely blinking at the nicks she took, she dished out punishment on a scale the soldiers had never seen previously, nor would they see again.

Her rapier the instrument of a lethal blend of mastery, preternatural speed and strength, a complete lack of mercy, and a colorful imagination, she cleaved limbs from bodies and made four kills in quick succession. The last man standing she ran through, shouldered to the ground, and drained of the blood that remained in his body. Then, with playtime having come to a close, she turned her attention to the skirmish that had enticed her to venture to the front line, and which continued to rage among the earthworks.

She saw a pack of six or seven ragtag guerilla fighters killing anyone who was wearing red who had the misfortune to cross their path, while also destroying every gun emplacement upon which they laid their hands. They were uncompromisingly ruthless, breathtakingly vicious, and careless of the futility of their mission—Louisbourg was doomed—and the fact their chances of survival were nonexistent. Standing astride the soldier whose blood had momentarily quenched her thirst, she savored their no-holds-barred style. Her relish turned sour, however, when she saw one of them, a grizzled man wearing a grimy white greatcoat and who was protecting a wounded teenager, punch a youthful British soldier in the face.

Shanklin Bridge went down, tangled up in his own arms, legs, and gear and lost his grip on his sword. His ears ringing, blazing cannons, sparking guns, flashing swords, and smoke swirled around and around in the shrinking tunnel that was his field of vision. In its center, a man in whose eyes the flames of Louisbourg burned was whipping his two hands and the sword they gripped downward at him from above his head. Transfixed, he watched the blade slice through its arc and wondered what it would do when it reached his head.

Shanklin supposed it would crack his skull and squish his brains. Oddly, it clanged and scraped and missed his melon completely. Stranger still, polished riding boots planted themselves in the dirt, one beside each of his shoulders, and he was left looking up at a wondrous pair of trouserless legs.

A split second after she bound the graying guerrilla fighter's blade with her rapier, Marquaisa had to slap away his backhanded riposte, then duck as the sharpened edge of his sword whizzed over her head. His follow-through exposed his ribs and she jabbed at them. But he recovered and bound her blade with his own. He then pushed them down so their points ground in the dirt, his between Shanklin's legs, and hers between Adélard's.

"I saw you kill those soldiers," Bonfils growled in his peculiar

Acadian-French dialect, locking eyes with her, "Why stop me from killing this one?"

"Because he is *my* soldier," Marquaisa snarled back at him in Spanish accented French. "I will decide when he is to be killed. Right now, I think I'll kill you, and your little pup too!"

"That will have to wait," Bonfils informed her, looking past her shoulder. "You have attracted some admirers"

"As have you," she said with a nod toward a gang of squaddies creeping up on Bonfils from behind. "Last one back gets to watch their brat die."

Bonfils scowled at her. Then, with a quick tug, freed her rapier and snapped instantly into a defensive stance, ready to counter her attack. Instead, she chuckled at him, making the hairs that had not been singed off his forearms stand on end. She then took a half step back and pivoted on her left foot to salute the quartet of cursing soldiers rushing her way. Only then did Bonfils turn and stand, *en garde,* between Adélard and the oncoming trio of troopers.

Each of them occupying a pole in a compact kill zone, he north and she south, Bonfils and Marquaisa stayed light on their feet, lunging and sidestepping, but never yielding ground. Marquaisa took on her opponents one at a time. After singling out one, she beat back the others while she fenced with her selection, briefly, before dispatching him to Oculus's burning halls of damnation. She then moved on to the next man in line. Meanwhile, Bonfils attacked and tried to kill someone with every stroke of his blade, turning back his enemies with force and fury and sapping them of their strength and will. He killed one by hammering on the soldier's hilt guard until his sword dropped from his hand, then slashing his throat. He took a second by feigning a trip and leaving his body exposed, then lurching away from the man's strike and driving the point of his blade up under his chin and out through the top of his head. Bonfils's third attacker retreated before he freed his sword from his second victim, which he extracted by letting the dead man fall, then yanking out his blade while the soldier was in his death throes. Unencumbered and no longer beset by men out for his blood, he spun around to see how his adversary was faring at the opposite end of their tiny corridor of death, and to check on Adélard's health. He found her standing over the boy, dead men fanned out behind her, with the point of her rapier poised above the artery pulsing in Adélard's neck.

"Do not," he said to her and dropped his sword.

"Why not?" Marquaisa asked him, cocking her head.

Bonfils sighed, his shoulders slumping, and turned his eyes to the sky then back on her and answered, "I made a promise."

"Fool," she taunted and narrowed her eyes at him. "You missed one."

The soldier who had retreated away from Bonfils had returned and, sword raised over his head, was charging the unarmed guerilla fighter. Bonfils cast a glance over his shoulder at the stampeding man, then took a last look at Adélard before closing his eyes and waiting for the end he thought he'd have met much earlier in the evening.

When it came, it sounded like a crack and a squish. But, when he checked the back of his head his hand came away damp only with his own sweat. Confused, he scuffled through a turn, and as he came around, he first saw the soldier's sword laying in the dirt a few inches away from his feet. Next, the trooper came into view, his hand and arm outstretched, his face in the ground, a sword lodged deep in the back of his skull. Further down the corpse, at its feet, a girl, her slight but strong body wrapped in rags, her straight blonde hair twisted in a French braid, stood staring at it. Her eyes were hard with hate, but brimming with sorrow.

"Clavonne?" Bonfils blurted, wondering how it was she still was alive.

"For Opsule," she said, choking back a sob and forcing the name passed her lips.

"Ahem," Marquaisa cleared her throat.

"What?" Bonfils started, then flinched as the pieces of his previous conversation clanged together in his brain. "Oh, no!"

"Oh, yes," Marquaisa sneered at him, the point of her blade still hovering over Adélard's throat.

Suddenly, she twitched her left arm. Her sword jumped in her hand, but flicked away from Adélard. In a flash, she brought the blade to her chest, its point aimed at the sky. In the next instant, she swept it down and away from her body in a wide arc. As she did, she tilted her head down slightly, slid her left foot back, bent her right knee, and sunk into an achingly graceful bow. She held it for a respectful few seconds, then stood to her full height and sheathed her rapier.

"Keep your promise," she commanded Bonfils and chased it with an order. "Go. Now, warrior."

"Merci" (Thank you), Bonfils replied, tilting himself into a ramshackle bow of his own invention. He then called over his shoulder to Clavonne, "Come and help me with Adélard."

Marquaisa watched the guerillas hoist their comrade off the ground, sling his arms over their shoulders, and start dragging him away, his toes etching lines in the dirt.

"Clavonne," she called after them, bringing them to a halt. "Your mistress, Haritha, is safe. But she will not soon be returning. So, you must tend to her business," she tasked the girl, then added, "She thinks highly of you. As do I. *Adieu." Farewell.*

"Au revoir" (Goodbye), Clavonne replied without looking back.

As they went on their away, Marquaisa overheard Bonfils ask Clavonne, "What business?"

In answer, Clavonne hushed him up and scolded told him, "None of your business."

"She is, indeed, someone to be reckoned with," Marquaisa told Shanklin, who was blathering about wondrous bare legs and tall leather boots. "Come fool."

Using her toe, she flipped the teenager onto his stomach. Bending at the waist, she grabbed him by the scruff of the neck, straightened up, and hauled him off the front line. As she humped back through the ranks, soldiers coming forward very helpfully pointed out where she could find the hospital station. She saluted their generosity, and after they passed by took a detour into a crater and propped Shanklin against its bank. She then nicked her lip with her fingernail tip and pecked him with a kiss that slid a drop of freezing ichor into his mouth, which spread over his tongue and slipped down his throat.

"You will live forever," she promised him, then vanished.

HMS BIENFAISANT

Prudent's fires dimmed as *Bienfaisant* was coaxed deeper into the fog on the ends of taut lines that reached out to a cluster of pinnaces that were eking their way further out into the harbor. Washington stood at her rail and watched as *Prudent* cut herself to pieces and crumble under the fury of the fires that consumed her. Shaking his head as a last few sporadic blasts rendered her unrecognizable, he turned away from the rail to attend to the salvage duties to which he'd been assigned by Wolfe, and with which Balfour had, enthusiastically, kept him busy.

Taking up a lantern, he set out alone on his inspection of *Bienfaisant.* Studiously avoiding the pools of gore left behind in the aftermath of the battle on her main deck, he assessed the damages to the ship inflicted by that selfsame battle. Satisfied she was intact, up top, he made his way below to the gun deck. Though less of the action had taken place amongst the cannons, as he made his way through and around the heavy barrels he squelched through some dark, slick spots that were riddled with bits and chunks of clothing, weapons, and people. None of the munitions appeared to be either sabotaged or at risk of exploding spontaneously, so he proceeded deeper into the ship's bowels.

At the top of the stairway that led down into the ship's hold, he paused when he heard the scuttling of what sounded like rats. Not the least bit interested in the prospect of rattling his saber at a riot of rodents, he cast the light from his lantern down to the base of the stairwell. A clear circle of planks reflected his lamplight, and content he would not soon be the target of an attack by a regiment of rats, he edged his way down the risers. When he reached the foot of the stairs, he raised his lantern over his shoulder to give himself as broad a view of the contents of the hold as the little light would provide. Its glow cast shadows into a chaos of stacked chests, barrels, casks, and bins that were marked in languages that were both familiar and foreign to him.

Ignoring the quiet scurrying that reached out to him from the darkness of the hold and safe in his bubble of lamplight, he picked his way through the containers. In the deepest section of the hold, nearest the ship's stern, his light fell on a pile of crates whose canvas wrappings bore an inscription that included the likeness of Oculus's three-headed pet hound. Intrigued, Washington crept in close to the tarpaulin and read the *lingua franca* jottings that spoke of supplies provisioned by the Kingdom of Spain.

"Huh, the Spanish buoying up the French. Who would have thought?" Washington mused as he pulled back the tarp.

Under the canvas, a few of the wooden boxes had toppled and cracked open. When Washington crouched down and pushed his lantern close to the split boxes, they threw back at him bright, reflected light. Blinking away the sting of the glare, he reached out and tugged on one of the loose lids. Overestimating the strength of seal, he pulled too hard, tore off the lid, and spilled the contents of the box onto the deck.

Washington covered his head with his arms and ducked for cover, fearing he'd tripped a booby trap. When the sounds of gunpowder exploding and water rushing up through the floorboards did not fill his ears, he quickly straightened himself up. Then, after a subtle glance to his left and right to verify no one had witnessed his moment of awkwardness, he crouched down and held his light over the goods that were emptied from the box, and caught his breath.

Gold bars, all bearing the stamp of the King of Spain, shone in the lamplight. Shocked, Washington recoiled and stood back an arm's length from the bricks, his lantern poised over the treasure. He then raised the light a bit higher, cast his eyes over the rumpled canvas, and envisioned the dozens of other, identical wooden boxes that lay beneath it. Unbidden, visions of previously unimaginable futures blossomed before his eyes. As they did, so did the beginnings of a plan to bring them to fruition.

Moving quickly, he righted the overturned box and refilled it, quietly, with the scattered bars. He then turned the corner of the canvas down over the stack of crates, and made his way hastily to the stairway that would take him up to the gun deck. He hustled along the aisle between the cannons to the narrow corridor that was lined with the officer's quarters. With a grunt, he kicked one of the doors loose from it hinges, then carried it back down the aisle. When he reached the top of the stairwell, he propped the door across it, lengthwise. He then used his dagger to scratch a rough skull and crossbones into the wood to label the hold as being poisoned, and then stood back and admired his makeshift blockade.

"Now, all I need is a crew," he said to himself, pensively. A heartbeat later an idea stormed into his brain. Without judging its merits, he put it into words, "If I give the job to my American friends, then perhaps they won't consider me so much of a *schweinehund,* after all."

While Washington mulled over possible solutions to the problem of manning *Bienfaisant* with a crew, Fortess scuffed his feet and cackled. Sitting on a short stack of boxes, each of which was marked with a three-headed dog, he rhymed to himself, "Thought you not, France join Spain? Then a block you have for a brain. Now Fortess has their loot. He'll make them galoots. Then end them, their hearts ripe with pain."

CHAPTER 46

CEREMONY

JULY 26TH

HMS AMELIA

P*rudent* having been burned to the waterline, *Bienfaisant* having been captured, Louisbourg was utterly defenseless. On that point the British army and navy agreed. They disagreed, however, on what to do about the French. The navy argued for allowing them to surrender with honor. The army wanted to wipe them off the face of the earth. Jeffrey Amherst, Commander-in-Chief of the British expedition, took the middle ground. The French, he decreed, would be given the opportunity to surrender, on his terms. But, if they weren't quick about it, then he would dispatch Louisbourg and everyone in it to Oculus's burning halls of damnation.

"Enter," Amherst replied to the knock on Boscawen's door without lifting his eyes off the documents that were scattered across the bureau behind which he sat.

Brock slipped through the door, closed it quietly, and marched to the front of the desk, where he waited to be attended by the general. When, at last, Amherst flicked the page he was reading onto a pile of similar pages and tipped back his chair to look at the major, Brock shifted nervously.

"What's that in your hand, Brock? Yet more administrivia with which I am to numb my mind and crush my soul? It really is too early in the morning for that," the general harangued the major, narrowing his eyes at the young man while concealing a grin.

"No, sir. I mean . . . yes, sir," Brock stumbled.

"Enough with the 'sir' business," Amherst quipped. "You were in Wolfe's command. As you may have noticed, he's not much of one to stand on ceremony, or to shrink from speaking his mind. Got those habits from me, I'm afraid." The general sat forward in his chair and reached across the desk and grated, "So, give it over. When we're done with it, you can regale me with the stories our dear James told you about me and share with me the pet names he has invented for me."

"Yes, sir," Brock cringed at the formality in his delivery, and then scrambled to recover. "It's a request. It just came in from Colonel Washington. He's asking your permission to take *Bienfaisant* to Halifax, for dry-dock and repair. He thinks she still may have some serviceable life left in her, despite the damage she took on last night."

"So, our backcountry colonel turned salvage-jockey now thinks himself a sea dog," Amherst chuckled. "Anything in the cargo of interest, or that can be put to immediate use?"

"The colonel says the stores in the hold that could be of use were sent to the depot for distribution to the men, or to the hospital to help treat the wounded," Brock relayed the information to which he had been made privy.

"He is nothing if not thorough, is our Washington," Amherst sighed. "Well, this kind of thing typically lands on Boscawen's pile. But, he's out gallivanting on dry land—got himself a bit stir-crazy cooped up on this tub for so many months—so let's handle this, shall we? When does he plan on leaving?"

"As soon as he receives your permission," Brock conveyed Washington's wishes to the general.

"Not wasting any time, is he. To be expected, I suppose. The man is depressingly efficient," Amherst looked one last time at the page on which the request was scrawled, then picked up his pen and defaced it with his initials. "There. Done. Good show, Brock. Send that back to

Washington, so we can be rid of him. Anything else we can knock down, while you're here?"

"Nothing else new, sir," he replied, then added a reminder. "As planned, Governor Drucour will be arriving to stand before you sometime this afternoon."

Amherst's eyes twinkled as he hatched a plot with his aide, "Very well. Let me know when he arrives, so I can let him stew for a while before we have our meeting."

"Capital," Brock said, mimicking a Wolfe-ism, and exited to the general's jeers.

After Brock closed the door to the office he had taken over from Boscawen, Amherst groaned and hunkered down over what remained of his paperwork. By mid-afternoon, he had completed most the items on his administrative to-do list. Chortling, he fixed his signature on the item that he relished most and which was sure to drive Boscawen into outrage. Undercutting the admiral and the navy in his report on the capture of *Bienfaisant* and the destruction of *Prudent,* he attributed the lion's share of the credit for the mission's success to himself and the army, "Too bad you weren't here to give your side of it, Eddie."

He had just started his review of a plan for a strategic military offensive, at the heart of which lay what Wolfe called a "craven" policy consisting of the expulsion of more Acadians, when a knock on the door broke up his train of thought. Setting aside the plan, Amherst rubbed the fatigue from his eyes and composed himself for the meeting that he had been looking forward to all day, and called back, "Enter."

Brock entered, approached the general's desk, and spoke quietly, "Governor Drucour is here."

His elbows on his desk, Amherst tilted forward and asked Brock, conspiratorially, "Been waiting long?"

"Nearly an hour, by now," Brock reported, secretively.

"Hot in the sun?" Amherst inquired, wanting details.

"He's sweating," Brock filled him in, straight-faced.

"Good enough," Amherst took the news with a sly grin. Then, wiping his face clean of all traces of amusement, he instructed Brock, "Show him in."

Brock left the general's quarters and then announced his return a moment later via another polite knock.

"Enter," Amherst said, grabbing a random sheet of paper and pretending to be engrossed in its contents.

Brock opened the door and allowed the governor to precede him into the room, then followed him and quietly closed the door. Amherst picked up a second sheet and looked back and forth between the two while his guests stood in silence, waiting for him. When, at last, he looked satisfied with what he was reading, he peered over the pages at Drucour and ordered him, "Sit."

Ignoring the governor, the general shifted his attention to his aide, and gave him further instruction, "Brock, I believe adequate time has been provided for her wounds to heal, so would you be so kind as to fetch the captain?"

When the door closed behind Brock, Amherst leaned back in his chair, looked at Drucour, ignored ceremony, and got down to business, "I've been told you don't like our terms."

"I do not," Drucour muttered. "I am here only because the people wish it. My men served with valor. They deserve to be granted the honors of war."

"Your people are being given terms that are infinitely more favorable than the ones you have imposed on them for the past three months," Amherst launched his attack on Drucour. "They are getting the peace they deserve. As for your garrisons, they're getting far better than what Montcalm granted us at our Fort William Henry. Or, perhaps some of your men and a few of your remaining women and children would prefer a good tomahawking and a bit of a scalping?"

"My men were not party to those actions," Drucour shot back.

"And that is the *only* reason why they are *only* being required to surrender themselves as prisoners of war, rather than being shipped off to toil in the bowels of East India Traders for the remainders of their lives," Amherst fumed at the governor in reply.

Drucour reddened and opened his mouth to protest, but was stifled by another knock on the door. He could only glare at Amherst as he beckoned Brock.

"Come in, major, and bring the captain with you," Amherst invited his officers to join him, a hint of anticipation in the scowl with which he favored Drucour.

Behind Drucour, the two officers entered the war room. One remained at the door, while the other stepped around the bureau and stood to Amherst's right, facing the governor.

Drucour kept his eyes trained on Amherst, and he was about to throw himself into the protest he'd been forced to swallow, a moment earlier, when the British general stopped him with a raised hand and insisted on a bit of ceremony, "A modicum of decorum, if you please, Governor Drucour. Allow me to introduce to you Captain Kai Race. Captain Race, this is Augustin de Boschenry de Drucour, *former* Governor of Île Royale."

Drucour cringed at the modification to his title, then looked at the captain and his jaw dropped. His face coloring, he jumped to his feet. As Brock's pistol pressed to the back of his skull he spluttered, "What mockery is this? Your so-called terms are insult enough. But now you have reached a low that I did not think was within even *your* grasp, Amherst. Forcing Lady Drucour to wear that ridiculous uniform is unbearable!"

"Remarkable. I wouldn't have believed it if I hadn't seen it with my own eyes," Amherst congratulated the captain, "Sit down, Drucour. That is not your wife."

Drucour stayed on his feet and accosted Amherst, "I know who I am looking at." He then looked at Race squarely, and softened his tone, "My dear Marie-Anne, when you did not return after your brave tour of the battlements, I thought the worst. I am so happy to see you, and I am thrilled that the worst of my fears have not come true. But, seeing you so, I cannot help but wonder what else they have done to you?"

Amherst stood out of his chair, planted his fists on the bureau and leaned over it toward Drucour snarling, "If you see the captain and I sidestep away from one another in the next instant, then it is because you have ignored my order to sit down. Major Brock is not so flippant, I assure you, and neither the captain nor I wish to be caught in the shower of gore that accompanies the ball that he blasts through your skull, on my order. Now, sit down."

Drucour lowered himself into his seat. Brock took a step back, but kept his pistol cocked.

"As I was saying," Amherst remained standing and talked down at the former governor, "That is not your wife, Drucour. Captain Race is a woman with many talents, not the least of which are her singular skills in the art of deception."

"Thank you, sir. It is a gift," Race accepted the compliments, sighing quietly at the tedium that went with being regarded as something akin to a carnival attraction.

"Indeed, and it is one that would have got you roasted over a spit, not that long ago," Amherst observed. Then, sensing Race's impatience, he returned his attention to Drucour. "How hard do you think it was for us to plant an agent in a busy port town like Louisbourg? Once planted, how hard do you think it was for that agent to come to know you and your wife's movements? Then, knowing those routines, how difficult do you think it was to cut out your wife, perhaps while she was at the docks collecting a shipment of seeds for her gardens, then bundle her off for safekeeping while replacing her with an imposter? In case you are wondering, the answer to every one of those queries is, 'child's play.' Well, I'll admit, you'd need Race's *unique* abilities to pull off that very last bit, but the rest of it was the very definition of simplicity."

Drucour looked at Race and searched her ice blue eyes, one of which winked at him, and he saw her for the heathen that she was. At last, recognizing his mistake, he shook his head in defeat and muttered, "Congratulations, Captain."

"Let us be clear, Drucour," Amherst butted in roughly, "It was not Race who defeated you. Her mission was to convince you to not mount what you knew all along would be a futile defense. She failed. Not for want of trying, but on account of your pigheadedness. No, Drucour, it was not Race, but *you* who brought about your own defeat."

"I hoped, only, to delay you until—"

"Until what?" Amherst abruptly cut off Drucour. "Until reinforcements arrived and chased us away? You knew that was a fantasy. France has no interest in Louisbourg. She hadn't been fully restored since the *last* siege in '45, and from what Race has been telling me, the captains whose arms you twisted to keep their ships in her port refused to defend her. With all of that in front of me, you will never convince me that you were so blind that you did not see you were on your own. Yet, in spite of that knowledge, still you refused to do the sensible thing and yield to our massive superiority in numbers and firepower. Instead, you made us use our advantages to destroy Louisbourg, holding on until you could claim your people forced you to capitulate."

Amherst paused, and then concluded his evisceration of the governor, "No, Drucour, you will not trick me in the same way that your little performance here this afternoon suggests you were tricked by Race. I know that the pigheadedness you would not let Race penetrate is a deceit *you* employed to conceal *your* ruthless willingness to sacrifice lives in order to preserve or, better yet, advance your personal reputation and interests. I can assure you, it will be my pleasure to see that you do neither of the two."

Drucour glowered at Amherst, hatred burning in his eyes. But rather than give it vent, he simply reached across the bureau, picked up Amherst's pen, and stated flatly, "The terms."

Amherst obliged by pulling a sheet of paper out from under the pile on his desk, thrusting it at Drucour, and providing a synopsis of that which was written upon it, "Allow me to summarize. They start at the top of the page with today's date, July the twenty-sixth. They finish a couple of lines later with, 'I surrender.' That's where you sign."

Without so much as a glance at the wording, the governor scribbled his signature on the page and stood up. He turned as if to leave, but was stopped by Amherst's raised hand and forced to listen to additional provisions, "As a first step in the retooling of your reputation and interests, as of this moment, you are a prisoner of war. You will be reunited with your wife, who is fine by the way, and who awaits you on a transport out in the bay. The two of you will be taken to England, where you will be detained until it suits us to do with you otherwise." Returning his attention to the documents on his desk, Amherst dismissed Drucour with a flick of his fingers, "Good day to you."

"*Bienvenue*," Drucour said, then walked to the door and was escorted out by Brock.

"*Bienvenue*," Amherst repeated, absently. "*Bienvenue. Bienve . . . bien . . .*" He rummaged around his desk for a moment, then turned to Race. "The message from Poisson that Boscawen's aide—Oswald was his name—translated. What did it say?"

"*Bienvenue* . . . 'good day,' the same as what Drucour just said," Race provided the general the reminder, immediately, uncertain as to why he needed it.

"Did you see it? The message, I mean," Amherst, his excitement growing, asked her to search her own memory.

"Yes, it was torn and smudged, but the first few letters were clear enough," Race told Amherst what she recalled of the soaked parchment Fortess had delivered to Boscawen.

"What were they?" Amherst demanded specifics, stepping in close to her and watching her eyes as she thought back to conversation between Boscawen and Oswald.

"Oswald said to Boscawen, 'Sir, I see the letters B—i—e—n—and —v,'" she repeated the major's words, verbatim.

Amherst's jaw dropped, "And I say we mistook for etiquette what Poisson really said in his message. A shameful cockup on our part, I'm afraid." His eyes then lit up, "And just when I was beginning to think life in the colonies was going to be a bore. An adventure! And it has fallen right into our laps."

He sat on the edge of his desk and quietly spoke to Race, "This one is off the books, Race. For now, it will be just you and I who know of it. We will bring others into the fold if and when they are needed."

When the captain nodded her understanding, he explained, "It appears as though Washington, our backcountry colonel, is not quite the bumpkin we took him for. In fact, he could be more cunning than any of us could ever have anticipated. I say this because it appears as though he has made off with something of value to His Majesty. Gold to be precise. Lots of it. Enough to do whatever he chooses with whomsoever he chooses."

Race raised an eyebrow and a question, "What do you think he has in mind?"

"Beyond my now knowing he is shrewd, I cannot claim to be inside his head. Not yet anyway," Amherst admitted. "So, we may have to wait until such time as we catch up with him to inquire of him as to his intentions. That is to say, when we catch up with him and *Bienfaisant* . . . *B—i—e—n—f—a—i—s—a—n—t!*"

RAJANI

Vishnu, Ganesh, and Yuval were snoring loudly on *Rajani's* poop deck after a long morning of instructing Haritha in the aptitudes documented in the Kāma Sūtra. By contrast, to refresh herself, under the watchful eye of Enriquez, Haritha was skinny-dipping and sunbathing with Suchika, in a cove that was shielded from chilly onshore breezes by the rocks of Gabarus Point. To his right, using the spyglass that was presented to him as a gift for passing the first stage in his apprenticeship—which consisted of lessons in raiding, pillaging, and prison-breaks—Erieux scanned the comings and goings of the British fleet, to and from Gabarus Bay.

Enriquez dragged his eyes off the ladies and checked on his pirate-in-training. The Acadian had been sullen and withdrawn ever since he'd wakened after the battle at the stockade in which, once again, he was briefly reunited with and then abruptly torn away from his cherished Raçielle.

"Your Raçielle is not a mermaid, Rio," Enriquez teased Erieux. "She will not leap out of the water and into your arms, no matter how closely or for how long you watch the waves."

Erieux ignored Enriquez.

"The closest things you will find to mermaids are lying on the beach, behind you. You will not need your spyglass to see what I mean," Enriquez persisted.

"Is that bulge in your pocket a happy side effect of your piratical instincts telling you that you have identified creatures of myth, or evidence you are a slave to your baser instincts?" Erieux responded, at last, to Enriquez's poking and prodding.

"Ha!" Enriquez laughed. "He speaks, and with a tongue as sharp as his eyes! Good to have you back, Rio. I must, however, decline to answer your question this one time, as I wish to neither dispel a cherished myth, nor have you think less of me."

"Neither is possible," Erieux landed another verbal jab, then changed topics, "We have been waiting here for five days. How much longer are we required to wait for our employer?"

"I am glad that you now consider yourself in her employ," Enriquez began, a contented smile filling the frame of his goatee. "The answer is, 'until we have good reason to leave.' Have we?"

"Well, unlike you, I have not been idling away my time ogling mermaids," Erieux said, looking out over Gabarus Bay, "I have been engaged in more piratical pursuits."

"What kind of pursuits?" Enriquez raised an eyebrow as a familiar tingling crept out of his crotch and up his spine.

Erieux nodded at the man o' war that was well off the point, taking a southwest heading, "When you look at that ship, what do you see?"

Enriquez looked out on the bay, over *Rajani's* rail and fell back on the answer Erieux had provided to the same question, not long ago, "A waste of good oak."

"Again, your thick-headedness impresses," Erieux imparted on Enriquez his assessment of the pirate's observation, then attempted to enlighten him, "Look at how she rides low in the water. What does that tell you?"

"She is sinking," Enriquez stated the obvious.

Erieux persisted, "Imagine you are a seafaring soldier of fortune—"

"A pirate, like you?" Enriquez interrupted, and turned away from the water to study Erieux more closely.

"—and you happen upon a ship that is in good repair, like that one, but it is weighed down. Other than your fear for the welfare of its crew, what would be your first thought?"

"Too much cargo," Enriquez ventured, grinning.

"Precisely, and being the pirate that you are, what type of cargo do you think would weigh so heavily on so sturdy a ship?" Erieux gave Enriquez a meaningful look.

"Gold!" Enriquez smiled, broadly. "Well done, Rio, you have entered the second stage of your apprenticeship. Let us go and see if we are deceived."

HMS BIENFAISANT

Standing in front of *Bienfaisant's* wheel, Washington looked at an open horizon that was free of obstacles and smiled. He savored the sea air and the feeling of a weight being lifted off of his shoulders for a few moments, then called down to the main deck, "Pilot!"

"*Herr Vazigtonne!*" the gravelly acknowledgement rolled up the ship's rails.

"Change of plan," Washington said, squaring his jaw. "Plot a course for Boston. We'll dock there, offload the cargo, and leave the ship for the navy. When that's done, you lot can go your own way with my thanks and a bit of cash."

"*Jawohl, mein herr!*" *(Yes sir!)* the pilot then rattled off a quick set of commands for the man at the wheel, and the ship heaved as they took hold of her.

His back turned to the British fleet, New France disappearing behind him, Washington didn't see the Mughal ship that eased from behind Gabarus Point and took a bearing on *Bienfaisant.* Unaware of the unwanted attention his ship had attracted, Washington's mind drifted. As he remembered the trials he had endured and the lessons he had learned in his lifetime of service to England, his expression darkened. But as he envisioned the life that lay before him, it cleared.

Washington's recollections of his past life and his visions of his future life left distinctly different tastes in his mouth. Preferring the sweetness of his prospects, he spat out the bitterness of his memories, then growled the motto that would beat at the heart of his political dogma for decades to come, "*Phoq the Empire.*"

FLAT POINT

Gutted, literally and figuratively, of their heart and soul, rumor had it the French had finally surrendered. Even so, stories about the deadly suicide attacks that took place during the final barrage, the previous evening, had all British soldiers keeping their guard up.

One squaddie, in particular, was on edge as he patrolled what was left of the stockpiles of crates strewn around the beach below Flat Point. Despite what he'd heard in camp about the siege being over, Private Shanklin Bridge stayed alert, anxious to avoid mishaps of the type that had left him with a scar on his neck and a blackened eye. That the wounds had healed, inexplicably, as he lay concussed in a crater on the Moor of Gabanes, during the final barrage, did little to calm his frayed nerves. In fact, the lack of reliable answers to the questions he had about his recovery, and his subsequent robust health served only to agitate them further.

As he plodded along in the darkness, in sand that partly buried stacks of smashed crates, Bridge gave the rubbish heaps a wide birth and kept his musket at the ready position. He told himself he was just being cautious. But he knew the leather-necked sergeant to whom he had recently been assigned would tell him he was being chicken-hearted. So, making a conscious effort to change his mindset, he started stumping his way, purposefully, past the scrap, but froze when a shadow darkened the edges of his vision.

"Who's there?" he croaked, his voice cracking, his musket rattling in his hands.

"Bridge. Shanklin Bridge," Marquaisa spoke his name, quietly, and walked slowly toward him.

"That's me. You're someone quite different, I think," Shanklin guessed. His voice hitting a falsetto high, his heels scuffing in the sand as he backpedaled away from her shifting shadow.

"Good guess," Marquaisa applauded him, crunching bits of rotten wood underfoot as she stalked him.

"So, it was you," he guessed again, tripped, then righted himself.

"Me, who what?" she asked, knowing the answer and closing in on him.

"Oh, I don't know," Shanklin abandoned his retreat and spilled, "gave me the best night of my life, a little while back. Saved it, for some reason, last night. Then did something to erase some of its hurt?"

"Do you guess, still?" Marquaisa probed, stepping to within his arm's reach.

Shanklin's heart quickened when she came into full view. Calm, rather than crazed. Clothed, rather than naked, albeit sparingly in a coat not unlike his own, but more battle-scarred. Booted, rather than barefoot, in the style sported by the mounted officers he'd seen riding around camp. She also wore an officer's tricorn hat backwards, imparting an air of playfulness to her demeanor. But, it was the boots, glimpses of which flashed through his memories of the preceding night, that convinced him.

"No, my lady, I am certain," Shanklin replied, finally, his voice softening, his eyes tearing up as he dropped his musket. *"Gracias."* Thank you.

"De nada" (You're welcome), Marquaisa accepted his thanks as she removed her hat and shook out her hair. "Now, help *me* remember, you must."

"Remember what?" he asked, puzzled, wondering why he still was alive.

"What it is like to *not* kill, even if I *want* to kill," she answered gritting her teeth and eyeing his throat.

"Do you want to kill me, right now?" Shanklin took a risk.

"I want to kill all the time," Marquaisa told him, simply and honestly.

"Very well. Kill me. Right now," Shanklin challenged her, stepping in close to her and looking her straight in the eye.

She growled, long and low, her lips peeling back wickedly. Then, suddenly, in a voice low and gruff, she rasped, "I cannot."

"Why not?" he pressed her for a reason and, daring her, stepped into her, pushing his chest against hers.

"I do not know!" she snarled and seized him by the shoulders, her teeth bared and ready to strike.

Shanklin held his ground, kept his eyes on hers, breathed slowly, and said quietly, "I will show you why not."

Carefully, Shanklin placed his hands on Marquaisa's arms and gently drew them down until her hands were at her sides. He then kissed her, lightly, on one cheek, then the other, then cupped her face in his hands and kissed her lips. When their lips touched she shut her eyes and, unwinding in his easy touch, savored the tenderness of their embrace. Holding their kiss, he stroked the hair that fell from her temples over her shoulders. Then, slowly, he lifted one of his hands until it balanced the back of her head, while lowering the other and easing it around her waist to the small of her back. His fingertips delicately kneading her scalp, he parted her lips with his tongue, and finding hers kissed her full on the mouth. Feeling her body rise into his, he undid the buckle on the strap that held her scabbard, unfastened the buttons of her coat, and feathered his fingers over her smooth skin, from her belly to her back.

Marquaisa shivered at the warmth of his caress and pressed her body tighter to his, sifted her fingers into his hair and kissed him back. His taste fruity, she sampled more of him with her tongue, and as his flavor saturated her mouth she felt her sweet spot begin to tingle. Carefully, without letting go of their kiss, she reached her hands down and with sure fingers loosened his belt, pulled open the buttons that held up his breeches, slid them over his buttocks, and grasped him in the palm of her hand.

Shanklin answered by taking her bottom in his two hands. He felt the firmness of her cheeks, tracing their roundness with one hand and guiding his fingers down the cleft that reached from the tip of her spine to the edge of her back passage. With the other he reached between the front of her thighs, and when he found her crease he teased her with his fingers, while she pulled his swollen package, making it thud faster than his hammering heart.

The pounding pushed across his chest and into his arms and sent tremors to the tips of his fingers. To stem the tide of urgency that was flooding the pit of his groin, Shanklin broke their lip-lock and gulped in swathes of cool air. As he settled, the stiffness in his horn slackened enough that he slipped from her grasp. Still, he ached for release, so he cradled her in his arms and dipped her down into the sand.

Her jacket fell open when she stretched her arms wide and, as he knelt before her, she spread her legs. Her eyes still close, Marquaisa licked her lips and wrapped her calves around the back of his thighs and tugged his hips closer to hers. With each of her squeezes, Shanklin grew longer and wider and when, at last, the tip of his hard head pushed past her soft outer lips he slipped his hands under her, held her tight, and entered her.

Marquaisa rumbled, happily, and tilted her hips up into his, drawing him all the way in. Then, gripping him with her legs, she rolled him onto his back, lay on him, and while kissing his lips began to rock, smoothly, in and out in an easy rhythm. His hands open across the back of her ribcage, as she moved Shanklin felt the satin of her skin slide under the calluses on his fingers and palms, and the silk of her hair course over the ridges of his knuckles. Her blend of softness and strength thrilling, he thrust his hips into her when she pressed hers against him, matching her cadence.

Flowing at first, their steady beat gathered more pace as they delved into the pleasures of their intercourse. Their coupling growing more urgent, Marquaisa pushed herself upright. Straddling him, hers knees sculpting furrows into the sand, she walked her fingers up the sinew of her stomach, smoothed them over the curves of her breasts, and combed them into her hair, Arching her back and lifting her chin she ruffled her tresses, feeling their ends swish against her buttocks.

As they whisked over her skin, Shanklin drew in a sharp breath and took her waist in his hands. Thumping the back of his head into the beach, he ground his teeth, bucked in excitement, and poured himself into Marquaisa, while she rode him effortlessly and climaxed in ecstasy. Feeding the moment, they tensed their bodies and kept them rigid for long seconds. Then, as their passions eased, together they softened, she shutting her eyes and chuckling, while he tickled her thighs and caught his breath.

Happy his lungs no longer were on the edge of bursting, happier still to remain entangled with Marquaisa, Shanklin squeezed the muscles of her thighs delicately and asked her shyly, "Did that help you to remember?"

"Remember?" Marquaisa muttered, rocking her body quietly on his.

"What it is like to *not* kill, even if you *want* to kill," Shanklin reminded her, gulping, as nervous over what she might say or do in answer to his question, as he was proud to feel blood rushing to the crown of his newly coronated warrior king.

"Not really. Not yet. So, do that again, we must, or kill you right now, I will," Marquaisa declared with an evil grin.

"If we must, we must," Shanklin heaved an exaggerated sigh and reached up to kiss her, but stopped when she placed her finger on his lips.

"Shush," she whispered to him and smelled the air, "You must go, now. Dead men ride the waves."

"Dead, or undead?" Shanklin asked, daring to presume, as Marquaisa spun off him and onto her feet. Then, seeing her persona shift to that of the killer she'd been on the first night they'd met, he buttoned his lip and buckled on his trousers.

"Undead?" she replied to him with a question of her own, facing him squarely and defying him to say what he meant. Without waiting for his answer, she turned away from Shanklin, lifted her sword out of the sand, and sprinted south toward the spot on the beach to which a torch bobbing on the water was headed.

The further she ran, the more it became obvious to Marquaisa that her boots were not made for sprinting. They gave her the opposite of traction, their heels sunk deep in the soft sand and their soles skidded on the loose grit. Their leather vamps became waterlogged and heavy, and their shafts wrinkled around her ankles. But, she liked them, so she overlooked the fact that, while running on the beach, they made her look like a horse clambering on glare ice up a steep mountain pass.

Equally awkward were the instructions a passenger, standing at the stern of the rowboat approaching shore, was jabbering at his crew. The craft was carrying five personnel, including two rowers and three passengers, two at the stern and one at the prow holding a torch to light their way. Passengers and rowers all were outfitted in standard British army gear: red coats, white trousers, and black tricorn hats. His hat taller than the others, indicative of either a bigger head or a higher rank, or both, the soldier whose voice was carrying over the waves was correcting his rowers' technique, insisting that if they did as he instructed they would reach shore in half the time.

"Dash it all, Woolly, we'd have got here in half the time if our oarsmen had angled their paddles nearer the water," Brigadier General James Wolfe persisted, when at last they ran aground. "We'd be at command by now, hiding the rum from Jenkins before he rotates off duty."

Chugging ashore ahead of Wolfe, Lieutenant Fulton Woolworth, short of leg, stout of girth, caustic of nature grated, "He still moping about Neah?"

"Aye, he is" Wolfe informed the lieutenant. "He's taken Neah's death much harder than most of us, I'm afraid. They were friends, after all, and he was right beside Neah when she murdered him."

"Hard lines, for Jenkins. We must've put a fright into Rollo's *Squog,* though. Haven't seen or—" Woolworth clapped his mouth shut when he heard a twangy, ringing sound.

He and the rest of the squad, Wolfe included, stopped in their tracks and looked high and low for the source of the metallic whirling, which was growing rapidly louder and approaching them at a blistering pace. Before they found it, it stopped suddenly, with a *thwack,* which was punctuated by a *thud* when the leading man in their line hit the sand, on his left side, as if he were a tree felled by an axe. The torch he'd been holding aloft bounced in the sand, yards away to his left, and fizzled out.

Eye's wide, the soldier immediately behind the dead man checked himself for wounds inflicted, but not felt. Finding none, he looked at his fallen comrade just as the sword that lanced his neck and pinned him to the ground was yanked free. In the same action, one of its sharp edges angled towards his throat and separated his head from his shoulders.

Still unsure of what was happening, the way of things was clarified for the third soldier in line when his mate's hat hit him in the face and his head bounced off his chest. Shock stole his voice, but training took control of his body and without thinking he drew his flintlock pistol from under his belt, raised it to shoulder height, and fired. A *smack* and a *grunt* told him he'd hit someone, so he pressed forward his attack, casting aside his gun and whipping his sword from its scabbard.

On his second step, he impaled himself on the gore-streaked blade that was on a collision course with his heart. Transfixed, he watched it travel its full length until its jewel encrusted hilt guard rammed into his waistcoat. The arm that held it level was as true and as hard as the blade itself, and the eyes that guided it burned as hot as the fires in which the blade was forged. They watched the spark of life die in his, then passed him by as the sword was jerked out the front of his chest and he was allowed to fall flat on the sand into which his blood was gushing.

Woolworth and Wolfe, who by now were standing side by side, fired their pistols into the space that was occupied an instant earlier by the soldier who now lay dead at their feet. His killer sidestepped and watched their shots sizzle past, sheathed her rapier in the scabbard strapped to her back, then charged the two officers. On her first step she slipped, but recovered and clamped her left hand in a vice-like grip around Wolfe's throat, while snatching a fistful of the lapels of Woolworth's red coat, just below the collar line.

Wolfe pounded on her hand and arm, so she squeezed his neck harder, until his face reddened. Then, positive he could see what she was doing, she bared her teeth and plunged her fangs into Woolworth's jugular. Wolfe battered her with his fists and his feet, but she held him fast. Woolworth squirmed, but he proved a savory treat so she took her time and drained him slowly. When he was empty, she licked her lips and watched his eyelids fall, then tossed him to the water's edge. His toes in the sand, his body face down in the water, his arms floated over his head and waved slowly, in warning to others, or as a plea for help, or to bid farewell to all.

"Wolfe," Marquiasa peered into the general's watering eyes, then looked him up and down. Unimpressed, she let go of her grip on him and shoved him away.

"Witch!" Wolfe rasped and ripped out his sword. In the same motion he made a vicious cut for Marquaisa's eyes.

To avoid it, she took a step back. When he missed her, his arm swung high and wide and he stumbled to his right. With him off balanced, she took two steps forward and drove her right fist into his left cheek, dropping him, dazed, to his right knee. His left leg splayed out, heel in the sand, toe pointed at the sky, his arms flailing, he wobbled in his angular stance and tried to organize himself for another attack. His intentions plain to see, she hit him with a roundhouse left that connected above the bridge of his nose and knocked him onto his back. His sword lost, his arms and legs flopping like fishes on dry land, she stood over him, one foot on each side of his hips, leaned over him, and slapped his face.

"Listen to me," she grabbed his chin and made him look into her eyes. "This is a warning. Leave this place and never return. If you do, you will die."

"So I've been told," Wolfe slurred. "It might be a welcome reprieve . . . from you."

His rebuttal went unanswered. Mystified as to why she let him have the last word, he propped himself up on his elbows and gazed down the length of his body, past his waist and beyond the tips of his toes, at empty dunes. She'd gone and left him in the dark, the lone living soul at the end of a line of dead bodies.

"I am no witch," Marquaisa said to herself as she trotted further away from him, south, towards Gabarus Point.

"Whateverrr you are, *trrrouble* are you," a girl's voice burred in the gloom that stretched before Marquaisa.

The demoness slowed to a standstill and sniffed the air, while waves lapped against her ankles.

"Hobnob, Witch of the Sea," she answered back, masking her relief over not succumbing to the urge to immediately kill whoever, or whatever caught her by surprise.

Swaddled in layers of fine cotton and soft wool, long tresses of silky curls and ringlets swaying with her fluid movements, Hobnob materialized from whisps of salt spray and, her bare feet swishing in the surf, slowly approached Marquaisa.

She stopped just out of Marquaisa's reach, smiled shyly, and said, "I like your boots."

"Me too," Marquaisa replied, scuffing the sand with her heels. Then she patted her head and, wondering why she felt only her hair, added, "I had a hat."

"Sorry you lost it," Hobnob consoled her. "But, at least you kept your new coat. It looks—

"Like crap," Marquaisa spoke the truth to spare Hobnob from having to lie. Keen to stack truisms, she tried to pay Hobnob a compliment, "You look tasty—shit—I mean, you look very . . . nice."

Hobnob giggled, quietly, at the flattery, then turned to face south, took a few small steps away from Marquaisa and invited her to follow, "Come, I have a little boat. It will take us to *She Wolf.*"

"She Wolf?" Marquaisa balked. "Where is *Rajani?* Where are Haritha, Enriquez, and Erieux?'

"They are fine," Hobnob assured her, and kept walking away. "Come, we will talk while the boys flex their muscles for us and *rrrow* us all the way to Gabarus Point."

Marquaisa took a few reluctant steps forward, then hurried to catch up. When, together, they reached the boat that was waiting for them, beached in the sand, she found that Hobnob had not overstated its size. It was, indeed, "little," with room enough on one bench for two oarsmen, as well as for herself and Hobnob on a smaller bench near its prow.

Minding their manners, the boys helped the ladies to their seat, then cast off, jumped on board, got their craft turned the right way round, and set themselves to work on the oars. Hobnob wrapped a cozy blanket around herself and Marquaisa, then snuggled in close to her.

"I know you don't feel the cold, but I do," she said, with a shiver, and added an admission. "I also needed to feel you again, and not through some silly blanket."

Marquaisa wrapped her arm around Hobnob and pulled her closer, so they could whisper to one another, and asked the girl, "How long?"

"From the moment you left," Hobnob confessed.

"Why?" Marquaisa pressed her.

"For Saro, it was because you saved him from Duvauchelle. For me, it was because you did to Sharkey and his crew what I wanted to do, but could not. We would follow you again. You could not stop us," Hobnob finished in a rush, her timbre peaked with a spicy blend of willfulness and devotion.

"Okay. Okay. It's okay," Marquaisa reassured Hobnob, giving her a squeeze. "Where *is* our Captain Saro?"

"He is on the path between Gabarus Point and Freshwater Cove, waiting for you. He will wait until morning, then return to *She Wolf,*" Hobnob conveyed Saro's posture and added, "He has grown."

"I expect he has," Marquaisa teased her. "Now, tell me of *Rajani.*"

"Enriquez took her to chase another prize," Hobnob reported.

"When?"

"Today."

"Well, credit him for waiting for me as long as he did," Marquaisa cut the pirate some slack. "I would not have waited as long for him."

"Credit Suchika, as well," Hobnob submitted. "She agreed to parley and told me she would have marooned Enriquez in a heartbeat —just like he abandoned her at Martinique—but not her friends, or you. She worships you."

"Suchika and I swapped a few recipes. She will be the death of Enriquez," Marquaisa predicted with a grin.

"I heard you foretell of a similar fate for your Wolfe, back on the beach," Hobnob reminded her. "Was it a warning, a threat, or your second sight."

"A warning, spawned by a vision, that was meant to sound like a threat," Marquaisa grumbled and turned away from Hobnob to look out on the water. "If it comes to pass, he will die here. But it is not to be by my hand. Otherwise, he would be dead by now."

"That is without question," Hobnob laughed and bopped Marquaisa on the shoulder with her fist. "So, what now? You came here for a reason. Do you wish to pursue it?"

"Ferdinand's gold. Yes," Marquaisa clasped her hands in her lap and stared at the deck of the boat, "But I have lost its trail."

Hobnob placed a hand on top of Marquaisa's, and leaning closer to her whispered, "I can help you with that."

Doubt tainting her reply, her voice hushed, Marquaisa prest Hobnob, "Think you so?"

"I do," Hobnob stood by her words, then backed them up. "One night, not long ago, the British allowed a French ship, *l'Arethusa*, to slip through their blockade. You would think, given her good fortune, she would head straight for home, to France, and away from this forsaken wilderness. But she did not. Rather than head east, she sailed north, up the coast. She stayed here, in New France. Who would do such a thing?"

"One who, because he has betrayed her, cannot return to France," Marquaisa replied, a grin tugging at the corner of her mouth. "Poisson."

"The one and only," Hobnob confirmed.

"He will have taken sanctuary in the *Citadelle (Citadel)* at *Québec*, on some pretense or other," Marquaisa concluded, releasing the tension in her shoulders. "You too are one of a kind, Hobnob with the curly brown hair. *Gracias." Thank you.*

"De nada" (You're welcome), Hobnob returned the courtesy, her eyes sparkling. "Shall we go and kill him, take his gold, and *burrrn* his ship?"

"Indeed, we shall," Marquaisa agreed. "But, first, I need to go home. I am not yet entirely myself after my time at the bottom of the lagoon. I need to recover in a place where I can rest, keep you safe, and with Xi's help further your education."

"Home," Hobnob pronounced the word whose meaning was, to her, beyond understanding.

"Yes, a city that floats on the water, and which lights up at night, and which is full of creatures of spirit," Marquaisa listed her home's virtues dreamily, "It goes by the name, *Venezia.*"

"Rrremarkable," Hobnob breathed and leaned against Marquaisa. "Who is Xi?"

"The most wondrous creature of all."

CHAPTER 47

DÉRANGEMENT

SEPTEMBER 30TH

HMS ROYAL WILLIAM

Wolfe clung to the webbing that was hooked to the rail of *HMS Royal William* with his left hand, while with his right he swirled the tip of his new cane in the waters of Gaspé Bay. As he stirred up tiny whirlpools, a skiff ferrying a squad of soldiers across the bay toward the great ship bobbed on the waves. Their faces sour, the soldiers' bleak mood juxtaposed the vibrant forest canopy by which they were backdropped and which was colored with rich reds, yellows, and auburns. It mirrored, however, the desolated village that had been built up between the forest's edge and the water-line and which now was littered with debris and was hung over by the smoke that was wafting from the shells of charred buildings.

When at last the skiff bumped against the hull of the ship, Wolfe swung away from the webbing and hopped into the midst of his troops, greeted them with handshakes, then got them started on their way up the ropes to the ship's deck. After the last of the enlistees was given a boost, Wolfe turned to their squad leader and sketched him a salute, which the leader returned to him in kind, just as another pair of boots thudded onto the deck of skiff.

Without turning to welcome the new arrival, Wolfe greeted the squad leader, "Jenkins, good to see you. Come to rescue me from my misery, eh?"

"Sir?" Jenkins grumbled, his hope for a reprieve from the business of expelling Acadians from their ancestral homes fading from his expression.

Ignoring Jenkins's peevishness, Wolfe made a half turn to allow him to see the person newly arrived onboard the skiff. He then commenced with the introductions, "Lieutenant Thadan Jenkins, allow me to present my new *aide-de-camp*, Captain Thomas Bell. Bell, Jenkins. Unlike you and me, Jenkins, Bell is of sound mind. But, like you and me, he wishes to see our current campaign—what are we calling it, Bell?"

"The Gaspé Expedition, sir," Bell reminded the general.

"Right," Wolfe gave his aide a thumbs-up. "As I was saying, he wishes to see our campaign of destruction and deportation through to a glorious and successful conclusion. However, I believe he agrees with me, secretly, that our purposes would be much better served, right now, by laying a good hiding on those Canadian hellcats over at Québec. However, he has not told me so, for I suspect that vestiges of a misguided respect for authority still are ingrained in his complexion. No doubt drilled into him by the relics of bygone campaigns who haunt our Academy at Woolwich. But, never fear, we shall cure him of that affliction. Shan't we, Jenkins?"

"Aye, we will, sir. Now, by your leave, I need to see to the men up top," Jenkins attempted to excuse himself, while avoiding making eye contact with Wolfe.

"Nonsense, Jenkins. *Gung-ho* Glastun—your right-hand man since friend Neil met his untimely demise at Louisbourg—will see to their needs," the general overrode his subaltern, then guided the lieutenant back to his seat in the skiff. "I need you to show me the site of your latest conquest, and to explain to Bell how to conduct a proper clearance."

Jenkins' shoulders slumped as he hunched over on the bench.

"So, let's away, shall we? Oarsmen, stand aside!" Wolfe shooed the seamen up the ropes toward the rail. "Gentlemen, give my regards to Glastun. Bell, you and I will now set about the task of clearing our minds of the drudgery of administration, whilst filling our lungs with the fresh September air of the *Gaspé!*"

Wolfe picked up an oar, plunked himself onto the bench beneath it, and shifted over to give his aide room to do the same. "Shove off, Jenkins. I mean that in a nautical way, of course. Now, put your back into it, Bell, and don't kill all the codfish with your paddle."

As Wolfe and Bell pulled the skiff over the swells toward the shoreline, the general prodded Jenkins with questions about his and the men's health, and listened to a few of the lieutenant's stories about the troops and their performances during the raid. The mission brief complete, Wolfe anticipated Jenkins by answering the questions he thought were on the lieutenant's mind.

"You are wondering what crime Bell committed that resulted in his being sentenced to serve under my command. Well, let me tell you," he began. "Bell's offences were to have served with distinction at Louisbourg and to have been judged, by an assortment of nincompoops more intelligent than I, to be suitably highly qualified for the position. His undoing was Amherst's snatching up Brock—with whom I know you were close—out from under my heel. He also was next in line for promotion. Although, by the time we're through with him, he may have his own very different label for the assignment."

"Good for Brock," Jenkins nodded. "He'll be buying me a drink, next time I see him."

"Too true," Wolfe agreed. "As for Rollo, he's off making mischief over on *Île Saint-Jean (Prince Edward Island).*

"Same as us?" Jenkins asked, ducking his head, slightly ashamed.

"Indeed," Wolfe pulled his oar from the water and heaved a sigh. "It's an ugly, but according to the nincompoops, necessary bit of business. I say the sooner we're done with it, the better."

"Aye, sir," Jenkins mumbled, looking at his hands. "Speaking of ugly, what of de Sade?"

"*Monsieur* de Sade was a panderer and a fop, and by my estimation completely mad," Wolfe minced no words, laughing as he uttered them. "I do believe the events at the stockade finally tipped him over the edge. Evidently, the French thought of him the same way as did I, seeing as they left him to rot in our prison. So, just to irritate them, we sent him back to them. Cut him loose in no man's land, on the Moor of Gabanes. No telling what's happened to him since then."

"And what of Lady Haritha?" Jenkins asked Wolfe, tentatively, glancing over his shoulder as they neared the shoreline.

"No sign of her since the raid on the stockade," Wolfe informed the lieutenant, his eyes wandering. "Damned shame."

Just as Wolfe expressed his regrets the skiff beached. When it ground to a halt, he vaulted into the surf and splashed toward shore, pointing randomly with his new cane, and prattling on, "Not at all like Freshwater Cove, eh Jenkins?"

"Not entirely, sir," Jenkins frowned, slogging his way onto the beach. "By the time we landed most of the villagers had run off into the woods. We rounded up the ones that stayed behind—somewhere between thirty and forty souls—and sent them out to the transports in the bay. We then fired houses, back there," he pointed to the blackened remains of a set of buildings that were arrayed along the tree line, "as well as the sawmill and the smith's forge, over there." He aimed his finger at collapsed structure that spanned a small tributary that emptied into the bay.

"I see," Wolfe said, impressed but unimpressed as he surveyed the destruction. "Well, let's make one last sweep for stragglers so Bell can state in the mission report, with a clear conscience, we did our due diligence."

The three officers completed a cursory search of the mill and forge, then quickly moved on to the burned out houses. All of the shacks had been razed to the ground. Bits and chunks of stone from fireplaces were the only indications the charred husks had once been occupied by humans. Satisfied they had carried out their orders, the three officers made an about-face and started back toward their skiff, but stopped when they heard rustlings coming from one of the wrecked houses and saw a pile of stonework crumble.

The three soldiers approached the shifting rubble, cautiously, keeping wary eyes on it as they surrounded it. The movement under the stones became more fevered as they watched, and taken by a sense of urgency, they all started grabbing rocks and pitching them off the pile. Suddenly, they caught a glimpse of colored fabric and they redoubled their efforts to clear the rubble. Little-by-little, an arm appeared, then shoulders, and then a head, which was face down in the rocks and sprouting a tangle of thick bronze locks.

Ashen-faced, Wolfe looked at Jenkins and forced himself to help his lieutenant and his captain gently remove the rest of the rocks that were piled on the body. When it was fully uncovered, it was clear it had been crushed under the weight of the collapsing fireplace, and despite their efforts, no longer showed no signs of life. Cursing quietly, Wolfe crouched beside the body, and dreading what he thought he might find, grabbed its shoulder and rolled it over. As he did, Haritha's wide, vacant eyes stared through him and he moaned in anguish.

"Is that all you can do?" a guttural voice rasped at Wolfe from a crushed windpipe, "Fuss, like a little child?"

The vacant eyes turned to jet-black orbs as Haritha's shattered face moved up to his, "I knew what you wanted when first we met, but I denied you."

She opened her mouth and a coarse, black tongue ran over razor sharp fangs as she grabbed the back of his neck and yanked him down, "Well, my love, I will deprive you no longer. Your wish is granted. Time to die."

"Holy shiiittt!" Wolfe roared the tried-and-true antidote for demon-infested nightmares.

Gasping, he threw off his blankets and sat bolt upright. Chill, September air bled off the waters of Louisbourg's harbor and through the open porthole of his cabin on the *Royal William*, making him shiver.

"She will live forever. You will die in one year's time," the fore-telling, spoken in a voice born not of nightmares but of battlefield terrors, clawed into his consciousness.

"So you keep saying," Wolfe replied, casually, to the pool of blackness floating at the foot of his cot. "Would you care to narrow it down to the hour?"

"That will be your decision," the specter prophesied, a hollow ring in its tone as it drifted nearer to the general.

"Very well, how about here and now?" Wolfe challenged it, scrambling onto his knees and sticking out his chin.

"I am not the one. If I was, you would be long since dead,"the shade stated, flatly, hovering a hand's span in front of the general's nose.

"I see, well, in that case take your useless information and bugger off," Wolfe blustered, leaning closer to his visitor. "Anyway, I doubt I'll remember it or you beyond my next bowel movement, which, given the quality of the food in the mess and my susceptibility to sea sickness, could happen at any moment."

A chuckle bled from the roiling pool and flowed, in sticky coils, around Wolfe's torso, telling him at each turn, "You are a fool."

Wolfe shuddered but grit his teeth. Darting a hand under his blankets, he snapped out his new walking stick and slashed at the wriggling tentacles, "Show your true self and we'll pick up where we left off on the beach, witch, only this time you'll get the real me."

Wolfe felt a touch of ice between his shoulder blades, and when he turned his head his world was consumed in a nightmare of fangs, claws, and a depthless blackness that resonated with a deep voice, *"Here I am."*

"What in blazes?" Wolfe shouted, regretting, momentarily, he'd got what he'd wished for. Then, on instinct, he somersaulted off the foot of his bed. The instant his feet touched the deck of his cabin he bounced off them and twisted in the air to land facing his bed. No sooner did he put down than, howling a battle cry, he leapt back on top of his mattress and sliced the open air above the blankets with his cane.

While Wolfe lunged, stabbed, shouted challenges, then spun and hacked some more, a pair of voices echoed in the inky pool that was dissolving around him.

"I knew I could use your second sight to make a *brrridge* to him,"

Hobnob chirped. "But, you were all, 'No way *José.*' And I was like, 'Yes way!' So, now, who's the witch?"

"Okay, okay, *you're* the witch," Marquaisa conceded. "But, what about me? Was I creepy enough? I mean, the dream was creepy, but I feel like I wasn't creepy enough."

"Oh, yes, you were *sooo crrreepy.* Look, I am totally shaking."

Epilogue

September 30th

Tracadigash Mountain

To reclaim all of the burned-out particles from the muddy floor of Barachois Lagoon, to make of them something new, to breathe life into it, and then to send it to a place where it could take the centuries it needed to grow and mature, required of Oculus the blink of an eye, a moment of inspiration, a puff of breath, and lastly a flick of the wrist. Proud of his progeny, but exhausted by his exertions, the Almighty flopped down in his gorge at the root of Tracadigash Mountain, fell back against its rock face, and soaked up what remained of the autumn sun.

A network of tremors rippled across *Gaspé* as Oculus nestled into his mountainous recliner, then dragged to within easy reach a vat of beer the size of a small lake. When, at last, he was comfortable, Kirby, his three-headed hound, padded over to him and curled up against his hip, sending a wave of aftershocks across the peninsula.

"Let's see what's on," Oculus said, scratching the backs of six fuzzy, black ears.

With the talon that jutted from his left big toe, he nudged the side of a clear, colorless crystal sphere whose diameter spanned the greater part of his field of vision. Slowly, the sphere spun on a pedestal that was fashioned from a vein of silver that stabbed the earth to its core. At each degree of rotation, a set of images took shape and came to life within the ball.

After a full turn of the sphere, he dipped a colossal stein into his vat of beer, took a pull of brew, then garbled through a burp that sparked an atmospheric disturbance, "Three hundred and sixty degrees, and nothing on."

Kirby huffed out a landscape-altering snore, and Oculus yawned and let his eyes droop. But, before they banged shut, he perked up, "Good thing I upgraded to the version that lets me turn that thing in the opposite direction. Maybe there's something good on over there."

With a grunt he nudged the crystal with the talon that jutted from his right big toe. Images of various species and genders copulating, warring, and reveling flitted across the crystal, and while Kirby lulled himself into a deeper sleep, Oculus grumbled at the passing images, "Lame, lame, lame." For variety, and to keep himself awake so as to neither scratch nor spill beer on his crystal ball, he threw in the occasional, "Give me a *phoqing* break."

Finally, at the one-hundred-and-eighty-degree mark, an image caught his attention. In one of the floaty, wooden tubs his humans spent so much time fussing over, but which always filled with water and sank, a man was using a stick to ward off a shadow that that looked vaguely like the demon who fried Owe-me and Show-me. Thus, necessitating his construction of a whole new species of monster. The man's feistiness was comical enough, but of real interest was the fact he and the shade were an ocean apart, and *it* had help.

"A demon and a conjurer," the divine one belched. "Fancy that. Looks, for sure, like they'd give my so-called wizards at Oculorius a run for their money. Well, we'll have to keep our eyes on them, won't we, Kirbster?"

With that grudging bit of acknowledgement chaffing his backside, Oculus tapped his crystal a few more times, until it returned an image of his favorite spot on the river the Anishinaabe called the *Kichi Sibi (Great River)*. Oculus liked best the place in the river where it was pinched between two islands. At the narrows, a steep waterfall named *Akikodjiwan (Cauldron Falls)* pitched the river into a deep basin. Powerful currents turned the basin into a giant stewpot full of massive whirlpools, the hissing and vapors from which could be seen and heard for miles. The Anishinaabe sent prayers and offerings into the mists of the cauldron to garner protection from their enemies. Oculus used it as the incubator for his monstrosities.

When he tuned in to the goings on at the cauldron, an Anishinaabe woman was kneeling beside it at midday, sprinkling tobacco on a plate and preparing to make her own special offering to her protectors. Above her, on a portage path, two voyageurs, down from Montreal and on their way into the interior to collect furs for the trade, spotted her through the mists. With a nod to each other, they lifted their canoe off their shoulders and lowered it carefully onto the path. Dropping their packs, they scuttled to the trail that led down to the earthen dais from which the woman was sending her prayers. Certain their approach would not be heard above the crashing water and hissing steam, they rushed the woman, tackled her to the ground, and clamped their grimy mitts over her screams.

"Time to answer some prayers," Oculus piped-up, causing Kirby to prick his many ears.

Peeling his back off the mountainside, he crossed his legs and rested his left elbow on the inside of his thigh and his chin on his fist. While he absently raked ditches into the valley floor, he looked through the mists that were clouding his crystal, down into the whirlpools that spun all the way to the base of the cauldron. On the floor of the basin, wrapped in a fresh cocoon, a thousand reconfigured shards of light pulsated with new life. With a click of his tongue, Oculus tore open the sack, and with a second click, wakened the embryonic leviathan it contained.

As the shards drifted out of the cocoon, the creature stretched its loosely knitted limbs, feeling their limits. It then clacked the claws on its fingers and toes and, pleased with their strength, spun playfully in the water. Stopping itself in mid-roll, it floated in place, face-up, searching through the whirlpools. Sensing its creator's unconditional joy its lips peeled back and it showed its rows of razor fangs through a broad smile. Oculus smiled back indulgently, and with a raised eyebrow asked his pup to grant him the first of what would become many interesting wishes.

Leaning forward, the divine one pulled Kirby closer to the crystal. Full of anticipation he urged his hound, "Watch this."

Overcome by the strength of the two voyageurs, the woman stilled herself and looked for an opportunity to strike back. As her eyes flicked from one spot to the next, she saw a change in the mists that were spinning out of the cauldron. Deep in the haze, points of light in all the colors of the rainbow stretched up and swirled in the vapors. As they spun, they wove themselves into sparkling, sharp-edged masses that turned into a pair of broad hands that reached out of the mist and hooked into the dais with jagged talons.

They clawed towards the woman and grew into thick arms that dragged a chiseled torso and two long legs out of the mists. When it stood, the blades of light that covered the creature sang in tune with the vapors out of which it emerged. At its full height, it shook its head and threw a shower of water back into the falls off cable-like locks of hair and sharply pointed ears. It then peered at the woman, through a pair of eyes that were made of innumerable shifting diamond chips.

Her eyes frantic, she kicked at the voyageurs, who laughed at her, until the gray-black shadows they cast on the dais swam in a pool of kaleidoscopic light. Together, the two men followed the woman's terrified gaze, turning their heads just in time to see two great paws reaching for their throats. Their skin flayed on contact with the monstrous hands, and they squirmed as they were lifted off their intended victim. When they were clear of her, the creature squeezed its fingers, rupturing its prey's veins and cracking their vertebrae.

The creature watched the men convulse and pour their lifeblood through its fingers and down its arms. Finally, when they went still, it looked at the woman, smiled at her, and quietly waited. Uncertain of what to do, the woman looked at her dead attackers and, pleased with their fate, smiled back. At the sight of the woman's smile, the creature howled, and with the two dead bodies firmly clasped in its hands, loped back to the edge of the dais and disappeared into the cauldron.

"Now, that's entertainment," Oculus said, turning to Kirby and pointing his finger at the crystal. Then, looking back at the crystal and into the depths of the cauldron, he watched his creation enjoy its first meal and praised it, "Good *Squogie*. Good *Squogie*."

Ode for a Jingo Undone

At last, moment granted to pen a note,
Gut sore, stone cold, near dead, stuck on this boat.
Behind, battles hard fought and won; Sweet spoils!
Ahead, fortune and fame, rewards for toils.

Up-down, left-right, forward, then back, good gravy!
Much more of this, welcome would be old Davey;
Jones's chest, bolt shut, held fast in mud to sleep.
No life, no death, but peace beneath the deep.

"Nonsense!" the cry from souls to war still drawn.
"Why doze, while blood and fire yet greet the dawn?"
Each day replete with test of strength and will;
Power the true hateful of mind who kill.

For king, for home, for those with whom arms lock.
In thin red line, flint-eyed, begging to mock,
Mad dogs and fools who play at words and worse,
Craft verse and rhymes would Grey suffer to curse.

— WOLFE

Milton Keynes UK
Ingram Content Group UK Ltd.
UKHW021544080424
440701UK00005B/133/J